TAROT
Crossing Worlds

RACHEL CLARKE

The Book Guild Ltd

First published in Great Britain in 2024 by
The Book Guild Ltd
Unit E2 Airfield Business Park,
Harrison Road, Market Harborough,
Leicestershire. LE16 7UL
Tel: 0116 2792299
www.bookguild.co.uk
Email: info@bookguild.co.uk
Twitter: @bookguild

This work is entirely fictitious and bears no resemblance to any persons living or dead.

Typeset in 11pt Minion Pro

Printed and bound in the UK by TJ Books LTD, Padstow, Cornwall

ISBN 978 1916668 607

British Library Cataloguing in Publication Data.
A catalogue record for this book is available from the British Library.

For my family, who are worth crossing worlds for.

Chapter One

Long Ago, There Lived...

When the last sunrays of the day kissed the grounds of Castle Wayan, fourteen-year-old Princess Maria hurried off the drawbridge into the medieval inner courtyard. Patches of copper-tinted hair stuck to her face as the girl's unsettled chestnut eyes fixed upon the entrance ahead.

Catching a breath of the humid air, she wormed through the livestock and crowds of people too preoccupied to notice her. Reaching the other side, she glanced at the yard before slithering into the grandiose entrance hall where a commanding staircase stood.

The girl bounded up two steps at a time as sweat trickled down her brow. She arrived on the landing and meandered right, down a dimly lit hallway with painted tapestries hung from gold hooks on the walls. They showcased an eclectic mix of images detailing swords, cups, pentacles and wands in varying shapes, colours and sizes.

At the far end, she pushed open a door and scrambled into her bedchamber. Princess Maria winced as the door closed with a loud bang. How careless could she be? She knew her family would expect her presence at dinner shortly.

She shrugged off her mishap, picked up a couple of pillows from her bed and placed them delicately on the floor in front of the doorframe. The princess thought she should hide any movement from peering eyes as she bolted towards the fading light from the balcony.

Pulling the drapes shut, she immersed herself in darkness and raised her Tarot deck in the air. With a subtle swoosh, the wondrous cards came to life. Their dazzling, deep-red energy radiated out as Princess Maria nervously shuffled them face down.

Underneath, the beautifully illustrated deck displayed an array of characters and objects with specific duties from Wayan's royal court. The women, men and children of varying ages and ranks took centre stage against day and night backdrops with symbols related to swords, cups, pentacles and wands. The princess breathed deeply as the Tarot cards continued to seep out budding energy.

Finally, she asked them when her mother and father would be murdered. "Please," the princess strained under her breath, "tell me everything. I need to protect them." But as the cards continued to conjure red magic, nothing else happened apart from the girl's growing frustration.

She wistfully removed the top card from the deck and turned it over. Her troubled eyes fixed on the upside-down image of a large wheel covered in pentacle symbols. It was the same card as last night, and the night before. She knew what it meant. A sinister change in circumstances was approaching. As her worries grew, the deep-red energy brewing inside her Tarot deck shot out. It whipped up a storm in the centre of the bedchamber and conjured a scene.

Shocked, the princess stepped forward, fighting back tears as she witnessed her severely wounded parents, Queen Anya and King Peter, lying on the cold stone floor in the inner courtyard of Castle Wayan. Covered in deep lacerations across their chest and stomach, blood seeped from their wounds, staining the ground.

Half a dozen armoured soldiers from the Tarot world, Naxthos, walked away from the injured rulers with their blood-drenched swords raised high. They stepped through a dazzling circular portal back to their homeworld.

Now completely alone, with no one from Wayan coming to their aid, Princess Maria's parents held hands as they closed their eyes and died together. The princess didn't know how much more she could take as she clung onto the vision for any clues that could help to prevent her parents passing.

A tap on the door diverted her attention. Shaking uncontrollably, Princess Maria instructed her Tarot deck to dispel the image, but they didn't listen. Asking them again, the cards continued to disobey their owner over the sound of a slightly louder knock. "What are you playing at?" urged the princess, but before she could attempt to retrieve her Tarot cards floating in the air, a concerned voice flared up in the hallway.

"Maria!" called Queen Anya. "I know you're in there. Those pillows don't fool me."

"Please," whispered Princess Maria at her Tarot cards, "disband the scene."

"Maria!" repeated Queen Anya.

"I'm fine!" strained Princess Maria.

"I'm coming in," replied Queen Anya, sensing the unease in her daughter's voice.

"Crap!" the girl muttered under her breath as the door was forced open. The Queen of Wayan strode in, her knee-high boots hitting the floor hard. The radiating red energy from her daughter's Tarot cards struck the garnet jewels nestled in the queen's crown. They glistened, as did the garnet embroidered on her velvet crimson waistcoat that hung loosely over Queen Anya's dark, lightweight trousers.

Ready to pounce, the queen's annoyance quickly subsided as her deep chestnut eyes cast a worried look upon the distraught princess. Drawing closer and taken aback by the future death of her husband and herself, Queen Anya fell hauntingly silent, deep in thought.

"Mother?" said Princess Maria softly. "Mother, are you okay?"

"Yes. It is you I'm concerned for."

"Why? You're the one in danger, not me."

"No, you're wrong."

The distress and torment plaguing the girl were undeniable, and the queen decided to end it. She willed her majestic Tarot cards to conjure strands of fantastical red energy which branched out and set alight the floor-standing pillar candles around the outer edges of the bedchamber.

As the soft warmth consumed the space, her cards disbanded the image her daughter's deck had cast. The queen stood in the centre of the room, staring hard at the girl, who avoided eye contact.

"This image you have witnessed may not be certain," said Queen Anya.

"But…" Princess Maria said hurriedly, clutching her Tarot cards, paranoia brewing.

"No, Maria," interrupted Queen Anya. "Look at you. You've lost all sense of reason."

"You saw the image too," replied Princess Maria, a little softer.

"Yes. It wasn't hard to miss."

"Then why are you so calm?"

"It's not the image that concerns me; it's where the scene came from, and that's you."

She stepped towards her daughter and gripped her tight. She encouraged her to meet her eyes and watched as tears poured down the girl's cheeks.

"Please, hear me out," said Queen Anya. Releasing her hold, the queen gestured for them both to sit on the sofa at the foot of the bed. Once comfortable, Queen Anya took her daughter's hand and squeezed it gently. "Your hunt for answers can feed into your Tarot readings," explained Queen Anya. "The desire to know your destiny or someone else's can be precarious."

"Yes, I understand that."

"Do you? Really? From what I just saw, dear daughter, you were falling down a rabbit hole."

"I…" mumbled Princess Maria.

"You need to come to terms with seeking the truth for what it is. Not driven by your version of the truth," stated Queen Anya, her voice firm.

"But what if the vision is true?"

"Well, the best place to start is to go back to the beginning."

Contemplating her mother's words, Princess Maria's eyes were drawn to her Tarot cards as they flew in the air with new-found eagerness. They circled the room, gaining momentum, until finally, after shaking off their owner's influence and negativity, they gained the strength to calmly whisper into the princess's ear, "Clear your mind. For both our sakes."

Pang!

Those words struck the girl's heart with shame as she realised her cards had been suffering too. About to spiral into a pit of guilt, a sharp snap from inside her head broke the self-punishment. She was beginning to understand she needed to take the advice of Queen Anya and her Tarot deck. If not for herself, for them.

Eyes closed, Princess Maria was determined to shut out the outside world and embrace the blank space. Succumbing to the peace oozing into her soul, she started to feel good again. Soon enough, her cards returned to their owner with glee.

Relaxing into the smooth motion of each card, intertwining through her fingers and travelling to the bottom of the deck, the girl focused on not jumping to conclusions. *Don't expect anything*, the princess reiterated to herself. *Just paint a picture of your mother and father. That's it. Nothing else.*

Ready to reveal the top card, she opened her eyes. The death card with the image of a skeleton was facing upwards looking back at her. *Okay, stay calm, don't react*, Princess Maria told herself. Clearing her mind once more, waiting for her Tarot to guide her, the deck flew out of the girl's hand and conjured a confident display of profound red energy.

While Queen Anya watched with pride, the cards circulated around the energy, willing it to grow in strength.

The princess smiled at her accomplishment, and the cards forged a scene in the centre of the bedchamber.

As the energy subsided, all became clear. Queen Anya and her husband, King Peter, were holding hands, smiling at the gathering of their merry people assembled inside the inner courtyard. Nothing seemed out of place or threatening as musical instruments roused the air, and there was not a single Naxthosian soldier in sight.

"Naxthos is our ally, dear Maria," said Queen Anya. "You don't have to worry."

Rising from the sofa, Queen Anya made her way to the drapes and pulled them open. She gestured for the princess to follow. Mother and daughter stood silently on the balcony, admiring the stillness of the night sky's serenity.

Now calm, the princess glanced at the queen, taking in every detail of her features, and in the blink of an eye her mother was gone. As she reflected on the memory, twenty-eight-year-old Queen Maria of Wayan stood on the same balcony as she and her mother had all those years ago.

Her parents hadn't suffered a brutal death at the hands of the Naxthosian army. Instead, many years later, they'd decided to journey out of Wayan through a gateway, crossing vast Tarot worlds and enjoying the rest of their lives together without duty or regime. They'd entrusted their daughter as Wayan's protector.

"I will encourage you to find peace," whispered Queen Maria in the present. She placed her hands delicately upon her well-rounded bump. The baby kicked its mother. "I take that to be a yes." Queen Maria chuckled.

Looking out from the exotic Island of Delqroix, the queen spotted an excitable crowd of fish quickly cutting through the waters. She watched them swim away from the epicentre in awe of their glistening, multicoloured scales reflecting off the clear, crisp lake.

Eager to show her soon-to-be newborn the wonders of their world, Queen Maria struggled to decide where to begin; the four clans that enclosed their home on the mainland harnessed and crafted fantastical sorcery using the object from their respective symbol.

The Land of Cups, comprised of esteemed sailors and water-bearers, was docked in a shipping town in the south-west. The expert sorcerers and sorceresses from the Land of Wands resided inside the rugged mountains in the north-west. The heavy-handed, combat-skilled Swords were in the north-east. Finally, the Pentacles. With a rich history in learning about the unity of the symbols and inspiring others to succeed, they lived in treetop houses in the luscious green forests of the south-east.

Deep in the trance, the abrupt sound of the bedchamber door closing startled her. She did not want to tear herself away from the beautiful landscape but knew she had to. She took one last look at the fish before carefully stepping off the sun-drenched balcony into the stale air.

Her husband, King Marco, born on the Tarot world Naxthos, stood perplexed on the other side of the room. His once uplifted sky-blue eyes looked riddled with worry, and his tall body hunched over from an invisible weight. Consumed with love for her partner, Queen Maria gave him room to explain, but it never came, and his anxiousness worsened.

"Marco?" said Queen Maria softly.

Edging closer, the king didn't answer, and when she finally joined him, Queen Maria held his hands tight, encouraging him to open up.

"It's Lillian," said King Marco.

"Lillian?"

"She's here."

"What! You mean right now?"

"Yes. She's just arrived from Naxthos with her children and the nanny. They are downstairs in the guest quarters as we speak," replied the King.

"How did she seem?"

"She seemed genuinely pleased to see me. Like the last three years of no contact hadn't happened."

"Marco, please don't blame yourself," urged Queen Maria. "She was the one who went cold. It wasn't your fault."

"I just don't want to get my hopes up," said King Marco, his tone subdued.

"Then don't expect anything. Keep a clear head, dear husband. Let's see how the events unfold."

Looking into his wife's spirited hazel eyes, her soft, comforting words made the King of Wayan feel more at ease. He stared down at the bump and felt all-consuming love for mother and baby. Taking refuge inside their little bubble, the minutes ticked by, and finally King Marco was ready to face his estranged sister again.

Unity established, the pair stepped out of their bedchamber and into the harmonious hallway, where the old tapestries hadn't changed since Maria was a little girl. At the far end, the queen caught a glimpse of an additional portrait: her mother and father stood smiling at the congregation around them in the throne room before they set upon their journey through a portal into other worlds. *Wherever they are*, Queen Maria thought, *all I hope for is their happiness.*

King Marco gently squeezed his wife's hand and guided her slowly down the grand marble staircase. When they finally reached the bottom, they took a sharp left towards an archway leading down a narrow passageway towards the guest quarters and through a door at the far end into a plush, regal living room with old stone walls and medieval-style furniture and architecture. The sun's rays beamed through a large stained-glass window and lit the room with multicoloured light.

The sound of children laughing filled the air. They seemed joyful, like they were running rings around each other. The queen and king hunted for the source; a separate door was open on the other side of the room.

The roars of laughter grew more robust. They stepped through into the dining room as a young boy, close to seven, with dishevelled strawberry-blond hair and covered in mud, chased a slightly younger girl. She had freckles on her cheeks and dark auburn hair cut into a blunt bob. They were goading one another as they ran around an amused woman in her mid-thirties, with long white striking locks and an energetic, whimsical spirit.

"You both!" said the woman playfully. "Where will you cause trouble next, I wonder?"

"The whole of Wayan!" called Anmos.

"You're silly!" chirped Aimesia.

The boy darted away and, without looking, *bang!* King Marco had the wind knocked out of him, and the scared young boy backed away.

"I'm so sorry! I didn't mean to run into you!"

Trying to keep a straight face, Queen Maria turned her attention to the nanny, who bowed, and waited dutifully with a warm, inviting smile.

"Hello," said Queen Maria.

"Your Highness," replied Sylvie.

"Please, no bowing," urged the queen. "What is your name?"

"Sylvie, of the Tarot world Rosa."

"You mean sorceress!" said Anmos.

"Sorry, Anmos." Sylvie chuckled. "Sorceress Sylvie of Rosa. It's a great honour to finally meet you both."

"And it is a delight to meet you, Sylvie," replied Queen Maria, instantly liking her.

As Queen Maria continued the pleasantries, King Marco nervously scanned the space around them, and the Sorceress of Rosa picked up on his restlessness.

"Is there anything I can help you with, Your Majesty?" encouraged Sylvie.

"We had hoped to find my sister," answered King Marco through gritted teeth.

"She told me she was heading to the jetty," said Sylvie.

"The jetty?" replied the confused king.

"Yes, there was something she needed to locate on the mainland, and so desired a boat to take her there."

"What was she looking for?" asked Queen Maria, as shocked as her husband.

"She didn't say. I was ordered to stay with the children and wait for her return."

Casting nervous glances at one another, the rulers of Wayan made an abrupt exit into the narrow passageway.

They picked up the pace, stepping into the radiating light coming in through the large entrance hall windows, and headed outside. Their mouths dropped at the sight before them, for Queen Lillian breezed through the yard, her forest-green cloak with gold flora lace embroidery trailing the ground behind her. Her rich green eyes with tints of yellow met her brother's.

"Everything okay?" asked Queen Lillian.

"Lillian?" asked King Marco, confused.

"Yes? Er, dear brother, you look unsettled? As do you, dear sister-in-law."

"We thought you were down by the jetty?" queried King Marco.

"Why would I be?"

"Sylvie told us?" asked King Marco.

"No. I never told Sylvie that. Why would she…"

As the last word left her lips, a dark, sinister cloud formed around the group. The nanny had lied, and they needed to find Anmos and Aimesia quick. Feeling sick as they drew nearer, Queen Lillian was the first to enter the empty living room.

"Mother!" shouted Anmos.

Now fearful for her children's safety, Queen Lillian followed her son's voice into the dining room, as did Queen Maria and King Marco. They watched in horror. The Sorceress of Rosa had already willed fantastical, multicoloured magic from her Tarot cards and wrapped the energy around Anmos and Aimesia. The children struggled to break free as they stood before a glistening circular gateway to another Tarot world.

"Sylvie!" pleaded Queen Lillian. "What are you doing?"

"Please, stop!" called Queen Maria.

Inches away from leaving Wayan, Sylvie ignored them. She forced the terrified children through the portal just as Queen Lillian ran for the gateway. It closed before she could reach it.

In hot pursuit, Queen Maria willed her agile Tarot deck to tap into the portal's energy, and soon their profound red power reopened the gateway. The three rulers strode through, preparing to take down the Sorceress of Rosa with their Tarot cards. But, on the other side, their mission was futile as countless portals leading off into vast worlds shimmered victoriously. Sylvie and the children had vanished.

Chapter Two

Twenty-One Years Later

Ping, *ping, ping!*

The next flurry of work emails landed in Andrew Hanes's inbox like a round of bullets. Close to 5.30pm, and with no prospect of leaving the baking middle-storey office block soon, the restless agent's assistant to the 'stars' felt the sweat trickle down his back, soaking his white, long-sleeved shirt. As he tried to psyche himself up, he took a swig of lukewarm tap water from the glass that had been sitting there all day.

He rolled his office chair closer to the monitor and his eyes fixated on the endless list of new requests from the 'talent'. Some were chasing updates on potential work, one wanted to amend last-minute travel logistics, and another needed help sourcing and arranging delivery of a new garden furniture set ready for Friday evening. It was Thursday.

Stomach slowly churning with anxiety, Andrew lost all sense of reason. He rose from his chair, grabbed his phone and hurried past the large windows towards the heavy glass doors. Pushing them open, feeling their weight, Andrew took a short, resentful glance at the 'Dream Myers Talent Agency' logo on the wall to his left before entering the waiting area.

Kyle, the receptionist, was engrossed in a dating app website. Andrew contemplated taking the lift, but instead he entered a narrow passageway cut off from the rest of the communal areas. At the far end was a large window and he gravitated towards it.

He paused for breath and buried his head in his hands. His mind was swirling with tasks when an uproar of laughter diverted his attention away. Staring down longingly through the glass, he watched clusters of people chatting and enjoying evening summer drinks along London's South Bank. It looked like their merry faces had been there most of the afternoon, and Andrew was jealous.

Buzz!

"What now!" Andrew shouted, assuming a notification on his phone was from someone at work. But, in this rare instance, he was wrong. Mouth agape, rereading Emily's WhatsApp message, Andrew was astounded. Even after the rescheduling and uncertainty, she'd still like a first date – tonight!

Her tone was upbeat, and a flicker of hope ignited within Andrew, but then, thinking about all the emails he needed to deal with, he feared he wouldn't be able to escape his desk in time. And so, with a sinking feeling, the hyped-up agent's assistant started writing an apology back. He felt she was going to think even less of him than she did before.

As he was about to hit send, a round of cheers from outside snapped him out of his thoughts. Andrew froze, looking out the window again, watching the smiley faces beside the waterfront set against London's majestic skyline.

He thought it was for the best. He was only going to waste her time. But something inside was holding him back from sending the message. Butterflies replaced the stomach churns, and before he knew what he was doing, he deleted his reply and suggested 6.30pm. SENT! "Shit," said Andrew.

Stepping away from the window, Andrew took a deep breath and returned to the scene of distress. He glanced at the wall clock; time was ticking.

"Andrew!" bellowed a tense voice from an enclosed office in the far corner. "Andrew, it's urgent!"

He didn't answer back. But Andrew's boss, Lanie Myers, owner and founder of Dream Myers Talent Agency, wasn't going to back down.

"Andrew!" shouted Lanie, now sounding wild and possessed. "It's urgent!"

"Everything's urgent," Andrew muttered through gritted teeth.

Shaking off the toxicity and putting on an elated front, Andrew lingered in the doorframe of her office, ready for a quick getaway. However, while waiting for further instructions that never came, he caught a lovely breeze from the only working fan inside her suite.

In the centre of the room, Lanie was typing frantically behind an oversized desk, the tip of her long nose inches away from the computer monitor. It looked only a matter of seconds before she would lose her head forever inside the screen. Finally, Lanie glanced up at Andrew, tucked her mad, curly hair behind her ears and returned to her emails.

"Hi, Lanie," said Andrew softly. "Sorry I didn't respond the first time."

"No time for pleasantries, Andrew. We have a potential client."

"A new client?" choked Andrew.

"She's a rising chef on daytime TV, specialising in minimal cooking. Quite literally a new one-pot wonder."

"That sounds interesting."

"Brilliant," said a pleased Lanie. "I'll add her to your roster. It's only fair."

"Er…" stuttered Andrew, taken aback.

"You need to grow just as much as our clients."

"Well…"

"It's okay, Andrew. No need to thank me."

Andrew thought she was deluded. Biting his tongue, he wished Lanie would fill the empty desks in the overspill with people who could help him.

"I've already sent you an email with a list of instructions for this weekend," said Lanie.

"Wait, what, this weekend?" said Andrew, a little rattled.

"Yes, of course," said Lanie. "I need you to go to the studios next door and go through the welcome pack with her. This chef is hot property, and we don't want to lose her. Do we?"

Envisioning a floating desktop monitor landing on her head and knocking Lanie out cold, Andrew walked away before saying or doing something he would regret.

Instead, he cursed under his breath, collapsed at his desk, and carried on working into the evening. Thankfully, he'd managed to push back the time with Emily to 8pm. It was 7.45pm.

Pausing mid-email, Andrew heard movement from his boss's office. Wearing a thick layer of newly applied liquid foundation, bright glittery eyeshadow and vibrant lipstick, Lanie Myers glided out of her office in a sparkly dress and pointed mid-heels. Clutching the handle of her burgundy, leather, designer handbag, she asked half-heartedly whether Andrew had any plans that evening.

"I… not much," answered Andrew, looking at Lanie as if she was on another planet. "How about you?"

"A networking event on a rooftop bar by Tate Modern. I've asked Nick to look after the kids," said Lanie, trailing off at the mention of her husband's name.

"That's nice of him," replied Andrew with caution, knowing there was tension in their marriage that was mainly down to Lanie's long working hours.

"Yes," answered Lanie. "He knows our agency doesn't run by itself."

As the last words left her lips, she finally left him in peace. So close to the finish line, all he now needed to do was categorise his emails in order of importance, ready for the early morning start. But, while he focused on getting the job done, a flicker of unusual red energy appeared in the top right-hand corner of the monitor. It expanded quickly, and before Andrew knew what was happening, a large crack appeared, and the computer turned itself off.

He pushed the button to restart his desktop and it burnt his finger. Wincing at the pain, he heard a crackling sound. Looking at the screen, the sound ceased, and the monitor caught fire. The flames spurted out with incredible force, nearly hitting him. He fell back in shock and wished he hadn't left his laptop at home. Andrew watched the flames change colour to a deep red, and for a split second he thought he'd seen them shimmer.

Grabbing a fire extinguisher beside the entrance, he spotted Kyle through the glass door collecting his belongings. Andrew blasted the screen with carbon dioxide, but instead of putting out the fire, it antagonised it. The flames whipped higher, and the shimmering was undeniable. He was at a loss and needed help! He managed to catch Kyle just in time before the lift arrived.

"Wait!" shouted Andrew.

"Andrew I can't stick around I have a…"

"Date? Well so do I. I need your help."

"But…"

Andrew grabbed Kyle's arm and dragged him through the foyer into the agency. They were confused.

"I don't get it?" said Kyle.

The fire had gone, leaving no trace of its existence. Andrew was about to speak when he heard a buzz from his phone. He picked it up off his desk and saw a message from Emily, saying she was at the pub already. Looking at the wall clock, it read 8.05pm.

"Gotta go, Kyle. I can leave you to this?"

"Leave me to what?"

Andrew grabbed his rucksack and walked away. At the lifts, he pushed the call button repeatedly until one finally arrived. He made his way downstairs, through the barren lobby and out into the pleasantly warm evening air.

Turning left down a built-up pavement, he concentrated hard on meandering through groups of giddy people towards the waterside.

The riverbank was packed to the brim as he fought his way through, desperately trying to locate the pub where he was supposed to meet Emily. Checking his watch, the time was now 8.14pm. So close. Keep going! Finally, Andrew clocked Ye Olde World Tavern and dived into the crowded bar area. He was panting heavily and worried he wouldn't be able to find Emily. He backtracked towards the entrance for a better view. Turning on his heel, Andrew collided with a woman.

"Sorry, I didn't see you there," said Andrew.

He met the deep hazel eyes of an understanding, middle-aged stranger who wore a loose-fitted blouse tucked into a smart pair of blue jeans. Her plain beige hairband tied her copper-tinted hair loosely in a bun, and she smiled at him warmly, not saying a word.

"I should have watched where I was going," continued a frazzled Andrew.

"No harm done. I'll leave you to enjoy your evening," answered the stranger. Soon after, she reached into the back pocket of her jeans, and a wave of concern spread across her face.

"I think I've lost something," the woman said.

"Are you okay?" asked Andrew.

"I… er." The woman stumbled over her words, her voice growing worried.

"Please. Let me help you."

"It's okay, don't worry," replied the woman, trying to keep a brave face as she scanned the floor around them.

Following her gaze, Andrew noticed a peculiar object near his feet: a playing card with the red emblem of a castle on one side. He knelt down and picked it up. A comforting aura started to seep through his skin. Relaxing a little, Andrew held it for the woman to see, and as soon as her eyes clocked the object, she looked relieved.

"Yes, thank you," said the stranger.

Just before he returned the card to its owner, Andrew looked on the other side. It was blank. The woman gently retrieved the card and slipped it back into her pocket. Leaving Andrew to it, she walked towards the other side of the pub. As a group of people broke apart to let the stranger through, he spotted Emily planting herself at the bar, laughing and joking whilst ordering a round of drinks.

He straightened himself up and wiped sweat from his brow before striding towards her. She seemed effortlessly natural and down to earth in a floral top and black jeans, and at that moment, he knew he liked her. Finally, Andrew was in the same room as Emily after meeting on a dating app, and it felt good.

Emily's energetic eyes met his, and she instantly lit him up. Lifting two pints of ale from the bar, she handed one to him and gave a toast to their first meeting.

"I'm sorry to have kept you waiting," stressed Andrew.

"It's okay, honestly. It gave me a chance to catch up, too."

Pointing at the flour stains on her trousers, Emily explained her pastry stall as they moved away from the bar. She had only set up her business a year ago, and it was becoming popular at Borough Market. Andrew was happy just to listen, taking sips of his drink, which tasted even better than he thought it would. Suddenly, the conversation shifted to him.

"So, you said you worked for an agency?"

"Yeah, a talent agency," answered Andrew, keeping it brief.

"That sounds like a completely different world."

"Yes, it is."

"Do you enjoy it?"

"Yes," answered Andrew, with a slightly delayed response.

"What is it you enjoy the most?"

"I…er… Well, I've always wanted something more. So, after completing my media degree, I moved to London for freelance work, and in the last few years I fell into talent management, looking after a wide range of artists in the TV world."

"Are any of them demanding?" Emily chuckled.

"Ha, yeah, some of them!" Andrew laughed. "I guess with any job, there are some downsides."

"I can understand," said Emily delicately. "Where are you from originally?"

"A small town on the Welsh…"

Buzz!

Crap! Andrew thought. Picking up on his anxiousness, Emily sensed there was more to his work than he let on as she watched his troubled eyes read missed calls, messages and emails on his phone.

"Andrew?" said Emily softly. "Are you okay?"

"I, er, yes, sorry. I forgot what I was saying."

"You're from a small Welsh town, moved to the bright lights of the big city in search of a different kind of adventure, and now, as time has passed, it looks like the life you wanted has caused you a considerable amount of stress."

Mouth dropping at her words, Andrew didn't know how to respond. His phone buzzed again. This time, it was a call from one of his 'starlets', who most likely needed a taxi amending for tomorrow morning. Meeting Emily's eyes, he switched his mobile to silent and placed it back in his trouser pocket.

"Yeah, there might be something in what you just said."

"Something?" teased Emily.

Grinning at each other, their conversation turned more light-hearted and flowed into the rest of the evening until, eventually, they needed to call it a night. Waiting for Emily, who had gone to the toilets, Andrew stood near the front door, resisting the urge to look at his phone. Out of the corner of his eye, he noticed the woman he had bumped into earlier slowly making her way over. She smiled at Andrew fondly before exiting the pub.

Much to Andrew's relief, Emily reappeared, and they stepped outside into the warm night air, relaxed, enjoying each other's company.

"This was fun. Are you free next week?" asked Emily.

"I…" Andrew stumbled over his words.

"It's okay," reassured Emily. "Whenever you get a chance."

"I'll definitely let you know. I'm a bit tied up this weekend."

Oh no, this weekend! Andrew suddenly remembered Lanie's bombshell. *What am I going to do about that? Why did it have to be this one?*

"Me too," replied Emily warmly. "It's going to be a busy one at the market."

"Best of luck," said Andrew, worried he sounded like an idiot.

"See you soon. I hope your journey isn't too bad," teased Emily.

Taking one last look at each other, they said their goodbyes and parted ways. Emily headed east to her small studio flat in Southwark whilst Andrew needed to catch a train back to Clapham High Street. But, approaching the entrance hall of Waterloo station, the mood inside didn't look inviting. Crowds of expectant commuters had gathered in front of the departure board, their smiles melting away at the long list of train cancellations. Other weary travellers, who had arrived much earlier, were on the platform waiting outside a severely delayed, packed train back to Clapham.

It was a joke. Andrew wondered how long it would take to clear. Cursing, he begrudgingly reached for his phone.

Just as he was about to reply to Lanie, he paused. Heart pounding in his chest, something inside him snapped. He wanted everything to stop, just for one night. He walked away from the glum commuters and exited the station.

Keep going! he reiterated. *But where?* called a part of him. *You still have a lot of work to do, and you'll only get more stressed and anxious!*

Please, no! replied the shaken Andrew as he passed the Southbank Centre and went down the steps towards the London Eye.

We need a plan, his conscience told him, but Andrew refused. Stopping abruptly, nearly taking down a cyclist, he darted towards the waterfront, where he slumped over the side of the railings in front of the River Thames. Resting his forehead upon the cool metal, he became lost in himself, unable to face the London skyline and its wondrous architecture lit up in an array of colours.

Further along stood the Queen of Wayan, keeping a safe distance from a troubled Andrew. *He looks broken*, she thought, her concern for him at an all-time high. Still wearing the comfortable, non-attention-seeking Earth clothes from the pub, she kept hold of the Tarot card she'd purposefully dropped on the floor for Andrew to pick up. It was the one her most esteemed necromancer had conjured on Wayan many years ago in her quest to find the long-lost children of Naxthos.

Since she arrived on Earth, taking her chance on a severely late bloomer, the card, much to her amazement, had started brewing with excitable, profound red energy, and even more so as it gravitated towards Andrew. It had even tampered with his desktop, ensuring he would leave his office and make contact with Emily.

But, seeing the stress that consumed the young man, she had to tread carefully. After twenty-one years of searching, she couldn't just show up and expect him to turn his life around. Sylvie's memory-wiping spell had done a severe number on him, and the thought of the Sorceress of Rosa, still in hiding, made Queen Maria nauseous.

She decided to sit tight and wait, looking away from Andrew before she felt worse about the situation. Then, turning her attention to the quaint city skyline, she started counting the colours on the buildings to help calm her frustrations when a large, dazzling, forest-green ball of energy appeared in the night sky.

Perplexed, Queen Maria cast her eyes around the oblivious humans on South Bank. She watched Andrew lift his head. He had not registered the energy either. She was the only one that could see the strange display, and as the queen watched the mystical sphere expand, it formed a glistening green ring, hovering over the river.

She prepared for an attack, and as she was about to connect with her Tarot cards and conjure a wall of defence spells around herself and Andrew, the ring dispersed, and the sky returned to normal. Wondering who or what had created the ring, all Queen Maria knew was that she wasn't going to let Andrew out of her sight. Not this time.

Chapter Three

The Answers We Seek

Standing on a small pebble beach close to the water's edge, twenty-six-year-old Amy Hanes cast her honey-tinted eyes out to the wild ocean and watched the waves making their way to shore. Her delighted, freckled face and long auburn hair were whipped into a frenzy by the energetic sea air. Zoning out, she accidentally let go of her oversized turquoise tote bag. As she knelt to pick it up, the sea foam soaked her long summer dress, but she didn't care. Straightening back up, she caught the strong smell of salt water.

The young woman finally tore her gaze away from the sea just as the August sunlight broke through the ever-changing Welsh clouds. She smiled at the sun's victory and strolled in her sandals across the small cobbles towards a set of old concrete steps. Gripping the worn iron railing, she slowly ascended, arriving on Aberaeron's promenade.

Amy spotted the early rising dogwalkers enjoying the start of a new day as she crossed the road into a narrow street. On either side, surrounding her, were colourful

Georgian houses with flowerbeds and quaint garden furniture next to their front doors.

With only a handful of people to divert around, Amy didn't take long to reach the bustling main road filled with local merchants parking their vans outside the array of shops, cafes and pubs in preparation for the customers.

Just as she was about to meander left, her phone buzzed from the pocket of her light denim jacket. Feeling a little unnerved, Amy removed it and inspected the screen. A flicker of annoyance spread across her face as she put the phone away.

Marching across the road, she nearly walked in front of a car and the horn bellowed, shaking Amy back to the land of the living. After apologising, she reached the other side in one piece.

"That Lanie will be the death of both of us!" said a frightened Amy. "Okay, get to your safe place, quick!"

Her heart started to return to normal as she approached a bright blue building. She looked up fondly at the hanging sign with 'Flint & Drift' edged onto an old piece of timber. Amy scrambled for the keys at the bottom of her bag and unlocked the stiff, rickety door. It needed a bit of force to push it open. She finally succeeded and instantly felt uplifted as she stepped inside the treasure trove.

Housing an eclectic range of seaside and nature artwork illustrations, handmade trinkets and kitchenware crafted by local and national artists, Amy was home. She passed the shelves with a grin as she gazed upon the colourful seashell bowls, clocks and ships.

She plonked herself on the high stool behind the counter and fired up the laptop. Opening the calendar, she contemplated whether it would be safer to cancel the events and exhibitions she'd pre-booked with her brother. Amy sat in silence.

Her eyes scanned the screen and she felt foolish. It was always the same with Andrew. He never says no to Lanie's demands and eventually, as usual, he decides it's for the best she doesn't visit him.

Noticing the time was 8.00am, Amy pulled away from making a rash decision and closed the browser, determined to start the day as she meant to go on. She opened her mailbox with anticipation and began sifting through customer orders and artist and merchant enquiries, whilst keeping tabs on emerging entrepreneurs on social media. She thought the creativity out there was awe-inspiring. She left the laptop and entered the back room, which was littered with packaged orders.

Picking up a wrapped seascape canvas, Amy strolled through the shop towards the entrance on a mission to deliver the item to its owner. She didn't bother to lock up as she closed the door behind her and flipped a sign hanging over the glass panel saying, 'Back in ten minutes'. A few minutes later she arrived at a quaint shabby-chic coffee shop called 'Bean Eazy' with tables and chairs outside.

The smell of inviting, roasted coffee hit her. Families with toddlers had already settled at vintage-style tables with their hot drinks and cake whilst the owner, Macey, who was in her early forties, busied herself behind the counter. Amy rested the protected artwork safely on a shelf and tiptoed away.

"Where are you going?" asked Macey.

"Hi, Macey. I didn't want to disturb you," began Amy.

"Don't be silly. Wait here!"

The owner asked her young apprentice, whose eyes looked bloodshot from a late night of online gaming, to make Amy a cappuccino – free of charge.

"And pop a croissant in a bag too," said Macey. "Thank you, Thomas."

Winking at Amy, who stood aside and smiled gratefully, the owner checked the tables whilst the dishevelled teenager tried to focus. His eyes squinted at three coffee machines when there was just one, and Amy thought it could take a while.

Her ears pricked up at the sound of a raised voice in the street drawing near, and a man in his mid-twenties, close to Amy's age, entered with a healthy stack of flyers.

"Mam, I'm trying, honestly!" the man said into his mobile. "I don't mean to be funny, but could you have told me who to ask? You'd have known in advance, surely?"

Soon after, the caller cut him off, and Amy watched him look around the cafe in frustration. He took a deep breath, and as he was about to say hello to Macey, she got in first.

"It's okay, Ben," said the understanding owner.

"I'm sorry," said Ben, cheeks flushed with embarrassment.

Taking the flyers, Macey chuckled with amusement as she read a promotion for 70 per cent off at Sea Mysticism, a magic shop one mile out of Aberaeron, further along the coast.

"Your mother's business going well, I see," quipped Macey.

"Yes, absolutely," replied Ben sarcastically. "She's become a bit more eccentric recently."

"How do you mean?" asked Macey, desperate for gossip.

"First, it was palm reading, and now it's Tarot cards. Her words were, 'It can't be that hard,'" Ben said, exasperated.

Chuckling to herself, Macey popped the flyers on a small table at the front, but her smile quickly dropped, for Amy still hadn't received her coffee or croissant. Marching behind the counter, a woman on a mission, Macey bulldozed Thomas out of the way whilst Amy and Ben stood awkwardly silent, fearing for the boy's life.

"Honestly, Macey, it's…" started Amy, but the owner couldn't hear anything around her. She was too far gone.

"It looks nearly ready," whispered Ben, reassuring Amy.

"I hope so," answered Amy, breaking a smile.

Standing side by side, the seconds ticked by, and Amy glanced at the flyers on the counter. But just before she was about to strike up a conversation with Ben, a subdued Thomas finally handed over the items.

"Thank you," said Amy. "Have a good day, everyone."

"Thanks, Amy!" called Macey, not taking her eyes off Thomas.

Turning on her heel and smiling at Ben, Amy took a sip of her cappuccino as she left. Her eyes beamed with happiness as she took another swig. Scrambling to open the paper bag, she bit into the butter-dripped croissant, not caring about making a mess on her clothes or the pavement. By the time she'd got back to Flint & Drift, she had eaten the entire pastry.

"Every time," muttered Amy, wishing Macey had given her another.

Buzz!

Okay, deep breaths, she told herself as she reached for her mobile. *You've had caffeine and a lush snack, so all is right with the world. Well, just about.*

As expected, the message was from Andrew, chasing a response. Now hunched over the counter, contemplating the situation, Amy needed to decide soon, for her own sanity. There would always be a risk, whatever weekend; she imagined Lanie, the hyped-up loon, scuppering Andrew's downtime at every opportune moment. Not this time!

Telling her brother she was going to visit anyway, Amy hid the phone behind the counter, out of sight. *Don't go back on your decision, Amy! It's final!* But a slight pang of guilt began to seep into her being, as she knew all too well the stress Andrew was under. *No, Amy*, she told herself.

Dodging her thoughts, she set her sights on the shelf furthest away and bolted towards it. She rearranged the trinkets to keep her mind occupied, and thankfully, soon after, a flurry of tourists entered.

As the day wore on, and after another onslaught of tourists, Amy took the opportunity to look up at the anchor-themed wall clock. It was 4pm. She placed a small, polished brass bell on the front desk and buried herself in the back room, logging and preparing the postal orders, ready for the next morning. A good hour passed until Amy had finished.

Content, she stepped back into the bright light of the store, soaking in her surroundings, when she noticed something peculiar on the counter that wasn't there before. A set of newly opened Tarot cards rested neatly on one of the flyers for Sea Mysticism's 70-per-cent-off sale. Looking around, there was no soul to be seen, and she wondered if Ben had left them. She thought it would be a little creepy, though, if he had.

She picked up the deck gently and set aside the cover card titled 'Rider-Waite' before she cast her eyes upon the image of a happy young man wearing exuberant medieval attire, standing close to the edge of a cliff with a merry dog at his side. "The Fool," said Amy aloud, reading the name on the card with the number zero. It reminded her of Andrew, apart from the medieval skirt and dog. She moved on and inspected the number one card showing a magician. She looked closely at the young, determined conjurer wearing majestic robes, holding a wand in his right hand, and pointing at the sky. Before him, a sword, a pentacle coin, a cup, and a wand rested on a table, and underneath was a garden of beautiful roses and lilies.

Continuing through the deck, Amy touched upon the beginning of a suit of cards with a pentacle symbol. There was a page, knight, queen and king. Sifting further, she saw numbers one to ten. Admiring the imagery, she felt compelled to delve deeper, and out of the corner of her eye, the flyer started to glisten with wondrous energy.

Watching the piece of paper, Amy wasn't alarmed, for the magic of an unknown force from the deck had successfully infiltrated her, making her comply. Without thinking, Amy gathered her mobile, purse, keys and an unopened pack of wine gums and threw them into the large turquoise tote bag. She kept hold of the cards as she locked up twenty minutes early.

As she reached the bus stop on the main road, she was lost in her own world, entranced by the cards. A bus pulled up and she stepped inside. She didn't engage with the driver, who didn't seem to mind she hadn't paid for her trip and found a seat midway up the aisle.

She waited absently as the bus pulled away and drove along the coast, where an isolated seaside village came into view. Before Amy could read the welcome sign, she'd missed it. Feeling compelled to get off, she pushed the call button, and soon enough the driver let her off at the next stop.

The mood was bleak as the grey clouds encased the area. Amy spotted, on the hauntingly quiet road, a handful of boarded-up shops long forgotten about, save for one. A bright yellow building, plastered in magenta, navy, and emerald green bunting, had clung to its lifeline with a determined force.

The words on a chalkboard sign came into view, *Please come in! Please! There's a sale!* As Amy reread the sign, she thought it was perhaps a desperate force rather than a determined one. Looking up at the name, 'Sea Mysticism', Amy wondered why the shop was in such a remote location. As she drew closer, she saw a metal plaque underneath the bay window – *In memory of Steven Jenkins.*

Turning the handle, a bell above the door rang across the vast space of the olde-worlde magic shop, announcing her arrival. Underneath the rustic wooden beams, Amy waited for someone to greet her as the door slammed, but no one came.

Unable to stand there, she started exploring the rows of quaint wooden shelves packed with antique and modern magic books on the mythology of magic, everyday magic, and even *Magic for Magic's Sake*, in big bold letters.

She cast her eyes over a colourful collection of crystals including rose quartz, gold tiger eye, purple amethyst and many others, that had been placed in various wicker bowls on a shelf close by. The labels beside them, describing their purposes, looked like they'd been written in a hurry. 'In need of a miracle, pick up a shungite' read Amy, as she looked at the black polished gemstones.

She caught a strong whiff of something. It came from patchouli and white jasmine incense sticks which had been placed inside tall glass vases. Next to the sticks were incense holders with miniature gold stars printed on. The rest of the shelves housed charms, runes and relaxation CDs, and gemstone jewellery in a variety of colours for each of the birth signs of the zodiac.

She had to admit that the owner, Ben's mum, was passionate about her business. The level of detail was evident. Amy gravitated towards a shelf full of unopened Rider-Waite Tarot decks and felt a little queasy. The sickness intensified and the realisation hit. She was not at home, packing for her trip to London. Instead, she was somewhere else utterly alien to her. *What just happened?* Amy thought, heart racing. *How did I get here?*

As her eyes darted around Sea Mysticism, she couldn't contain her nerves and decided to make a quick getaway. Pacing across the floor, she saw a hand appear from the centre of a floor-length curtain, startling her. Its dumpy fingers, covered in silver-plated rings with an eclectic mix of gemstones, pulled the curtain back, and its owner, Susan Jenkins, popped out.

Wearing a coral dress, a rainbow-coloured scarf and a crescent moon hair scrunchie, Susan's wild, grey-tinted hair was all over the place. Her bright blue eyes widened, and her mouth dropped at the sight of Amy. "Hello," said Susan.

"Hello," said Amy nervously.

Perplexed, Susan looked like she couldn't believe a customer had finally walked through the door, and as her eyes clocked the Tarot cards in Amy's hand, a big grin spread across her face. "Aw, brilliant. Well done, Ben!" said Susan, trailing off with excitement. "This way, dear; follow me. You're in for a treat."

Too slow to escape, Amy was dragged through the curtain and into the cosy, candlelit back room, with wood-scented incense filling the air and soft cushions in various colours littering the carpet.

Amy wondered how she had managed to end up there. She clocked Ben talking to a slightly older man whose features looked similar to his, with jet-black hair, a short, straight nose and an oval chin.

"Right, lovey, gotta go," said Susan. "I need to check something quickly before we start. Help yourself to nibbles and juice."

Bubbling with annoyance at Ben for landing her in this mess, Amy watched the men pause mid-sentence. Sensing her presence, they turned to face Amy, and Ben's face dropped with shock.

"Amy! Hi," said Ben, a little embarrassed.

"Hi, Ben," muttered Amy.

"I'm surprised to see you here."

Meanwhile the older man, his brother James, took a step back with a smirk just as their younger sister Lucy, and her best friend Amanda, were gawping at Ben and Amy further away.

"Oh, I thought the cards were from you?" replied Amy, voice much lower. "If it wasn't you, who was it?"

Before Amy and Ben could talk further, Susan bolted to the front, asking the group to make themselves comfortable on the cushions.

"Hello, everyone. What a great turnout," started Susan. "So, I just wanted to introduce everyone. So firstly, my eldest son James. Pop your arm up, stop slouching. Next, my younger son Ben. I mean, try to look a bit more enthusiastic, Ben. Finally, my youngest daughter, Lucy. Thank you for smiling. Good job."

Everyone, apart from Susan and Amy, registered how ridiculous her introduction sounded, including Amanda, as three-fifths of the room were her children.

"So, we are here for an intro to a basic Tarot reading," continued Susan. "Never fear; I read a beginner's guide and followed it up on YouTube, so we are all set. Who would like to volunteer first?"

Scanning the room with hope, Susan Jenkins soon realised no one seemed keen and Amy looked intimated. Trying to stay positive, she gestured for Lucy's friend Amanda to join her and watched the twenty-year-old with messy, unbrushed hair seem highly put out as she sulkily made her way over.

"Brilliant. Thank you, dear," said Susan delicately.

As they sat on the cushions facing one another, and sideways for the onlookers to get a clear view, Susan handed the girl an unopened Tarot deck. Amanda ripped open the plastic like a Christmas present, whilst the anxious shop owner asked the blasé guinea pig to shuffle the cards face down.

"You need to connect with these cards, Amanda. Focus your energy on them," explained Susan.

James, Ben, and Lucy shared amused glances with one another at their mum's best efforts, and just as Susan was about to explain the workings of a single-card spread, high-tempo club music blasted out of Amanda's trouser pocket. Remaining silent, the room waited and finally the noise stopped. Returning to shuffling the cards, Amanda had forgotten what Susan had told her, and the music erupted again from the girl's back pocket.

"Should I take the call?" asked Amanda.

"Yes, dear. I think that might be for the best," urged Susan.

As the girl rose, she reached for her mobile and walked away, disappearing behind the heavy curtain onto the shop floor. With the owner of Sea Mysticism now alone at the front, her children studied each other's faces, deciding who should take the hit. Suddenly, to their amazement, Amy volunteered.

"Are you sure?" Ben whispered.

Amy was in a daze and didn't respond. She made herself comfortable on a cushion across from Susan, still holding the cards she acquired at Flint & Drift.

"Thank you, Amy," began Susan, trying to contain her annoyance at Ben, James and Lucy. "Please shuffle your cards face down. Ease into the rhythm. Perfect. Ask the cards a question but keep it to yourself. When you're ready, reveal the top card, and rest it on the carpet for us to decipher."

The room watched a compliant Amy close her eyes. Breathing deeply, she felt a crackle of energy transfer out of the cards and into her fingertips. Still, Amy wasn't scared. She kept going, and in her mind she could see astonishing forest-green energy dancing around the room in front of her. Hearing a whirlwind of whispers in the distance, Amy strained to make out the words until, finally, the voices settled and told her to ask the question she needed an answer to.

Will my brother be okay? Amy thought. Overwhelmed with worry for Andrew's well-being, her question seeped out of her soul, and the Tarot energy instantly latched on to it. Soon after, brewing with intensity, the forest-green power shot out of her Tarot deck and struck her body. The Jenkins family were in complete shock.

"Make it stop, Mam!" called Lucy.

"It's not me!" shouted Susan.

Amy cried out in pain as she released fantastical energy from her hands. It swirled around the room and conjured a magnificent green ring.

"That must have been one hell of a YouTube channel, Mam," said James.

Desperately firing up her laptop, a panicked Susan hunted for the video she'd seen online, whilst James told Ben and Lucy to stay away from Amy. Ignoring his brother, Ben attempted to reach her, but James pulled him back as the wondrous power consumed the ring. A scene unfolded, and the family saw an anxious young man, standing at the water's edge of the River Thames, next to the London Eye. He was hunched over, about to hit the railing with his forehead.

The scene flickered and the ring disappeared. Amy lost her balance and dropped to the floor, exhausted. Breaking free from James's grip, Ben rushed to her aid, with Lucy chasing after him.

"Mam?" asked James, who joined Susan as she continued to hunt for answers online. "Mam, please, you're shaking." Taking the lead, James closed the laptop and wrapped his arms around her. She couldn't speak. For the first time in her life, the owner of Sea Mysticism had witnessed a magical gateway, and she was terrified.

Chapter Four

Awakening

Slumped on the carpet, battling to regain consciousness, Amy heard a mishmash of voices in the distance. Struggling to make out what was being said, she knew they seemed panicked, especially Ben, whose shaky voice drew closer.

Someone else, perhaps James, urged Ben to stand back, and soon after the same voice told Lucy to make a run for it, but she resisted. So, with an argument on the horizon among the Jenkins siblings, images around Amy slowly returned to normal.

Overwhelmed with nausea, she inhaled and exhaled deeply and eventually mustered the strength to lift herself and sit upright with Ben's help. Grateful for the assistance, her relief soon turned to concern; he looked as white as a sheet.

"Ben?" said Amy. "Are you okay?"

Unsure where to begin, Ben's eyes darted across the room to his mum, and as Amy followed his gaze, she immediately sensed Susan's unease.

"What happened, Mrs Jenkins?" asked Amy.

"I, er," stuttered Susan, releasing her grip from around James's waist.

Amy's eyes darted to the floor. The Tarot cards she'd brought to Sea Mysticism were strewn everywhere and she didn't understand why. Bewildered by the display, a faint flicker of light drew her attention. She hunted for the source while the Jenkins family looked on anxiously, hoping the forest-green energy and the gateway wouldn't make a second appearance.

Amy found the light. One of the cards showed an elderly gentleman standing on a cold mountain peak. He wore a cloak and held a lamp. Inside the lamp was a shining star, and the flicker of wondrous light emulated from the star. Then, out of nowhere, it happened again.

"Did you see that?" said Amy.

"See what, Amy?" asked Ben delicately.

"The flicker coming from the lamp."

Pointing to the 'IX – The Hermit', the Jenkins family knew, without a shadow of a doubt, that was the one Amy had selected in her Tarot reading. Of course, they couldn't see anything out of the ordinary, but Amy was sure it was real.

"Dear," said Susan, "we can't see anything."

"But…"

"Maybe something to eat and some water will make you feel better," said Susan. "You fainted, and it was a nasty fall. It could have happened to anyone."

There it was, much to their children's disbelief; their mum had told an all-out lie, and it would be difficult to backtrack. But Susan, whose fear turned to worry for the young woman, felt this was the best way to protect her, at least for now.

However, Amy's insides couldn't let go of the flickering star. Instead of saying something, she fell eerily silent as Lucy sprang to action. The youngest sibling left through a door into the kitchen, where the clanging of glasses, slamming cupboards and running tap water dominated the air.

The chaos subsided and Lucy bulldozed towards Amy, who was jolted back to reality when the girl planted an opened packet of ready salted crisps and lukewarm tap water in her hands.

"Crisps? Seriously?" quipped Ben.

"It's all I could find," protested Lucy.

"Yeah, I bet it was," replied Ben, unconvinced.

"It's okay," interrupted Amy, not wanting to cause another family row. "Once I've finished with these, there are some wine gums in my bag."

A glimmer of her old self, Amy watched Lucy beam at her words and even Ben couldn't help but chuckle. The three started to relax a little, but Susan was growing more restless on the other side of the space. She tried to hide it, but his mum didn't fool James. The owner of Sea Mysticism had wanted to ask a burning question, and it was the opportune moment.

"Amy, dear," began Susan, taking a gentle step forward.

"Yes," replied Amy, munching on a crisp.

"Out of interest. Where did you get your cards from?" asked Susan.

"Well, er, originally, I thought they were from Ben. I was packaging orders in the back room at work, and after

I'd finished the cards were waiting for me on the counter with one of your sale flyers."

"One of our flyers?" asked Susan, a little unnerved.

"Yes," answered Amy confidently.

"Where do you work, Amy?" continued Susan.

"Aberaeron."

"And so, you just decided to come out here?" queried Susan, growing increasingly intrigued by the young woman's story.

"Yes. I, er, I don't know how to describe it. It just felt right, me coming here."

"Well, Ben was the only one visiting Aberaeron today," said Susan.

"Then I don't understand who else it could have been," continued Amy, checking to see if the lamp on the card had flickered again.

"It's okay, Amy," said Susan. "Lucy will fetch you something more substantial to eat. I think you need to rest now."

"Do you know what the Hermit card means?" asked Amy, unable to let go.

"It's, er…" Susan didn't have the answer.

"It's okay, Mum," James reassured her, handing Susan one of the many Tarot booklets she'd impulse-bought online. Cheeks flushed with embarrassment, Susan accepted the booklet and flicked through the pages earnestly until she finally found what she was looking for.

"The gentleman on the card represents slowing the pace of hopes and dreams and being open to the bigger picture. Otherwise, you risk loneliness and isolation like a hermit," Susan trailed off.

"And that's the card you drew," added Lucy, eager to help.

"I drew that card?" asked Amy, struggling to remember.

"Yes," confirmed Lucy.

"Lucy!" said Susan, wishing her daughter would stop.

"What?! It was that card, though," replied Lucy.

"Please, Mrs Jenkins," said Amy. "If there's anything else, please tell me…"

Ring!

The welcome bell pierced the silence of the shop floor from the other side of the heavy, draped curtain. The front door closed with a bang, as if on purpose, and Susan was stunned. Another customer! Were they all arriving from Aberaeron in one night?

However, to James's dismay, she instinctively gripped his arm for moral support and started dragging him towards the curtain.

"Thank you for volunteering," Susan said.

"No problem," replied James through gritted teeth.

"Everyone else, just relax," said Susan. "Well, at least try to. We won't be long."

Lifting the curtain and pushing him through, Susan followed after taking one last look at Amy.

In the shop, mum and son heard the thundering clouds outside as the rain beat down heavily upon the windowpanes. The fleeting summer weather had been bullied into submission. Across the shop floor, Susan and James scanned the soaked visitor who stood in the centre of Sea Mysticism, shaking her battered brolly.

"Hello," chimed Susan.

Startled, the woman, wearing a light beige coat, navy top and light, smart jeans, looked a little younger than Susan, possibly mid-forties. She turned to face them, and her rich green eyes with tints of yellow looked instantly relieved.

"Hello. Are you Susan Jenkins?" said the woman, hoping the answer would be yes.

"Er, yes," Susan answered, trying to remember if she'd met this woman.

"Ah, good," replied the visitor. "I'm Diane. I hope I'm not too late for the beginner's Tarot session?"

"The Tarot session?" said Susan.

"Er, yes," said Diane, a little confused.

Holding up the flyer to Sea Mysticism's sale offers, the woman pointed to the spot where it mentioned 'Intro to Tarot' beginning every Thursday at 6.15pm. The time was 7pm.

"Oh yes, that Tarot reading, of course," said Susan.

"Phew! I hope I'm not too late. Unfortunately, there were so many travel delays, and the bus journey here wasn't the smoothest. But I was determined to make it."

"Oh, I really am sorry," began Susan, "but we needed to cancel at short notice."

"That's a shame," answered Diane, looking disappointed. "May I ask why that is?"

"We didn't have enough people. Again, we are so sorry you came out all this way. Is there something I can get for you in the shop? Free of charge, of course."

Mrs Jenkins didn't care how much it cost, as long as it appeased the woman. But Diane didn't want an object. Instead, she wanted to know if anyone had stayed behind. Confused by the odd request, Susan said no, and Diane's soft, understanding demeanour slowly evaporated.

"Are you sure about that?" she asked, rather direct.

"Yes," said Susan, a little shaken.

"It's just I wanted to meet others interested in Tarot, and that would seem more valuable to me now than anything else."

"Honestly, no one stayed behind," continued Susan, quickly realising she needed to defend herself.

"Not even from Aberaeron? Where I'm from?"

"Not even from Aberaeron," added James politely, but underneath the visage, he was determined to stop the inquisition. "And I can safely vouch for my mum, as I've been here too – no one stayed behind." Joining his mum's side, the eldest Jenkin sibling cemented their camaraderie, while Diane turned back into the sweet woman they had met minutes ago.

"We're sorry, we have to close up soon," said Susan. "A family commitment. You understand."

"Yes, I certainly do," replied Diane as she glanced out the window.

"If there's anything you want…" added Susan.

But before Mrs Jenkins finished her sentence, the visitor said farewell and left. Confuddled by the abrupt exit, Susan and James rushed to the window and peered out. The rain had eased as they watched Diane catch a bus in time. Soon after, it pulled away into the night.

"Well, that could have been much worse," James said, chuckling.

"Yes, especially after what just happened tonight," said Susan.

"Magic might exist after all," teased James.

"Well, after what we endured, I think it bloody well does!" said Susan.

She marched across the shop floor, followed by an anxious James wondering what mood his mum would be in next. She pulled the curtain back with such force that the railing above rattled, and her mouth dropped at the sight of Ben and Lucy, who looked rather sheepish.

"Mum, before you say anything, please don't get mad," said Lucy.

"Where's Amy?" asked Susan. Her eyes travelled across the room into the kitchen, where there was an exit door at the back.

"Look, she needed to leave," stated Ben.

"But you could have kept her here longer!" shouted Susan.

"And keep her hostage?" quipped Ben. "At least she didn't leave on a flying broomstick!"

"She could have! Or through a gateway or something," said Susan.

"We checked with Amy, but she insisted on getting the bus," replied Ben.

"You are chivalrous, Ben," scoffed James.

"We've only just met. It would have been a little full-on, don't you think? Trying to control her every move?" asked Ben.

"Honestly," said Susan.

"But, Mum, hear me out." Ben tried to reassure her. "Amy admitted she would have asked a question during the Tarot reading about her brother."

"Did she hint at him having any interest in magic?" asked Susan.

"No. Her words were 'he wouldn't be caught dead around this stuff'," answered Ben.

Looking sullen, Susan made her way into the kitchen and ransacked the cupboards. Eventually, she found a bottle of wine, loosened the screw cap and poured the liquid haphazardly into the largest glass she could find – a gin goblet.

Her children fell eerily silent on the other side of doorframe, watching Susan take swig after swig. When she topped up her glass, she removed her phone from her dress pocket.

"Mum, wait a minute," urged James, trying to be a voice of reason.

"But, I just want to check she's okay. Especially after what happened to Amy, who is now alone on her way back to Aberaeron, thanks to Ben," said Susan, resisting.

"I know, Mum, but you know she needs some space. So, we all agreed," begged James.

Susan longed for her eldest daughter to be in the same room with James, Ben, and Lucy. But she knew James was right. She needed to quash her desire to send a message, however unbearable it was.

"Mum," said Ben delicately, trying to make amends, "I know we can't do anything if she doesn't want our help, but we could help Amy."

Resting her glass on the counter, Susan fought back the tears as Lucy moved in and wrapped her arms around her mum. Finally, after another sip, Susan was ready to engage. She learnt from Ben and Lucy that Amy's brother, Andrew, lived in London and planned to visit him this weekend.

"That makes sense, from what we saw on South Bank. The guy next to the London eye must have been him," said James.

"He could be the Hermit," added Susan.

As her children breezed past their mum's comment, still getting to grips with the possibility of Tarot reading or magic truly existing, they knew they couldn't stand back and leave Amy to it. And so, while the Jenkins family were setting a plan in motion, further north, along a bumpy, winding road, Amy's mind was riddled with uncertainty as she sat alone at the back of the bus.

From the moment she discovered the Tarot cards – now safely tucked away at the bottom of her tote bag – to leaving Sea Mysticism, Amy was desperate to remember every detail. But, instead, a whirlwind of images came and went. It was like pieces of a jigsaw, thrown into a bag and shaken violently.

And so, drawing nearer to home and still no closer to unravelling the whole picture, Amy removed the mobile from the pocket of her denim jacket and tried ringing her mum. It went to voicemail, and as she listened intently, her mouth dropped. She'd found out her parents were on a cruise! Amy tried ringing and texting, but still no word until, finally, she gave up.

Confused by their odd, whimsical behaviour, Amy stared out the window into the abyss of the remote countryside. Retreating into herself, she hadn't noticed Diane, who sat quietly behind the bus driver, look around and cast her a fleeting, innocent glance.

Returning her gaze to the front, Diane, also known as Queen Lillian of Naxthos, was trying to hold it together. But, from planting the Tarot cards at Flint & Drift to orchestrating Amy's attendance at Susan's shop, she knew she had to be sure. And now, it seemed like she had finally found Aimesia.

Closing her eyes, the Queen of Naxthos willed fantastical forest-green energy, the colour of her Naxthosian heritage, inside her mind. Next, she visualised Amy's Tarot cards in the centre, and as the power consumed the deck, Queen Lillian focused on connecting with their aura and tapping into their memories.

Flash!

Transported to Sea Mysticism, she watched the memory scene intently. First, the volatile forest-green energy seeped from Amy's eye pupils while the Jenkins family looked on in fear. Then, taking a step back, the queen witnessed the young woman crying out in pain as she conjured from her hands the magnificent gateway.

"Make it stop, Mum!" called Lucy.

"It's not me!" shouted Susan.

"That must have been one hell of a YouTube channel, Mum," said James.

Ignoring the chaos surrounding her, Queen Lillian fixated on the forest-green ring. She caught a glimpse of Andrew at the water's edge and hoped he was Anmos. She drew closer, unable to look away.

Without thinking twice, she crossed through the portal and manipulated the scene so that she arrived safely on South Bank, next to Amy's brother. But, as soon as relief spread across her face, unease struck, for she'd detected a different kind of energy close by. One that was both familiar and uninviting. Hunting for the source, she eventually found it and cautiously approached the Queen of Wayan, who was spying on Andrew in the distance.

Growing more unsettled by her presence, a raging fire erupted inside Queen Lillian's stomach. No way was she going to let her sister-in-law find her children first.

Chapter Five

Separation

The wind's howling mourned across the wild fields as night fell over the desolate Scottish coastline. Twenty-seven-year-old Cassie Jenkins, who wore sturdy hiking boots and dark rainproof clothing, cautiously made her way along a rough, unmarked path.

Her frizzy blonde hair was tied back securely. Susan's eldest daughter cast glances behind her to check no one was following. Eventually, she reached the base of a sharp, hilly incline. Kneeling on her hands and knees, she crawled to the top of the slope. Before peering over the edge, she pulled the dark scarf over her nose to conceal her face.

As the wind grew more intense, she saw an uninterrupted view of an imposing, decrepit-looking farmhouse. The structure looked long forgotten, with no light coming from inside, but Cassie was determined to reach it.

Making her way along the top of the slope, she found a clearing into a build-up of woodland. Thankfully, her shoes had a good grip as she wormed around uneven terrain and climbed over fallen tree trunks. To anyone else, it may have been a struggle, navigating through the forest in pitch darkness, but Cassie was able to see everything.

Adrenaline pumping, she arrived at the bottom of the hill. But before she exited the trees, she steadied her pace. She fixed her eyes on the farmhouse from a hidden vantage point, paused for breath and scanned the area to check the coast was clear.

Once satisfied, she pushed forward. Crouching as she approached the large house, she caught a glimpse of a well-looked-after, khaki-coloured Jeep parked in one of the battered stables. There were no registration plates, and the vehicle looked recently cleaned and polished.

Blood boiling, she hurried across the complex and immediately hunched under the nearest windowpane. Slowly and carefully lifting herself, Cassie saw through the dirt-covered glass, broken kitchen appliances, mould-ridden walls and cupboard doors hanging off their hinges. There was no sign of life in the dark space.

Cassie stayed close to the wall as she circled the farmhouse; again, there was nothing out of the ordinary. But, instead of walking away, she repeatedly rechecked the ground-floor windows. Eventually, she saw something dart across the living space. The figure looked human as it rushed out of the room and into the hallway.

Cassie had finally exposed her prey. She dashed to the back door and turned the handle with such force the lock ripped clean off. Unfazed by the little effort it took to break in, she travelled through the murky hallway, casting glances sideways, checking that no one was in the living room, kitchen, or dining space.

After one last look behind her, Cassie stood at the foot of the rickety staircase leading to the first floor. A glimmer of light covered the soles of her boots, damping the creaking noises as she made contact with the first step.

The unusual energy continued to conceal Cassie's trespassing as she slowly and carefully made her way up the stairs. Halfway up, the banister curved sharply right to a second set of steps. She kept going and arrived on the first floor. The hallway was dark and cold, bereft of life, with two doors on either side closed securely and another at the far end slightly ajar.

Listening intently, Cassie waited and waited. A slight scuffle in the distance alerted her to the door on the left, and she gravitated towards it. Now planted in front of the closed entryway, she pressed the side of her face against the wood. Straining to hear further movement, soon after, there was a loud bang! Cassie stood back, inhaled and exhaled deeply, and took the door off its hinges with one powerful kick. Swooping in as the door flew across the space, her face scrunched angrily at the scene before her.

A scared young boy, aged no more than ten, struggled to break free from the rope tied around his wrists and ankles. His captor, a burly, clean-cut man wearing an expensive-looking berry jumper and dark-washed jeans, looked out of the place in the wilderness.

He gripped the boy's shoulders violently, making the child wince through the tape secured around his mouth, and looked up at Cassie with hatred. She approached, fists clenched as the man dragged his victim across the room and threw him down hard into a closet. The boy's head made contact with the floor, and the impact was severe.

Dazed and unable to react in time, the door to the cupboard soon closed behind the child. Now trapped, he got into the foetal position, shaking as he struggled to understand what was happening on the other side.

Smash!

The sound of furniture being thrown about, glass smashing, and wails of pain pierced the air. All of a sudden, the boy scrambled back in shock as he witnessed a shimmering, fantastical beam of light through the cracks in the doorframe. It was unlike anything he had seen before. As quickly as it had appeared, it disappeared.

Silence. The commotion had evaporated, and the fearful child waited anxiously into the night as no one spoke or made a move. Exhausted and on the verge of passing out, the sound of a police siren in the distance shook him back to consciousness.

The boy's fears reignited. Desperately hoping he would be found soon, he edged closer to the door, straining to hear anything from his captor on the other side. But there was nothing – the man had been knocked out cold.

Cassie needed to leave. She hurried across the hallway downstairs towards the entranceway she'd forced open. The same glimmering light was following her, expertly wiping away footprints and traces of evidence of her presence as she left the farmhouse.

Once outside, the energy diminished, and she bolted across the complex, passed the stables and was soon back in the woodlands. The police sirens amplified in the background, and the sharp pang of guilt returned.

Remembering the terrified look on the boy's face, Cassie had contemplated opening the closet and hugging him, but she knew she couldn't risk it. "You need to keep going," Cassie muttered under her breath. She climbed back up the slope, heart beating frantically.

When she reached the top, instead of doubling back towards the unmarked path, Cassie ventured away from the coastline, crossing a couple of miles of wild terrain not usually tackled by hikers, even experienced ones. She picked up the pace, refusing to slow down in case her legs stalled, and after reaching mile six, Cassie looked relieved when she drew closer to a grove of deciduous trees on her left.

A gentle wall of shimmering light revealed itself, and Cassie crossed the mystical border into the grove that kept those inside hidden from the outside world.

Surrounded by a circular wall of energy, Cassie removed her scarf as she made her way towards a small, outdated caravan in the centre. Turning the handle and opening the door, she winced at the cuts on her hands. It was from when she threw the man into the floor-length mirror and the glass had smashed. But it was safe to say the boy's captor had come off worse. Much worse.

Closing the door gently, Cassie looked out the window, checking the forcefield was still active.

"It's okay," whispered a soothing voice inside her mind, "we're safe."

"I'm sorry," replied Cassie.

A wondrous light flickered from the inner lining of her waterproof jacket. As Cassie unzipped the pocket, a dazzling, energetic array of Tarot cards flew out and circled the caravan, whipping up an air of victory at completing their mission.

"Don't apologise, Cassie," urged the delicate, whispering voice of the Tarot cards. "You did amazingly tonight."

"No, we did amazingly," replied Cassie, choking back tears. "It's exactly how we'd read."

"And now you need to rest," urged the Tarot deck. "Please."

Nodding, Cassie walked past a large foldout table littered with ordnance maps of the area and a detailed floor plan of the farmhouse where the man had kept the boy.

Soon after, she slumped upon a tiny settee under the large bay window, lifted her achy legs and stretched them out fully along the cushioned seating.

Reaching for a bottle of newly purchased scotch on the drab carpet close by, Cassie unscrewed the cap and took a large swig. Well, after what happened that night, she thought she deserved it, so another swig soon followed another until, finally, the warming sensation helped ease her nerves.

"We'll be close by," whispered the cards in her mind. "You get some rest."

"Thank you," murmured Cassie.

"And Cassie."

"Yes?" she asked, starting to become a little subdued by the alcohol.

"Please, go easy."

As the Tarot deck floated away, Cassie lay there, silent, closed her eyes and embraced peace. She drank some more of the scotch on autopilot and, as she was about to drift off: *Buzz!*

Her momentary bliss was swiftly interrupted. She reached for the mobile she'd left behind on the floor nearby and opened a message with anticipation.

Her mum was drunk, texting her, desperately wanting to make sure she was okay, but Cassie couldn't reply. She took another swig of scotch and fought back the tears.

"Of course, I want to see you, James, Ben and Lucy," she muttered to herself as Susan continued to fire off text after text, unable to hold back from declaring how much she wanted Cassie to go home.

"But I'm trying to protect you," Cassie said aloud. "From what I know, and you all don't!"

So, while her head spun with guilt and alcohol, the concerned Tarot deck returned to Cassie, hovering in the air, ready to help.

"Cassie? What did your mum say? Are you okay?"

"I, er…" Slurring her words, Cassie closed her eyes, and the excess alcohol forced her into a deep, dream-like state. All was hauntingly quiet, to the point she couldn't hear the Tarot deck anymore.

Feeling a little scared by the emptiness surrounding her, Cassie needed help. She didn't want to feel alone, and her inner longing fed off her desires. For a moment, she was inside a memory from nine years ago.

"Come on, Cassie!" called the familiar voice. "Hurry up!"

Rushing onto an empty, sandy beach at the crack of dawn, seventeen-year-old Cassie struggled to carry an oversized, newly bought stand-up paddle board under her left arm. Tripping up and nearly dropping the paddle in her right hand, the anxious teenager tried to keep up with her father, Steven Jenkins, who was eager to keep the momentum going as they approached the shore.

He threw his board onto the sand close to the water's edge, turned around and waited expectantly for Cassie to join.

Drawing nearer, she kept her head down, unable to meet her father's eyes, and he knew she was upset. But, instead of asking what was wrong, he encouraged her to get into the sea.

"You can do it, Cassie. You love the water. It'll be fun, promise," he reassured her.

Unconvinced, Cassie watched her father push his board into the placid water and secure his paddle on top with natural ease. Biting her bottom lip, she looked away.

In a matter of months, her father's illness would win, and he would be gone. So, it wasn't about how comfortable she was with the sea, it was about never seeing him again. On the verge of exploding, Cassie suddenly felt awful and held back.

"What the..." she muttered, disappointed in herself. She couldn't cause a scene. What kind of daughter would she be? Well, the selfish kind. She couldn't prevent him from trying to live his life to the fullest.

Too caught up in the whirling of deep, saddening thoughts, Cassie hadn't realised Steven was dragging his board out of the water and dropping it on the floor next to her. As he waited patiently for Cassie to snap out of her spiral, he quickly realised he needed to intervene, for both their sakes, if they were to have a good day. He gripped her hands and squeezed them gently, telling her to let go of the paddle and board and return to him.

"I, er, Dad, I'm…" Cassie was too choked to speak.

"It's okay," he reassured her.

"But…"

"We can still have a good day, Cassie," continued Steven, encouraging her to let go. "It doesn't have to be all doom and gloom."

"I'm sorry, Dad," she exclaimed, finally releasing the paddle and board on the sand.

"You shouldn't be apologising," he replied firmly.

"I can't even go out on the ocean for you. It's pathetic. I'm pathetic."

"Sweetheart, you're not pathetic."

"I'm not as strong as James."

"Cassie, each of you has your strengths."

"Huh, I'm not sure about that, Dad."

Ignoring her, Steven wrapped his arms around Cassie and hugged her tightly. He always knew it was dangerous to tell his children too early before the end. But what choice did he have? There was no choice. He and his family were all backed into a corner, with time ticking away.

Finally, letting go of his daughter, Steven urged Cassie to sit down on the sand and embrace a fleeting moment of stillness. They sat side by side and watched the sun break through the clouds. Unable to move from their spot, father and daughter made the most of each other's company while locals and tourists began to descend on the stretch of beach around them.

Laughter erupted as families pitched their sunchairs and set up their picnics. It seemed like any other fun-filled outing, where the day was a chance to bring loved ones together for some escape from the daily grind.

But a day wasn't enough for Steven and Cassie. However, some would say it was better than nothing, and the intoxicated Cassie in the present remembered her time with Steven as if it was yesterday.

She understood her father didn't want to ruin their time together by revealing the secret he'd kept from Susan and everyone else. But Cassie wished he'd told her on the beach that day, so she didn't feel like such an outsider.

"Cassie?" called the Tarot deck in the distance. "Cassie, please wake up."

As dazzling, mystical light wiped away the memory of Steven, it shocked Cassie back to consciousness. Panting profusely, she looked wildly around the caravan, battling to make sense of her surroundings.

"What…" began Cassie.

"We suggest you put your mobile away first, Cassie," stressed the cards.

"I, I saw my dad," she stuttered, unaware of what the cards said.

"We know," they replied, sounding upset.

"He should have said something then."

"We're so sorry he kept us hidden."

"I know. I know you are."

"We never wanted to keep anything from you. Yet, even now, after so many attempts, we are still unable to tell you or show you where Steven is truly from. Steven's will was unbreakable."

Cassie was speechless. After all, what was there left to say? She had spent nine years literally keeping the cards close to her chest and, to that day, had still learnt nothing about her father's past before he'd met Susan.

"Think of the boy you helped tonight," interjected the cards. "At least we are doing some good."

Placing her head in her hands, Cassie soaked in their words. She took a deep breath and readjusted her body to lie on her side. With her face pressed against the settee, she forced her mind to stop and slept into the early hours.

While she slowly regained her energy, unknown to Cassie, the mystical forcefield outside began to flicker. It emitted brighter and brighter, stopped, and the light caused a mighty rumble beneath the earth. The force intensified then, *bam!* The trailer shook violently, and shimmering, fantastical light consumed the cabin inside, blinding Cassie as she opened her eyes.

Thrown off the settee and landing on her front, she looked around, straining her eyes, but she couldn't see her father's Tarot cards anywhere. "Get up!" Cassie told herself. "Come on!" Pushing hard off the carpet, she reached for the door, turned the handle, and landed on the grass outside.

Struggling to understand what was happening, the Tarot cards circled frantically above. Cassie was awash with fear as the forcefield energy swiftly changed colours. The rotation continued, from glistening white to forest green and a deep red.

"Stay back, Cassie," urged the cards.

"What's happening?!"

"The field has detected another Tarot force, possibly two of them."

"What do you mean, 'another Tarot force'?"

"From other worlds," whispered the cards.

"Worlds?!" Taking a step forward, Cassie gazed upon the wondrous forest-green energy and the profound deep red. "Do they have anything to do with my father?"

"No."

"Are you certain?"

"This isn't Steven's energy," replied the deck.

Her mind whirled with intrigue as the colours diminished and everything returned to normal.

"Cassie?" asked the cards, now hovering in front of her.

Unable to reply, Cassie retreated into herself, knowing she couldn't let go of this.

"Cassie? Cassie?"

"I'm sorry," she answered finally, "I know you're scared, but I need your help. I need to know where that power came from."

Chapter Six

Worlds Apart

On Friday evening, less than twenty-four hours after meeting Emily, Andrew was on the other side of the River Thames, dishevelled and out of breath. He'd left Dream Myers Talent Agency dead on 5.30pm, and as usual, Kyle the receptionist was nowhere to be seen.

Once outside, unable to face taking the underground, he decided to power walk underneath the baking sun for about forty minutes north. Sweat dripped from his body as he dodged absent-minded tourists from the opposite direction.

Soon enough, he caught sight of a sign for Euston station across the busy main road and pushed the button for the traffic lights with more force than needed. He grew more agitated. The lights changed to red, but instead of crossing, he was rooted to the spot. His mobile vibrated in the back pocket of his jeans. Removing it, his face scrunched up in annoyance at an incoming call from Lanie.

He dived back, trying to escape the onslaught of pedestrians coming at him from all sides, when he accidentally bumped into a pram. The baby's mother gave him a look of disgust. He apologised for the mishap, but she was having none of it; her child could have been seriously injured. Retreating into the sanctuary of a quieter side road, Andrew called Lanie back.

"Hi, Lanie."

"I came back, and you weren't here," replied Lanie sharply.

"Sorry, I assumed you had gone home."

"Well, I assumed you would be here, and I could count on you," quipped Lanie.

"I, er…"

"You need to be at the studios at 8am tomorrow. Do you understand? I've emailed you the additional notes again, as you never replied to my first email."

Pulling the phone away from his ear, Andrew inhaled and exhaled deeply, waited a few seconds, and returned to the call. "Understood, Lanie," he replied, steeling himself before hanging up. Eyes ablaze, he sifted through his inbox and cursed aloud; Lanie had sent her first email only twenty minutes ago.

Popping his phone away, he bolted for the crossing. Once on the other side of the road, he meandered left and stopped abruptly. A woman, his age, lost in her own world, had accidentally blocked his way. She had long, blonde, frizzy hair and wore sturdy walking boots, plain clothes, and a waterproof jacket tied around her waist. She looked prepared for a day out of London with a hiking group – but Cassie Jenkins wasn't a local, eager to escape to the countryside. She was too preoccupied hunting for the fantastical energy she encountered earlier that week in the remote wilderness of the Highlands. It had been quite a shock, and Steven's Tarot cards had guided her to that spot, where she felt the same power close by.

At first, Andrew considered asking Cassie if she needed help with directions, but time was ticking. Amy's train was only ten minutes away, and he couldn't risk leaving his sister waiting. So, walking away from Cassie, he left her to it.

"Cassie," whispered the cards, "please, stay alert."

"I promise," she replied, voice low.

"Any sign of trouble, we are taking you away from this place. Immediately."

"Yes, understood."

Casting her eyes across a sea of bodies scuttling in all directions on the pavement, she felt a tingle of light from the Tarot deck in her stomach. They guided her away from the traffic lights, and she took a sharp right into Euston station's outdoor drinking and food complex. Swarms of tourists and commuters were packed into such a tiny space, but Cassie fixated on the entrance ahead. She picked up the pace when a family of four barged into her, dragging their suitcases towards the underground.

Once the dust settled, she arrived inside the station, but was surprised to find it fairly empty. Individuals were leaving, but no one was desperate to enter.

"Slow and careful, Cassie," warned her father's cards.

The cautious Tarot deck guided her across the ticket hall, where she clocked a row of signs next to the platform entrances. Gazing down one ramp, she couldn't see any station staff.

The tingle in her stomach returned. She strolled along, reaching the sign, 'Platform 7 – Arrival – Birmingham International'.

"The Tarot energy can't be arriving on a train, surely?" said a bemused Cassie. Checking over her shoulder, she realised she was now the only one inside the station apart from a couple of individuals darting across the ground floor further back.

"A little odd, don't you think?" she whispered. "Outside was bustling."

"Yes," replied the deck sharply.

"Have you detected anything else?"

"Not yet. Whatever this energy is, Cassie, they are making a strong effort to conceal it," said the cards. After taking in their words, she descended the ramp to platform seven, where no soul could be seen. On the train from Birmingham International, however, the carriages were packed full of passengers, including Cassie's anxious brother Ben and complacent sister, Lucy. They sat together in front of the luggage rack in the fifth carriage from the front.

Peering out of the window as the urban skyline came into view, Lucy's eyes widened with awe, while Ben, in the aisle seat, looked straight ahead, focused on the task at hand.

"Look, Ben!" urged Lucy.

Poking her brother, Lucy felt a rush of excitement at their oncoming approach into Euston.

"Lucy," said Ben.

"What? Amy's fine. She's still in the carriage behind us. No way has she got off the train."

"Still…" continued Ben.

"So, we won't miss her when we arrive," added Lucy.

Thankfully, since Amy had left Aberaeron that morning with her signature turquoise tote and a small, bright blue suitcase in tow, Ben and Lucy's secret stalking had gone undetected. But Ben couldn't let his guard down; one wrong move and they could quickly lose her.

"You haven't been to London before?" asked Lucy, still engrossed in the views outside.

"I'll tell you later," replied Ben.

Shuffling awkwardly in his seat, he checked his mobile, hunting social media for anything Amy might have posted. Nothing. Ben hit refresh. Still nothing. Switching his search to her brother, a low, weak announcement from the train's control room struggled to penetrate the air around them.

Straining their ears, Ben and Lucy made out they were arriving at the station, and Lucy's energy grew giddy again. The light outside evaporated, the train slowed, and they had arrived.

"Right," Ben muttered. "Here we go." Attempting to lift himself, he felt strange. Looking down, his eyes widened with fear as shimmering, forest-green energy covered his waist, preventing him from leaving his seat.

"Lucy," choked Ben.

Next to him, his sister wrestled with the same ordeal, and across the carriage, other panicked passengers tried desperately to get up too, but the energy wouldn't let them.

"Ben…"

But before he could reply, he felt drowsy. Losing feeling in his legs and arms, Ben was about to fall into a deep sleep when, *jolt!* A flash of profound red power appeared and struck the green energy with such force that it was immediately dispelled.

Released from his trance, Ben gasped for breath, lost his balance and fell sideways into the aisle with a loud thump. The red power had also set Lucy free. She escaped her seat, knelt before her brother and placed a hand on his shoulders, just as Ben met her shaken eyes.

"Did you see what happened?" asked Ben.

"The green and red?" replied Lucy.

"Yes."

They looked up and down the carriage. The other passengers were hunched over, sound asleep, and the mood was eerily silent. Were all the carriages like that?

"We're the only ones still awake," said Lucy.

"So, we should find Amy."

Nodding, they rose from the floor, strode past the luggage rack and attempted to push open the entryway, but the sensor didn't work. The door refused to budge, and Lucy decided to break away. Rushing to the other end of the carriage, she passed the endless stream of unconscious bodies. Heart racing wildly, she reached the end and pressed her hand against the sensor, but with no luck. The door remained shut.

Failed attempt after failed attempt and no closer to exiting the train, Lucy's panic took over. Banging hard on the glass, no sound came from the other side. She pushed hard against an emergency call button nearby and began working her way back to Ben. She checked the window on her left. No one was on the platform, and her anxiousness worsened. Finally, she switched sides, looked out of the other window, and her mouth dropped.

Through the glass, a few metres back, a perplexed Cassie was standing on the spot, staring hard into her sister's eyes.

"Cassie?" said Lucy.

"Lucy!" called Ben, his back still facing her as he tried again to break into Amy's carriage. "Lucy, are you okay?"

Silence. Lucy's hands shook as she removed the mobile from her pocket and searched for Cassie's number. Then, hitting the call button, the phone rang, and Lucy watched her sister scramble to take the call.

But, as she was about to answer, Cassie heard footsteps approach in the distance and paused. The energy being emitted by her father's Tarot cards was chaotic. They were scared.

Taking a deep breath, she turned her back on a trembling Lucy and watched the outline of a figure making its way down the ramp onto the platform. Coming into view was a woman, in her late forties, wearing a plain blue top and light jeans. Nothing seemed out of the ordinary as she made her way towards Cassie.

"We're leaving now," said her father's cards.

"But what about Lucy?" said Cassie. "I can't just leave her."

The Tarot deck glowed inside her jacket pocket. They conjured small, fantastical energy currents and willed them to travel through Cassie's clothing and into her skin. Unnerved by their takeover, she felt compelled to turn her back on the woman and sprint towards the other end of the platform.

"We're going to escape onto the tracks," warned the cards.

"Wait!"

Reaching the second carriage from the back, she regained feeling in her legs and fell forward onto the concrete.

"What happened?!" asked Cassie, wincing in pain on the cool, hard ground.

No answer. The footsteps in the background grew louder, and a shot of adrenaline encouraged Cassie to rise from the floor and face their owner. The woman had followed her and was only a few metres away. Her rich green eyes with tints of yellow gave Cassie a look of concern.

"Are you okay?" asked the woman.

"I, er." Cassie paused.

A feeling in her stomach told her to step away, so she hurried towards the nearest train doors and attempted to open them – but they wouldn't budge. Instead of giving up, determination rose from the depths of her being. Cassie sought to reconnect with her father's Tarot deck, and as the desire grew in strength, whatever was suppressing the cards' energy was now momentarily beaten down.

"Cassie," said the cards, "are you okay?"

"I am now you're back."

"I don't think for long," stressed the deck. "Here, just in case." Before anything strange happened to them again, the cards transferred energy into Cassie, and glistening light radiated from her hands. Feeling a surge of power, she gripped the side of the train doors, wrenched them open, and jumped onto the train.

Inside, she closed the entryway securely behind her and immediately felt the unsettling mood in the air. She turned left and began tearing open sliding door after sliding door, working her way through the carriages while casting glances at the benumbed passengers slumped in seats.

When she arrived at the interconnecting walkway from the seventh carriage towards the sixth, she detected a shaky voice up ahead. Slowing down, she peered through the glass. A young woman with freckles on her face and long auburn hair was standing further back, talking desperately to someone on the phone.

"You can't get out?" asked Amy.

"No. The barriers are down everywhere," answered Andrew on the mobile. "I can't leave through the entrance or come to your platform."

"Have you found anyone else?" Amy asked.

"I've searched both floors. There's no one here. Are you sure everyone in your carriage is unconscious?"

"Yes," replied Amy. "I had hoped Lanie was one of them."

"And the woman you saw outside? Who followed the other?" asked Andrew, unable to process the mention of his deranged boss. "Have they come back?"

"No," said Amy, checking through the window again. "They've disappeared. This is unusual, right? I mean, this kind of thing doesn't normally happen in London?"

The phone went dead, and her brother was gone. Amy tried to call him back, but her phone failed to connect. To make herself feel better, she imagined Andrew's boss sprawled unconscious on the floor, unable to cause trouble. She revelled in the imaginary scene as the door behind her opened, making her jump.

"Who are you?!" called Amy as Cassie breezed in. "How did you manage that? I've been trying to..." Pausing mid-sentence, Amy clocked the minor cuts and patches of blood on Cassie's face and hands. "Wait, are you okay? What happened to you?"

Choking at the questions, Cassie welled up. The reality of the situation she'd landed herself in had finally hit. "Yes, I'll be fine. And I fell over."

"You ran away from the other woman?" asked Amy. "Yes. That was you. Are you in trouble?"

"I don't know her," protested Cassie, anger building, "and I don't know what is going on here. I just need to reach my sister. She's trapped in the next carriage along."

"Okay, okay," said Amy softly and delicately, sensing Cassie's distress. "I'll come with you."

"Wait, you can't," replied Cassie, taken aback. "You don't even know me. Why so eager to help?"

"Yes, I know I don't know you. But, right now, I'm sure we both feel and look like crap, so we might as well endure it together."

Soaking in her words and warming to Amy's spirit, Cassie realised she might be useful once Lucy was saved. Yes. They could leave together and protect one another.

"What do you think?" asked Cassie inside her mind, but the Tarot deck had succumbed to another disappearing act. Unable to wait any longer for an answer, she decided for the both of them.

"Okay, well put," replied Cassie. "What's your name?"

"Amy. And you?"

"Cassie. Let's go."

Amy quickly grabbed her oversized turquoise tote bag from the empty seat and swung it over her shoulder. When they reached the far side, Cassie dived in front of

Amy, disrupting her vision while craftily prying open the entryway with glistening energy. Amy's attention, on the other hand, was somewhere else entirely.

Breathing heavily, her mind started to feel weighted by a voice in the distance. It told her she was finally safe, but Amy looked around the carriage at the unconscious passengers and thought it must be a joke.

"Safe?" said Amy. "I'm anything but safe."

"Amy!" called Cassie. Having already entered the interconnecting walkway, Cassie paused when she realised Amy hadn't followed. "Amy? Is there something wrong?"

Amy didn't answer back. It was like she hadn't even heard the question. Sensing something off, Cassie returned, but before touching Amy's shoulder, the train shook violently, and shots of fantastical, forest-green energy pierced through Amy's bag.

An array of Tarot cards charged out of the bag and Cassie's mouth dropped. She watched as they wistfully circled Amy, conjuring fantastical, growing energy. Without warning, the deck transferred their power to Amy, who started to scream while the rumbling around them intensified.

Across the carriages, comatose passengers fell out of their seats onto the floor. Still trapped in the fifth carriage from the front, Ben and Lucy lost footing near the luggage rack. They grabbed hold of the metal rails, and once they could steady themselves, looked at each other anxiously as they heard the screams in the distance.

The cries amplified and Lucy felt so useless. She knew it was Amy. Starting to well up, she couldn't look at Ben, but her brother didn't succumb to guilt, for he'd spotted something unusual at the far end of the carriage and couldn't take his eyes off it.

A flickering of profound red energy had appeared. It travelled up and over the doorframe, brewing itself into a frenzy then, *click!* The door opened.

Blinking, Ben realised the red power had vanished, and rather than face Lucy's emotional turmoil head-on, he grabbed her arm and pulled her along the aisle.

Confused and shaken, Lucy tried to resist, but Ben encouraged her to keep going. The rumbling around them started to ease a little. Once they made it through the archway, they noticed the exit door leading on to the platform had also opened. Ben pulled Lucy out of the train and into the polluted air.

They heard the faint chugging of the engine as their eyes travelled down the outside of the train. All the doors were open, including Amy's carriage, but no one was getting off.

"The screaming's stopped," said Lucy.

"It might not have been Amy," replied Ben.

"Liar. We both know it was her."

"Lucy, wait!"

Striding forward, Lucy dodged Ben's attempt to restrain her, making her way to Amy's carriage. "No! I can't be seen as a child all the time!" Arriving outside the open doorway, she peered inside, and what she saw next terrified her.

"Lucy? What–" said Ben.

"It's Amy!" Darting away from the train, she barged into a perplexed Ben.

Strike!

An incredible burst of forest-green energy ploughed into Cassie's chest. She flew back from inside the train, missing a collision with her sister and brother. Hitting the ground hard, Cassie was knocked unconscious before rolling to a stop.

"Cassie!" called Lucy, tears trickling down her face as she reached her sister.

"Why is she here?!" asked Ben, also arriving at the scene.

"How would I know, Ben!" shouted Lucy.

"I'm not blaming you," said an angered Ben as he checked Cassie's pulse. "I was just… Wait, she's breathing."

"It looked like the same green energy at our mam's shop," blurted Lucy, stroking her sister's forehead.

"What were you about to say, Amy?" cut in Ben.

"She wasn't herself," stressed Lucy.

Strike! Strike! Strike!

Volatile shots of the same green power flew out of the entryway. Soon, Lucy and Ben saw Amy emerge and land on the platform. Releasing the energy from her hands, Amy fired a final monumental surge of power, and her inner self resurfaced. She looked around the station, terrified, and completely unaware of the damage she'd caused.

Nausea quickly consumed her stomach and Amy slumped to the floor. She watched the Tarot cards she'd acquired from Flint & Drift fall from the air and scatter around her.

"Andrew," said Amy, wishing her brother was present more than anything.

Hearing footsteps approach as Lucy's voice protested in the background, a set of arms wrapped themselves around Amy, and a male voice whispered that it was all going to be okay. Wiping her deep auburn hair away from her face, Ben tucked it behind Amy's ear as she met his eyes.

"I'm sorry," said Amy. "Whatever I did, I'm so sorry."

"I know," reassured Ben. "I'm here."

As Ben hugged Amy, Cassie began to stir next to a teary Lucy, and the group, riddled with hurt and confusion, hadn't registered that the woman who'd approached Cassie had re-emerged onto the platform, short of breath.

Raising her hands, Queen Lillian conjured swirls of forest-green energy that rose from her fingertips and shot up. The magic merged and whipped into a frenzy, generating a glistening circular portal out of the floor.

The group was awestruck, including Cassie, who was awake. They worried about what would happen to them, but Queen Lillian didn't care about Ben, Lucy or Cassie. Instead, she grabbed Amy's wrists and dragged her away from Ben with great strength.

"Get off her!" said Ben.

Strike!

Queen Lillian released forest-green energy from her right hand and hit Ben's shoulder. Wincing, he watched as Amy was overpowered and taken through the portal. He chased after them, not caring if he was about to leave his world behind. But Lucy and Cassie cared.

"Ben!" shouted his sisters.

Desperate to reconnect with Steven's Tarots, Cassie hoped they could help stop him, but they didn't. "Please!" she said aloud.

"Wait! Lucy?!" shouted Cassie.

Her sister had risen from the floor in pursuit of Ben, and Cassie had no choice but to follow them. But, before Lucy entered the portal, Cassie noticed the forest-green energy consuming it changed to a dazzling white. She raced through the portal anyway after her sister.

Chapter Seven

Back to Basics

Trapped inside the cold, dreary station, Andrew was standing in front of the arrivals board, with no luck getting a signal. He considered taking a walk, even though he'd already explored the shops, newsagents, and eateries on the ground floor and up the escalator to the first floor. He'd even nosedived inside some of the stockrooms and kitchen areas, but the staff and customers were absent everywhere.

He caught sight of a signal bar on his phone. He dialled 999, but the line went fuzzy. Hanging up and trying again, a delicate-looking, olive-skinned hand crept up behind him and squeezed his right shoulder. Caught off guard, he flinched. His heart raced as he turned to face the woman he'd met at the pub last night.

"Hi," said Queen Maria innocently.

"Where did you come from? I've searched everywhere."

"Well, you couldn't have searched everywhere," she replied with an undertone of playfulness. "Otherwise, you would have found me."

"Right," he replied, unconvinced. "Where were you, though? I saw you last night too. Didn't I?"

"You look a little panicked," said Queen Maria.

"And it looks like you're darting around my questions?"

"I'm not darting," she replied coyly.

The Queen of Wayan took a sly look above. Her majestic, crafty Tarot cards flew silently around the station. Ducking and diving around pillars and beams, they'd successfully beaten off Queen Lillian's magic on Amy's train, and now their mission was to stay alert for any sign of a breach into the station.

"Okay," continued Queen Maria, staring hard into Andrew's eyes, "maybe I'm darting a little. I fear for my safety."

"Sorry, what?" asked Andrew, thrown by her comment.

"Someone wishes me harm, and I'm afraid you might be caught in the crossfire."

Well, technically, it was the truth. Her sister-in-law would relish the opportunity to hurt her or, better yet, kill her to acquire Andrew.

"Someone is after you?" said Andrew, still trying to process her words.

"Yes."

He scanned her meticulously for anything that could help him figure out her deal. She seemed normal last night, but a niggling feeling told him it couldn't be a coincidence, bumping into her twice in two days. And now they were alone together? Maybe she was a stalker trying to get on Lanie's talent roster. If so, he hoped she would admit to it so that he could warn her to steer clear.

"Are you okay?" asked Queen Maria, interrupting his wealth of conspiracy theories.

"Sorry, who are you running from?" asked Andrew.

"Someone I've known for a long time. Let's just say the past has caught up with me."

Face scrunched in uncertainty, he kept staring at Queen Maria who, for a moment, glanced behind him. He noticed her calm manner had been rattled for the first time since she'd appeared, and he was confident it was something serious. Spinning around, he froze on the spot. He was unable to comprehend the sight in front of him: a fire had ignited across a concrete wall. It whipped into a silent frenzy, and as the flames grew livelier their colour transformed into a deep, glistening red.

As the flames died down, fear seeped from Queen Maria's stomach and consumed the whole of her insides. Managing to contain it away from Andrew, she silently wondered why the spell used to cast the invisible protective forcefield around them was failing. Her necromancers on Wayan promised her it would do the trick.

High above, the queen's Tarot cards rallied together, for they knew, just as their owner did, they couldn't keep their world from Andrew any longer. It was time to go. Raising her arms and closing her eyes, adrenaline pumped through Queen Maria's being as a swishing sound soon followed a mighty swoosh.

Andrew dived back, shell-shocked as he watched a flurry of cards, driven and confident, shoot past him in the air. They circled Queen Maria dutifully, conjuring fantastical red energy that entered her body.

Not sticking around for an explanation, he sprinted across the ticket hall. Reaching the escalators, seeking higher ground, he bounded up them two steps at a time. He refused to look back as the red mystical power grew in strength and started to eat the air around him. Vision distorted, he paused. In the background, a faint gleaming sound came into earshot. It grew louder, and the red power dissipated around him.

Turning to face the source, he was gobsmacked by a gigantic, dazzling red ring in the centre of Euston station. Inside was a mirage of a deep blue crystal lake and a geo-Gothic stone fortification behind it.

"I meant what I said," called Queen Maria, staying close to the portal. "It's not safe. We need to go."

The entirety of the station's outer edges caught fire, and like the wall he'd seen moments ago, the flames glistened and died out. Finally, the whole forcefield was disbanded, and a fatal blast of forest-green energy cleaned off a metal shutter leading to the platforms. The screen flew across the waiting area and, seconds later, Queen Lillian entered from platform seven. Clocking Andrew, she started to advance, but Queen Maria blocked her. Charging fantastical red magic from her hands, the Queen of Wayan opened fire at her sister-in-law, who deflected her magic with ease.

Watching both women locked in mystical combat, Andrew continued his quest up the escalators, out of harm's way. At the top, he darted right and ducked as a fireball of energy swooped over him, hitting the sign of a burrito eatery. Heart pumping, he rose from the ground and made a run for it. As he tried to enter the newsagent's, he felt a tingle in his hands. The red emblem of a castle, the same image on the card he picked up last night, appeared across his palms. He was unaware it was a spell Queen Maria had cast. It intended to bind him to Wayan.

Staring in horror at his hands, he had no time to react. The glistening red gateway had homed in on his whereabouts on the first floor. It whipped itself into a frenzy behind him and charged. Scooping Andrew through, the portal vanished.

"When did you play that dirty little trick?" asked Queen Lillian, deflecting her sister-in-law's energy attacks. "Binding him to your world! He's my son, not yours!"

Their battle ceased as they locked eyes. The many years of distrusting one another led to that moment. Finally, finding Andrew and Amy made everything real.

"Amy's next," said Queen Maria.

"No. That I know is wrong," said Queen Lillian.

Flames rose from the floor and encased Queen Maria in a Wayan-made forcefield. Her Tarot cards flew above the entrapment, attempting to dispel the fire with their wondrous power, but their owner couldn't escape her homeworld's protection spell.

"We know for certain this is from our world," answered the deck.

"An innocent mistake or a traitorous act," said Queen Maria. Anger brewing, she'd had enough of the theatrics. Her sister-in-law was coming after Amy, and she needed to solve the mess she'd landed herself in. Mind racing with ideas, the queen removed the card she'd given Andrew last night from the pocket of her jeans. One side still had the castle emblem, while the other remained blank. "How about we…" began Queen Maria.

Before she could finish the sentence, her Tarot deck sprinted into action. Working together to immerse the blank side of the card with their energy, the emblem of Queen Maria's castle appeared. The magic travelled out of the card into her being, and the deck cast the binding spell. Finally, Queen Maria felt in control as she connected with the forcefield around her.

"Dispel," said Queen Maria. She was free. Charging forward across the ticket hall, the queen kept going. She reached the gap where the shutter used to be, sped through it, and continued down the slope. The stale air hit as she raced towards platform seven. Reaching the first carriage, she continued along the outside until, finally, she slowed and stopped. She was too late. Amy was gone.

Still angered by the farcical forcefields, Queen Maria instructed her Tarot cards to conjure a portal home. As the deck formed the shimmering ring, she heard a commotion on the other side. It was apparent Andrew wasn't enjoying his time on Wayan.

Taking a deep breath, she crossed through worlds and arrived at the end of a wooden jetty within a small harbour. It connected to Delqroix Island, the home of Castle Wayan, a small but mighty, medieval-esque structure perched on top of a luscious green hilltop. Romantic, geo-Gothic stone walls encased the harbour, with two small stone lighthouses positioned at the far ends where a narrow gap allowed fishing boats to enter and leave.

As the hot afternoon sun beat down, Queen Maria enjoyed, for those brief few seconds, the warmth on her face. Casting her eyes upon the armed soldiers lined up at the water's edge, the queen maintained that she was pleased to see them. Internally, however, she wondered whom she could really trust.

Stood at the entrance to the jetty, dividing the infantry, was her husband, King Marco, trying to suppress the deep weariness of the trouble his sister had caused. Patches of grey hair bedevilled his fair locks, and his sky-blue eyes had changed to a steely grey over the years.

Blocking out Andrew's meltdown between them, he looked into his wife's soul and knew instantly something was wrong. Even though it pained him to see her troubled, it wasn't the time or the place to discuss what happened on Earth; they had Andrew to deal with.

"Where am I?" demanded Andrew.

Eyes darting wildly from the soldiers to King Marco and then to Queen Maria, the crystal-clear water with the deepest blue, turquoise and cerulean dazzled, and his mouth dropped. A flurry of fish with multicoloured scales of pinks, yellows, oranges and purples jumped up out of the water and back in again.

"Please, hear me out," answered Queen Maria, moving towards Andrew slowly and delicately. "The main thing is you're safe."

"Safe! I never needed to be safe in the first place until I met you."

"Okay," agreed Queen Maria. "Yes, I understand that."

"Please, just answer the question. Where am I?"

"You've arrived on a Tarot world called Wayan," she began, preparing for the worst reaction from Andrew. "The woman who attacked me is Queen Lillian from a different Tarot world called Naxthos. We have a bitter feud."

"A Tarot world?"

"A world where its inhabitants can harness mystical energy from our Tarot cards. I am Queen Maria of Wayan."

"Tarot?" said Andrew. "The cards you find in crappy tourist shops?"

"That's Earth, Andrew," continued Queen Maria. "Here, it's a little more serious than that. You had a taste of it at Euston station."

Andrew fell silent. There was no denying what he'd seen and felt on the other side of that crazy, determined ring that had charged at him. He couldn't dismiss any of it. But, if he tried to, he worried whether denial would make it even worse.

"Andrew?" asked Queen Maria, silently worrying she was losing him. "Andrew, are you okay?"

"How do you know my name?"

Before she could reply, he took a step towards her and the infantry by the water's edge sprang to action. Fantastical red magic was being emitted from the swords and shields in their hands. A single command from their queen and they would fire energy bursts from the points straight into him.

She gestured for her soldiers to stand down. Stepping towards Andrew, she was as quick in her mind as she was on her feet, explaining her Tarot cards had told her his name.

"Told you!" said Andrew. "I want to leave. Right now."

"As you wish," answered Queen Maria, taking a fleeting look at King Marco. They knew if she resisted

Andrew's demands, it would cause way more animosity. So, he would just have to learn the hard way.

In the distance, a stirring sound grew. It became louder until, finally, a dazzling gateway was summoned at the far end of the jetty on the exact spot where Queen Maria arrived. The queen and Andrew turned to face the portal straight on, and she gestured for him to return home.

Not looking back, Andrew made a run for it. The hope of returning to his life propelled him, but a small part of him felt sad at the prospect. Burying that inkling of doubt, he tried to pass through the ring but was pushed back by an invisible force. Landing on the wooden planks with the wind knocked out of him, he steadily rose from the floor, his joints and muscles aching from the impact.

Everyone remained silent and subdued as he attempted to cross over to Earth but failed again. Not backing down, he continued, but every time he was on the verge of leaving Wayan, he was thrown back. Finally, on the floor, his face and hands bloodied and bruised, he rolled onto his back in distress.

"Andrew," whispered Queen Maria, "you need to stop now."

Knelt before him, the Queen of Wayan waited patiently for an answer. After a few seconds of silence, Andrew inhaled deeply and met her eyes. Fighting back the tears, he recognised the sincerity in her demeanour, and they felt a mutual understanding.

"I want to help you, but, unfortunately, you are now bound to Wayan," began Queen Maria. "The only way to leave is by tapping into the energy of our world." She sensed the cogs going inside his mind. Silently hopeful, she reached out her hand. "Let me help you," she urged.

He hated to admit it, but she was right. What other choice did he have? He was powerless. Casting his eyes across the soldiers standing to attention, he looked back at Queen Maria. He promised himself to stay alert as he accepted the hand of the queen, who breathed a subtle sigh of relief.

Helping him up, slow and steady, Queen Maria guided him along the jetty. When they reached the entrance, they were joined by a guilt-ridden King Marco. Keeping his feelings hidden, he wanted to tell his lost and confused nephew that he wasn't alone, that he was in the presence of his uncle, but he couldn't.

Andrew sensed his solemness, but before he had the chance to speak, the king cut in and introduced himself as Queen Maria's husband. The abruptness snubbed any more interaction, and Andrew felt strangely hurt.

Quickly moving on from the change in mood, the queen continued alongside the whitewashed harbour, passing the guards staying in position as King Marco and Andrew followed close behind.

Catching sight of the verdant, rolling hills and luscious green forests on the mainland across the waters, Andrew wondered how big this world truly was. He thought he heard a shrieking noise high above, like a bird of prey but deeper and more menacing. Hunting for the source, he stopped abruptly. The queen had paused in front of a diamond-shaped stone archway. She was checking Andrew was focused on where they were going. Once she knew he'd snapped out of his curiosity, she continued through the archway.

On the other side, Andrew looked above in awe. They were encased in a canopy of tall, rich, tropical vegetation where an unusual mix of flowers and fruit was growing. Marvelling at the colourful flora, Andrew began to fall behind as Queen Maria and King Marco arrived outside a hexagon-shaped cabin made of thick-cut crystal. It glistened wondrously, expertly hiding what it housed.

"That is where we need to go," said the queen.

Andrew joined them and all three entered the hut. A colourfully mesmerising, stained-glass display dominated the wall space in front of them. Stepping forward, Andrew's stomach danced unusual, excitable somersaults. It was nothing like he'd ever seen before. His eyes travelled from left to right; the first section of the wall had a backdrop of cerulean blue with the edging of waves spread across and an array of gold chalices in varying shapes and sizes floating in the 'sea'.

"There is one word for our world, and that is balance," said Queen Maria, gesturing for Andrew to continue soaking in the images in front of him.

A simple, hardy sword took centre stage on the next glass display. Behind the weapon were edgings of snow-capped mountains amid a steely grey. Next to that, a rugged mountainous range set the backdrop for the third section, where an array of wands hovered in the air, spouting colourful fireworks. The final part on the far right showcased a warm orange coppice. Gold circular coins with a five-point pentacle engraved in the centre covered the tree trunks.

"Wayan's built on ensuring a harmonious balance between our magical symbols: cups, swords, wands and pentacles," continued Queen Maria. "Each wall represents the four lands that look after and harness each symbol. The Land of Cups resides on the south-west mainland. The Land of Wands is located in the north-west. The Land of Swords dominates the north-east, and the Land of Pentacles looks after the south-east. You are on Delqroix Island, the centre of the world."

Eyes darting across all four segments, Andrew fought wildly to remember every detail. Unable to tear himself away, he hadn't noticed Queen Maria gravitate towards a small, delicate-looking stone basin resting on the crystal in the centre of the hut.

Kneeling before the empty bowl, the queen placed her hands on the ridge. Looking inside, she saw a wonder of bright colours whipping and swooshing in merriment within her mind. They were in a tizz at the prospect of conjuring a new Tarot deck for Andrew.

But, on the outside, King Marco and Andrew couldn't see anything. They waited in silence. Even Andrew sensed the cue to stay quiet. Finally, the Queen of Wayan opened her eyes and rose from the crystal floor.

"This basin will give you a Wayan-made Tarot deck of your own," began Queen Maria, "and the cards will enable you to tap into our world's energy for you to return home."

"Great," said Andrew eagerly. "As easy as that then."

"Not quite," said Queen Maria. "Because you are not from this world, you will need to earn the basin's respect."

"Respect?"

"Yes," she answered coyly.

"Seriously?"

"Careful, Andrew," said Queen Maria. "Your attitude is bordering on a little disrespectful."

"I, er…" stuttered Andrew. "Okay. What do I need to do?"

"You will need to help each land with a particular problem they've encountered. And to clarify, they are individual problems, not collective. Once you've succeeded, the basin will give you your cards."

"So, as simple as that?" said Andrew sarcastically.

"Yes, as simple as that. I'm glad you're taking this well."

"How do I…"

"My daughter will help you."

Lurking in the entranceway behind Andrew was a stoic woman in her early twenties with olive skin and dirty, strawberry-blonde hair tied back securely. Her eyes were a deep hazel like her mother's, with tints of electrifying blue reminiscent of her father's. She wore thin, highly resilient armour that covered her body. A sword was placed securely over her back, and her Tarot deck was nestled in a drawstring bag hanging from a belt around her waist.

"Hi," stuttered Andrew.

"Hello," answered the queen's daughter, low and tenacious.

"This is Evie," said Queen Maria. "She will be accompanying you."

Rooted to the spot, Andrew glanced around the family of three, unsure how he was supposed to act next. Evie didn't seem friendly, and no one gave him further instructions. As the mood in the hut grew more awkward, the queen interjected and nodded at her daughter.

"Let's go, Andrew," directed Evie.

Surprisingly shaken, Andrew stepped away from the Queen and King of Wayan and followed Evie outside, leaving the rulers alone inside the crystal cabin. King Marco held his wife's hand and, squeezing it gently, urged her to tell him what had happened on Earth.

"I could have reached Amy too," said Queen Maria, her frustration overspilling everywhere. "There was a chance to get both of them."

"And?" asked King Marco.

"And something went wrong. The protective forcefield dispelled and it re-emerged, trapping me inside. Only briefly, but it was enough time for Lillian to snatch Amy."

"You don't think it was a mistake?"

"No. Lillian was on cue for my entrapment. I suspect someone is helping her on Wayan."

"Then, we will find them. At least we have Andrew."

"We could never tap into her plans," said Queen Maria, working herself up. "All those years of trying to read into the complexities of her being, our Tarot cards failed repeatedly. All we saw were clouds. Nothing else."

Wrapping an arm around his wife, King Marco registered the fear in her eyes for Andrew and Amy's safety. All the years of animosity between them and Queen Lillian in their search for the long-lost children had conjured a toxic web. However much Queen Maria took a step back and re-evaluated, she was always thrown back into the melting pot. And now, the liquid was well and truly overspilling into one destructive mess.

Chapter Eight

Swords

Positioned at opposite ends of the vessel, Andrew and Evie spoke no words as they sailed out of the marina on a small, agile fishing boat. Behind the helm, Evie guided them through the opening between the lighthouses and away from Delqroix Island onto the calm, open lake with ease.

It was like second nature to her as she relished the gentle bobbing of the waves crashing against the hull. As they started their journey towards the north-east side of the mainland, Evie looked straight ahead, avoiding her shell-shocked passenger.

Left alone, curled up at the front of the boat, Andrew was staring at the scorch marks on his hands from attempting to break through the gateway. While his whole being felt disjointed on Wayan, he clung to fragments of his life on Earth.

Relieved Amy was safe on the train when it all kicked off between Queen Maria and Queen Lillian, he hoped she had taken refuge at his flat in Clapham. But, above everything, he didn't want her to assume his disappearing act was because of Lanie. Of course, Andrew wouldn't stoop that low, but would his sister think differently?

As his anxiousness grew, Andrew's body took matters into its own hands and shut down. As his mind caught up with the outcome, he closed his eyes and waited. Eventually, his head released a speck of uplifting energy, a memory of his date with Emily. To his surprise, he felt at home in her presence, however fleeting it was.

While lost in the moment, a greyish mist encased the vessel, and the clear skies evaporated. Andrew soon noticed and looked over the side. He saw the outline of a steel-clad dock drawing closer, and just as his anxiousness started to return, he met Evie's eyes. She was towering over him, her face expressionless and detached. She wore a thick, hardy cape with fur sewn into the inner lining, and in her hands was a spare shawl for Andrew.

"It will get colder," she said.

Wrapping the protective garment around him, he watched Evie return to the helm. She expertly manoeuvred the boat to dock safely near the water's edge. Then, unpicking a rope mountain from the deck, one end was securely tied to a metal hook embedded in the wood.

Shortly after, a quick succession of clip-clops hitting the ground hard came into range, and Andrew strained his eyes through the mist. Half a dozen horse-drawn soldiers wearing fur-lined, argent-coloured capes arrived on the jetty. Their light and agile armour covered their bodies, and a sword engraving dominated the centre of their breastplates. A metal holder that contained their

Tarot decks was underneath their plackarts, close to their hearts.

One of the horse riders jumped off their steed and caught the rope Evie threw him to tie the vessel securely. Once satisfied, she instructed Andrew to follow her as she leapt over the side and landed on the steel platform with a powerful thud.

With Andrew in close pursuit, Evie picked up the pace. She breezed past the soldiers from the Land of Swords while nodding to them respectfully. All six knew her and reciprocated. When she reached the back, two riderless horses waited for them, and Evie instructed Andrew to mount one. He was a little hesitant, as he didn't have the best track record with horses. The last time he rode one was when he was a teenager. His mother encouraged him to try it inside a wild west theme park. It started well. Journeying up and down the centre of the town set, he began to relax a little, until the horse dropped to the floor. Andrew panicked and dived off as the mare rolled onto its back and over his left toe. It was sore and bloodshot, and since that day he'd never been too fond of horses. To him, they were unpredictable.

"You need to," said Evie.

As Andrew struggled to get on, Evie took matters into her own hands and forced him securely into the saddle. She mounted the other horse and told the soldiers they were ready to depart.

They left the jetty, closely followed by the riders, and entered a clearing into the depths of a snow-capped forest. Swiftly inclining along a bending pathway, the landscape changed to rugged mountains where the temperature started to drop.

Unexpectedly enjoying the biting chill whipping his cheeks, Andrew started to process the adventure surrounding him as they rode on. An hour passed, and Evie slowed down. She pointed ahead to a medieval-esque castle smaller than the Wayan one, perched on a soaring, snow-covered mountaintop with an argent flag of their symbol raised proudly from the highest tower.

The horses bounded across a stone bridge shortly after a sharp, uphill climb. Below, Andrew saw the descent, and his insides felt nauseous at the terrifying drop. He looked ahead, attempting to suppress the sickness, as his horse galloped over the drawbridge and into the desolate main yard of the sturdy fortification.

The mares slowed down just as two individuals appeared through an archway to greet them. Sir Stephan, the leader of the Land of Swords, his hair wild and unkempt, walked with a limp as he smiled warmly at the sight of Evie. Next to him was his wife, Lady Selene. Her hair was straggly like her husband's. They were covered head to toe in warm, fur-clad clothing.

"Greetings, dear Evie. I trust your mother is safe and sound?" said Sir Stephan.

"Yes, she is safe, thank you," answered Evie with fondness.

Andrew was taken aback; it was the first sign he had of any emotion from her. He watched as she readily accepted Lady Selene's offer to dismount. She landed on the ground confidently and, without indecision, hugged the Lady of Swords tightly.

They broke away, and as they turned their attention to Andrew, both women registered the perplexed look on his face. He'd piqued Lady Selene's interest, and she walked towards him, offering the same help to alight, but he froze.

Behind Sir Stephan, Evie had planted herself out of sight from the Leader of Swords. She pursed her lips at Andrew's behaviour and gestured for him to accept the offer as if his life depended on it. Weary of holding everyone up but more scared of Evie, he gripped the lady's hand and attempted to get off the horse. He landed haphazardly on the ground, and Lady Selene smiled. Not saying a word, she knew he needed to catch his breath, and as soon as Andrew's balance returned, Sir Stephan commanded his horse riders to venture back into Wayan, scouting for any sign of trouble.

"So," Sir Stephan said once his soldiers left, "you're not from this world?" He addressed Andrew head-on.

"I, er…"

"It's okay. I already know about the little mishap. Let's hope you can help us," said Sir Stephan.

Shaking a little, Andrew was shown towards a separate archway on the far side of the complex. Evie stayed by his side as the Leader of Swords carefully descended an old spiral stairwell that led into pitch darkness. Pausing in his tracks, Andrew realised Lady Selene hadn't followed and looked behind to check she was okay, but Evie told him to continue inside. She didn't want to stick around any longer than needed.

They left the Lady of Swords alone in the centre of the yard, scanning the remote grounds meticulously. Nothing appeared out of the ordinary, but she wasn't fooled. Placing a hand on her breastplate armour, she began to connect with her Tarot cards, securely contained close to her heart underneath.

Wondrous, steel-grey energy shone out through the metal, and as Lady Selene desired more fantastical magic to help guide her, her eyes grew ever so weary when she saw a faint flicker of another colour: deep blue-green. It was a reminder that the Lady of Swords wasn't from Wayan.

"I'm here," called a discordant voice in the distance.

On a platform above the castle walls, a hesitant teenage girl with streaks of teal hair tied back aimlessly revealed herself. She gripped a basket filled with unusually large eggs, and patches of dirt covered her face, tunic and trousers. Her deep, sandy eyes, with a subtle pang of longing, looked upon Lady Selene.

"Let's be honest, you're not collecting eggs," quipped Lady Selene.

The girl ignored her comment as she rested the basket on the wooden plank. Then, slowly and carefully, she descended a rickety ladder to join her in the centre of the yard.

"Are you having a meeting? Now, I mean?" asked Gwyn.

"So, you were waiting for an opening?" replied Lady Selene.

"I rarely see you," answered Gwyn with unease. "I'd hoped we could discuss Gorda."

"It's not the right time," said Lady Selene.

"Excuse me, my lady, but it's never the right time. My mother, however, would always make time."

"Don't talk about…" Lady Selene was rattled by the girl's comment.

"My dead mother? Your closest friend?"

"Gwyn," cut in Lady Selene, her anger building.

"Gorda is our home, too."

"It's not mine anymore," sniped Lady Selene, "and it never will be."

The Lady of Swords couldn't face the girl. She looked so much like her mother when she was her age, and it pained Lady Selene to know she would be witnessing her closest friend growing up all over again in the image of Gwyn.

Turning her back on the girl, Lady Selene made her way towards the archway leading to her husband and the others. As she descended the staircase underneath the castle's depths, Sir Stephan, Evie and Andrew had already reached their destination inside a small, rectangular chamber. Forged swords and shields of varying lengths and sizes dominated the walls, radiating mystical energy. Flickering from one colour to another, they lit up the room.

In awe of the sight, Andrew eventually broke his gaze away and joined Sir Stephan and Evie at a large, circular, steel table within the centre. The top was littered with maps marking out the hotspots where portals could open and close in Wayan. It also showed the positioning of the queen's defences in case of a possible breach from another Tarot realm.

Scanning the mainland surrounding the Island of Delqroix, Andrew felt a rush of adrenaline. Still, before he could ask questions about the detailing, Sir Stephan drew his attention away.

"Over the last two months," began Sir Stephan, "someone or something has been taking our swords, shields and other weapons from our armoury room."

"Sir Stephan," cut in Evie, unaware this had been happening.

"It's okay, Evie," reassured the leader. "It's not been too detrimental, just a nuisance. I assigned a team to keep watch for anything suspicious, but it's still a mystery. A handful of weapons go missing every few days. But no one sees or hears anything." Sir Stephan looked down at his breastplate armour, and the outline of his cards shone through the metal in dazzling, steel-grey energy. "I asked for guidance, and my deck homed in on the Wheel of Fortune card," said the Leader of Swords.

"The Wheel of Fortune," began Evie, aware Andrew was confused, "depicts a wooden wheel similar to one attached to a horse-drawn cart, and around the outer edges are the symbols of our four lands. But, to clarify, this depiction is based on our world. There are thousands of Tarot worlds with uniquely depicted cards associated with what makes up their homes. It's not just the pictures that differentiate – it can also be the meaning. Not every being in existence will interpret their Tarot decks the same way. On Wayan, the Wheel of Fortune is associated with change; an action that could lead to turning the tables on something initially thought of as inevitable."

Absorbing Evie's words, Andrew was intrigued by the complexities of the Tarot and, deep within, a tiny flame came into existence that he'd never expected to ignite. "So, by stealing armour," said Andrew, finally able to process a sentence, "it could turn the tables on something?"

"Possibly, but it depends on how Sir Stephan felt when he asked his cards for help," said Evie, meeting Sir Stephan's eyes.

"Sorry, how do you mean?" asked Andrew.

"Well, internally, Sir Stephan may have already decided who hadn't taken the armour at the point he read. And so, the Wheel of Fortune might be warning him that what he thought was certain could actually be the opposite."

"I, er…" Sir Stephan stumbled over his words.

"Reading from Tarot cards can be tricky," continued Evie. "If you risk forcing or influencing the deck, then the answers may not be an accurate reflection."

Andrew looked from Evie to Sir Stephan, and while the Leader of Swords seemed slightly embarrassed at the notion of self-sabotaging his own Tarot readings, hurried footsteps approached in the distance. Moments later, Lady Selene breezed into the chamber. Her eyes were puffy and swollen, as if she'd been crying.

"My lady," began Sir Stephan, detecting his wife's unrest.

In close pursuit, Gwyn entered the space. The pent-up frustration she'd kept silent throughout childhood had taken its toll, but just as the girl was about to confront Lady Selene in front of her father, she paused. The sight of Andrew threw her off. From one grievance to the next, Gwyn's toxicity rose. What made an audience with this odd-looking outsider more important than her?

"Gwyn?" asked Sir Stephan delicately.

"Father," answered Gwyn, "what's happening?"

"My dear, we have a guest," replied Sir Stephan, slow and firm.

The girl cast her eyes from a confused Andrew to a concerned-looking Evie, and then finally, she homed in on the coldness coming from Lady Selene. The sets of eyes staring at her made Gwyn feel alone in their presence, and instead of fighting back, she retreated into herself.

"Another time…" began Sir Stephan.

I need to leave, Gwyn thought. It was all too much hearing another round of her father's excuses. Closing the door to the chamber, the girl was alone in the passageway, and as she walked into the shadows, she hoped those around her would finally listen one day.

"Sir Stephan? Lady Selene?" asked Evie. "Is everything…"

"Yes." Sir Stephan rose, shutting down Evie's concern for them and Gwyn.

"Okay," replied Evie, swiftly moving on. "What do you need Andrew to do?"

"We need him to guard the armoury," answered Sir Stephan. "Immediately. My guards have been wasting their time with this nonsense, and I need someone inconsequential to take the post. However long it takes."

Growing weary of the timescale, Andrew's face fell sullen, just as Evie rose from her chair and nodded.

"Absolutely," she said.

Motioning Andrew from his seat, Evie made haste towards the exit. She released the latch and exited the chamber with Andrew following close behind. They travelled through the damp, low-level tunnels under the heart of Castle Sword. It was as cold below as it was above, and the desire to return to the warmth of Delqroix Island pervaded Andrew.

"We are close now," explained Evie.

Pulling his shawl up close around his neck, Andrew fell back from Evie a little, and as hanging, flamed torches lit the space up ahead, he stopped. Eyes widening with concern, he was confused as to why Evie hadn't reacted, for splodges of a glistening turquoise liquid were spread across the floor in front of them. Kneeling before a patch closest to him, Andrew touched it.

"Andrew?" asked Evie, unsure why he'd stopped.

"Can't you see it?"

"See what?"

"It's like a sparkling liquid. A mix of blue and green. There are splodges spread all over the ground and up ahead. It's warm," he explained.

"I can't see anything."

"I can see it as clear as day."

Evie strained her eyes, kneeling beside him, but there was still nothing. Why could someone from another world see something she couldn't? Racking her brains for an answer, Evie asked Andrew to follow the trail.

Taking the lead, he guided her through the underground passages in search of the source until, eventually, he heard a faint groan coming into range, but Evie was oblivious. "You can't hear that either?"

"No," answered Evie, her voice shaking a little.

Turning a corner, Andrew stopped abruptly, and Evie barged into him. Wondering what he'd seen, she instantly sensed something terrible had happened from the look on his face. Slumped against the wall in front of them was an injured figure covered head to toe in the Land of Swords armour. A metal section across their midriff had been melted off, revealing a deep cut. The bluish-green, shimmering liquid oozed out of the wound, and Andrew realised the patches had been blood.

"Andrew, what do you see?"

"An injured soldier in Wayan armour."

"Okay, tell me everything."

Kneeling before the stranger, Andrew did as Evie asked. He removed their helmet. The figure was a dishevelled young man with bright turquoise hair, deep sandy eyes and a marking of a small sea creature tattooed into the side of his neck. It had broad fins that ran its full body length, giving the animal a flat, roundish shape.

"What happened?" asked Andrew.

The man was cut up, and it wasn't just the wound. His whole demeanour seemed distraught, as if he was hurting from the inside.

"Please, let me help you," said Andrew.

"No," spat the man. "You and them, none of you helped us."

"Us?" queried Andrew.

"At least I made a difference. However small the spoils were from your wretched armoury," said the man. As his life ebbed away, a menacing, mystical force came into existence. It started to melt away the armour covering the man's body and, when the magic finished, it worked to disintegrate his flesh until nothing was left.

Welling up in shock, Andrew lost his balance. He fell back onto the stone floor, and Evie instantly checked he was okay. After everything he told her, she was confident the stranger was from the Tarot world Gorda and was responsible for stealing the armour.

"But," stuttered Andrew, "that's not everything. He was attacked."

"Yes, he was."

Reaching for her Tarot cards, nestled securely in the pouch tied around her waist, Evie gazed upon them with the utmost respect. Their relationship was a meaningful, unbreakable bond, and as she cleared her mind, the wondrous deck began radiating an amaranth light. The energy expanded out, feeding off their owner's state of mind into a space of calmness and, above all, clarity.

Whip!

The cards flew from Evie's hand and circled the spot where the Gordan once lay, and as they continued to work their magic, shimmering amaranth light was conjured in the centre of their circle.

Andrew watched in awe as an image was formed out of the energy. It showed the bank of a river in the remote wilderness and a decrepit-looking warehouse at the other end of a wharf. The cards homed in on the structure, and as they drew closer to the large entrance doors, Evie fixated upon the symbols littered across them. There were outlines of small-scale fishes and chalices and hidden among them was a small sea creature similar to the marking on the Gordan.

"Do you know where that is?" asked Andrew.

"Yes," answered Evie. "It borders the Land of Wands with Cups. An area called Forta. There hasn't been any activity there for a hundred years, and I'd like to know when that animal symbol was added. It doesn't look Wayan."

Facing Andrew, Evie let out a concern bothering her since they'd left Sir Stephan and Lady Selene in the chamber. Why couldn't she see or hear the Gordan?

"Maybe–" began Andrew.

"Perhaps," cut in Evie, "it's because you are not from Wayan, whereas I was never meant to see him, just like Sir Stephan's soldiers who kept watch over the armoury."

"So..." replied Andrew, hoping to give some helpful input.

"So," said Evie, "in retrospect, you have helped the Land of Swords; you found the culprit, and he is dead."

After the last word left her lips, Evie watched her Tarot cards dispel their magic and return safely inside their owner's pouch. Her demeanour seemed so matter-of-fact that Andrew fell unusually unsettled. He knew Evie was right. He had set out to do what he was told to, but a man, or being, died in front of him.

"Andrew?" asked Evie, silently hoping Andrew's conscience would shine through.

"It's not done," he said. "I can't just turn my back on this."

A slight smile spread across Evie's face, and for the first time since they'd met, she began to warm to him.

"So?" asked Evie.

"So what?" answered Andrew.

"What shall we do?"

Chapter Nine

Forta

Tears rolled down Gwyn's face as she rocked back and forth on the creaky floorboards underneath the dark, abandoned warehouse in Forta. She hadn't meant to hurt the Gordan, who was her friend. All she'd tried to do was warn him about Evie's arrival and the strange man accompanying her. But out of nowhere, she'd changed and, with unnerving strength, pushed her bewildered friend hard against the stone wall, causing him to release the sack of weapons he'd stolen from the Land of Swords armoury. The Gordan couldn't speak. He was in shock. She grabbed the loot from his hands and withdrew one of the swords. Before she knew what had happened, she plunged the sword through his armour and into his stomach.

The metal melted away, revealing his bare, lacerated skin. Gwyn dropped the blade and the weapons that made a crashing sound on the stone floor. And, soon enough, the girl was herself again and panicked.

Knowing his life force was ebbing away, the Gordan was more concerned for Gwyn's safety. Straining his words, the injured being tried to tell her it wasn't her fault and encouraged her to help him through the tunnels to escape outside.

Unable to move and utterly broken, Gwyn couldn't think straight as voices in the distance drew nearer: a male and a female voice. The Gordan gripped the girl's shoulders and told her to snap out of it. Coming round, she helped to support his weight as he limped along while holding tightly on to the sack of weapons in her left hand.

After ducking and diving through the narrow cold passageways, the pain was too much, and he needed to stop. The voices in the distance echoed louder, and Gwyn's eyes widened with terror as she heard Evie question why Andrew could see the dazzling liquid on the floor but she could not.

Gwyn and her friend looked upon the trail of blood he'd left in his wake, and he knew he couldn't continue. Before the girl could speak, he told her to take the weapons and go.

"But—" said Gwyn.

"No," stressed the Gordan. "This is for your mother's homeworld. You need to do this."

"Honestly, I don't know what happened back there…" said Gwyn.

"And that's another reason why you need to go," said the Gordan. "To find out why."

Evie and Andrew were mere seconds away from arriving, so Gwyn ran from the scene towards the increasingly bitter chill and ascended a spiral staircase.

The air pierced her cheeks as she reached the top. Slithering around the outer edges of the courtyard, with only a handful of footmen present, the girl made it around the back of the stables and snuck inside.

Without looking back, Gwyn acquired a horse and left Castle Sword hastily over the drawbridge and into the snow-capped mountains. She knew only one place where it would be safe, and she needed to reach it fast.

It was a long, arduous day's ride down the mountainscape and into the barren forests of the Land of Wands in the north-west. Gwyn reached the border of the Land of Cups, and after she hunted down and ate a plentiful meal of game, she instructed her steed to return to the castle.

Once the horse was ready to return, the wild-eyed girl emerged from the forest and cautiously approached the warehouse nestled eerily next to the ghost-like wharf in Forta. Finally, Gwyn arrived outside the large storehouse entryway doors, where the small sea creature sigil of her mother's homeworld instantly illuminated and let her inside.

Taking refuge through a trapdoor and down a set of stairs deep underground, the exhausted teenage girl dropped the bag of weapons and fell to the floor. Her mind was consumed in fear. Gwyn did not know what had possessed her to kill her friend.

Removing the blade she'd used, now stained with dazzling bluish-green blood, Gwyn rested the sword before her and fixated on the tip. She couldn't see a way out.

"Gwyn?" asked a shaky voice in the distance.

She reached inside the inner lining of her tunic and removed her Wayan-made cards. Feeding off their owner's distress, they started to glow erratically as a steel grey mixed with pigments of teal – the colour of her mother's homeworld – was fighting to shine through.

"They need them, Gwyn," said her Tarot deck.

Across the space of the dank, abandoned storeroom, a mesmerising protective barrier showed the depths of Wayan's lake. The colourful aquatic life went about their mundane daily routine on the other side, swimming circles towards the magical transparent wall and cutting away into the crystal-clear waters.

"The opportunity will be any moment now," continued the deck. As the last words left their lips, the energy from Gwyn's cards grew stronger, and in an instant, a hefty amount of power shot through the air and latched on to the diaphanous cover. The magic targeted a small school of multicoloured fish from the deep and reeled them in against their will. The scared fish wriggled frantically, desperate to escape, but the mystical energy overpowered them.

Watching her cards take the lead jolted Gwyn to act. Picking the bloodied sword off the floorboard, she sprinted across the far corner of the space and hid it securely inside one of the shipping containers. Then, rejoining the weapons she'd stolen from her father's castle, Gwyn placed her hands on the floorboards and closed her eyes. Concentrating hard, she waited for an inkling of energy, hoping to connect with her from the Tarot world, Gorda. As the minutes ticked by, Gwyn was confident she hadn't missed her opening and wondered if something had happened on their side.

"Come on," she said, tears forming.

The Tarot deck continued to lock their magic around the defeated fish, sure the time would come. Then, much to Gwyn's relief, she felt the calling, joined forces with her mother's homeworld, and created a fantastical flaming portal before the mystical aquatic barrier.

Whip!

The cards propelled the fish through the gateway while Gwyn suppressed any detection of their plan from within Wayan due to her Wayan-Gordan blood. Once the food crossed worlds, the portal sucked in the bag of weapons. All the supplies Gwyn could offer for the malnourished inhabitants were complete.

The flaming circle vanished, leaving fresh scorch marks on the wood. The magic from her cards dispelled, and the deck flew sombrely into their owner's hand, for they and Gwyn knew it was never enough.

The girl planted herself before the protective transparent wall and gazed at the deep water. There were no other fish or life to be seen, and Gwyn had never felt so alone, even though her cards were still with her. All she could do was stare hard into the lake and release a trickling of tears.

Gwyn would soon realise she wasn't alone, for high above, on the preternatural land, Evie and Andrew had already docked and were hurrying across the wharf, eager to reach the decrepit-looking storehouse.

"This area belongs to the Land of Cups?" asked Andrew, trying to keep up.

"Yes," answered Evie.

"That might be good."

"Why?"

"Technically, I might end up helping their land, too," replied Andrew, eager to talk his way into making some kind of deal.

Ignoring him, Evie soon arrived in front of the warehouse doors, hunting for the aquatic animal engraving among the cluster of goblets, but she couldn't find it. "Can you see the creature?" asked Evie.

"No."

"Then I suspect it was wiped off recently. Stay close." Reaching for the sword secured on her back, Evie gripped the handle as they entered the building. Mould and cobwebs consumed the empty space. Evie's intuition, as did her cards, told her to stay alert.

Positioning themselves in the centre, searching high and low for anything unusual, Andrew caught sight of something in the distance. Darting to the source, he knelt before a small splatter of dazzling teal liquid, similar to what he found in the tunnels underneath Castle Sword.

Much to Evie's annoyance, she was suffering from the previous problem. She didn't know what he'd seen and, sensing her frustration, Andrew was straight in there, telling her what he'd discovered.

"Okay," whispered Evie.

In an instant, Evie's Tarot deck flew out of her drawstring bag, homing in on the patch of the floorboard. They delved into the intricacies of the mysterious liquid, cross-examining the magic with other Tarot worlds. Finally, they sensed it was Gordan blood, and their shimmering amaranth light started to eradicate the concealment magic hiding the entrance to a trapdoor with a rusty handle.

Signalling for Andrew to pull back the now exposed entryway, Evie stood firm with her sword raised. Once opened, all was silent inside the pitch blackness as they slowly descended a stairwell into the depths of the warehouse. Guided by the light being emitted from Evie's deck, they reached the underground level littered with dusty cargo boxes.

Andrew's eyes widened with amazement at the shimmering aquatic wall on the other side of the space. They were protected, like a submarine. Drawing closer to the magical barrier, he was quickly lost in the moment. Evie, however, wasn't fazed. She kept her guard up and wondered whether they were alone, but Andrew flagged something on the other side before she stepped away from the transparent wall. They leaned in closer, and a fish approached at high speed. It was volatile as it collided with the barrier. It quickly swam away and struck again. The fish wanted to break through, and Evie sensed something terrible must have happened to make it hell-bent on entering the storehouse.

"Please," she asked, "what's wrong?"

Shaking erratically, the animal stared hard at Evie and gestured for her to look at a particular spot on the transparent wall. Straining her eyes, she saw a flicker of steel-grey energy, a remnant from Gwyn's Tarot cards.

"Andrew," warned Evie, "stay behind me." Evie faced the darkened space and called out to those suspected of hiding to reveal themselves. Silence. She tried again, but still no movement, and as she threatened to advance, the amaranth energy from her cards invaded every nook and cranny of the darkened room, and there was Gwyn, clinging tightly to the blood-soaked blade. In her other hand were her Tarot cards, desperately trying to conjure mystical energy into the sword as a means to help defend their owner, which frightened Gwyn even more. She had never asked for or wanted a showdown, especially not with Evie.

"Gwyn, what is going on here?" demanded Evie.

"Please, it wasn't me."

Evie turned to Andrew, who confirmed the same dazzling liquid on the weapon in Gwyn's hand.

"It-t-t," stuttered Gwyn, overcome with anxiousness and losing her balance, "wasn't me…"

"Gwyn, give me your cards," instructed Evie.

"Please," cried Gwyn.

"How do you explain the Gordan blood? And the stolen armour?" asked Evie.

"I…"

Evie took a careful step towards Gwyn, who was on the verge of collapsing. "Gwyn," continued Evie, "please don't do anything."

"Evie, you saw her in the chamber with her father and Lady Selene. All she wanted was to be taken seriously."

Seeing the empathy in Andrew's eyes, Evie's respect for him reached new heights, and they nodded. Turning to face Gwyn, they watched with unease as her Tarot cards failed attempt after attempt to will magic into the sword. The scene was too much, and Evie and Andrew knew they needed to intervene.

Slowly and carefully, they knelt before Gwyn. Evie asked her to tell her side of the story, but the teenager didn't respond. The toxicity endured clouded her fragile mind, so her cards took matters into their own hands.

Their energy shone brighter and brighter, conjuring an image of the moment Gwyn was about to warn her Gordan friend inside the tunnels. Cries of pain pierced the air inside the warehouse as Andrew and Evie fixated upon the girl changing demeanour within the memory and plunging the sword through the Gordan's armour. The more they witnessed, the more Andrew and Evie soon realised Gwyn and her friend were trying to help her mother's homeworld and that an invisible force had made her do something she didn't want to.

"What we have seen shows you weren't the murderer," began Evie, "but it shows you conspiring against Wayan. You stole from your father and took fish from the Land of Cups."

"There wasn't a choice!" blurted Gwyn, her inner anger rising to the surface. "There's never a choice! Not for my mother's homeworld. You all just leave them to starve."

"Gwyn, that's not…" started Evie.

"True? Is that what you were going to say?" sniped Gwyn. "That's not 'true'!"

"Gwyn, please, let's talk," said Evie.

"Now is the time for talking?"

"Yes, Gwyn, now is the time for talking," replied Evie.

"What's the point? You're just going to hand me in or send me off to Gorda and be rid of me!"

"No, Gwyn. I'm going to give you an opportunity," replied Evie firmly. "You want to be taken seriously? I will arrange for you to join your father's counsel."

"Why?"

"Aren't you tired of hiding?" asked Evie. "Don't you think you can do more good making the necessary changes from inside Wayan instead of fighting it?"

"It's a trick," said Gwyn.

"No, it's not, Gwyn," said Evie. "In the long run, it is better to help your mother's homeworld through honesty and gaining respect over time on Wayan. Then you can really make a difference."

"But I still don't know what happened to me in the tunnels! It could have been someone from my father's castle!"

"Then, the more reason to work with your father, rather than being alone in an abandoned warehouse waiting to be picked off," answered Evie.

Gwyn was silent.

"Andrew, we're leaving." Evie said decidedly.

"But–" protested Andrew.

"No, we need to move on from this and leave Gwyn to decide. In the meantime, we can still push forwards."

Evie approached the stairwell while Andrew hung back. He watched the teenager slump to the floor. She began to sob. Andrew hoped she would eventually come around to accepting Evie's offer, for it was time for Gwyn to stop carrying the weight of her mother's homeworld on her shoulders.

Chapter Ten

Welcome Home

$\mathcal{A}$ loud rumble permeated Naxthos's night sky and wintry rain struck the tops of ten large, foreboding stones standing in a circle on a remote, grassy mound. The sacred rocks protected an ageing, raised altar in the inner circle, and while the weather worsened, a gateway opened beside the altar.

"Let go!" Amy screamed as Queen Lillian pulled her through the portal. Looking ahead to the ripple between worlds, she panicked. The Tarot cards in her left hand willed an erratic burst of incredible green energy out of her right hand.

The power narrowly missed Ben, who'd leapt through the portal after her before it closed.

"I can help you," said Queen Lillian, letting go of Amy to give her space.

But Amy couldn't stop releasing forest-green energy; she was out of control, and her insides felt like they were about to explode! Tears descended on her face. She clocked Ben, trying to hold it together as he cautiously approached her.

"I'm here, Amy," said Ben delicately.

"Stay away!" shouted Amy. "I'll hurt you."

"But you don't want to hurt me," replied Ben. "Please focus on that!"

"I'll try," said Amy, as she felt the rough edges of her cards.

Thinking of Ben and not wanting to strike him, Amy desperately willed her deck to die down her powers. Finally, after further pleading, the cards ceased, and she felt the wintry chill pierce her skin. Casting glances from the altar towards the standing stones, Amy and Ben struggled to make sense of their strange surroundings. They realised the woman who had forced Amy here against her will was now cautiously approaching.

The Queen of Naxthos raised her hands, welling up at the sight of her long-lost daughter.

"Amy," said Queen Lillian, stuttering a little, "please hear me out."

"Who are you?" asked Amy. "What does anything of this mean?!"

"There's no easy way to say this," said Queen Lillian.

As Amy urged Queen Lillian to continue, she felt light-headed, and Ben had to catch her before she fainted. A blinding light consumed Amy's mind, and a flashing of images rocked ferociously around her in an attempt to awaken the memories that Sorceress Sylvie had quashed into the deep depths of her being. Floods of feelings and experiences from when she and Andrew were small children living on Naxthos came back into existence and her brief visits on Wayan.

The standing stones disappeared, and the turbulent

unravelling had settled on a scene from the past. Amy was inside a plush, regal living room with old stone walls, and medieval furniture and architecture. The sun's rays beamed through a large, stained-glass window and lit the room with multicoloured light.

Heart beating frantically, she touched the top of an old, outdated armchair. It felt real.

The sound of children laughing engulfed her. They seemed joyful, like they were running rings around each other. Amy spun around and hunted for the source. It was coming from another room.

Edging closer, the roars of laughter grew more robust, and she stepped nervously inside. A young boy, close to seven, covered in mud with dishevelled, strawberry-blond tousles, chased a slightly younger girl with freckles on her cheeks and dark red hair cut into a blunt bob. They were goading one another as they ran around an amused young woman with striking, long white locks.

Amy's eyes bulged out of their sockets when the girl paused for breath. That child looked exactly like her when she was her age. And when she saw the boy better, he was the spitting image of Andrew's younger self.

Amy felt familiar energy enter her body. However, she didn't know why it was there, and the opportunity to explore it frightened her.

"You both!" said the young woman playfully. "Where will you cause trouble next, I wonder?"

"The whole of Naxthos!" called Anmos.

"You're silly!" chirped Aimesia.

"When you have done with Naxthos, what then?" said the young woman.

"Well, nanny Sylvie, another world!" said Anmos eagerly.

"There was a world I'd hoped to show you one day. But so much different to this one," said Sylvie with excitement.

"How different?" asked a captivated Anmos.

"It's hard to describe, but it's extraordinary," said Sylvie.

"Show us!" said Anmos, without thinking.

"What would your mother say?" said Sylvie.

Anmos couldn't be discouraged; his heart was now set on adventure, and after further begging, Sylvie promised to show them a brief insight into the other world from where they were standing. She turned her back on them and willed from her Tarot cards a gateway out of Naxthos. Taking hold of little Anmos and Aimesia, she encouraged them to look closer.

Amy watched from the sidelines as Sylvie quickened the pace. Anmos and Aimesia looked out of breath. Unexpectedly, there was the sound of the main door opening, and a group of tense voices entered.

Hearing her mother's voice, little Aimesia called out to her, but a troubled Sylvie quickly placed a hand around the girl's mouth, telling her to keep quiet. After that, the mood dropped considerably, and Anmos picked up on the nanny's change in character.

"Mother!" shouted Anmos.

That was the final straw for Sylvie. Her face changed to pure resentment of the world around her. She willed multicoloured energy from her Tarot cards and instructed the power to wrap around both children as they struggled to break free.

Amy watched as a younger Lillian rushed into the room. Upon seeing the horror in front of her, the princess demanded Sylvie release her children. But Sylvie forced Anmos and Aimesia through the portal. The gateway closed. The children were gone. The image disappeared, and Amy woke up. High above, the rain had eased, and Ben's face came into view as he knelt on the muddy moss beside her.

"What did you do to her?" demanded Ben.

"I'm sorry you saw that," said Queen Lillian, her voice soft.

Amy met the queen's eyes, and, for a split second, she felt something strangely intimate between them.

"We should leave," said a concerned Ben.

"Ben–" began Amy.

"Are you okay? What happened?" asked Ben.

"I think…" said Amy. "I think I might be connected to this place."

"Connected how?" asked Ben.

Taking his hand, Amy was about to explain when, *poof!* Ben disappeared. She searched wildly around the inner circle, but he was nowhere to be seen.

"Ben!" shouted Amy.

She was alone. Queen Lillian had also vanished. But the standing stones were still very much present, and the ancient altar hadn't moved from the centre. She looked up at the clear night sky. The rain had ceased. The air felt warm and rather muggy. Amy suspected she was back in the past.

Hurrying across the dry, grassy mound towards an opening between the sacred rocks, Amy heard the sound of hooves approaching. Two horses bounded out of the nearby forest, heading towards her. They carried concealed riders on their backs, and Amy needed to hide from them, fast!

Seeking safety behind one of the rocks, she dropped to the floor and peered around the rough surface to get a better look. The two horses entered the inner circle, and their pace hurried to the very end, until they stopped abruptly before the altar, nearly throwing the riders off.

One of the figures scrambled to the floor and lifted a small child off the saddle. A separate figure did the same on the other horse. Finally, the two adults removed their head masks, revealing a man and Princess Lillian.

"Do you think we were seen?" said Princess Lillian.

"I doubt it," said the man. "But we don't have much time. The court will know if we've been missing for too long."

"Sweetie, it's okay," said Princess Lillian delicately, trying to console the two-year-old girl, who looked upset, while the man knelt before the boy and told him he was brave. The princess removed a piece of parchment from her tunic, rolled it out, and studied the many symbols and inscriptions.

The scruffy, desperate man looked lovingly at his wife, who reread the parchment, taking in every detail for the upcoming spell they were about to try. Finally, she paused, met his sparkly yellow eyes, and smiled warmly at him.

"Father?" said four-year-old Anmos. "Mother?"

"It's okay," said the man.

But the man was suffering from shortness of breath as the family settled before the altar. He released little Aimesia's hand and clutched his chest tight. The girl screamed, and Anmos wrapped an arm around his sister to console her.

"Nicholas!" said Princess Lillian, kneeling before her husband.

Behind them, the children shuffled awkwardly, and their faces became sullen as if they knew something terrible would happen next. They were right. Shimmering, foreboding forest-green energy radiated out of the children's bodies, expanding, and they could not control it.

Further back, Amy watched as the energy pierced into Nicholas's chest, and their father was awash with pain and suffering. Princess Lillian begged them to stop, but Anmos and Aimesia didn't know how.

"It's the worst it's been," screamed Nicholas as his life ebbed away.

The children sobbed as their mother hastily picked up the parchment. She desperately read off the magic that would help to suppress the children's ability to draw star energy away. But as Princess Lillian reread the instructions, nothing happened. Nicholas was close to death.

"I'm sorry," said Nicholas. "As long as I'm a part star, this will continue to happen."

His wife looked at their guilt-ridden children and decided to take matters into her own hands to save her family. She willed her Tarot cards to conjure a portal to another world and carried Nicholas through in time.

"I will bring you back," whispered Princess Lillian as she kissed Nicholas on the forehead.

The portal gateway closed, and she rejoined Anmos and Aimesia, sobbing in the background.

"Where did he go!" said Anmos.

"Somewhere safe, I promise," Princess Lillian encouraged them.

Then, as the forest-green energy calmed and retreated into their bodies, the children disbanded their ability to draw star energy. At that moment, the family mourned Nicholas's absence, and Amy felt a sinking feeling that it was all her fault.

Swish!

She woke up from the memory with a thumping headache, surrounded by darkness, with only the light from the stars to help her focus. Not aware how long she'd been out, Amy breathed deep and exhaled to calm herself, but as her body rested upon the cold altar, a chill travelled down her back.

"Ben!" called Amy, but he didn't answer. Reeling from the past, Amy wondered if Nicholas was her biological father. Lost and confused, she called out to Queen Lillian to show herself.

"Amy, dear," said Queen Lillian, emerging from behind one of the sacred rocks.

Lifting her body, Amy swivelled around and dangled her feet off the altar. Staring directly into the queen's eyes, she waited.

"This is your home, sweetie," said Queen Lillian, on the verge of tears. "Sylvie took you from me. I've been searching for you all this time."

"My life, everything I've known," cried Amy, shaking uncontrollably, knowing she couldn't deny the awakening of her memories.

"Because of her," spat Queen Lillian, referencing Sylvie with such venom. "All because of her."

"And Nicholas?" asked Amy, dreading the answer.

"I haven't found him either. But I forgive you for what you did to your father. I know you couldn't control your star powers. He was a beautiful star who decided to fall to Naxthos and live amongst us. We fell in love and had you and Anmos."

Lost for words, Amy fell eerily silent, but Queen Lillian cut through her dismay and offered them some hope.

"I found a way to control your powers, sweet daughter, so we can locate Nicholas safely and bring him home," explained Queen Lillian. "I promise."

Having caused so much pain, Amy's mind was whirling with heartache and uncertainty about her entire existence.

"Amy," said Queen Lillian softly, "it's all going to be okay." The Queen of Naxthos looked lovingly at her daughter and asked her to pick up her Tarot cards from the altar. She encouraged Amy to shuffle them while fixating on the stars above. And when the moment felt right, she selected the card she felt most connected to from her deck.

As Amy kept taking in the sky, she stopped shuffling her deck and revealed her chosen card. Looking down in awe, Amy scanned the image of a woman kneeling with one foot in water and the other on land while a star above shone brightly.

"The Star card," said Queen Lillian, relieved. "This is it, Amy. We can now work to locate Nicholas." Queen Lillian's heart danced somersaults as she willed a fantastical, illuminating spell from her Tarot cards. Corporal symbols of the swords, cups, wands and pentacles shone and levitated. They swirled and swooshed until, finally, they combined and released mystical green power out of the Star card and into Amy's body.

"I don't feel so good," said Amy.

The Queen of Naxthos expertly manipulated the power out of Amy's body, awakening star energy, and instructed it into the altar and the sacred standing stones. As the ancient structures lit up with fantastical, forest-green magic, all at once they released great power into the sky.

"It hurts. I need it to stop," called Amy.

Ignoring her pleas, Queen Lillian stood back and watched anxiously. High above Naxthos, the energy acquired a large band of stars and directed them towards the castle.

While Amy struggled to break free from the spell, her eyes widened in fear. Levitating before her was a twinkling star, and from behind, Queen Lillian appeared and fastened a thin gold chain with a pentacle-shaped pendant around her neck.

The chain burnt into her skin, and as Amy wrestled to get it off, the delicate star above the altar had transformed into a small amethyst crystal. It flew through the air and nestled itself safely inside the pentacle pendant.

A haunting sensation took hold, and Amy felt herself leaving her body. Her face turned to joy as the star was now in control.

"Thank you for bringing me down from the sky," said Star Maya in Amy's body.

"You are welcome," chimed Queen Lillian, now a completely different person from the loving, maternal figure. Giddy with excitement, the Queen of Naxthos wasted no time. Picking Amy's cards off the floor, she told the star her guards would take care of them.

"Excellent," said Star Maya.

"Please tell me," said Queen Lillian. "How was the transformation?"

"It felt good. Amy, however, won't be leaving the crystal anytime soon."

Chapter Eleven

It's All in the Past

$\mathcal{A}$ group of musicians carrying an eclectic range of instruments filed through a broad, semi-circular archway enriched with zigzag and roll mouldings. Once inside the great medieval-esque banqueting hall of Naxthos, the merry band assembled in the middle of the forest-green marble floor. Their warm faces watched as the eager Naxthosian court approached the long wooden tables on the outer edges. As the court sat, a loud buzzing sound from the buisine shot into the air. The room roared with laughter at the timing, and subsequently, the other musicians joined in, blasting out merry tunes, bringing the room to life.

The castle's staff immediately appeared through various lower entranceways carrying trays full to the brim with meat and vegetables. Behind them, the cupbearers entered, determined to fill each goblet to the brim with a silky-smooth, sweet, fermented berry liquid called Naxed.

As the magnificent feast was about to begin, numerous Tarot decks sprang to life. They flew away from their owners around the hall. Circling above, the cards released different colours of astonishing energy, casting a mini firework display over the space in celebration.

Sat in the middle of the top table overlooking the banqueting hall was King Nate of Naxthos, and his wife Queen Henrietta. On the queen's right sat their daughter, Princess Lillian, and the empty seat next to her at the far end belonged to their son, Prince Marco. Shuffling awkwardly, the young princess, who had just turned twenty-two, cast a troubling look at the open spot.

"Is there something plaguing your mind?" asked Queen Henrietta.

Caught off guard, the princess fell silent, but before she had the chance to come up with an answer, her mother had already jumped to a conclusion.

"Don't worry, your brother is safe," she said. "He'll be back soon."

Princess Lillian couldn't care less about Marco. Biting her tongue, she waited and, with a dutiful, daughterly stare, nodded at her mother.

"Wayan is easy to return from," said Queen Henrietta. "You need to find that smile inside you. One of our guests is starting to notice."

Straightening her back, Princess Lillian took a casual sideways glance to the left of their table. Next to King Nate were twin brothers Sima and Samo, the high fairies of the Tarot world, Rosa. They'd only arrived that morning, and even though their visit was short, they were determined to enjoy every moment. Their tiny fairy wings protruding out of their backs fluttered cheerfully while the brothers watched the performers begin their dance routine in front of the musicians.

Next to Samo, at the other end, was the final guest from Rosa: a promising sorceress in her early thirties, with striking, long white hair cascading over her shoulders and no visible fairy wings. The princess's solemn and withdrawn face had immensely piqued the sorceress's curiosity.

"Why doesn't she have fairy wings?" whispered Princess Lillian, looking away from the sorceress at the musician playing the buisine.

"Because she's adopted," answered Queen Henrietta, her voice low.

Princess Lillian paused and bit her lip. She couldn't get distracted. Then, after a couple more minutes ticked by, Princess Lillian knew it was now or never. Preparing to ask her mother to be excused, she was interrupted by a sudden presence. The Sorceress of Rosa had already left her seat and was standing before them. Her kind eyes looked at Queen Henrietta, and her gut instinct told her she was a humble and respected ruler.

"Greetings, Your Majesty. I'm Sylvie of Rosa," said the sorceress.

As the young Sylvie bowed before the queen, Princess Lillian struggled to contain the brewing anger inside, and the sorceress sensed she'd struck a nerve.

"Thank you for your hospitality," said Sylvie.

"The pleasure is ours, Sorceress Sylvie of Rosa," replied Queen Henrietta, with genuine warmth in her tone. Then, she nudged her daughter.

"Sorry," blurted Princess Lillian.

"Princess Lillian, it is an honour to meet you," said Sylvie, calm and collected.

"Thank you, it is an honour to meet you, too," answered Princess Lillian through gritted teeth.

"Apologies if the room and I are keeping you from something more pressing?" said Sylvie. The sorceress had purposely dangled a carrot in front of Princess Lillian, who had no choice but to accept it.

"Yes, you're observant," said Princess Lillian.

Queen Henrietta was taken aback by her daughter's words.

Ready to pounce like a wild beast, Princess Lillian quickly mentioned Prince Marco to throw her off balance. "I'm worried about him," said a sincere Princess Lillian. "I conducted a Tarot reading, and it guided me to uncertainty for his safety. So, it's been troubling me all evening."

"When did you conduct the Tarot reading?" said Sylvie, trying to catch her.

"Just before we congregated inside the banqueting hall," said the princess, staying in character.

"Dear, you should have said," answered Queen Henrietta.

"Please, can I be excused? It would make me feel better if I waited inside the portal room for his return," said Princess Lillian.

"Deep down, I know he is fine," said Queen Henrietta, "but if it makes you feel better, then you're excused."

A wave of relief washed over the princess, and she smiled gratefully at the queen. The unbreakable bond between a devoted mother and her baby girl had prevailed, and Sylvie was impressed by the princess's tactics. The sorceress was convinced the girl was hiding something important.

Pacing around the back of the top table towards the broad, semicircular archway, Princess Lillian fought back the tears as she got closer to leaving the feast behind. The world she had grown up in and loved suddenly felt alien to her, but it had never been her intention.

Veering off, Princess Lillian turned abruptly down one of the narrow passageways while the merriment grew fainter. She continued down the long stretch of corridor, and a sudden chill hit her. Eventually, the princess stepped through an entranceway and pushed open an extensive set of polished oak doors.

Inside the well-insulated barn made of strong, hearty Naxthosian oak, Princess Lillian looked around at the array of horses nestled safely in their pens. Eyes darting wildly, looking for her jet-black, sort-of-noble steed called Nightgaze, she found him sleeping on the floor at the back, snoring with contentment.

Kneeling before the horse, she stroked his side, but Nightgaze didn't stir. He was too far gone. The princess then decided to nudge him, but that didn't work. Finally, she pushed him so hard that the jet-black horse woke up, startled. Realising his owner wanted to go on an adventure, Nightgaze couldn't be bothered. But Princess Lillian persisted until her disgruntled, noble steed gave in, knowing he'd lost the fight.

With the door to the barn open and his saddle securely fastened, the Princess of Naxthos got on Nightgaze and commanded him to leave the castle immediately. They rode through the desolate courtyard underneath the pitch-dark sky with only a faint flicker of starlight in the distance. Over the drawbridge, the air was chilly, and it pierced her face, but she didn't care; she loved the cooling sensation it gave, as she felt connected with the outdoors.

Riding away from Castle Naxthos, they drew closer to the edge of the Royal Forest. They entered through a clearing, making their way deep into the heart of the woodland. Ahead, she spotted a small fire and choked at the sight. This was where she so desperately needed to be.

Nightgaze cantered towards the small camp and stopped to let Princess Lillian off. Delicate flames licked outwards. She jumped on the hard soil with a thud and looked wildly around. A figure in the distance approached. His shaggy black hair was all over the place, and his sparkly yellow eyes looked at her with all the love in the world. Hugging each other tight, she hoped she wasn't too late.

"Has it happened yet?" she said.

"No, not yet," replied Nicholas, voice trembling.

She held him tight, for she knew he needed her now more than ever. Then, from above, a beacon of yellow light came closer. It expanded and floated at eye level in front of the couple.

"I think something is about to happen," said Princess Lillian. Releasing their hold of one another, Nicholas faced the floating entity that kept order among the stars in the Naxthosian night sky. That entity was called Mystic, who said nothing. All was silent in the woods save for Nightgaze chomping on a branch in the distance.

Unsure if they were meant to make the first move, Princess Lillian and Nicholas were about to say something at the same time, but the hollow voice of Mystic filled the air. She took hold of Nicholas's hand and squeezed it gently.

"You need to make a choice, Nicholas," said Mystic. "I granted your fall from the sky because you were growing bitter up there."

"I'm sorry," said Nicholas.

"Shush. Your toxicity started to affect other stars, and I had no choice. You have immersed yourself in the world you so desperately wanted to be a part of. So, I need your final answer."

"I want to stay on Naxthos," said Nicholas, looking at Princess Lillian lovingly. "Please, grant me this."

Mystic contemplated Nicholas's decision, for it wasn't an easy wish to grant. Much thought had to go into the plan, especially as the entity knew it wouldn't be around forever. The stars above countless worlds across the vast Tarot universe would need help at some point; Mystic needed to ensure Naxthos would still be protected even after it was gone.

"I will grant your wish. But, on one condition."

"Anything," said Nicholas.

As Nicholas and Princess Lillian waited, the entity told them it would need to give Nicholas the power to draw energy away from the stars. Confused by Mystic's request, the two lovers didn't know how to broach the subject, especially since they didn't want to risk changing its decision.

"There could be other stars, like you, who grow bitter because they couldn't live amongst the Naxthosians. But I can't allow all of them to fall."

"I'm sorry," said Nicholas.

"So, if, for whatever reason, I would need to leave Naxthos, then you would protect this world. With the power to draw energy away, you will be the one to squash any star threat," said Mystic, its tone final.

"Wait," Princess Lillian muttered under her breath. "What dangers would Nicholas face if he was to become Naxthos's protector?" A plague of worry encroached on her mind as she began visualising unpleasant outcomes. Nicholas squeezed her arms gently.

"It's okay, Lillian," he reassured her.

"But…"

"I love you. That's all that matters."

He accepted the deal. But, before Mystic cast the spell, Princess Lillian had a sudden urge to speak up. From inside, she'd been worrying about Sylvie. What if the sorceress, and possibly others, decided to hunt for the truth about them? She couldn't afford to put her family in harm's way.

"What's wrong?" asked Nicholas, worried they might miss their chance.

"It's okay," Princess Lillian reassured him. "Trust me." She stepped away from Nicholas and planted herself in front of the entity. Back straightened and chin raised, she knew she couldn't lose face. The princess needed to become someone Mystic would take seriously and accept.

"All we ask in return is to cast a spell that will distort anyone who wishes to conduct a Tarot reading on ourselves," said Princess Lillian. "We need to keep this a secret."

"That's a well-considered request, young princess," answered Mystic.

"Yes. If you need Nicholas to become Naxthos's protector, you wouldn't want to blow his cover, would you?"

A sudden pang of love overwhelmed Nicholas's heart at her words. After centuries of living in the sky among other stars, he had never felt anything like this – pure joy. He didn't interfere. Instead, he just watched. They observed the entity that continued to float in the air. Even though there was no inclination towards what it was about to do next, Princess Lillian refused to submit.

Mystic's dazzling energy grew outward as it told the young lovers, "Yes." With a mighty flash followed by a gentle rumble, the yellow power vanished.

Alone in silence in the middle of the Royal Forest, except for a loud fluttering snort from a startled Nightgaze, Princess Lillian and Nicholas looked at each other. Relief sprang across their faces, and the realisation Nicholas had been allowed to stay on Naxthos started to feel real. Tears of joy escaped down her cheeks while he hugged her tight. Immersed in the embrace, they became one, and that was the beginning of the rest of their lives together.

Their love continued to grow each day, and on an ordinary evening five years later, they were still as bright as the night they'd successfully bargained for Nicholas's soul. High above the south-facing tower of Castle Naxthos, the sound of laughter and excitement brought their candlelit, archaic living quarters to life.

Nicholas was in the centre, playing gentle tag with their cheeky four-year-old son, Anmos. Unfortunately, the clumsy boy hadn't dodged his father in time, so Nicholas grabbed the chance to ruffle his son's strawberry-blond hair. Anmos lost balance and face-planted onto the shaggy rug, but instead of crying, the boy rolled over, giggled, then dangled his arms in the air, waiting for Nicholas to lift him.

While father and son continued to play, behind them, Princess Lillian stood smiling in front of a great forest-green bookshelf made of marble and with row upon row of children's fables. In her arms was her shy two-year-old daughter, Aimesia. Eventually, the princess chose a mustard, leather-bound book inscribed with *Volume Three of the Naxthosian Tales of Old*. She carried the book and the girl, whose light auburn hair stuck out in all crazy directions, towards the oval window and sat on a comfy armchair.

The warm light of dusk began to stream in through the window and illuminate parts of the stone walls. Princess Lillian delicately stroked the faint freckles of the little girl's cheeks as she looked up at a relaxed, happy Nicholas. Once everyone around her seemed content, she opened the book and began to read the opening line of a fable titled *The Quest of the Sorceress and the Wheel of Destiny*.

Nicholas paused. He felt an ache in his chest and let out a slight groan, barely noticeable to his family. The pain withdrew, and so he carried on playing tag with his son. But, after a minute or two, the pain re-emerged. It had spread to other parts of his body, and Nicholas began to worry. Standing still, he took a deep breath, but the agony wouldn't subside.

"Father?" asked Anmos. "Are you okay?"

"Yes, I'm fine. Don't worry."

Nicholas collapsed on the shaggy rug and cried out. Star energy had consumed his entire being and, from his eyes, he saw a scene where a small ball of burnt-orange energy had entered Naxthos's atmosphere from another Tarot world. It drew nearer, slow and calculating, and then, *swish!* It grabbed the opportunity and landed quickly in a remote area where an abandoned ancestral shrine rested nearby.

Without warning, the vision was gone, and Nicholas was back in the room. His worried family knelt beside him, and as Princess Lillian and Anmos took turns asking what had happened, he felt the star's presence near the shrine and a wave of fear consumed him. Whatever had arrived meant to harm Naxthos, and Nicholas needed to disband it fast.

"A star has arrived," he said.

"Arrived?" asked Princess Lillian.

"From another Tarot world. It wants to dominate."

"It's finally happened," said Princess Lillian, fighting back the tears.

"You need to stay with the children."

Kissing the panicked children, Nicholas hugged Princess Lillian and reassured her he would be back soon. An uneasy feeling rose from the pit of her stomach, but she had no other choice but to keep silent.

Turning his back on his wife, Nicholas couldn't look at his family again for fear he would change his mind. He bounded out of their living quarters and sprinted down the commanding spiral staircase, two steps at a time. Through the castle, he ducked, dived and weaved to avoid being noticed, and eventually snuck into the barn and found Nightgaze blissfully snoring, as always when night fell.

Stroking the magnificent horse, Nicholas encouraged him to wake up and after further cajoling and prodding, the steed jolted and locked eyes with the secret protector of Naxthos. Seeing the desperation in his eyes, Nightgaze knew the troubled being needed help and encouraged him to prepare his saddle for their journey.

Camaraderie developed and they rode out of the stable and through a narrow clearing, avoiding the castle's life. Under the clear, muggy night sky, they travelled through the Royal Forest and found an opening to a desolate, grassy mound where, ahead, ten prominent stones stood in a circular formation.

The hurried canter of Nightgaze caused the ground to shake underneath them, and as the noble steed bound towards the sacred stones, Nicholas spotted an ancient, forgotten altar in the centre. The horse's pace hurried to the end, where he stopped abruptly before the shrine, nearly throwing Nicholas off.

Resisting the urge to throw up, Nicholas lifted himself off the pillion. His sparkly yellow eyes looked wildly around the space, for this was the exact spot the star energy had led them to.

The air fell hauntingly quiet and Nicholas and Nightgaze stayed in position with no sign of life. After a few more minutes, they thought they'd seen a dazzling shadow dart between two standing rocks in the distance. But still, nothing was visible, and it could have been a mind trick.

They were about to explore another part of the grassy mound before a rapid burst of burnt-orange energy came out of nowhere and struck Nightgaze. The steed fell to the floor with a loud thud, and as Nicholas knelt to check, the star released a more powerful energy blast, and Nightgaze was reduced to ash.

"He's gone," Nicholas cried, feeling the grey powder on the spot where the noble steed rested. Another blast struck the back of the protector of Naxthos, who didn't fall. Instead, it angered him. Turning to face the entity as it stepped out of the shadows, Nicholas came face to face with an enlightened being in the shape of a Naxthosian with no unique features or skin.

Thirsty for blood, the star mercilessly fired at Nicholas, who was still unaffected. But, not taking any more chances, Nicholas raised his arms and muttered an incantation into the sky. The air around him was whipped into a frenzy and a jolt of yellow star energy appeared and entered his hands. Nicholas willed the power to draw star energy away from the harmful being, who stood surprisingly still and compliant.

A feeling of nausea overcame Nicholas, who had to stop and catch his breath. The star unleashed a mystical onslaught of a different kind of star power. It burnt Nicholas's shoulder badly and he was thrown off guard.

Avoiding withdrawing further star energy in case it weakened him further, Nicholas dodged and blocked other attacks. Finally, he grabbed the opportunity to manipulate his power and strike incredible energy back. The star fell back and hit one of the standing stones. It landed on the floor, as Nicholas approached with caution. The entity wasn't able to get up. Scanning the volatile being, the protector of Naxthos knew he needed to extinguish the star, and the quicker he did it, the sooner he would be able to reunite with his family in Castle Naxthos.

On the other side of Naxthos, inside the south-facing tower, Princess Lillian was hoping for his safe return. Looking out of the commanding oval window, she reassured herself Nicholas would be fine for it was his responsibility, and Mystic gave him the tools and spells necessary to succeed.

As she calmed herself, a creak from behind the door that led to the children's bedrooms diverted her attention. Rooted to the spot, she strained her ears, but all was silent. "So, the children must still be sleeping," she whispered, sighing in relief.

Turning to look out the window again, the princess sensed a presence enter the space, and she welled up at the sight of a concerned and dishevelled Nicholas closing the main door behind him.

"Are you okay?" she said, hugging him tightly.

"Yes, just about. I don't know where that star came from, but if there are others like it, we are in trouble."

"We can work it out together."

As they embraced, she felt Nicholas wince in pain and pull away.

"What's wrong?"

"I think another star has arrived."

Hunched over in agony, unable to meet his wife's eyes, he pointed at the oval window, and once Princess Lillian turned to inspect the night sky, it all happened so quickly. A delicate gold chain with a pendant shaped like a pentacle was forced around the princess's neck.

"Nicholas! What are you doing?!" called Princess Lillian, panicked.

Nicholas pushed Princess Lillian hard against the stone wall, and as she faced her husband, the chain was burning into her neck. Struggling to unclasp it, the jewellery wouldn't budge, and before her, the person she thought was her husband began to transform. Patches of skin turned into illuminating, burnt-orange energy, revealing the same star entity that had fallen to Naxthos earlier.

While scanning the room for a weapon, Princess Lillian was overpowered by the star. This time, it threw her so hard against the wall that blood oozed from her forehead. Looking up in fear, the princess watched as the entity transformed into a quaint amethyst crystal. It flew towards the necklace and placed itself inside the pendant.

Desperate to get the necklace off, the chain continued to burn into her skin as a weird and frightening sensation took over. She was losing control of parts of her body until, finally, Princess Lillian's asomatous state was trapped inside the amethyst crystal, and Star Lisa commanded her body.

The pleased star inspected its new form and walked around the living quarters, taking in every detail of the princess's family life. Toys and books littered the floor, and as it reached the marble bookshelf, the entity saw row upon row of children's fables. At the top, out of reach of Anmos and Aimesia, was a selection of scarier encounters, most notably, *Tales of Barbaric Customs*. Opening the cover, Star Lisa flicked through its contents and homed in on the names of Tarot worlds the universe feared most. One of them was Lixus.

The star thought those names would be useful, especially for what it intended to do to Anmos and

Aimesia, which required time, patience, and careful planning. Scanning the room, the star saw a rolled-out piece of parchment showing the family tree of Naxthos on a low oak table nearby. It was about to approach the family tree when a gentle tap on the door startled the entity. It stayed still, not making a sound. But the tapping continued with more determination, and once Star Lisa realised the being on the other side wouldn't retreat, it released the latch, and the heavy door swung back.

Sorceress Sylvie of Rosa stood to attention and cast a look of deep concern over Princess Lillian.

"Is everything okay, Your Highness?"

"Yes," answered Star Lisa.

"Your head? It's bleeding?"

Star Lisa had forgotten the wound it had inflicted on Princess Lillian. But instead of an explanation, the entity didn't answer back; rather, it sought to stare at Sylvie, making her feel uncomfortable.

"Are the children okay?" said Sylvie, desperate to look inside the living space.

"Of course."

"Shall I go check on them?"

"Why?" said Star Lisa, rather abruptly, trying to contain her annoyance.

"It is my duty, after all," said Sylvie, with a more delicate tone.

The silence was unnerving as Star Lisa refused to move from its spot, and for a moment, Sylvie thought she'd seen a book on a table nearby titled *Tales of Barbaric Customs*.

"I wouldn't be the best nanny in the world, would I," said Sylvie.

The penny finally dropped; Star Lisa realised the annoying woman in front of her was the children's nanny. The star forced a smile and nodded. But just when Sylvie thought she'd be allowed in the room, Star Lisa told her, "No. It's getting late. Tomorrow morning would be better."

"Er, okay. Where's Nicholas?"

"He took a trip."

Star Lisa shut the door in Sylvie's face. The Sorceress of Rosa was perplexed. Even though she'd always suspected Princess Lillian harboured a secret, there was never a moment she'd felt concerned for the children's well-being. What if the princess was starting to go down a path of inflicting abuse? If she thought the situation would get out of hand, Sylvie swore to herself she would do whatever was necessary to protect Anmos and Aimesia from harm, even from their own mother.

Chapter Twelve

Wands

Their journey from Forta was undoubtedly sombre. Andrew and Evie's encounter with Gwyn underneath the decrepit warehouse had thrown them both. But, as their resilient vessel entered choppy waters towards the north-western mainland, Evie wanted Andrew to let go of his feelings for the teenager. She needed him ready for the wonders he would witness next within the Land of Wands. But before that time came, the waves grew increasingly volatile, rocking the boat and forcing them to support one another as they stood beside the helm.

Fast approaching a small, isolated landing bay amid a high cliff face, Andrew was surprised to find no one to greet them. As Evie manoeuvred the boat, it struck the side of the metal dock, causing a loud bang and, like lightning, she jumped off, not caring about the turbulent waters underneath. She battled the uprising of prevailing winds and tied the rope to one of the handful of steel rings welded into the floor.

Evie hurried along the platform towards the cliff face without waiting for a hesitant Andrew. Standing before the rough-edged formation, she placed her hands on the surface. It instantly recognised her energy and conjured mystical stones that started to protrude from the bottom to the top.

"What do we do now?" Andrew asked, hurrying over.

"We climb."

Andrew raised his head at the sheer, imposing height, while Evie began her ascent. He looked straight ahead, trying to block out everything around him.

"Hurry up!" called Evie.

Andrew grabbed the first set of stones, lifted himself off the ground, and started shaking.

"Come on! Andrew! You need to keep going."

Unsure what was worse, the thought of the climb or hearing Evie grow more frustrated at him, he tried to rise slowly and carefully. Minutes felt like hours as he drew closer to a quarter of the way.

Taking a breather, he noticed the light from the sun had dropped significantly and they were entering the early evening. The mystical stones glowed, determined to help guide him up before the sky descended into darkness.

Looking up, he couldn't see Evie. She must have reached the top already, and he was holding her back, as well as himself. Something inside told him to get on with it, but he nearly lost his footing as he quickened the pace. Pushing his bodyweight close to the rock face, Andrew breathed heavily. The visibility grew worse around him, but before he attempted to complete the last phase of the ascent, he heard a faint swooshing noise in the distance.

Straining his eyes above, he couldn't see anything, but the whirling note grew louder, and he thought he saw an array of piercing yellow circles flying through the air.

Finally, reaching the top, he was about to lift himself onto the cliff's surface when, *swoosh!* A flying being darted past, causing him to nearly stumble back over the side.

Evie reached for his hand and pulled him towards her just in time. Reunited with her, Andrew's heart was racing, but a magnificent sight knocked the wind out of him.

Five majestic, panther-like creatures with raven wings protruding from their backs stood proudly on all fours. Their coats were silky and as pure as the night, and their eyes dazzled like yellow stars. So substantial in size, large enough to transport two people, the beasts were beautiful and intimidating.

"What are they?" asked Andrew, eyes widening in amazement.

"They are called rapas," said Evie, amused at Andrew's reaction.

Three residents of the Land of Wands sat comfortably on the saddles of their rapas, each wrapped securely around their creatures' torso. They held long wooden staffs that glowed wondrously, lighting up the scene before Andrew and Evie.

Andrew saw the remaining riderless rapas and turned to Evie, a little hesitant.

"And you were nervous about horses?" she quipped.

Taking a gulp, waves of uncertainty for the unknown consumed Andrew's insides, but Evie didn't stop to discuss it. Instead, she approached a young man in his early twenties, whose eyes were warm and inviting.

"Hello, Evie," said the young man, smiling at her.

"Thank you so much for greeting us, Nathaniel. How's Missy?"

"Missy's good," said Nathaniel as he patted his rapa tenderly on the neck. "She's still a little scared of the fireworks, but we're getting there."

"Fireworks?" blurted Andrew.

"Yes," answered Nathaniel, slowly and carefully, acutely aware of Andrew's true identity. "We'll be able to show you soon enough."

Evie placed her hand on Andrew's back and marched him to the free rapa closest to Nathaniel.

"Now, remain calm and don't just flap around. The rapa you'll be riding on is called Tricksy," said Evie.

"Tricksy?"

Tricksy turned her imposing panther head and looked down at Andrew. Her body remained deathly still. He was wary of her sizeable paws and claws, and then, as he cast his eyes up, he gulped at the saddle tied around her back.

"Er…" Andrew stuttered.

Tricksy gripped the back of Andrew's vest collar with her teeth and hoisted him up. His feet dangled awkwardly as she manoeuvred him to land on her saddle. Holding tightly to the leather handle before him, he started shaking while Evie smirked. She jumped onto her rapa and signalled Nathaniel to take them to Mount Wayan, the home of the Land of Wands.

On their journey, Tricksy and her fellow rapas glided effortlessly in the air. The mood was calm and serene around them, taking in the beauty of the night sky. Andrew, however, was far from at peace. His eyes were closed, desperately hoping he wouldn't plummet to his death.

"Andrew," called Evie on the rapa next to him, "you're going to miss it if you keep being a baby."

Opening his eyes and looking straight ahead, he spotted a breathtaking mountainscape in the distance. Drawing closer, he could see clearer individual balconies made of white quartz crystal constructed horizontally and vertically on the outside of Mount Wayan. Out of sequence, the residents stepped onto each balcony from inside the mountain. They held wooden staffs that lit up in their hands.

"Our home," called out Nathaniel.

Andrew looked on in awe as the shining, mystical light looked like a sea of stars guiding their people home.

"It's incredible," called back Andrew, starting to feel surprisingly more relaxed.

Nathaniel and Evie smiled as all five rapas flew high over the balconies and positioned themselves directly above Mount Wayan. Underneath was a mystical round forcefield that disappeared as the creatures lowered themselves through the summit. As soon as they were inside, the forcefield re-emerged above them.

As Tricksy descended inside the monumental space, Andrew saw the top of a gigantic quartz crystal spiral staircase that travelled all the way down to the depths. On one side were hexagonal doors that led to people's homes, while on the opposite side of the mountain were individual stables that housed each family's rapa.

In awe of the scene, Andrew hadn't noticed Nathaniel and his two companions break away while he and Evie continued to one floor below. Their rapas landed in front of empty stables, waiting patiently for their riders to dismount.

Evie's rapa went to the barn on the left, while Tricksy was at home in the compartment on the right. Andrew watched with amusement as she knelt on a bed of hay, tilted her head, and sank to the floor in contentment. Tricksy fell asleep within seconds and instantly started to breathe heavily, until she finally started snoring loudly.

"You're beautiful, Tricksy," said Andrew.

"I'm glad you eventually enjoyed the experience," said Evie.

"This place is…"

"Incredible?"

"Yes."

"It never gets old."

Andrew smiled at her words. To live each day surrounded by wonder and adventure. But, before he could reflect on his life in London, Evie urged him to follow her up the spiral staircase, where Nathaniel greeted them on the floor above.

"My uncle's inside," said Nathaniel warmly. "He's looking forward to seeing you."

Evie smiled as she entered the large, open living area where a burnt-orange rug shaped like a pentacle dominated the centre of the white quartz crystal floor. Luxurious cushions in various shades of purple were littered everywhere.

On the far side, a tall brass stand held a long wooden staff, and next to it were four marble steps leading to the open-aired balcony. An anxious man in his early eighties appeared from outside, nearly losing his balance as he descended the steps to greet Evie and Andrew. His fierce brown eyes, showing years of experience, now looked gaunt and haunted, and his long brown tunic had holes.

"The door, Nathaniel, quick," said the man.

"Yes, Uncle," replied Nathaniel as he reached the front door and closed it.

"Please… please sit, Evie and Evie's companion," said the man.

Evie lowered herself onto one of the plush cushions, as did Andrew. Once everyone was settled, Evie was the first to speak. "Hello, Sir Gregory. My mother mentioned you'd reached out to her for help."

Sir Gregory, the Land of Wands' leader, lowered his head in shame. He was silent for a few minutes until his nephew, Nathaniel, touched his shoulder.

"Uncle, do you want to tell them, or shall I?" asked Nathaniel.

"Er, it might be better to show them," Sir Gregory replied with dread. The leader removed his sleeve and showed them his right arm. Under his skin was a sepia-coloured line that had branched out. "It's expanding. It's now reached my shoulder."

"What happened?! Does it hurt," asked Evie, concerned.

"I feel weak," said Sir Gregory.

The group's attention was diverted to the sound of happy and merry residents cheering in anticipation from outside their balconies, but Sir Gregory was on the verge of tears. "Every night, I give the people their fireworks to celebrate the passing of another day, but…"

"Sorry, Uncle, but we haven't got much time," said Nathaniel.

The young man rose from his cushion and accepted his uncle's robe. Then, ensuring the hood concealed his face, Nathaniel removed Sir Gregory's wooden staff from the brass stand and marched up the marble steps onto the balcony.

He held the wand proudly and, soon after, there was an uproar of excitement. *Flash!* The mystical object conjured multicoloured waves of fantastical energy, igniting the night sky with colour and spectacle. Families cheered and applauded from their balconies, while Nathaniel gave a sigh of relief.

Andrew and Evie positioned themselves under the archway, gazing wonderfully at the display, but Sir Gregory hadn't moved. He felt ashamed of himself and couldn't bear to witness the fireworks.

After the spectacle had finished and another day ended, Nathaniel rejoined the others inside and placed the staff back delicately on the stand. Soon after, he sat beside Sir Gregory, wrapping an arm around his uncle, hoping to make him feel better. "Two weeks ago," said Nathaniel, addressing Evie and Andrew, "Uncle Gregory lost his powers. The line you saw on his arm is poison, and it suppressed his magic. Since then, I have managed to pose as him every night to conjure the fireworks so his people wouldn't suspect."

"Sir Gregory, I'm so sorry. Do you suspect anyone who could have done this?" said Evie with care.

"No, no one. I thought the people were happy, content. It's upsetting because the colour of the poison is similar to the energy my people conjure from our Tarot cards. I couldn't bear it if it was someone from inside our home."

"It might not be them, dear Uncle," Nathaniel reassured him.

"Exactly," said Evie. "We don't know for certain. Do you remember where you were when it happened?"

"Er, I flew back from the water's edge of Lake Wayan with Margot."

"Margot is his rapa," said Evie to Andrew, who'd looked confused.

"She landed on the staircase as normal and went to her stable. I entered my living space, had a cup of hot mint tea that I'd conjured from my staff, took a couple of sips, then I felt uneasy. That's when I noticed a vein on my hand turned a rich, dark brown, and it had grown out. As a result, I'm getting weaker and unable to use magic."

"So, you were the only one in your home? You conjured your drink from your staff?" asked Evie. Meanwhile, her Tarot cards circled the room, hunting for anything that suggested foul play, but nothing was apparent.

"Yes, and because my magic has disappeared, I can't ask my Tarot cards for guidance. Nathaniel has tried to use his deck, and they keep showing us the death card."

Andrew turned to Evie, concerned, but she shook her head at him to dismiss his assumptions. "No, Andrew, it doesn't necessarily mean actual death. But it could mean the end of a chapter and the beginning of a new."

"Exactly, Evie, someone seeking to overthrow Sir Gregory," said Nathaniel. "I am just his nephew, not his son, and it wouldn't take much to overthrow my authority without first earning the respect of the people."

Evie looked at Sir Gregory, who started to cry, and she gestured for Andrew to make their way to the front door to give them some space.

"We are going to stay and keep watch," said Evie, her eyes filled with rage at seeing the leader of the Land of Wands broken. "I promise we'll find the culprit."

Nathaniel nodded gratefully, and as Evie and Andrew closed the door behind them, Andrew was straight in there.

"Who could have..." he started to say.

"Shush. Remember, no one knows."

"Sorry."

"It's getting late, and the lights will go out soon on the staircase, so you return to Tricksy and keep watch over Sir Gregory and Nathaniel, and I'll start at the bottom and work my way up to the top."

"You can't be serious. I can't even see the bottom of the staircase. It will take you forever!"

"We've got all night," said Evie, making her way down the glistening quartz steps while her Tarot cards flew in front.

Andrew thought she was mad to cover that distance and considered following her and pushing for a new plan, but he couldn't leave Sir Gregory and Nathaniel. Now alone on the stairwell, the mood inside the towering cavern was silent, save for the rustling of hay in the stables and groans and grunts from the sleeping rapas. Finally, Andrew reached Tricksy's stable, hid inside and kept watch.

The next night, Nathaniel continued to pose as Sir Gregory and after successfully setting off the fireworks, Andrew and Evie repeated their actions. Evie and her

Tarot cards inspected the staircase again, seeking out any wrongdoing energy from inside people's homes, while Andrew kept watch from Tricksy's stable. Similarly, they saw no one attempt to cause any harm.

The following day, Evie's patience wore thin, and Andrew was desperate to unravel the mystery and get one step closer to claiming his Tarot cards and returning home.

The situation grew more peculiar, for Sir Gregory's arm had begun to heal, and his Tarot cards started to give his powers back. Moreover, he could feel the magic flowing through his wand again.

"I don't understand," said Evie. "We've seen nothing out of the ordinary. No one has tried to make a move on Sir Gregory, and now he is making a speedy recovery!"

"So do we still need to wait?" replied Andrew, his frustration also bubbling. "Otherwise, the same person might try to poison him again." Andrew paced around Tricksy's stable, feeling helpless.

"Andrew, I'm annoyed too. I want you to claim your cards just as much as you do."

"Sir Gregory conjured the drink himself, and he was alone. He'd only just returned from the Lake Wayan on his..." Andrew paused, his eyes widening with curiosity.

"What?"

"Have you seen Margot?"

"No, I haven't. Sir Gregory hasn't been anywhere. He didn't want anyone to suspect his magic had gone."

Andrew made his way out of Tricksy's stable and ran up the flight of stairs to see Margot slumped on the hay, asleep. He knelt beside her and noticed she was still wearing her saddle, so he undid the belt under her chest and removed it.

"What are you doing?" said Evie.

"What if someone poisoned Sir Gregory before he'd returned to Mount Wayan? And the colour of the poison was a ruse to focus our search from within the Land of Wands?"

He hung the saddle on one of the large nails protruding from the wall and inspected it. He didn't notice anything odd until he flipped the saddle around. Underneath the leather handle, a speck of sepia energy glowed innocently.

"Look there," said Andrew.

Evie inspected the mark and nodded. "When Sir Gregory held on, the poison must have transferred onto his skin," said Evie.

"But now he is better? Who would go to all that trouble to hurt him, only for him to make a speedy recovery?"

"What if the person never meant to hurt him?" said Evie.

Without warning, the poisonous magic glowed brighter and brighter, and as Evie told them to leave the stables immediately, it generated an electrical current and struck Andrew's back. Falling to the floor, Andrew was knocked out cold. Panicking, Evie knelt beside him, and as she asked her Tarot cards for help, the ill-intended magic disappeared from Margot's saddle.

Chapter Thirteen

The Unfolding of Time

The sun's rays easily permeated through Andrew's bedroom curtains, casting light across his unconscious body. Laid on his stomach on his single bed, he began to stir a little as a firing round of notifications from his mobile encroached the air around him.

Disorientated and wearing the same clothes he'd left in, Andrew squinted, recognising the familiar box room within the cramped two-bed flat he shared with George in Clapham. He started to remember fragments of his time on the Tarot world Wayan, but he was uncertain what had been real. Suddenly, dehydration hit, and he desperately needed water. He stood up straight on the floorboards when *ping, ping, ping* – a second round of notifications shot from his phone. He moved towards the side table. The screen read 8.15am, Saturday the 14th of August – the day after he was meant to collect his sister from the station.

Andrew checked his phone, and his eyes widened at no word from Amy, only Lanie. His hyped-up boss had fired numerous emails, dialled a dozen times, and the final onslaught was a WhatsApp voice note. He hit play and listened as her erratic voice threatened to sack him because no one could contact him after leaving work early yesterday.

Andrew slammed his thumb hard on the screen and deleted the message. He marched across the bedroom, turned the doorknob, and threw the door back violently. It hit the wall with a loud bang and broke the silence, all apart from Andrew's heavy, panicked breathing.

"Amy!" shouted Andrew. Checking the living room, kitchenette and living space, no one was there, and there was no sign of Amy's luggage. "George?!" shouted Andrew.

He opened the door to George's bedroom without caring about disturbing his flatmate. But, taken aback by the empty space with no furniture or evidence of occupation, he knew something was very wrong. There was no way George, or his belongings, could have disappeared into thin air!

Andrew stood in the hallway, anxious and paranoid. He tried to call Amy but couldn't connect. What was happening? He stressed as he fought back the tears. Was the air around him some cruel trick? Had he actually returned to Earth?

Of all the people Andrew wanted to see, to help him make sense of his surroundings, he needed Evie. He wanted her to be real, even if she didn't exist and he was about to be escorted to psychiatric care.

Taking deep breaths, he tried to envision her tenacious presence, and as his heartbeat started to slow, he whispered to himself that Evie would tell him to explore and push forward. Never dwell on the moment long enough to risk losing yourself. Wiping away the tears, he made his way towards the end of the hallway and released the latch. He opened the front door to his flat, ventured onto the second floor's landing, and passed another apartment directly across from him.

There, he lost his balance after meeting a set of concerned, rich green eyes with tints of yellow. Falling back onto the floor, Andrew stared up at her as she leaned against the wall with such innocence.

"Hi, Andrew," replied Queen Lillian softly. But to those very few in the know, it was Star Lisa. "Please, don't be frightened," she continued. "I chose this place as I didn't want to alarm you. I never wanted to cause you harm." Kneeling before him slowly, Queen Lillian locked into Andrew's eyes, hoping to put him at ease, but he was still rattled.

"Queen Maria didn't seem to think so," he replied. "You were the one who struck first."

"I was trying to save you, Andrew," said Queen Lillian. "One of my necromancers managed to find a crack in Wayan's defences and poison Sir Gregory's saddle. I'm sorry, I was desperate to reach you."

"Why go to all that trouble for me? I've nothing to do with this. Wait," he said, the cogs churning in his mind, "Sir Gregory's saddle was poisoned two weeks ago, before I'd even met you."

"Exactly, Andrew," said Queen Lillian. "You need to know who you truly are." She placed her hands on either side of his head, and fantastical, forest-green energy seeped out of her skin and entered Andrew's. Unable to resist, he started to shake violently on the floor as the magic fought hard to penetrate Sylvie's memory-loss spell.

The pain in his head grew more intense, unravelling the intricate web of his false life on Earth and reawakening the one he was destined to journey along. Finally, he saw the exact moment in his childhood when nanny Sylvie snatched little Aimesia and himself from Wayan. Anmos's distraught mother, uncle and auntie tried desperately to prevent it. But it was too late: Sylvie escaped through a portal. She ducked and dived across countless Tarot worlds until, finally, she'd found Earth – a world very much in its infancy and, overall, inconsequential.

But, instead of leaving the memory there, Queen Lillian replayed the moment repeatedly in Andrew's mind. As a result, he suffered countless reruns of his birth mother's distress and King Marco and Queen Maria, all resulting from Sylvie's ill intent.

While Andrew was burdened with making sense of his true identity, Star Lisa inside Queen Lillian's body was relishing cementing Sylvie's blame for everything. It held the memory over and over, tormenting him until he was completely broken.

"Anmos," said Queen Lillian softly. "Anmos, I'm so sorry you had to see that."

Andrew's eyes opened. He couldn't move. His entire world had been squashed and realigned into one horrific nightmare, shattering his belief in everything he thought he'd known.

"Sylvie took you from me," said Queen Lillian delicately, "but the pain she caused, we can work through it together."

Andrew toyed with the memories but, deep down, he couldn't deny what he'd seen and felt. The realisation his birth mother had been trying to reach him all that time was heartbreaking. She had been suffering through trying to find her children while he was unnecessarily worrying about his stupid career and looking after some mediocre talent. How pathetic were his troubles compared with hers? The difference was at opposite ends of the scale.

"It's okay," Queen Lillian soothed him, "everything will be okay." Reaching out her hand, Star Lisa, in Queen Lillian's body, patiently waited for Andrew to take it. The entity was so close now to solidifying its connection with the long-lost child of Naxthos and extracting him back to his homeworld. The first thing it would do would be to give Andrew a Tarot deck and subject him to the same fate as Amy.

While revelling in the future, the star hadn't noticed a sudden change in Andrew. Still lying on his back, he started shaking again, but this time it was as shocking to Star Lisa as it was to him.

Something unexpected had happened, and the star was angry. It tried waking Andrew, but he was forced to return to the depths of his mind. Cool evening air that felt surprisingly real filtered in through a commanding oval window and hit the back of his neck.

In a child's bedroom within the south-facing tower of Castle Naxthos, little Aimesia was fast asleep, immersed in forest-green energy. The sleeping magic coating Anmos had suddenly evaporated, causing him to wake up to the sound of voices from their living quarters on the other side of the stone wall.

This is unnerving, Andrew thought as he watched his younger self gingerly creep out of bed, tiptoe across the rug, and peer through a small gap in the bedroom door. Andrew pursued him and hovered over the boy, where he was also able to make out the scene before them.

In the main doorway into their living quarters, Sorceress Sylvie of Rosa cast a deep look of concern over Princess Lillian.

"Your head? It's bleeding?" said Sylvie.

Star Lisa had forgotten the wound it inflicted on Princess Lillian. But instead of an explanation, the entity didn't answer; rather, it sought to stare at Sylvie, making her uncomfortable.

"Are the children okay?" asked Sylvie, desperate to look inside the living space.

"Of course," said Star Lisa.

"Shall I go check on them?"

"Why?" said Star Lisa, rather abruptly, trying to contain her annoyance.

"It is my duty, after all," said Sylvie, with a more delicate tone.

The silence was unnerving as Princess Lillian refused to move from her spot.

"It's getting late. Tomorrow morning would be better."

"Er, okay. Where's Nicholas?"

"He took a trip."

Andrew watched his birth mother shut the door in Sylvie's face and cast a deep, hateful look. Straining his ears, he heard Princess Lillian whisper under her breath that, the first chance she had to dispose of Sylvie, she would take it.

The toxicity surrounding her is unnatural, Andrew thought. Having reconnected with his childhood, he understood Princess Lillian as a kind, warm soul. But the woman before him seemed different, and it scared him.

Andrew's hand trembled on the doorknob. Before he entered, the world around him evaporated. Sitting upright on a four-poster bed, Andrew panted profusely. He had returned to Wayan.

Looking around wildly within a medieval-esque bedchamber, he saw long, velvety, maroon curtains hanging on either side of a monumental floor-length window. A man sat on a velvet-cushioned armchair at the back of the room.

"You're awake," said King Marco.

Andrew locked eyes with his uncle and started welling up. He slowly pulled back the covers.

"Careful, Andrew," said King Marco, who rose from his chair and met his nephew in the middle of the room.

Andrew couldn't formulate a sentence, but instead of speaking for the both of them, the King of Wayan remained silent and gestured for him to look out the window. As he did so, he soaked in the world of Wayan, as if seeing it for the first time in a long while.

Remembering back to when he was a child, he'd loved visiting his auntie and uncle during the hot summer months. It was just as beautiful then as it was now, and he needed every ounce of beauty before facing the harsh truth of his heritage.

Eventually, he turned to face the king. "I can't seem to make sense of anything anymore," he said, drained of energy.

"Andrew…" began King Marco.

"Uncle," added Andrew, with pain in his voice.

"Your birth mother awakened your memories. But her method in doing so was very harmful to you. After you were struck down in Tricksy's stable, your cousin Evie brought you back to the castle. We managed to infiltrate Queen Lillian's magic and unknot all of your childhood memories, not just the ones she wanted you to fixate on."

"She was different in one of my memories, like it wasn't her at all."

"A lot has changed since you last saw her," answered King Marco, trying his hardest not to fall apart. "Your mum is not the same person anymore." The King of Wayan fell silent, looked out the window and remembered the happier times when he and Lillian were children. He knew she had been kind-hearted, and a small part of him hoped his sister could redeem herself.

"I never wanted this," said King Marco. "I tried to convince Maria that Lillian wasn't destructive. But your birth mother continued to execute terrible things, and I couldn't keep making excuses for her actions."

"So, do you believe Sylvie was actually trying to save us?"

"Yes," stuttered the king. "I do."

Uncle and nephew stood in silence, unable to discuss the matter further, for they both felt devoid of energy. But, clinging on to anything that could give him an uplifting light, Andrew thought at least Amy was safe on Earth.

"There is no good time to tell you," cut in King Marco. "Your birth mother took Amy against her will."

"What?!" said a bewildered Andrew.

"Yes, and we want you to claim your Tarot cards. Not to return to Earth, but for helping to protect Amy when the time comes."

"And when is that?" snapped Andrew.

"Gwyn came forward, which means you've helped the Land of Swords and Cups. It turns out Lillian managed to hex Gwyn into killing the Gordan. And you have assisted Sir Gregory, so the final land you must visit is Pentacles."

Head in hands, the thought of losing his sister made Andrew feel sickly numb. But, again, what had possessed his birth mother to act out like this? Those eyes he saw at Euston station had not stemmed from love. Instead, they sought to exact pain.

"Andrew?" said King Marco gently.

"I'm with you, Uncle," replied Andrew, snapping out of his trance. "We need to save Amy."

Chapter Fourteen

Far from Home

Once, a long time ago, the Tarot world of Naxthos was a happy melting pot blended with laughter, merriment and fond memories with guests of other worlds. Now barely recognisable, screams of distress pierced the cold, wintry night air inside the castle's grim inner courtyard. Taken from their homeworlds, half a dozen scared and bewildered beings of different shapes, sizes and colours were huddled together on the cold stone ground.

Shaking uncontrollably from the blistering chill, the prisoners wondered why Queen Lillian had taken them there against their will. They wore tightly secured mystical handcuffs around their wrists that glimmered with delight at their captivity. Further away from the group, a blazing campfire with a gigantic hanging cauldron bubbled and brewed fantastical forest-green energy.

A tall, slender sorcerer, Saxthos – with a shaved head, crooked nose and deep orange eyes – raised his arms and willed individual strands of incredible burnt energy from his Tarot cards. He instructed the power to wrap around and take their Tarot cards from each being. The cards' images resembled their owners. Ignoring their pleas to stop, Saxthos immediately willed the decks into the pot. The water bubbled violently. The cards vanished.

Having trapped the Tarot decks in another realm, the prisoners were alone, without their powers to help them. But before they could mourn their loss, the sorcerer moved wistfully on to the next phase of his plan. He conjured delicate, pentacle pendant necklaces made of gold, and they flew through the air rapidly and wrapped themselves around the hostages' necks. As the group struggled to release the chains that burnt into their skin, Saxthos saw something that piqued his interest.

A quizzical-looking, human-sized reptilian, covered head to toe in red scales, from the Tarot world Skala, cast a glance in the shadows behind Saxthos. As soon as he knew Saxthos was aware, he dropped his head, avoiding eye contact. Turning, the sorcerer strode towards the shadows, not wanting to take any chances.

Nothing was visible in front of him except the stone wall. However, the Skala reptilian kept quiet, for he knew precisely what he'd seen: the face of a scared young teenage boy with short, light brown hair and rainbow eyes. His name was Calum, and he'd lost focus, keeping his invisibility a secret. Now the boy had regained his composure, he was again fully shrouded in a soft, protective light that hid his presence from everyone around him.

Staring hard at Saxthos, with hatred in his eyes, Calum dared not move, but the opportunity was right there. Hoping for no sudden action, the boy knelt and attempted to delve into the pocket of the sorcerer's tunic. Soon enough, Saxthos concluded the nerves must have got the better of the reptilian and decided to move swiftly on.

Calum retreated from the sorcerer and watched as he returned to the hostages. Trembling at the ordeal, the boy, with bags under his eyes that made him look like someone much older, took a gentle step forward. He had his chance to swipe the keys but failed!

Thrown by a volatile swish that struck the courtyard, Calum saw a portal open, and five Naxthosian soldiers piled out with three other afflicted beings from various worlds. The boy muttered about their next set of victims as he painfully witnessed them being subjected to a lashing with a whip. Fighting back the tears, he had to hold himself together.

A burst of commotion came in from the drawbridge. Kicking and punching outwards, Ben's face, neck and hands were covered in cuts and blood as he scrambled to break free from the soldiers' grips. Shouting for Amy's whereabouts, no one answered back, which made him even more frustrated.

"Get off!" roared Ben, his heart beating wildly.

He refused to give in, but inside the ancient, foreboding complex, his mouth dropped at the horrific scene before him. The distressed and injured hostages threw off Ben's bravado as he couldn't understand what would possess someone to oppress these beings. He was rattled, and a dark cloud consumed his mind. He was beginning to understand there were bigger things at play than Amy and him.

With his muscles loosened, the soldiers could restrain Ben more easily, and they wasted no time shoving him hard before an amused Saxthos. The latter stood transfixed at the cauldron, enjoying the bubbles on the surface. Their eyes met, and Ben was unnerved by the delight of the sorcerer. After a minute or two of haunting silence – for Ben didn't know where to start – Saxthos took the lead and planted his face close to Ben's.

"You were wrong," declared Saxthos.

"Wrong?"

"You called for Amy before. Her real name is Aimesia, Queen Lillian's daughter."

"No. This is all a big mistake."

"Soon enough, you'll accept her true identity. Until then…"

Smack!

Ben's head suffered a heavy blow from the hilt of a sword. Dazed and confused, he fell to the floor, and the soldiers lifted him and marched him away. As Ben's vision returned, he thought he'd seen Saxthos's tunic move on its own for a split second. Eyes blinking, the image was gone, and his attention turned to the whipping flames from the hanging torches that cast shadows of the violent skirmishes in the courtyard.

Before Ben was forced through an archway, he felt a sharp cut on the back of his neck. He probed the wound with his hand, and the tip of his finger started to emit a soft white light.

"Wait?! What was…" said Ben.

The soldiers led him down a narrow spiral staircase. Craning his neck, he could still see darkness below, and vertigo started to make him feel a little queasy. Continuing into the depths of the castle, rats scurrying nearby made Ben jolt, and as they were coming to the end of the long, arduous downhill trek, he saw lit torches coming into view.

At the bottom, a line-up of soldiers guarded a large, menacing metal door. As soon as they saw Ben, the guards pushed open the door and allowed them to enter a high, commanding cavern, the home of Castle Naxthos's prison. Ben took a big gulp as he looked up at the endless, row upon row of drab, highly secure, stone-walled cells next to a gently sloping stairwell that travelled to the top of the formation.

The rainwater's splashing noise escaped into the prison, repeatedly hitting the rock's rough edges. And soon after, the monotonous sound was shaken up by the cries for help from beings that were locked away. But an anxious Ben needed to block out the turmoil around him, for he'd noticed the soft white light had spread up his arms. Pulling his shirt sleeves down, he tucked his hands into his pockets to avoid unnecessary attention as the soldiers handed him over to one of the guards.

A delicate voice whispered in Ben's ear, out of reach of the entrance door and the arsenal, telling him to step back into the shadows when the moment was right.

Jolting, Ben looked wildly around for the source, but no one was there. Had that been a figment of his imagination? In this instance, that was the most likely answer. Yes, a weird part of his subconscious was now taking over.

"Listen," stressed the delicate voice, "do this for Amy."

Guilt struck his heart, and he started to well at the mention of her name. He knew he was at a loss, with no other choice. However much it uneased him, he decided to do as the voice said.

The guard beckoned Ben into a fortified walled space, and as instructed by the voice, he moved back into the shadows, out of sight, where the soft light was beginning to turn him invisible. Just as the guard was about to close the prison cell, the sharp fall of a rock nearby diverted his attention.

A camouflaged Calum willed his invisible Tarot cards into the room, and they wrapped themselves around Ben. The deck pulled him out with incredible force, just before the guard slammed the entry shut.

Ben came face to face with Calum. Bemused, he could see the teenage boy, whose face looked burdened with a heavy weight. Slightly unnerved by the maturity spread across his skin, Ben kept silent as the boy gestured for him to stay quiet. They moved back, out of earshot from the guards and prisoners, and slowly and carefully headed towards a small archway.

Inside was a cesspit of rat bones and dried blood. Turning, Ben and Calum knelt and peered from their vantage point of the prison. Finally, it was safe to talk.

"Who are you?" asked Ben.

"Calum, and just to be clear, I'm on anyone's side apart from Queen Lillian's."

"That I can agree with. How did you escape?"

"I wasn't detained, but my auntie was. I stowed away, waiting for the opportune moment to save her."

"Is she in one of these cells?"

"No. Somewhere else highly guarded. I heard you in the courtyard. I know you arrived with Amy. Or Aimesia. It's the same person."

Mouth agape at Calum's words, it was becoming harder for Ben to deny Amy was tied to this place. Digesting everything he'd heard and witnessed, it was now making sense in a weird, profound way. Calum knew the cogs were churning, but he couldn't wait for Ben forever. Removing the set of keys from his waistcoat that belonged to Saxthos, the pleased teenage boy felt hopeful. Sifting through them, he paused at the one he needed.

"This key, mixed with Saxthos's blood, unlocks the door to the cavern where my auntie's cards are held captive," said Calum. "Our best chance is to reunite them and, with their help, save Amy."

Before Ben could answer, Calum darted towards a large pile of rat bones in the far corner. Sweeping away the remains, the boy knelt and pulled up a mucky, tattered piece of hessian fabric. Underneath was a trapdoor, and he gripped the circular metal handle tight. He managed to lift the trapdoor and instructed Ben to get inside. A little hesitant, Ben slowly joined the boy. Calum's Tarot cards took the lead and conjured incredible multicoloured energy. The power wrapped around Ben and forced him in anyway.

Landing in a heap, one floor underground, the sudden impact made Ben groan in the darkness, while Calum easily touched the floor. Above, the boy's Tarot cards worked together to close the trapdoor skilfully, and their soft, radiating energy lit a pathway for the group to follow.

Ben mustered the strength to rise, holding on to his aching ribs for support, while Calum travelled down the corridor, beckoning him to follow the light.

"Okay, I'm coming."

They wormed their way through endless passageways and sharp, narrow tunnels within the most remote area of the castle. Tired and covered in sweat, Ben and Calum finally reached a set of small, green, marble doors. *This is it*, Calum thought, *the place we are meant to be*. He removed a vial of Saxthos's blood from his waistcoat pocket.

"That's Saxthos's blood?" asked Ben, wondering how Calum acquired it.

"Yes. This wasn't too difficult to get. He's the cause of daily conflicts."

"Fair point," quipped Ben.

Immersing the key inside the vial, it started to glow a crisp, burnt-orange, the same colour as the sorcerer's energy, and Calum nodded with satisfaction – it had worked. Easily unlocking the door with the glowing key, they cautiously entered.

Ahead, a long wooden suspension bridge dominated the cavern's centre. On the far end was a raised platform where a calm floating sphere imprisoned a Tarot deck. Ben and Calum watched as the anger-fuelled cards continuously smacked against various parts of the magical forcefield, determined to break free.

"Those cards belong to my auntie," said Calum.

"How can you be sure?"

"I can feel their energy. There's no other feeling like family."

"Wait. Why didn't they go in the cauldron?"

"Her cards refused to disappear," answered Calum, not giving anything away.

"Refused to disappear?"

The boy walked away.

"Wait!" called Ben. "What about your cards? Can't they show us what to do?!"

"No. They can't," answered Calum, now on the defence. It was too painful to think about, and he didn't want to explain to Ben why his Tarot deck couldn't see into the past or future. So, instead, Calum fixated upon the sphere while Ben followed him. The boy made his way across the drawbridge, gaining momentum. "Come on, nearly there!" he told himself as he reached the halfway point.

Calum paused in his tracks as he heard a faint swoosh in the background, his ears straining for the source. A loud bang rattled the air, and a quick, powerful shot of mystical energy came out of one cavern wall and struck the wood in front of Calum's feet. But the boy kept going as Ben pleaded for him to stop. An endless onslaught of magical power from all corners of the cavern fired on them.

"Calum!" shouted Ben. "Come back!"

But the boy refused. His auntie's life depended on it. Struck in the back, wincing in pain, Calum hoped his Tarot cards could deflect the attack, but they were too caught up worrying about their owner, and Ben knew it.

Ben reached for the boy as the drawbridge swung violently, grabbed hold of Calum and dragged him back. Kicking and jarring, the stubborn boy struggled to break free, but Ben wouldn't let go.

"Absolutely not. This is for your own good."

"Get off me," cried Calum.

Stumbling off the bridge and landing on the ground near the green marble doors, they wrestled with each other as the attacks subsided around them.

"Look!" stressed Ben as he held the boy's face. "Look around. And do you hear that? Nothing!"

Panting and spluttering, Calum digested Ben's words and realised he was right. Ben's anger withdrew, and Calum felt a little unnerved.

"I, er," stuttered Calum.

"I understand you feel the world's weight is on your shoulders. But after what just happened, you need my help," said Ben.

"Okay, I'm listening."

"Well, I think I need to be the decoy."

Getting off the floor, Ben helped Calum up, and as they stood side by side taking in the orb across the space, Calum realised Ben was right.

"I can defend you with my cards if I stay in position," said Calum.

"Exactly," replied Ben, pleased they were working together.

"Are you sure you'll be okay?"

"I'm going to have to be," smiled Ben, a little warmer.

Unity reached, Ben stepped away from Calum, taking deep, nervous breaths out of range from the boy. Coming to terms with what he was about to endure, he tried to suppress the thought of changing his mind. Maybe, come to think of it, send Calum in, but Ben couldn't back out now. He had already tried to set an example. Shaking his body to warm his muscles, Ben began sprinting, and as soon as his feet landed on the bridge, the spectacle of mystical energy reappeared and fired at him.

He dodged the magic, but soon enough, Ben was hit. The impact travelled through his skin and struck his shoulder blade. Calling out in pain, Ben looked up as Calum's Tarot cards continued to conjure multicoloured energy, pastel in tone, and help deflect the mystical assault. Finally, much to Ben's relief, he reached the end of the drawbridge and arrived on the rock home to the orb.

"Yes!" called out Calum as his mood elevated.

But as the boy lost focus, his Tarot cards did too, and for a split second they missed, and an energy blast nearly took Ben's head off. Fortunately, Ben dodged it and shouted at Calum to keep concentrating, but the boy noticed something peculiar. While Ben was inspecting the sphere amid the chaos around him, Calum realised the magic released from the walls had accidentally scarred the orb.

"Ben!" shouted Calum.

Trying to warn his comrade, Calum kept flapping his hands, but Ben couldn't hear. The Naxthosian magic had manipulated the air around them to stay silent just as Ben touched the object. It generated explosive shockwaves and sent him flying back.

Rolling along the ground, Ben came to a halt, and as the sound of a magical tirade of swish, swirls and bangs consumed the space, Calum instructed his cards to change the airflow course and redirected the energy attacks at the orb. Soon, the forcefield broke down, and the object shattered. The freed Tarot cards flew into the air with ferocity and meandered around Calum's deck, ready to protect it.

"We did it!" said Calum, joining a terrified Ben on the other side of the drawbridge. "It's okay. You can look up now."

"Are you sure?" panted Ben, wincing at the injury on his shoulder.

"Yes."

Still not entirely convinced, Ben mustered the courage to rise from the floor and surveyed the suspiciously calm cavern. He spotted the two Tarot decks levitating and dancing around each other in delight and felt their happy reunion.

Ben turned to Calum, who remained silent. Sensing the boy was on the verge of breaking down and letting go of everything he'd endured, Ben looked away to give him some space. He wondered, though, where they needed to go next.

"Calum?" asked Ben, finally speaking.

Spinning back to face the boy, Calum had disappeared, along with his cards, and a concerned Ben couldn't find them anywhere.

"Calum!"

The recently freed Tarot cards, whose aura seemed confident, hovered in front of him. He sensed they had a plan for him, and within seconds they transported him to a cold, dark, depressing space.

Confused and shrouded in the same soft, protective light as Calum and the Tarot decks, Ben was about to ask what had happened. But the scared, emotional boy gripped his mouth shut and pointed at the outer circle, where an array of armed Naxthosian soldiers stood to attention.

Realising the soldiers couldn't see them, Ben nodded at Calum and remained silent while the freed Tarot cards levitated slowly across the room towards their owner –

a hunched, concealed figure lying on the ground. Their neck, wrists and ankles were imprisoned in heavy metal shackles.

Placing an arm around a traumatised Calum for support, Ben watched the freed cards identify themselves in the figure's limp, injured hand. The covered face groaned at the contact, and multicoloured light started seeping out of the Tarot deck and into the figure's body.

Gaining strength, the figure removed its hood, and Ben's mouth dropped at the sight of the gaunt, frail woman.

"Wait for it," whispered Calum.

Then, as his auntie's Tarot deck whipped itself into a bloodthirsty frenzy, their magic tore apart the shackles and worked to break the containment spell this woman had endured since she'd been caught.

Just as the rattled soldiers were about to advance with mystical nets and spears, the multicoloured magic was too quick. They revitalised Calum's auntie back into her true self, as her striking, long white hair glistened.

Her nephew watched, determined, as his auntie, Sorceress Sylvie of Rosa, was finally restored. Eyes filled with explosive rage, her Tarot deck fed off her anger, conjured incredible multicoloured energy, and opened fire on the Naxthosian army until every soldier in the detainment room was dead.

Chapter Fifteen

The Villain Within

The fighting stopped, and the dust settled. Surrounded by carnage from Sylvie's offensive on the Naxthosian soldiers, Calum and Ben stayed close together. They didn't know where to look first as they hesitantly stepped over the bodies, burnt to a crisp. Calum tripped on a gaping dismembered arm still holding a spear. The startled boy nearly lost his balance, and Ben swooped in and gripped him tight.

"It's okay, I've got you."

They made their way towards the sorceress, who was reeling from her new-found freedom in the centre of the oval space. She felt good as she watched her steadfast Tarot cards circling the room. They scanned for any potential threat while ensuring no one on the outside intended to breach the entry point.

As the mood seemed momentarily quiet, the esteemed Sorceress of Rosa let down her guard slightly and began to shake with adrenaline. She saw Calum and Ben and slowly moved towards them, half expecting the shackles to hold her back. But, instead, the sensation felt unnatural. She gazed upon the bruises across her milky, sun-deprived skin, and tears started to well behind her eyes.

Seeing her nephew, a pang of love hit her, and a sudden conflict of relief and annoyance grappled from within. Sylvie never wanted Calum to place himself in harm's way. He was the only family she had left. The boy registered his auntie's hesitation and waited, but the sorceress knew she had to say something soon. Unfortunately for Calum, her responsible side won.

"You shouldn't have come to Naxthos," blurted Sylvie, a little sharper than intended.

Calum's cheeks flushed a deep crimson red, and he kept his head down. Ready to start a lecture, her heart melted. Wrapping her protective arms around the distressed young boy, the sorceress hugged him tightly.

"I couldn't just leave you," stressed Calum, growing a little more confident.

As tears rose between auntie and nephew, Ben kept away, not daring to disturb their reunion. But, soon enough, Sylvie released her grip and asked Ben if he was okay.

"Er, to be honest, I'm not sure how to answer that."

"That's understandable," replied Sylvie, her tone delicate.

"But it's Amy I'm worried about," said Ben. "Sorry, Aimesia, I guess." Riddled with worry, Ben explained what had happened near the shrine and the moment he was led away from Amy. The sorceress's Tarot cards listened silently and intently in the background to every detail. Sylvie encouraged Ben to keep going, even with the horrors in the courtyard, until Calum broke him out.

"Wait," added Calum. "You forgot about the necklaces."

"What necklaces?" asked Sylvie.

"Saxthos forced the hostages to wear thin gold chains with pentacle-shaped pendants. The metal burnt their skin," explained Calum.

"Well, now that's another problem we need to unravel," said Sylvie. "But we need to find 'Amy', or Aimesia, first."

"Why does her mother want Amy?" asked Ben. "What is your involvement in all of this?"

"I, er…" Sylvie stumbled. A resurgence of memories consumed her mind of her time with little Anmos and Aimesia. She had grown to love them like her own, and to this day she still believed she had done the right thing. However, lurking at the pit of her stomach was a speck of regret and, consequently, fear. When she faced the children again, would Andrew and Amy hate her for what she did?

"I was their nanny," began Sylvie. "I was worried Queen Lillian would hurt them or even use them for a darker purpose, so I chose to take them."

"Take them?" said Ben.

"I planted new memories and gave them new lives on Earth. I kept running through Tarot worlds for many years and thought I could finally rest. But I was wrong."

"You took them?" repeated Ben, fighting disgust at Sylvie's actions, "So Amy had no idea why she was mixed up in all of this? She was scared and felt alone!"

Calum blocked Ben from coming any closer to his auntie through fear his comrade was about to lose it. Ben sensed the desperation in the young boy's eyes, and the red mist started to evaporate.

"I just..." Ben began.

"I know you care about Amy," said Sylvie. "Queen Lillian is the villain here, and we need to stop her. Please, Ben."

"I... Okay, what do you need."

"Thank you," Sylvie said delicately. "When you arrived on Naxthos, was it just you and Amy?"

"Yes. We were separated from Andrew, if that's his real name."

"Anmos," whispered Sylvie. "But Andrew also. Where did he go?"

"I don't know," said Ben.

"Can you remember anything else?" said Sylvie.

"A red energy appeared. It helped us escape the train," said Ben.

"A red energy?" said Sylvie.

It could have been from the Queen of Wayan, Sylvie thought, and as she resisted the urge to not get carried away, her Tarot cards took the lead.

They whipped themselves high and conjured great, multicoloured, fantastical power that set to work on locating Amy. But as the magical energy continued to seep out, no image was visible, and the sorceress sensed something was wrong.

"Something, someone, or both, is preventing us from finding Amy," said Sylvie.

And with no way of knowing from inside those walls, they had no choice but to venture out the shrine. But, just as her cards were about to generate a portal, a rattled

Calum jolted forward, telling them to stop. Confused by the young teenager's outburst, the sorceress turned to Ben, who looked just as perplexed.

"Please! Don't make a portal!" called Calum.

"Why?" Ben asked.

Sweat pouring down his face, Calum took a step away from the group, trying with all his strength to hold it together.

"I saw a being attempt to escape through one," said Calum. "They disintegrated on the spot."

"That doesn't mean we will suffer the same fate," Sylvie stressed, but Calum wasn't convinced. As Ben watched a heated argument develop between auntie and nephew, something stirred in the background that diverted his attention. Looking at the soldiers littering the floor, no one moved. However, a faint rustle crept into the air, and Ben didn't feel so good.

His stomach started tying itself in knots, and an unknown force pulled his other organs in opposite directions. Finally, Ben couldn't stand up any longer and collapsed. Briefly, while crying out in pain, he heard the rustle transform into a dazzling sound in the distance. An explosive lightning strike punched the air as heavy rain overcame the ten monumental standing stones. Slumped in the mud, panting and sobbing at the extreme pain he'd endured, Ben didn't know where he was, and as the soft voices of Sylvie and Calum came into range, they quickly dispersed.

Across the mound, Sylvie placed her hands on the smooth altar, trying to establish a connection with the ancient rock, while a concerned Calum hunched over a dishevelled Ben.

"What happened?" Ben asked.

"Auntie Sylvie's Tarot cards interrupted our squabble," explained Calum. "Instead of a portal, they teleported us here."

As Ben sat upright, realising they were away from Castle Naxthos, Sylvie kept hunting around the space for answers, but a devious kind of magic was blocking her attempts. She decided to start from the beginning. There had been Ben, Amy and her cards. Her Tarot cards! Where were they?

Before she could speak, Sylvie's card deck shone brightly and encouraged their owner to follow them away from the shrine and towards the edge of the dreary coppice of broad oak trees. Drawing closer, Sylvie could hear her nephew call out, asking if she needed help, but the sorceress refused.

"Stay with Ben and keep hidden," she commanded.

Hair and face soaked, the sorceress strained her eyes inside the forest, where her cards sprang to attention, meandering through the trees more deeply into the heart of the woods. Sylvie, pursuing them, continued until a faint glimmering of forest-green energy was visible ahead.

"Stay alert, my dear comrades. Dim your light and don't make yourself known."

Through a clearing, she spotted a group of half a dozen Naxthosian soldiers, covered head to toe in sturdy armour and sitting around a bubbling cauldron. Approaching with care, Sylvie noticed a guard clinging tightly to a small drawstring bag, and the sorceress's cards from above could sense Amy's Tarot deck was inside.

"Okay, easy does it," she muttered, willing her cards to surround the soldiers from behind the cluster of trees. They grouped to select their respective victim and conjured a strand of multicoloured energy from each team. On the count of three, the power shot out and wrapped around the soldiers' necks. Struggling to breathe, they scrambled around on the moss, desperate to connect with their Tarot decks. But, as their lives ebbed away, so did their cards.

Stepping into the inner circle beside the cauldron, Sylvie had a fleeting moment of enjoyment at seeing the soldiers in despair. Looking down at her injuries, she thought nothing was wrong with an eye for an eye, but the sudden snap of a twig nearby broke her appeasement.

Calum and Ben followed her, and Sylvie saw the horrified looks on their faces. "I think that's enough now," the Tarot cards whispered in their owner's ears, and she knew they were right. The multicoloured energy eased, separated, and tied the soldiers to tree trunks, preventing escape.

Sylvie kept her head down, avoiding eye contact with Calum as she made her way towards the guard, still holding on to the drawstring bag. *Swipe!* Sylvie seized the load from their hand and removed an innocent-looking deck of Tarot cards. They reached out to the sorceress with words of distress and told her they belonged to Amy but couldn't remember what had happened and where she had gone.

"It's okay," whispered Sylvie, holding the deck protectively. "I'm here now. I will keep you safe. I promise."

Turning to face the cauldron, Sylvie watched the volatile, forest-green energy bubble with glee and remembered Ben and Calum's account in the courtyard. She could only assume the soldiers had been lying in wait, ready to dispose of Amy's Tarot cards.

Kneeling before the soldier, the sorceress removed his helmet. The cold, steely man avoided her eyes.

"I need to know where their owner went," said Sylvie.

Silence. The soldier refused to answer, and Sylvie instructed her cards to hunt for answers through his eyes, but as the deck delved into the man's past, they found he had arrived at the shrine when Amy had already left.

"Rest assured," commanded the sorceress as she faced the rest of the group, "you'll be next."

Making her way around the camp, Sylvie conducted the same interrogation on each soldier, with her cards backing her up. But, just like the first, no one had been present at the shrine, and her patience, along with that of Calum and Ben, was wearing thin.

In the background, one of the detained was getting twitchy, to the point of looking wildly into the trees, desperate for an escape route. Unfortunately, too engrossed in the forest, the soldier had failed to notice Sylvie was now looking down at their bright, blue, fearful eyes.

Removing the helmet, a mop of dirty blonde hair fell to their shoulders, revealing a scared young woman with icy-coloured skin and delicate freckles. She pushed hard against the tree trunk, not daring to speak. But what had intrigued Sylvie more than anything was, just before the woman's hair fell, she spotted a delicate necklace around her neck.

"It's okay," Sylvie encouraged her, kneeling before the woman. "We're here to escape this world. We are just looking for a woman called Amy. But unfortunately, Queen Lillian has captured her."

A look of disgust spread across the woman's face at her words. "Captured!" she said aloud. "No way was that redhead caught. She went with Queen Lillian, as free as a bird."

Ben thought he detected a German twang in her accent. As he took a step forward with Calum, he felt something strange. The lifeless Tarot deck he'd been carrying around since Sea Mysticism had conjured a crackle of energy in the back pocket of his jeans.

"What do you mean?" said Sylvie, urging the woman to continue.

"I saw that redhead and Queen Lillian cross through a portal to a world I believe was called Lixus," explained the woman.

"Lixus!" called out Calum.

"What's Lixus?" asked Ben, confused.

"Where do I start..." replied Calum.

"It's a barbaric Tarot world. And one of Queen Lillian's favourites," answered Sylvie.

"Well, it looked like Amy's, too, from their buddy up," said the woman. "But I don't get the obsession."

"How do you mean?" asked Sylvie.

"These necklaces. Amy was wearing one too. Hers shone purple, though. Very odd," said the woman.

"Who are you?" interrupted Calum. "I've been hiding out here the entire time. How did you get the necklace around your neck in the first place?"

Shying away from the question, the young woman's mind was on the verge of losing all sense of reality. Detecting her torment, Ben gestured for Sylvie and Calum to hold fire, to let him try.

"We don't want to be here any more than you do," said Ben. "Please, at least tell us your name?"

Looking up at Ben, the woman took in his features and noticed he was both different and familiar at the same time. It was an unspoken, mutual understanding neither one had prepared for or considered possible. But at that moment, separately, they wondered if they were both from the same world.

"Erika," said the woman. "My name's Erika."

"And why do you wear a necklace?" asked Ben. "Can't you just remove it?"

"I was captured, like the other beings, and forced to wear a necklace that burnt into my skin. It won't come off. When the guards brought me before the sorcerer and threw my cards into the cauldron, he said I wasn't of any use."

"Why?" asked Ben.

"I don't know. All I know is the cards and myself were a disappointment. I had to bargain for my life. Either die or join their army in the firing line."

As the mood in the camp fell sombre, Sorceress Sylvie of Rosa grew unsettled from the information they'd been given. The safe bet would be to demand a gateway into Wayan and seek Queen Maria's help before pushing forward to Lixus. But Erika had thrown her considerably. There were still hostages on Naxthos, alone and taken from their homes. So, if she could just unravel the importance of the necklace, then at least Wayan would have something to go on.

Turning to face the group, who waited patiently for her to speak, Sylvie willed her Tarot cards to release Erika from custody. Holding out her hand, the young woman took it and smiled warmly at the sorceress.

"I can try to send you home now," said Sylvie. "Just tell me your world."

"It's…" started Erika.

Bang!

A thunderous force shook the trees around them. As the Naxthosian soldiers looked up with relief, Sylvie and her comrades kept close, hunting for the source of the impact. A magnificent portal grew outwards before them. Its outer edge glistened a burnt orange, and on the other side, Sylvie could make out the hurtful, grim space she'd been imprisoned inside.

Her group looked on nervously as the portal drew closer, determined to send them through. "Enough!" the sorceress said aloud, instructing her cards to manipulate the destination to Wayan. Conjuring incredible multicoloured energy, the Tarot deck tried but understood it wasn't an easy request. Wayan's barriers were up, and the only way to cross was to be granted permission on the other side.

"Keep trying!" commanded Sylvie.

As the portal drew nearer, Erika felt the necklace around her neck burn into her skin. Crying out in pain, Ben and Calum went to her aid, but there was nothing they could do to remove it. The latch wouldn't budge.

"Run!" the sorceress bellowed as her Tarot cards continued to fight back against the gateway.

Sprinting through the woods, desperate to avoid capture, the group kept going. Panting and aching, they couldn't afford to stop. "Keep looking ahead," shouted Sylvie, "don't lose your nerve!" High above, Sylvie's cards worked tirelessly to send a message through realms to Queen Maria.

Flash!

The portal propelled forward and consumed Sylvie and her comrades in seconds. They arrived deep underground, inside a monumental cavern housing row upon row of prison cells. The mood was eerily quiet as the hostages neither spoke nor rose from their cells.

"We're back inside the prison," said Ben, confused.

Inspecting the space around them, Sylvie noticed a hostage lying unconscious on the floor inside one of the cells. Releasing the latch, she stepped inside and carefully walked towards the body. But before she could inspect their neck, Calum cried out to her.

Turning, the sorceress exited the cell, and her mouth dropped at the sight of a delicate, floating light hovering in front of a perplexed Erika. It had drawn her necklace to the prison, and the light turned into an amethyst crystal and nestled inside the young woman's pendant.

"What is it?!" said Erika, backing away.

But before the group could act, Erika lost her balance, and a wave of fear washed over Sylvie, for she knew what the light was.

"It's a star," answered Sylvie.

Chapter Sixteen

The Calling

Inside the towering, ancient cavern underneath Caste Naxthos, row upon row of deep purple energy shone brightly out of every prison cell. To an outsider, they would have no idea what the energy meant or where it came from; they would only see a beautiful, wondrous display. But for the Sorceress of Rosa, she knew better than to accept the light so willingly.

Tearing herself away from the unsettling scene above, Sylvie looked down at Ben and Calum, tending to a scared Erika on the floor. The young woman's bright blue eyes fixated on the necklace, now housing an amethyst crystal that emitted purple energy. She wrestled with the latch to release it, and a terrifying sensation took precedence.

"We need to take cover, quick!" instructed Sylvie.

"Follow me," said Calum.

Crying out, Erika lost all sense of feeling in her legs. Sylvie and Ben swooped in to help her as Calum guided them across the other side of the prison and into the safe space he'd initially taken Ben. Once inside the rotten, bone-infested room, the distressed Erika was laid gently on the floor. She grappled with the chain, but it still refused to budge, and the amethyst crystal glowed brighter.

"Stand back!" Sylvie whispered to the group. Ben and Calum nervously kept their distance, and the sorceress's Tarot cards sprang to action and encircled Erika. They accelerated and hunted for a way to release the chain but paused mid-flight. Startled by their actions, the sorceress needed answers, fast!

Taken inside a vision of the future, Sylvie saw the moment her magic expertly broke the chain around Erika's neck. Instead of seeing the relief in the young woman's eyes, her face scrunched up in annoyance. *The star would have complete control*, Sylvie realised. *But why go to so much effort with the jewellery?* As soon as the question left her mind, the sorceress saw the star, unable to conjure incredible energy. *They would be powerless without their host*, Sylvie stressed.

Outside the vision, she accepted the proposed future without question and decided to hang back, not wanting to risk Erika's life. Soon after, the young woman stopped flapping about and rested her front on the floor. Eyes closed, lying motionless, the air fell hauntingly silent around Erika and the group.

The young woman's eyes snapped open, pupils filled with hate. She bolted off the ground and went for Ben. Both hands clenched around his neck. She was surprisingly strong, choking him easily and enjoying the pain she inflicted. As Ben struggled to break free, a sharp crackle of white Tarot energy sprang out of Erika's fingers and pierced Ben's skin. Bloodthirsty and feral, Erika was under the control of an ill-intended star, and Ben didn't know how to respond. So, Calum stepped in and dragged the young woman off him, and as the entity kicked and punched outwards, Ben rose and managed to armlock the being, taking the pressure off Calum.

"Dispel," said Sylvie.

The sorceress's Tarot deck listened to their owner and expertly conjured a convoluted spell on the star, who finally fell, restrained, at Sylvie's magic.

"That should keep it subdued for the time being," said Sylvie.

"How could she have generated energy without Tarot cards?" said Calum, concerned.

"It's not Erika, dear Calum, but a star, and it doesn't need a deck to generate power," explained Sylvie. "I bet that's why Saxthos threw all those cards belonging to the hostages into the cauldron from the very beginning."

As the words left Sylvie's lips, she checked the inner lining of her tunic to ensure Amy's Tarot cards were still there. No sooner had relief set in that the cards were safe, when Sylvie realised her comrades were in jeopardy. The prisoners on each cavern floor had opened their eyes and risen from the ground. Their amethyst crystals shone brighter and brighter, and Sylvie strained her neck up and took a big gulp at the countless hostile faces peering through the bars.

As the sorceress retreated inside the room's safety, she gestured for Ben and Calum to go closer.

"The cards warned me not to break Erika's necklace with our magic," explained Sylvie.

"Why?" asked Ben.

"Stars from above have transformed into amethyst crystals. This allowed them to switch and control their hosts' bodies. But unfortunately, the original owner is now trapped inside the crystal, in a realm called the amethyst plane. By removing the chain and thus the crystal, the owner's astral existence cannot be reunited with their body."

"So, if we broke the chain, Erika wouldn't be in control again?" asked Calum.

"Correct, and the star would be powerless. It would be impossible to feed off the owner's spirit."

"How could a star wish to cause harm?" asked Ben, recounting internally all the beautiful nursery rhymes, children's shows and films where the star was an emblem of hope.

"We don't have the answer just yet, but what we do know is they only need the astral state of the person, not the owner's Tarot cards. They've essentially managed to remove an obstacle."

"So, what can we do differently?" asked Ben.

Sylvie went over the processes in her mind, and as her head was about to explode, she asked her cards if they could tap into the crystal's energy. The sorceress needed to see a version of the amethyst plane.

In a flash, a whirl of purple mist rose from the floor and whipped around Sylvie. The energy encased her inside a mystical, malevolent forcefield devoid of life. She stepped carefully around the fabricated space, searching for a way out. The sorceress, placing a hand on the purple floating mist in front of her, realised the energy wouldn't budge. It was like a prison. Then, contemplating multiple scenarios, Sylvie decided on the one they should try and asked her cards to conjure a doorway.

"Where to?" the cards whispered delicately in her ear.

"The place I love the most."

Dutiful and resolute, the Tarot deck knew immediately where Sylvie meant as they expertly generated a shimmering doorway on the edge of the forcefield. Cries of laughter and merriment came from the other side while she drew nearer. The familiar sounds were intoxicating and made Sylvie's heart dance with joy.

Even though she knew it wasn't real, a part of her longed for her adoptive homeworld: Rosa. She imagined her fairy family waiting for her on the other side, their bright auras and dazzling wings immersed in a rich, colourful world showcasing every rainbow colour. But before Sylvie delved deeper, a stir in the background broke her concentration.

"My dear owner," whispered the cautious Tarot deck, "you know it is not real. It never will be."

"I…" began Sylvie.

"That world is gone," said the Tarot deck.

"Yes, I…"

"Queen Lillian destroyed it searching for you."

"I know!" bellowed Sylvie.

In a heartbeat, the last Sorceress of Rosa exited the vision. Now resting on the floor, back inside the cavern, she was unsure how long she had been out. Realising Ben and Calum were by her side, they told her to take it easy, but Sylvie refused.

"I think I've found a way to help Erika," said Sylvie.

"How?" asked Ben.

"She is trapped inside a purple-misted forcefield, but if there were a way to break out, Erika would have the opportunity to take back her body."

"You found a way," said an assured Calum.

"Yes. We bring down the forcefield and create a doorway for Erika to feed off her heart's desire. Through it would be the place she loves the most," explained Sylvie. "Please, help me up."

Sylvie went over the plan repeatedly, working out in her mind the intricacies involved in conjuring such a superior spell. While she was heavily involved in the processes, Ben and Calum kept quiet to give her the breathing space she needed. Finally, after a couple of more minutes in silence, Sylvie looked at Ben and Calum with hope on her face.

"Right, let's give this a try," said Sylvie.

Arms raised and eyes closed, the Sorceress of Rosa willed multicoloured energy from her Tarot cards and told them to focus on the image of the amethyst-plane forcefield. The deck illuminated wondrous power as they worked tirelessly, envisioning bringing down the shielding inside Erika's crystal. Finally, they were successful, and as Sylvie and her cards waited nervously, the young woman fell unconscious.

"Is she okay?" asked Ben.

"Erika should soon find a door out of the forcefield," answered Sylvie.

"And then what?"

"She will come face to face with the star, a mirror image of herself, and they will fight."

"Fight?"

"Yes, to claim back her body. It's a battle of physical strength and willpower."

"Was there no other way?"

"I'm sorry, Ben. The host's fate is sealed as soon as that star turns into an amethyst crystal. But Erika has spent only a short time in the forcefield, so she won't feel as weighed down in captivity. This will work to her advantage, I promise."

As Sylvie, Ben and Calum looked down at the young woman, hoping she would make it, the groans from the prison cells above amplified the cavern. "They are getting irritable," said the sorceress, "and no one from the Naxthosian army had come to check in on them. So, what was Saxthos playing at?"

"Can we bring down the forcefield for each of them, Auntie?" asked Calum.

"I'm worried we won't have enough time. But I can certainly try to dispel them for now. And I'm going to need your help, nephew."

"What is it?"

"You need to cast your invisibility magic over us both while I work my way up the cavern. And you, Ben, stay with Erika."

"Wait, what if the star wins?" asked Ben.

"We will need to destroy it."

From her hands, Sylvie generated and manipulated bright multicoloured energy. First, she split the power into two separate strands and forced each strand to change colour. One became white, and the other purple. Next, the energy was torn apart and broken down into two powders. Holding out two small drawstring bags, the sorceress willed the powder into their respective pouches and handed them to Ben.

"Open the bag with the purple powder if the star wins. It will take care of the entity. If Erika wins, open the bag with the white powder, the colour of her Tarot energy. It will reach out to her and help guide her home."

Ben accepted the two pouches without question. Sylvie gave him a brief look of fondness before she directed Calum towards the central space of the cavern. The anxious teenage boy placed a hand delicately on Sylvie's arm. He willed dazzling, protective energy from his Tarot cards, ensuring they were both shrouded in invisibility magic.

Once satisfied, they made their way up the commanding spiral stairwell, where Sylvie and her Tarot cards set to work on the lengthy process of dispelling each being. Row upon row they kept going, and when they reached the fifth floor, the two large entrance doors on the ground floor burst open. Sylvie grabbed her nephew and pulled him into the darkness against the nearest stone wall. While Calum strengthened the invisibility magic, they watched a group of twenty intimidating armed Naxthosian soldiers march into the cavern carrying rolled-out pieces of parchment.

With no time to waste, the infantry split up and inspected the lockups on each level, cross-checking the beings controlled by stars with the assignments they'd been given on the paperwork. Soon after, whispers of concern spread across the vast space, for the soldiers had noticed a pattern; the hostages were standing like vegetables, subdued and non-responsive, even though their amethyst crystals shone brightly.

The army fed this back to the guard commander on the ground floor, who seemed just as perplexed. He instructed one of his comrades to send a message to Saxthos.

Meanwhile, out of harm's way, an anxious Ben stayed close to Erika, hoping the Naxthosian army wouldn't want to venture towards them as the curiosity spread. Taking one last glance in their direction, Ben looked down as the young woman started to stir.

Staying alert, he held the drawstrings tight. One wrong move and its hands could be wrapped around his neck again. However, when their bright blue eyes opened, they cried. Shaking from the ordeal, the young woman didn't know where to look or what to do next as she felt in control of her body again.

Ben knelt beside her, and as their eyes met he instinctively felt Erika's presence again. Her hands shook as she removed the necklace with the dead crystal and placed it on the floor beside them. Ben opened his arms, ready to hug her. She fell into them, heart pounding with gratitude that she had survived the amethyst plane. But he knew they couldn't stay like that forever. Ben released his grip and gestured for her to keep quiet, showing Erika the pouch containing the white powder.

"This will guide you home," he whispered.

"Thank you so much."

"Where are you from?" asked Ben, desperate to know before she left him.

"Earth," replied Erika, intrigued by Ben's roots. "And you?"

"Earth," he replied, feeling elevated.

"I'm from a small coven south of Munich, in the Upper Bavarian district of Garmisch-Partenkirchen," explained Erika as Ben's eyes widened with wonder. "My family built a small, simple altar within Ettaler Forest about one hundred years ago. Over time we've been able to successfully master the basic art of Tarot and awaken some powers."

"I..." Ben stumbled over his words.

"My great-grandmother is the most skilled. If you need anything, we are always here for you and your family."

"Thank you. I just needed to know."

"It's quite all right."

Ben opened the drawstring bag containing the white powder. It fizzed delicately, rose and covered Erika in sparkling magic. The young woman felt lifted, and as the sorcery reached out and asked her to envision home, Erika started to fade away. Staring at a blank space, Ben felt a pang of longing he hadn't prepared for, and it unsettled him a little. He had only just met her, but the bond was undeniable.

Tearing himself away from his feelings, the soil under Ben's feet started to rumble violently. Sorcerer Saxthos unleashed shots of ferocious, fantastical burnt orange energy high up from the ground floor. He scanned each row, hunting for something in particular as his soldiers assembled around him out of harm's way. Anger brewing, Saxthos fired another attack at random points on the stairwell, but as the dust settled, there was still no one.

"I know you're there, Sylvie," goaded Saxthos.

The sorcerer unleashed another bout of energy and lit up parts of the staircase in flames. As Saxthos continued, his Tarot cards circled him, hoping to tap into Sylvie's whereabouts. Drawing closer, the deck were about to reveal where she was, but the sorceress had already brought the fight to them.

With a swish, an invisible Sylvie worked her way around the soldiers, wrapping strands of multicoloured energy conjured from her Tarot cards around their necks. As each combatant fell, Saxthos directed a wall of energy towards the commotion and hit Sylvie head-on. The sorceress cried out in pain as Calum's invisibility magic wore off. Stumbling back, she managed to steady herself as she looked up at Saxthos with contempt.

"Where did your Tarot cards go, Sylvie?" quipped Saxthos. "They flew away in such a hurry."

Silent and focused, the Sorceress of Rosa straightened up and conjured power from her hands. However, considerably weaker without the full backing of her Tarot cards, Sylvie knew there was no other way, for she had instructed her deck to rejoin Ben with Calum.

"She needs you!" said Calum, rattled with worry on the other side of the cavern as more Naxthosian arm soldiers filed into the prison through the entrance doors, ready to advance on Sylvie.

But his auntie's Tarot cards refused to budge. They emitted brighter and brighter light, for their only concern was to gather everything they had to break through Wayan's defences and send a message to Queen Maria. "Queen Maria, help us," urged the cards. "Please, Sylvie doesn't have long. We need you."

Across worlds, seeking sanctuary inside the grand council library, the engrossed Queen of Wayan stood over a desk, shoulders hunched. Her tired eyes fixated upon a regal piece of parchment that illustrated all the access points into Wayan. She had been surveying the map all night and into the early hours. Unable to rest, through fear of an attack from Naxthos, Queen Maria hadn't noticed her Tarot cards twitch anxiously upon the table beside her.

Their unease grew to a point where they started glowing a deep red, and out of the corner of her eye, she observed their oddity. Then, *shriek!* A piercing sound rocked her ears, and words of distress infiltrated her mind. Holding her head for support, Queen Maria strained to make out the random words.

"Help! Sylvie! Amy! Lixus!" shouted Sylvie's Tarot from Naxthos.

"No," said Queen Maria, knelt on the floor, fighting to keep hold of herself. "It's a trick. I will not allow you to cross."

"Amy has been taken to Lixus," said Sylvie's cards more clearly. "Sylvie needs you."

Grappling with her emotions, Queen Maria couldn't help but detest the sound of Sylvie's name. But as the pleas continued, she started to separate herself from the bigger picture, for the cries seemed genuine.

"I can't risk the safety of my people," said a troubled Queen Maria.

"They are already at risk," replied Sylvie's Tarot cards. "We need to work together."

Conflicted, Queen Maria had been placed in a difficult situation, and the safe part of her considered blocking the messages from Naxthos and dismissing the voices inside her head. Still, as Sylvie's Tarot cards grew more desperate, she heard the Sorceress of Rosa scream from the battle and the voices of Ben and Calum rushing to her aid.

"Set aside your differences," urged Queen Maria's Tarot cards.

Looking down at her deck, Queen Maria choked at their words, and without thinking further, she instructed them to remove the incantation. Suddenly, the defences dropped inside the library, and Sylvie's cards formed a dazzling portal out of thin air. Queen Maria kept her guard up as shots of mystical energy were fired on the other side.

Rushing through the portal, Ben and Calum held on tight to a severely injured Sylvie. Bloodied, burnt and bruised, she had given everything she had, and the sorceress couldn't hold on for much longer.

"Now!" hollered Queen Maria, and in a heartbeat, the Queen of Wayan and Sylvie's Tarot cards managed to dispel the portal together.

"Send a message," instructed Queen Maria to her cards, "to the High Council. Tell them what happened here and to maximise the defences. Now!"

As the deck flew away from the scene, their owner knelt before a fallen Sylvie. She delicately placed a hand on the sorceress's head, reassuring her that her help was coming soon. But the queen's words faded out, and as Ben wrapped an arm around a distraught Calum, they watched as Sylvie closed her eyes.

Chapter Seventeen

Divine Honour

"Cassie? Do you know where we are?" said Lucy, shielding herself from the scorching desert heat. How can it be this hot? Her fair skin wasn't built for it. She was going to burn in seconds.

"Are we sure Ben is even here?" asked Lucy.

Through gritted teeth, Cassie told her to keep looking for any sign of life, including Ben, but with no clear direction, the Jenkins sisters wondered where they were supposed to go within the barren wasteland that confined them.

"Wait! Why were you at the station? How convenient of you to be there at the right place and time when we barely see you!" said Lucy.

"James mentioned you were visiting," said Cassie, keeping the lie short.

"He never mentioned speaking to you," replied Lucy, unconvinced.

"Well, believe what you want! Ben needs us right now," said Cassie, avoiding her sister's gaze.

Turning her back to Lucy, she didn't know how long she could contain her anger. What a mess her Tarot cards put her in! They acted out of character and risked exposing her powers. Before Lucy headed through the portal, Cassie felt the shimmering white energy tamper with the destination. But why scupper their chances of reuniting with Ben?

Anxiety building, she resisted the urge to inspect her deck, hidden in her trouser pocket. Cassie wasn't ready to reveal her secret, but the pit of her stomach told her she would be exposed soon enough. Out of everyone, it looked like Lucy, whom she barely tolerated at the best of times, would find out first. She needed to remind herself not to kill her sister; her mum would be fuming if she found out.

"Cassie!" shouted Lucy, pointing up at the sky. "Cassie, can you hear me?"

"Remember, don't kill her," Cassie muttered under her breath as she followed the direction Lucy pointed to. A cadre of flying creatures descended towards them. Their mighty, outstretched wings cut through the burnt-orange sky like a carving knife. Their legs and feet, resembling a bird of prey, shifted position, ready to land on the hot desert sand in front of them.

Three sets of talons hit the ground hard, and the small quartz stones knitted across the entirety of their arming doublets rattled furiously underneath their cuirasses.

"Keep quiet, Lucy," whispered Cassie.

As Cassie surveyed the creatures, she saw weapons in the shape of axes tied to their backs and no visible Tarot cards on their person. She had a fleeting moment of hope. What if her Tarot cards could match these three brutish-looking creatures? Her powers could potentially overthrow them, but what if her deck refused to help? That was a considerable risk.

"Show us your Tarot cards," instructed the first creature, its human face, arms and torso stern and menacing.

"We don't have any," answered Cassie, voice low and calm.

"How did you cross over?" asked the first creature, which announced its name as Gama.

Falling silent, Cassie's insides were being swirled around in a ginormous, heated melting pot, unable to cool down and think of a rational, innocent explanation. So, instead, she toyed with the notion of revealing her powers to Lucy.

"You stand before the Royal Guard of King Hargvar of Lixus. However, you failed to report to Lena Arena on arrival, and you must be punished," said Gama.

Before Cassie had the chance to react, she was struck across the side of the face by one of the other Lixusians called Hela. Falling to the floor hard, she was shell-shocked. Protecting herself in the foetal position, while reeling from the hit, Cassie could hear Lucy throw words of protest in the background. But in a matter of seconds, she listened to her sister land on the floor with a loud thump. As she looked up, Cassie saw Lucy had been knocked out cold.

Cassie had no other choice. She removed her Tarot cards. "Please help me!" she whispered. "After everything we've been through, this should be the moment we become one. I promise, if there is anything I have done to make you dislike me, I will fix it."

Eager to connect and embrace their power, Cassie released her grip and watched as the cards flew high. The deck was about to generate shimmering white fantastical energy for Cassie to manipulate from her hands, but just as the power was about to unleash, it quickly disbanded.

Looking up in dismay, Cassie called out for help, but the cards didn't respond. Instead, they fell from the blood-orange sky, and when one landed in front of her, she picked it up, and her eyes widened with horror. The figure on the cover transformed into a creature like Gama and the others.

Scrambling off the sand, she inspected the rest of the cards around her. On each one she collected, the figure had also changed shape, and her worry escalated. Finally, as her mind pumped frenzied explanations, Cassie spun around to face the three creatures.

"What are you?!"

"We are Lixusians, and you have entered our Tarot world, Lixus, unannounced," said Gama, who came forward to inspect the card deck in her hands.

But as Cassie attempted to block it from sight, Gama snatched the cards out of her hands. Moving forward, ready to square up to the Lixusian, Cassie was quickly apprehended by Hela, and the third Lixusian called Alana.

Inspecting the image meticulously, a sudden familiarity hit and ignited within Gama an explosive rage.

"It's Jakar," said Gama, looking up and meeting the eyes of his camp.

Hela and Alana fell hauntingly silent at the word and mutually understood why their leader reacted the way he did. All three Lixusians reached an aphonic agreement.

"Is Jakar bad?" asked Cassie, sensing the negativity oozing from the creatures.

Backing away as Gama and Alana advanced, Cassie tried to resist, but they overpowered her. Kicking and struggling to break free, she hadn't realised what was happening in the background. The third Lixusian, Hela, removed a set of sturdy alloy handcuffs from her waist strap. She forced Cassie's hands around her back and locked the handcuffs around her wrists.

"What does Jakar mean? Please tell me!" Cassie called, but as soon as Gama placed the Tarot cards he'd acquired securely under his armour, the Lixusian wrapped his arms around her chest and squeezed tight. Finding it difficult to breathe, Cassie tried one final resistance but failed.

With a loud, hard kick off the floor, Gama released his enmity with a roar as he carried Cassie into the blood-orange sky. The harsh sun reaching its afternoon peak distorted her vision as she tried to lock in Lucy's location below, but she couldn't see her or the other two Lixusians. It was just them, alone in the air.

With nothing new to see for miles around, Cassie wondered where they could go from there. Without warning, a distant sound alerted her to an outcry of something hostile. Straining her eyes into the distance, she saw something. As Gama drew nearer, Cassie clocked a six-storey-tall elliptical stone structure that dominated the vast expanse of the desert.

They reached the outer edges and her mouth dropped. Legions of Lixusian creatures, all with the face and upper body of a human, and a bird-like lower body with powerful wings, roared with avidity inside the open-air Lena Arena:

the heart and soul of Lixus and home to mystical combat competitions between various clans.

"What are they doing?" whispered Cassie, unable to process the sight below.

"Deciding their destiny," answered Gama, whose astute ears heard her. "Through bloodshed," continued the Lixusian proudly.

Cassie realised the pace had slowed as her captor waited for a guard to approach. The Lixusian that addressed them looked at Cassie with suspicion.

"This one looks unusual," said the guard. "Not of any Tarot world I've come across."

"Which is why it's important we must have an audience with the king immediately," replied Gama.

"You look rattled," said the guard.

"Yes, but I can't explain here."

"Okay, I'll see to it," answered the guard, knowing it was safer to agree than aggravate him.

As the guard flew away, Gama dangled in the air for a moment and watched the crowds cheer frantically around the arena. Two competitors from the districts of Bara and Sina entered through separate archways on the ground floor. They locked eyes from opposite ends, crossed the sand towards each other and paused in the centre.

Their imposing wings swiftly extended, and their powerful legs pushed hard off the ground. Flying above the stadium, circling one another, the competitor for Sina narrowly missed Gama, and Cassie was ready to throw up from the close contact.

Deciding to retreat a little further away from the contest, Gama noticed Cassie was about to faint, so he shook her and told her to keep watching. Unable to escape the view of the barbarous spectacle, Cassie saw the competitors remove their Tarot decks from the leather pouches attached to their waists.

The two Lixusians willed shimmering white mystical energy from their cards and channelled the power into the weapons left for them on the arena floor. The competitor for Bara claimed the mace, which flew up into his hand.

The Lixusian from Sina claimed her intended weapon, the warrior scythe, and now both creatures were ready, they didn't wait for permission. They charged at each other while members of the royal court circled the arena on the outer edge. They dropped bloodied carcasses for the crowds to feast on, and Cassie noticed that some limbs resembled a human form.

Unable to breathe because of her captor's tight grip, Cassie's sickness worsened until Gama eventually decided to abandon their station. He carried her to the other side of the structure towards a gap in the roof. Hovering above, Gama began to descend. Travelling down, they entered a tight space surrounded by four walls made of clear quartz crystal.

Continuing into the depths of the construction, they arrived within a subterranean area, and a brief pang of wonder threw her off balance. Cassie was entranced by the view below as they soared across an esoteric, multicoloured river. For the first time since she'd arrived on that cruel Tarot world, Cassie felt something good from the beautiful, majestic water. And, for a fleeting moment, she'd also felt her cards come to life under Gama's armour.

Snapping out of the brief, euphoric moment, Cassie realised they were about to land on the other side of the river. Eyes wincing at the thought of crashing into a commanding set of quartz crystal doors built into the rock, her heart beat wildly. Narrowly missing, Gama and Cassie touched the floor inches away from the crystal. It glistened with white shimmering energy, and the Lixusian removed his deck of Tarot cards from his waist pouch.

The cards circled Gama quickly and generated the same-coloured energy as the doors. In an instant, the doors came to life and swung back, permitting them to enter the Lixusian throne room. Once inside, Cassie scanned the room as they walked across a smooth, clear quartz crystal floor. Suspended in the air was a steely, foreboding throne hanging from an array of chains dug into the ceiling.

Feeling a little dizzy from its menacing presence, Cassie looked away and saw a pile of small, half-eaten bones in one corner. She wondered if that was where she was heading next, or possibly her sister? Lucy had no Tarot cards, and she was of no use to any Lixusian other than as food.

Footsteps approached from a doorway at the far end, and Cassie watched as the commanding King of Lixus, Hargvar, entered the throne room. Covered head to toe in tattoos displaying quartz stones, his mouth opened and revealed the same crystals had replaced teeth.

The king glared at Gama and Cassie. What could have been so imperative that he had to leave the contest?

"My apologies for the interruption," said Gama, "but I needed to speak to you immediately."

Removing Cassie's Tarot deck, Gama raised them high for King Hargvar to see. He told the king the figures on the cards transformed into Lixusian form, and after analysing them, there was no doubt in his mind the deck belonged to Jakar. "And this inferior being arrived in the desert with no idea how or why," said Gama.

Contemplating his words, the king swiped the cards from Gama's hand and looked over them himself. He inspected each card and grew unsettled. "When did you take these from him?" said King Hargvar, advancing upon Cassie.

"Who do you mean?" said Cassie, turning for the set of quartz crystal doors, ready to try to make a run for it. But Gama gripped Cassie's handcuffs tight and forced her to kneel.

"I think she's been kept in the shadows all this time," said Gama.

King Hargvar soaked in his words and thought for a moment about the next course of action until he finally made up his mind. He wanted an image of the past extracted from Cassie's cards.

The king's Tarot deck flew up into the throne room with an anxious swish and a swoosh. They circled him from afar, not daring to be anywhere near their angry owner. Instead, the cards channelled shimmering, fantastical energy and made the tattoos across his body come to life.

Immersed in light, King Hargvar relished the power trip, and as Cassie's Tarot cards levitated, he struck them with the energy coming from his crystal tattoos.

Cassie let out a cry for him to stop. *Thump!* Gama struck her on the side of the face, telling her to keep quiet.

Dizzy from the hit, she struggled to focus on what was happening around her. *What if my cards are about to be destroyed?* Cassie thought as tears streamed down her cheek.

"You need to see this," instructed Gama, forcing her to look up at the display.

Blinded by the shimmering white light, everything started to calm down, and as Cassie squinted hard, she saw a faint scene from the past form. Then, as her sight returned to normal, her mouth dropped. With the wings and lower body of a mighty bird of prey, her father, Steven Jenkins, flew around Lena Arena with a blood-drenched sword in his hands. The crowds were chanting 'Jakar' as the Lixusian revelled in his victory.

Out of nowhere, an announcement was made: Jakar had achieved Divine Honour, and the world of Lixus would forever regard him as the greatest champion that had ever lived. A loud eruption rocked the structure, and the image of the past was gone.

"I'm assuming you recognise him now?" quipped Gama.

But Cassie couldn't hear him. Her world was crumbling around her, and she didn't know what to trust right now. It was too much to take in.

"The moment Jakar achieved Divine Honour," King Hargvar spat, "and it didn't take long for the traitor to abandon our world."

"Wait? Abandon?" asked Cassie.

Looking up at the intolerant king, Cassie instantly regretted her outburst, but to her surprise, he answered back.

"Yes," said King Hargvar, changing tactics.

"And Divine Honour?" continued Cassie, growing more confident.

"The destiny of our inhabitants is built upon the foundations of mystical combat," explained King Hargvar. "Those who survive a contest are one step closer to achieving Divine Honour. The highest form of respect one can obtain. It can make or break a Lixusian's social standing."

My father was a warrior, Cassie thought, racking her memories for any sign of his old life. But there was nothing. Steven was her dad, and that's all she'd ever known him as.

"So, how do you know Jakar?" asked Gama.

Cassie looked at Gama and King Hargvar. They waited for an answer, but she couldn't say anything. The truth was, Cassie didn't know where to start first. But at the same time, why did she have to explain herself to them? After everything these vile creatures put her and Lucy through!

The only thing she'd felt a genuine, honest connection with was the multicoloured river, and as she looked behind her, Cassie was desperate to catch a glimpse of its welcoming energy. Her inner strength rose to the surface, and she decided to make a run for it.

Sprinting away from Gama and King Hargvar, she kept going. Reaching the water, Gama swooped in the air and gripped her tightly. Drawing her back, they wrestled with each other on the riverside. Then King Hargvar commanded them to cease.

"So, you were drawn to the water?" he said, with a menacing grin. "It awakens our Lixusian powers from infancy."

Awakens! Cassie thought. Desperate for another way out, her eyes darted around the space, and she heard the faint, familiar crackling sound. Not wanting to build her hopes up, Cassie took a deep breath. Her Tarot cards appeared and flew above the river. Their energy felt uplifted by its aura, and soon enough, the water recharged the deck's power.

"What happened in the desert?" Cassie whispered.

"We loved Jakar," the cards whispered back. "But our desire to see him again meddled with the portal magic. We are sorry."

"It's okay," Cassie said, wiping away tears.

She backed away from King Hargvar and Gama, who remained surprisingly calm and collected. The first thing Cassie asked her cards to do was destroy the handcuffs around her wrists.

But as they were about to conjure sensational energy strikes, the cards unintentionally demobilised. King Hargvar picked a distressed Cassie off the floor and whispered in her ear, "The cards are mine, as are you."

With no time for her to react, the king threw Cassie into the river. The cold water pierced her skin as she wrestled to get out. Screaming in pain, the water dragged her back in. *Stab! Stab! Stab!* Her anatomy was changing against her will. Cassie's legs and feet transformed into a bird of prey, and her spine felt like it was being sliced open. The searing pain continued as a set of wings grew out of her back and extended out.

As the process continued, King Hargvar and Gama watched with satisfaction. The king's guard would soon detain Cassie and send her into Lena Arena for her first, and hopefully last, contest.

Chapter Eighteen

A Fighting Chance

Wayan's moon was a blood-red disc hanging in the summer sky. Beams of moonlight turned the lake aglow like flames flickering as they surrounded a small, dishevelled boat no one would care to miss.

The craft sailed away from Delqroix Island, the centre of the Tarot world, and a light evening breeze encouraged it towards the south-easterly patch of the mainland.

Queen Maria and Evie, the only ones on board, stepped onto the deck and watched their home, Castle Wayan, disappear into the distance. Knowing King Marco needed to stay, especially as Queen Lillian had awakened Andrew's memories, didn't make the separation any easier. Finally, however, the family had made a mutual decision: their voyage was necessary.

"Mother?" whispered Evie.

But Queen Maria remained silent as she turned her back on the castle and fixated on the forest-covered mainland. *You are not running away from Sylvie,* Queen

Maria thought. *And you will have a chance to speak to her when she recovers from her injuries.*

As Queen Maria's rationale came full circle, she looked up at the blood moon, and her anger returned. Sylvie snatched two children and forced them to live a fabricated life. In all honesty, Queen Maria didn't know how she would react when she met Sylvie again.

"Are you okay?" asked Evie.

"Yes. I'll be fine," said Queen Maria.

Resting a hand on her daughter's arm, Queen Maria scanned every part of Evie's face. The thought of a life without her would tear her apart. And Evie, sensing her mother's distress, needed to intervene.

"I'm here, Mother. And we are going to do this together."

Queen Maria hugged her daughter as they crossed the lake in new-found serenity. They were close to the mainland in a matter of minutes, and Evie stood to attention.

"I'll prepare to dock," said Evie, voice raised and confident. She took the helm and manoeuvred the boat expertly and safely docked their craft at the side of the elm jetty. But, before she could throw a rope over the side, the sound of a branch snapping diverted her attention away.

While mother and daughter leaned over and inspected the jetty, a figure emerged through the opening on the edge of the luscious green forest. Concealed head to toe in plain, dark clothing, the masked loner wore a long, thick cloak over the top.

Queen Maria and Evie didn't seem threatened by the sudden presence. Instead, they jumped over the side of the boat, landed confidently on the elm, and worked together to secure the vessel. Once satisfied, they waited patiently for the figure to get closer.

A strand of blonde hair escaped the head mask, and a set of hazel eyes looked upon Queen Maria and Evie with mischief. Once the figure stood before them, they removed the concealment, revealing a woman of similar age to the Queen of Wayan. Her eyes darted with intrigue at Queen Maria and then at Evie.

"You needed a private audience?" asked Lady Helena, the leader of the Land of Pentacles.

"Yes, thank you for coming alone," said Queen Maria, stepping forward and hugging Lady Helena tightly.

"We wouldn't want the other leaders seeing this. They might get jealous," quipped Lady Helena, smiling warmly at the Queen of Wayan and Evie.

Releasing her grip, a dark cloud formed inside Queen Maria's mind for the impending journey, and the leader of the Land of Pentacles felt her dismay.

"What do you need, Maria?" asked Lady Helena.

"Queen Lillian took Amy to Lixus."

The mention of Lixus sent shivers down the queen's spine. Ten years before, she visited the barbaric Tarot world. She was fresh, eager, and determined to build relations, especially as she'd been appointed Wayan's youngest ruler. Yet, her advisors warned her to step back and leave Lixus alone. Finally, after constant denial, Queen Maria realised her advisors were right.

"Evie and I will go alone. We don't want to escalate matters," continued Queen Maria. "I will need you to wait for the signal. Once Amy is back on Wayan, you need to take care of her."

"But why Lixus? And what did your tone mean by 'take care of her'?" queried Lady Helena, a little unnerved.

"Because we suspect a star has taken control of her body."

Taken aback by the instruction, Lady Helena wondered what the best course of action would be once Amy returned, but her question about Lixus still hadn't been answered. She sensed Queen Maria was skirting around the subject.

"And why Lixus?"

"Queen Lillian might want to control a Lixusian army," said Queen Maria. "So, they might be useful puppets."

"What about your cards, Maria? What did they say?"

"You're wasting time," said Queen Maria, dodging the question.

"No. I won't budge. What did your cards show? Did they tell you why Queen Lillian took Amy to Lixus?" pressed Lady Helena, refusing to back down.

"I'm not going to consult my cards."

Evie's mouth dropped at her mother's words. How were they meant to bring Amy back if her mother hadn't even asked her cards for guidance?! What was she thinking? Raising a voice of concern, the queen shut down Evie immediately, leaving her daughter exasperated and cheeks flushed. Before Lady Helena could chip in, Queen Maria shut down both women.

"In this instance, there's no point consulting my cards."

"But the Lixusians are devious, cruel creatures," said Lady Helena.

"Exactly, and I wouldn't expect anything less, which is why Amy is the focus. I can't have extra layers to think about. My cards and I will react better in the moment."

Lady Helena and Evie fell eerily silent. They looked away nervously, accepting their defeat, for no amount of protesting would change Queen Maria's mind.

The queen was sure she knew what she was doing and her decision was final. So, blocking out the negativity around her, she raised her hands and willed her Tarot deck from the inner pocket of her tunic. The cards flew with majestic confidence. They radiated profound red energy, and Queen Maria felt their support as they whispered in her head that they understood why she decided against a reading. Her chestnut eyes were awash with love, and she thanked them for their camaraderie.

The profound red energy gathered momentum, and a dazzling gateway emerged before the three women. So, this was it, Queen Maria decided, unable to turn back now. Casting one final look across the water at Castle Wayan, she bid a momentary farewell to her Tarot world. "I will see you soon," she told herself. Approaching the portal, Lady Helena reassured her she would be ready for Amy.

"Thank you," said Queen Maria.

The leader of the Land of Pentacles watched as mother and daughter exited Wayan, and on the other side, a fervent outcry rocked the bone-dry air. "What was that?" Evie muttered under her breath as the gateway closed behind them. Feeling suffocated by the windless heat, she breathed to steady her nausea. Feeling a little better, she walked across the sandy floor towards the edge of a rock-formed balcony. Peering over, Evie realised they were high above the ground.

Eyes wide with shock, she saw row upon row of feral creatures howl around an imposing stadium. Their volatile raucousness grew as individuals flew above and released bloodied carcasses with flesh still hanging off into the crowd. Evie felt sick, and it wasn't just the heat.

"Welcome to Lixus," Queen Maria said.

Disinterestedly looking away from the open-air crowd, the Queen of Wayan inspected the three stone walls that encased them. On each side was a set of large Lixusian wings carved into the rock and a bulging clear quartz crystal resting in the centre. All three crystals began to glow, and Queen Maria sighed in relief.

"Queen Maria and Princess Evie of Wayan, reporting to Lena Arena," said Queen Maria.

In an instant, the three crystals glowed brighter and brought the wings on the walls to life. They flapped and whipped up the sand, generating a small blizzard around them.

"What's meant to happen next?" called Evie.

"Just wait," encouraged Queen Maria, "and I'd suggest you keep taking deep breaths."

Instantly, they were transported three floors down to the royal balcony where King Hargvar of Lixus was lurched over the side, immersed in the atmosphere around him.

As Evie took in the shimmering white banners with the emblem of the Lixusian wings, she noticed a bucket of half-eaten bones resting on the floor next to the King. The foul stench mixed with the heat unsettled her insides.

Remember to breathe, she told herself, looking away from the sight.

Blocking out the vileness around her, Queen Maria approached and announced herself and Evie. But King Hargvar ignored her. He was still as cold and unsufferable.

"I'm here to help you," said Queen Maria.

The king chuckled and looked up at the royal guards. "No threat here," said King Hargvar. "As you were."

"This is serious!" said Queen Maria.

Marching towards the king, the Queen of Wayan placed a hand on his shoulder and demanded he turn to face her. With a savage roar, King Hargvar grabbed her neck, ready to squeeze the life out of her.

"Your subjects are in danger," said Queen Maria. "Queen Lillian is coming here, and she's found a way to draw stars from the sky and ensnare other beings."

Releasing his grip, King Hargvar stared into her eyes, hunting for any sign of deception. Finally, he let go and faced the crowds again. "When this is over, we can discuss," sniped King Hargvar. "But for now, just watch."

Knowing Queen Maria hated Lena Arena and everything his Tarot world stood for, the king revelled in making her uncomfortable. Queen Maria thought, *If I had my way, I would will my cards to strike him down instantly*, but she knew better than to antagonise a horde of vicious Lixusians.

Joining his side, Queen Maria looked down at the masses and hoped the contest would end quickly. But rather than be subjected to the torment, she silently withdrew from everything around her, including Evie. She fixated upon her Tarot cards and was about to tell them their task. Instantly, the cards whispered back, "Search for Amy?"

"Yes," said Queen Maria, her voice low.

Silent and steady, Queen Maria's Tarot cards snuck out of her tunic. They travelled away from the balcony and through an archway out of sight. Determined to keep tabs on their progress, the king's outburst thwarted her attention.

"Lixusians! The daughter of Jakar has arrived!" boomed King Hargvar.

He whipped the crowds into a frenzy as the competitors were allowed into the arena. The Lixusian from Sina impaled Bara in the previous day's contest, and she begrudgingly made her way across the sand, muttering to herself, "The human is not a champion!"

Queen Maria knew something was off. Where was the other competitor? Had Lillian arrived? But just as the crowds died, they ignited with delight when a nervous Lixusian stepped out of an archway underneath the royal balcony.

The Queen of Wayan watched the competitor shake uncontrollably, clinging on to her Tarot cards for dear life. As the terrified creature turned to face a section of the crowd, Queen Maria remembered King Hargvar called her the daughter of Jakar.

"Jakar achieved Divine Honour," muttered Queen Maria.

"But his daughter, Cassie, won't. She'll be dead before nightfall," sniped King Hargvar.

"How did you find her?" asked Queen Maria.

"She accidentally transported herself to Lixus." King Hargvar smirked. "From somewhere called Earth."

Across the stadium floor, Cassie crushed the sand between her talons as she tried to force her Lixusian wings to extend. They wouldn't behave but she had to keep trying! Especially as the disgruntled Sina looked ready to butcher her on the spot.

Seeing the blood-soaked weapons on the ground from yesterday's fight, Cassie took a big gulp. Her rival kicked hard off the ground without warning and flew dispassionately into the air.

"Wait!" Cassie called out. "Have we begun?"

But Sina ignored the question and, with ease, conjured mystical energy from her Tarot cards and channelled it into the scythe. Weapon aglow, it flew up into the Lixusian's hand, and Sina circled the arena, dutifully rallying the crowd into excitement.

Cassie, however, hadn't managed flight or claimed the battleaxe with her Tarot cards. Lena Arena was against her, and Sina was preparing to strike. Knowing she needed to pick up the axe, she knelt beside the weapon, and the crowd roared with laughter at her incompetence. Swiftly, Sina dived into the stadium, unleashed the warrior scythe through the air and willed the Tarot energy to pierce Cassie's flesh.

Cassie grabbed the axe, rolled on her side, and dodged the attack. She instructed her cards to charge the weapon, which finally worked. After that, she stood firmly in the centre of the arena. She radiated an aura of new-found confidence, and the crowd's raucousness died in shock at her quick defence.

From the royal balcony, Queen Maria smiled as the warrior inside Cassie emerged, but she knew the half-human couldn't keep up forever.

"Any sign of Amy?" asked Queen Maria inside her mind.

"Not yet," replied the cards.

"Please, keep looking."

A sharp crackle of energy erupted inside her stomach, and the queen felt a little uneasy. Suspecting her deck had found something important, she waited anxiously.

"I found a girl from Earth," whispered the cards.

"But Cassie's here?"

"No, there's another. Her sister, Lucy. She's imprisoned in the cells underneath the arena. I worry she won't make it."

"Okay," the queen whispered. "I need you to speak with Evie's cards and guide them and my daughter to Lucy's whereabouts."

"And then what?"

Looking around at Evie, who was too engrossed in Cassie's predicament, Queen Maria took in her features and fought back the tears. She knew, in this instance, it was better to send Evie and Lucy back to Wayan unscathed. She told herself she wasn't Sylvie. This was different. Burying thoughts of the sorceress, Queen Maria gave the signal. "Go!"

In a swish followed by a mighty swoosh, the bewildered princess watched as her Tarot deck leapt out of her pocket. Their outburst caught King Hargvar's attention, and his steely stare made Evie uncomfortable.

She backed away, and as she did, the princess was unaware she was retreating through a portal. Catching sight of the enchanting, shimmering outer edges, Evie's mouth dropped. Before she had time to call her mum, her Tarot cards pushed Evie through the gateway.

"I sent her back to Wayan," lied Queen Maria.

"Too weak to stomach a children's match?" sniped King Hargvar.

"Yes," said Queen Maria through gritted teeth.

As the king was about to take another swipe, he fell unusually quiet. He was unnerved by the sky, where a dark cloud began blocking the intense Lixusian sun, and Lena Arena was slowly shrouded in darkness.

"That's impossible!" roared King Hargvar. "Guards!"

A squall of Lixusian guards hunted around the stadium for an explanation as to why their sun had been tampered with, and while they continued the search, King Hargvar saw pops of stars awaken in the night. They twinkled innocently, then shone brighter and started drawing nearer to Lena Arena. As desperation grew, King Hargvar left Queen Maria alone on the royal balcony, and finally, now he was gone, she could help him, much to her annoyance.

Hoisting herself onto the balcony, she saw her cards approach. They cut through the centre of the arena with determined force, and when they reached their owner, she instructed them to try the multiply spell.

"Are you sure?" whispered the cards.

"Yes," said Queen Maria, voice a little shaky.

"We've never completed it successfully."

"Yes, I know," said a desperate Queen Maria.

The Tarot deck whipped around their owner and generated incredible deep-red energy. The power consumed the queen's being, and with a loud rumble, they conjured multiple copies of her on every row and inside every stadium balcony. Some shimmered, struggling to stay in position, while others were fully formed.

With eyes and ears everywhere, Queen Maria told her copies to hunt for Lillian and Amy. "Keep going!" she called out. "Anything you find, tell me!" The red magic continued to whip around her body, helping to boost the spell.

Someone cried out, "Here! I've found them!"

But before she could react, another copy said, "No! They are standing before me!" Queen Maria grew tired as more versions around Lena Arena chimed in.

Finally, one said, "I'm starting to disappear!"

She'd had enough. Instructing her cards to fall back, she looked at the night sky and immersed herself in the magic that plunged Lixus into darkness. Taking in every intricate detail of the spell, she asked her deck to power up the Sun card.

"Unleash!" bellowed Queen Maria.

With immense force, the queen's Sun card emitted an onslaught of profound mystical energy and hit the centre of the dark cloud. A speck of sunshine escaped for an instant, and Queen Maria told the card to keep going.

Bash!

A blast of forest-green energy pierced through the air and struck Queen Maria in the chest. The impact sent her flying across the royal balcony, and she landed in a heap, out of breath. Rolling onto her side, three sets of footsteps approached, and as the Queen of Wayan looked up, she met the eyes of her sister-in-law, Queen Lillian.

"Finally, you've come out of hiding," said Queen Maria.

"The same can be said for you," replied Queen Lillian. "You remember my daughter, Amy?"

Queen Maria scanned Amy from top to bottom, and all she could think was the young woman looked like a cold statue devoid of life.

"That's not Amy," sniped Queen Maria.

As the group fell silent, the third person, Emerea, knelt before Queen Maria. The sorceress forced the queen's head back and dug her nails into her scalp.

"But you're Emerea," said Queen Maria, refusing to give in to the pain.

Ignoring the comment, Emerea willed from her Tarot cards a small mystical ring that burnt into the back of Queen Maria's head. "The next portal you go through will be final," whispered Emerea with delight, "make sure it's the right one."

Releasing her grip, Emerea joined Queen Lillian and Amy, and as all three women looked upon Queen Maria, a ferocious roar drew nearer. King Hargvar and his guards soared over the royal balcony. They saw the uninvited guests and were preparing to charge.

Using the distraction to her advantage, Queen Maria conjured a portal behind Amy and struck her with red energy, forcing her through the gateway. "Right, that's one," muttered the queen under her breath. "Now, where's the other? Most likely hiding away on the ground floor. Let's go!"

Sprinting towards the balcony's edge, Queen Maria dodged Queen Lillian and Emerea's mystical attacks. As she reached the ledge, she hoisted herself up and, without looking back, jumped off.

Stepping onto one of her levitating Tarot cards, Queen Maria travelled down a makeshift staircase made out of the entirety of her deck. Halfway down her pace quickened, and soon enough, she landed on the soft sand unscathed. "Cassie!" Queen Maria called aloud, retreating underneath the roof of the stadium.

"Cassie!" called Queen Maria. "Wait, there you are!"

Seeing the scared half-human hidden under an archway nearby, the queen approached her. But as she got close, she felt a burning sensation on the back of her scalp. What had Emerea done to her? Queen Maria placed her hand delicately on the spot where it hurt. She called out for Cassie again, who turned to face her when the burning sensation intensified, and she saw Cassie suffering similarly. The pain was unbearable, and before they could make contact, a portal appeared behind Cassie and sucked her in.

Without hesitating, Queen Maria turned, hoping to escape the same fate, but the energy locked onto her too, and before she could fight back, the gateway sucked her and her Tarot cards in. Latching onto the portal's edge, Queen Maria attempted to pull herself out. A blast of forest-green energy nearly struck her hands, and she looked up in horror at Queen Lillian and Emerea standing side by side, determined to banish her through the gateway.

She watched as her sister-in-law initiated another strike. Finally, the Queen of Wayan lost her grip and was sucked through the portal that closed abruptly behind her.

Surveying the space in front of them, Queen Lillian held Emerea's hand and squeezed it gently. There was an intimate warmth only those two shared as they relished the moment they'd successfully ensnared Queen Maria in a Tarot world of their choosing.

Chapter Nineteen

The Amethyst Plane

Lady Helena stood to attention in the centre of a carved, elm octagonal chamber. With her arms raised, ready to channel her fantastical yellow Tarot energy, the leader of the Land of Pentacles scanned the vast space looking for any sign of a portal opening from Lixus. Her hazel eyes, with a tint of shimmering yellow, strained for anything noticeable while her Tarot cards were flying above. The deck circled the room hunting for any sign of activity, while Lady Helena's group of necromancers had taken their positions on the outer edges. The leader drew another breath and waited as the dazzling light from her cards flew over her, illuminating her light blonde hair.

Further back was Andrew, who was grateful to Lady Helena for letting him be present. He knew this was one of the most complicated challenges he would ever face: seeing his sister Amy controlled by a star.

A loud eruption rocked the chamber, and Lady Helena knew it was the cue. Telling everyone to remain alert, the leader watched as a fantastical gateway formed in the centre. In Amy's body, Star Maya was forcefully propelled back into the room.

Instructing two of her necromancers to close the portal immediately, Lady Helena and the rest of her team connected with their Tarot cards as they circled their owner. The energy from the cards transferred into their bodies, and from their hands, the necromancers directed their mystical yellow power onto the floor.

At the same time, Andrew edged closer with a possessed look to disarm the star, but Lady Helena was too quick for him.

"Andrew, stay back!" shouted Lady Helena.

Just as he paused, Star Maya scrambled off the cold marble floor and was about to generate forest-green energy and unleash an attack. But the power the necromancers conjured came to life and transformed into a pentacle shape under the star.

The pentacle glowed brighter and brighter while the necromancers fought to restrain Star Maya with mystical energy. At the same time, Lady Helena skilfully extracted and manipulated amethyst energy from the crystal Star Maya wore around its neck.

Looking on in amazement, Andrew stood back. He watched as the amethyst energy separated into five strands, and each strand travelled outwards and struck each point of the pentacle on the floor.

"Let me go!" screeched Star Maya furiously, trying to resist Lady Helena's efforts as the amethyst energy shot up from each point, creating a mystical forcefield around the star, trapping it inside. Anger erupting, Star Maya fired forest-green energy from her hands and tried to hit Lady Helena, but the forcefield blocked its attacks. Once all the necromancers were confident the prison was strong enough, Lady Helena stepped forward.

Going face to face with the star, the leader of the Land of Pentacles fell deathly silent, taking in the harmful being, actively trying to make Star Maya feel unsettled and insignificant. The minutes ticked by, and when the star finally broke and attempted to punch through the forcefield, Lady Helena ceased her silence too.

"You need to release Amy," said Lady Helena, who tried to keep her voice calm and steady as she fought back her rage.

"Did you hear me?" asked Lady Helena.

The room was silent as the necromancers and Andrew waited for an answer, but the star didn't respond. The tension escalated inside the chamber, and Andrew couldn't take it anymore. The torment the star inflicted on his sister was unbearable.

Andrew was about to step forward, but he was interrupted. One of the large, foreboding oval doors behind him opened, and Calum popped his head around. He looked at Lady Helena, then at Andrew, and nodded confidently at both.

"Thank you, Calum, we're coming," said Lady Helena as she placed her hand upon Andrew's shaky arm and guided him away from the agony.

While Star Maya was left to wonder what could be more critical, the door closed, and within the hallway Calum removed Amy's Tarot from his pocket. He handed them to Lady Helena, who knew, as well Andrew, that Sylvie had retrieved Amy's cards from Naxthos.

"Thank you," said Lady Helena, who'd orchestrated the moment for the boy to enter and disrupt Star Maya's interrogation.

"Let's be hopeful. Sylvie will wake up soon," encouraged the leader of the Land of Pentacles, placing a hand on Calum's shoulder.

As the group waited in silence, casting unsettled glances at each other, Lady Helena wanted the brief interlude to instil some paranoia in Star Maya. Finally, she gave the signal, and all three returned to the chamber, calm and collected.

At the front, Star Maya watched intently as Lady Helena, Andrew, and Calum made their way slowly towards the star, who looked slightly unnerved at the sight of Amy's Tarot cards.

"One of my necromancers is close to tapping into Amy's cards and channelling their energy into the amethyst plane. She would be able to use the energy to fight back," explained Lady Helena, trying to keep the lie convincing. "So, you have a choice: either return to the sky or let Amy kill you."

Locking eyes with Lady Helena, the star soaked in and contemplated her words. Star Maya smiled.

"You're lying. No entity in existence has been able to connect with their cards from the amethyst plane," said Star Maya. "I won't be returning to the sky. So, either we continue to wait while Amy remains trapped inside the forcefield, or I fight her."

A wave of fear struck Lady Helena. She was desperate to try anything else, but nothing came to mind. Instead, she grew concerned for Amy's life as she toyed with the amethyst plane forcefield. Then Andrew appeared at her side.

"We need to. There's no other choice right now," said Andrew, a decision firmly made.

"There could be another way, Andrew," said Lady Helena.

"I know you're trying to protect her, but if Erika managed to defeat the star that took over her body, I need to trust my sister can overcome this," explained Andrew.

"But it's not as simple as that. Each star is different in terms of abilities and intent. The one Erika overcame could have been weaker or even refused to hurt her!"

"Refused to hurt her?" said Andrew, curious about the sudden diplomacy from Lady Helena. He was about to ask what that meant but stopped himself. He had to focus on Amy.

"Still, Amy will give everything she has," Andrew said.

Lady Helena digested his words. Finally surrendering to the idea, she instructed her necromancers to carry out the act. And while the forcefield was disbanded, inside the crystal Star Maya wore, the star gave a menacing look at Andrew.

"I'm coming for your sister," goaded the star, who fell to the floor, motionless, as the group looked at Amy's body. All they could do was wait and hope.

*

Deep inside the innocent-looking amethyst crystal, Star Maya's final words echoed throughout the purple, fog-walled forcefield that encased an afflicted Amy. Sat in the centre, cradling her knees, she rocked backwards and forwards, waiting for even more uncertainty.

Nerves running away with her, Amy had to think of a coping mechanism and fast. She managed to latch on to the image of the dinner table at her parents' home in Aberaeron. It was her family's meeting point and the epitome of love and belonging. Welling up at the familiarity, she started to feel a little better. She was able to bury her worries in the hopes they wouldn't resurface and become alert in case something happened soon.

Raising her head, Amy saw the same mist surrounding her since she was first imprisoned, and instead of feeling sorry for herself, she rose from the floor. Cautiously, she made her way around the prison, inspecting patches of purple mist.

Something unexpected happened: a section began to evaporate on the other side of the space. Amy hesitantly made her way towards it – an array of clouds formed, and seagulls squawking and sea waves crashing could be heard in the distance. The familiar sounds struck her like an oncoming boat, and she was overwhelmed. Eager to cross, a small part worried it was a trap. She was already in one prison – it didn't matter.

Amy stepped through the clouds as she gave one final look of hate at the purple, mystical energy. On the other side, she was on a rickety wooden footbridge and light rain drizzled from above. Even though the rain distorted parts of her vision, Amy instantly recognised an array of colourful Georgian townhouses next to a Gothic-style church on the other side of the bridge. She saw a harbour on her right that brought tears to her eyes. She was back in Aberaeron.

"I'm back," she said aloud with joy. "This is real, isn't it?" Amy wasted no time as she power walked over the footbridge and made her way into the heart of town. She spotted Flint & Drift along the high street, but it had a sign in the window that said 'closed'. Peering through the glass, there was no life in the shop and the lights were out. She crossed the road towards Bean Easy, but upon arriving she spotted another closed sign.

It occurred to her that she hadn't seen or engaged with anyone since her arrival. She attempted to turn a corner and was transported back to the harbour. Her mouth dropped at the rapid change in location, and she felt the eerie mood around her bubble to the surface.

Realising there were no boats, people, or parked vehicles, it looked like the entire town had been stripped of life. As the clouds released heavier rain, the droplets shimmered a mystical purple, and the seawater inside the harbour changed to purple too.

"Where am I?" said Amy, resisting the body's need to shake uncontrollably.

There was no one there. As she was about to try reaching her parents' house again, the loud foghorn receiver from a lighthouse stopped her in her tracks.

Aberaeron didn't have a lighthouse. Confused, she sprinted towards the other end of the harbour and came to a set of stone steps leading down to the beach. Looking out at the sea view, she couldn't see a lighthouse. She did, however, see the sea change into different colours from the rainbow. It settled upon the colour purple and glistened, as slowly, out of the water, a mystical, amethyst-made jetty rose from the sea.

Her eyes widened with amazement as an array of magic swished into the sky and, with determined force, conjured a small, delicate lighthouse at the far end. Revelling at the structure in front of her, she had unintentionally let down her defences.

A set of sharp, irate footsteps drew closer from the harbour, and with one brisk kick to the back of her left calf, she lost her balance. She was disorientated after stumbling down the steps, landing face down on the sand. Managing to roll onto her back, Amy clocked her attacker, and her eyes widened with horror, as Star Maya looked exactly like her.

Wild with rage, the star wistfully travelled down the stone steps and picked up a large rock from the beach. Ready to inflict a heavy blow to Amy's head, Star Maya was thwarted.

Pumped with adrenaline, Amy rolled onto her side, dodged the attack, and kicked hard against Star Maya's ankle. The star landed on the ground, caught off balance, and Amy jumped on it. The two hit and kicked each other, neither one backing down. But the sudden sound of the foghorn inside the lighthouse drew Star Maya's attention away. Eyes scanning the mystical lighthouse meticulously, as if looking for something of value, Star Maya clocked what it was after.

The foghorn receiver moaned again but much louder, which jolted Amy to look up at the structure. When she caught her breath, Amy saw a bright purple beacon at the top of the lighthouse. Noticing the longing in Star Maya's face, she grabbed hold of the star's shoulders and pushed it back onto the sand. But Star Maya managed to trip her up, causing her to fall over. In an instant, the star sprinted across the beach towards the jetty.

Groaning in pain from cuts and bruises, Amy got up from the sand and followed the star under the greyish clouds as they released heavy, shimmering rainfall upon the seafront. With no idea where or what Star Maya was running towards, she just had to follow. Managing to catch up, even though the pain from her injuries slowed her down, Amy and Star Maya scrambled around the structure and found an entryway.

Star Maya bolted inside first, pushing Amy hard against the lighthouse wall. A little disorientated from the impact, she took a deep breath and followed the star inside. Looking up at the decaying spiral staircase to the top, she saw the bright purple light glow brighter.

Giving everything she had, Amy proceeded up the staircase two steps at a time. Drawing closer and closer, she kept going until, midway up, Star Maya paused in its tracks. With one swift movement, the star planted a heavy rock into the side of Amy's head. Falling back onto the staircase, she hadn't time to react as Star Maya stood over her and repeatedly hit the back of her head with the rock. Bloodied and beaten, she sprawled over the railing while Star Maya left her for dead.

Amy rolled onto her back in shock and moaned in agony at the shooting pains. It was becoming unbearable as tears started to stream down her cheeks. As she closed her eyes, she saw the purple light above fading away.

While the waves outside crashed violently against the structure, she was trapped inside her mind, battling to wake up from the attack. Panicked and desperate to move, she couldn't muster the physical strength.

Another wave on the outside crashed violently, and as her longing for home fed into the amethyst plane, something unexpected happened. The purple mystical seawater had risen and entered the entranceway into the lighthouse. It rose majestically, and when the water reached Amy, it began to lift her.

Feeling immersed in the cool liquid, inside her mind, she could see the slight flicker of forest-green energy in the distance. The energy crackled and grew more substantial, and before she could reach out and touch it, her consciousness was reignited. Eyes open, she looked up in wonder as the sea water rose and carried her to the top of the lighthouse.

She felt energised. Her wounds had fully healed, and the blood had been washed away. Amy remembered that flicker of energy; she'd sworn she'd seen the outline of a Tarot card. Contemplating what was possible inside the amethyst plane, she arrived at the top of the landing. The water placed her delicately on the floor next to the spiral staircase, and the sea level dropped.

She was amazed at the spectacle, casting a glance upon the shimmering liquid below, but her focus needed to shift, for Star Maya had already found what it was looking for. In its hands was a small glass beacon, the source of the purple light, and Star Maya was determined to break it apart.

Edging closer, Amy scanned the beacon, understanding its importance, and caught sight of a small amethyst crystal encased within. She realised the star wanted to claim the crystal first. Adrenaline pumping, she found the opportune moment. As soon as the star attempted to smash the glass on the floor, she knelt and wrapped her arms around its neck, squeezing tight. Wrestling to break free, Star Maya was unable to release itself from her grip. Amy kept going. Refusing to get sentimental, she looked away from its face, the spitting image of hers.

At last Star Maya lost consciousness, and as she released her grip, the star dropped to the floor in a heap. Unable to look at herself, she turned away from the body and slowly regained self-assurance. She told herself she was so close now.

Now alone in the lighthouse, she had no choice but to try to claim the amethyst crystal. She picked up the beacon and smashed it against the wall, but the glass didn't break. She tried again. But, after a few more failed attempts, she grew restless and desperate. She didn't understand why it wouldn't break. Was she doing something wrong?

Growing concerned, she hadn't noticed the mystical seawater rise again, and as it reached the landing, she felt the water begin to consume her feet and knees. In an instant, the sea whipped her into a frenzy, and she screamed. Holding the beacon tight, Amy looked up and saw she was close to making contact with the ceiling. She couldn't see a way out.

Minutes felt like hours as she tried to stay afloat, and finally the water devoured her head and consumed her entire body, trapping her in a makeshift water tank inside the lighthouse.

Her energy was depleted. She couldn't hold on any longer and started to sink to the bottom. Her desire for home intensified, and the power grew more substantial and filtered out of her consciousness into the seawater.

The forest-green energy re-emerged and pierced the beacon. The glass broke instantly, and as the crystal floated away the power transformed into Amy's Tarot cards. Their corporal state had managed to break into the amethyst plane momentarily, and the deck manipulated the current for the crystal to land safely in her hand.

The instant contact sent a shock wave throughout Amy's body, and she could see the outline of Andrew's face for a brief moment. He smiled back at her, encouraging her to keep going, and as his face disappeared, she heard his voice calling out to her repeatedly.

*

Inside the carved, octagonal, elm chamber, Andrew sat on the cold marble floor racked with worry as he peered through the gap to the mystical pentacle prison. Inside, Amy's body still lay unconscious, but he refused to stop speaking to her.

"Amy, can you hear me? Amy, please focus on my voice. You can do this. Keep going."

Behind Andrew, a concerned Lady Helena and her necromancers remained alert in case of Star Maya's return. The leader of the Land of Pentacles refused to take her eyes away from the amethyst crystal Amy wore around her neck. "It's still glowing," Lady Helena muttered under her breath. "No, wait!" Straining her eyes, she thought the light had subsided. "Come on, Amy," the leader said aloud, unable to hold it in any longer.

The crystal stopped glowing, and the chain released itself from Amy's neck. As the group watched nervously, the energy from the pentacle prison evaporated. Andrew looked to Lady Helena, who permitted him to step forward towards Amy. He knelt beside his sister, whose eyes were still closed, and rested his hand on her arm, squeezing it gently.

"Amy?" said Andrew, tears forming. "Please, Amy, wake up."

After a minute of silence, she began to stir, and a wave of relief struck him as he scooped her up in his arms and hugged her tight. She mustered the energy to open her eyes and stare up at her brother. Unable to contain the hurt, Amy burst out crying while Andrew cradled her tight.

Lady Helena kept back and gave the siblings some space. She stared down at Amy's Tarot cards nestled safely in her hands and felt reassured that, soon enough, they would be reunited with their owner.

Chapter Twenty

Naxthos

Alone in a grotto deep underground, the King of Wayan looked upon the gentle blue waters as they came to life. Shimmering and casting mystical light along the rough surfaces of the walls, the mood exuded peace and serenity. Still, his mind was riddled with worry at the impending mission to Naxthos. Slowly, a delicate ripple emerged from the depths of the water and travelled across the vast space. He couldn't take his eyes away. He reminded himself his sister was gone. She chose her path, and there was nothing he or their parents could do to save her from herself.

But just like the ripple, he hoped his sister would find a way to rise, however small it might be, and return to the person she once was – how he'd remembered her, not the villain other Tarot worlds feared and hated. He never wanted that for Lillian. He loved her, but enough was enough.

Breathing deeply, the King of Wayan awoke from the past and built up the courage to ask his Tarot cards for help. They flew out of his tunic, circled him in the air and conjured an array of forest-green energy strands, the same colour as his sister and his niece's Tarot deck energy. Surrounding King Marco's body, the cards fed comforting energy into his soul.

Once the light disappeared and he felt grounded, he stared back down at the water, but the ripple had disappeared. *And so has my sister*, he thought, choked up and ready to explode with anger and frustration. He didn't understand how it had come to this. At what point did she start to fall apart?

His Tarot cards swooped in again, determined to calm their owner, as they had seen him on the verge of breaking many times over. Some days it was a little easier, but that day, before King Marco was about to address his army, the deck needed to work harder than ever. The forest-green energy circled and consumed him, and as the warmth returned, the noise of a pebble travelling across the rough terrain broke their concentration.

The cards meandered in the air and turned to face the archway leading out of the grotto, and King Marco tore himself away too. Standing under the exit was one of Wayan's most experienced and sought-after necromancers, Reenie. Her hair was tied back tightly in a bun, and her tawny eyes looked eager.

Keeping her entire body concealed with a long, deep brown cloak, the necromancer's demeanour appeared solid and capable, hiding the injuries and torment with ease from the battles of the past. Yet, she hadn't been deterred. Instead, she was ready for the next fight. Reenie's head bowed in respect as she waited patiently.

"How long were you standing there?" asked the king, a little more abrupt than intended.

"Not long, Your Highness," answered Reenie confidently, looking up to meet his eyes. "Everyone's gathered in the portal room."

Nodding at Reenie, he gestured for them to exit the grotto, into a narrow passageway. He paused, looking back, and imagining the ripple in the water. He suddenly had a thought. "Wait, Reenie."

Facing the king, Reenie's eyes were awash with sympathy for she knew he needed every ounce of support.

"Once on Naxthos, if you or your necromancers find my parents, you must bring them back to Wayan," the king instructed.

Taken aback by his request, Reenie was desperate to know more but held her tongue. Sensing the urgency, the king kept it brief.

"I don't care how much protesting they do. Their daughter is gone, and they need to be kept safe here. No more excuses," he said.

"Yes, my King, of course. I will relay that to my necromancers," answered Reenie with determination in her eyes.

That's if my parents are still alive, King Marco wondered, for the last time he'd seen them was six years ago on their homeworld. They'd refused to leave Lillian, believing good was still inside her. But it was all smoke and mirrors. There was no easy way to say it, but it wouldn't surprise him if his sister had already murdered them.

Nodding, Reenie stood aside and watched as he moved cautiously down the passageway. Once the king reached the end, he stepped onto a high platform made of exuberant quartz crystal and, from his vantage point, looked down at his comrades within the vast space of the cavern.

As daylight filtered in from above, he saw Sir Stephan and Gwyn from the Land of Swords. They stood side by side as equals, admiring their line of soldiers with pride, for each individual was dressed head to toe in resilient Wayan armour, with a sword engraved across their chests. Forged from the energy of all four lands, the strong metal protected them from mystical attacks, and under the breastplate each soldier kept their Tarot decks safe.

The cards were their power source, enabling the soldiers to charge their swords with mystical steel-grey energy and fire at the enemy. The energy also expertly charged the pentacle-shaped shields they held on to and protected them from mystical onslaughts.

Satisfied by their unity, King Marco's eyes travelled elsewhere in the cavern and landed upon Nathaniel from the Land of Wands. The king admired the young man, who humbly addressed his soldiers as they sat on their rapas.

In return, each member of their clan looked at Nathaniel with respect, as if he'd proved himself to them time and time again. They encouraged him to continue his battle plan from the sky while proudly checking their wand-engraved armour. Once satisfied, Nathaniel's army held up their mystical wands and conjured from their Tarot cards rich brown energy, the colour of Mount Wayan, their home.

Across from the Land of Wands was Lady Helena's younger sister, twenty-five-year-old Maid Ella, who seemed on edge. She tried to block out her surroundings, a sign of inexperience, and focus on earning the respect of her sister's pentacle army. Row upon row of soldiers stared at her blankly as she raised her arms. Eyes darting around their faces, Maid Ella was about to lose all sense of reason until she finally closed her eyes.

Then, with sheer determination, she willed her Tarot cards to light up the pentacle tattoos that covered her arms. The tattoos glowed a wondrous burnt orange, and expertly conjured a mystical mace with the head in the shape of a pentacle and a pentacle-shaped shield.

As both objects hovered in the air at eye level, Maid Ella reached out to take hold of them. She willed the burnt-orange energy from her tattoos to conjure the same weapons for Lady Helena's soldiers. All efforts were successful.

While Maid Ella attempted to calm down from the ordeal, King Marco set upon the final leader, Commander Merdan from the Land of Cups. Agitated, with a stormy undertone the seafarer cast his deep turquoise eyes over his sailors, 'The Water Bearers'.

Instructing them to ensure their powers were working properly, his comrades willed profound blue mystical energy from their cards and conjured water out of thin air. As everyone completed their task, the rough-edged commander asked them to gather around him as his voice lowered.

"When we cross over, there should be no hesitation. Just act," instructed Commander Merdan. "Any sign of wrongdoing on Naxthos, and you warn me immediately."

Falling silent, he looked behind him and gave Reenie, who stood on the platform next to King Marco, a look of suspicion. The commander caught sight of the king staring at him and instantly told his Water Bearers to line up, ready to advance.

As the portal room fell silent, they watched King Marco command the space high above. He told everyone they would shortly cross to the prison under Castle Naxthos. Their mission was to detain the rogue stars. Soon after pausing, the king instructed Reenie to continue.

The necromancer stepped forward, confident in her leadership abilities, and gestured for four other necromancers who'd recently appeared from the passageway to join her on the quartz crystal platform.

"We have found an opening into the prison," began Reenie. "Once the stars have been detained, they need to be brought back to Wayan. Afterwards, my necromancers and I will work on their amethyst crystals."

"Wait!" called out Commander Merdan, unable to hide his true feelings any longer.

"Commander Merdan?" said King Marco, confused by the interruption.

"Let's do another reading right now, just to ensure this mission is as straightforward as it first appears," said the commander.

But before King Marco could react, Reenie immediately chimed in, determined to end doubt and paranoia. There was no room for backing out now.

"I can assure you, Merdan, that my necromancers and I have everything in hand," said Reenie, ensuring her voice echoed from every corner of the cavern. "Our cards have guided us to victory, and we are not too late to prevent the stars from escaping."

Her firm words shut down any rebellious replies from the commander, who angrily bit his tongue. As he looked at the other leaders, desperate for support, they avoided his gaze and turned all their attention towards King Marco.

With trust and confidence in his heart, the King of Wayan commanded his necromancers to open the gateway. In a swish followed by a forceful swoosh, five sets of Tarot cards belonging to the necromancers flew around the portal room in a dazzling array of multicoloured energy. As the force intensified, they opened a portal on the ground floor and a smaller one on top of the quartz crystal platform.

King Marco took the lead and went through the portal closest to him, while the leaders of the four lands stepped through the other portal, closely followed by their armies. Reenie was the last to cross, and without hesitation she closed both gateways behind her, leaving the cavern in deathly silence.

On the other side, King Marco stepped onto a muddy puddle, and as the heavy rain beat down violently from the dark skies above, the water soaked his hair instantly. Facing the edge of the ominous Royal Forest, the King of Wayan knew where he was. Turning to face the muddy wasteland that led to Castle Naxthos, his rage ignited as comrades looked around the scene, confused and bewildered.

"What happened, Reenie?" demanded King Marco as he inspected her face for any hint of wrongdoing. "You're our best necromancer. So, what went wrong?"

"I don't know, honestly, my King," replied Reenie, her eyes consumed with fear as she looked around at her fellow necromancers, who gave innocent looks. Before she could continue, Commander Merdan appeared at her side and cut her off.

"We need to return to Wayan immediately," he said, but as soon as he'd finished his words, Maid Ella appeared.

"But we've only just arrived! We need to try, at least!" she said.

"Wait, hold on!" called Gwyn, but quickly retreated, realising she'd interrupted her peers.

"It's okay, Gwyn. What are your thoughts?" asked King Marco.

"If the necromancers were wrong about our destination, they could have been wrong about the prison. What if the stars have already escaped?"

"Exactly," added Commander Merdan with a tired breath. "One of those necromancers could have an amethyst necklace around their neck right now." As the commander finished his sentence, everyone around him, including Sir Stephan, Gwyn, and Nathaniel, suddenly felt aligned with the logic. They looked upon Reenie and her necromancers with a vital air of suspicion, and King Marco knew he needed to act fast.

"We were promised the prison underneath Castle Naxthos?" said King Marco.

"We are just as confused as you are, my King," answered Reenie, whose voice trembled with worry. Reenie instructed her necromancers to try again, but King Marco stepped in.

"Wait!" he said. "For everyone's safety, I command the five of you, on the count of three, to reveal your necks to me."

His words rang through the air as the necromancers were taken aback by his instruction. Sir Stephan, Nathaniel and Commander Merdan turned to their armies and instructed them to prepare for signs of danger. Maid Ella didn't act. Instead, she was baffled by King Marco's approach.

Unsure what to do, she waited while one of her soldiers, Erik, scrunched his face in annoyance. Stepping forward while raising his voice, Erik commanded the Pentacle army to prepare for an attack. Looking directly into Maid Ella's eyes, the young rebel watched with delight as her mouth dropped in shock. But before she challenged the soldier, Maid Ella realised her sister's army had already followed Erik's orders.

Taken aback, she grew restless, and re-evaluated the situation as all eyes, especially King Marco's, were on her. *If I agree with Erik*, Maid Ella thought, *I will look like a failed leader who couldn't keep my sister's army in line. But if I challenge him, I worry I will look like a time-waster.*

"Thank you, Erik," she said, through gritted teeth.

"Everything okay, Maid Ella?" asked King Marco. "You looked hesitant."

"No, er…" she stuttered.

"Come now, share your thinking with us?" urged the king.

"It's just, can we be sure one of your esteemed necromancers is the culprit?" she queried, glancing at the commander, Sir Stephan and Nathaniel.

"Why are you looking at us? But, of course, it's not one of us!" said Sir Stephan.

"Maid Ella never said it was one of us, Sir Stephan, so you came up with that all on your own," quipped Commander Merdan. "Are you hiding something?"

Not getting involved in the paranoia brewing, King Marco kept his attention on Reenie and her group as his gut instinct told him that a star had taken over one of their bodies. "I will not ask again. Reveal your necks," he instructed.

Everyone fell silent and all eyes rested upon the nervous faces of the necromancers, who formed a line and surveyed each other. Each pulled down their tunics to reveal their necks from left to right. So far, no one was wearing an amethyst necklace, and finally, it was Reenie's turn. King Marco wished more than anything for her to be innocent, and as she revealed her neck, she was not wearing a necklace either. As soon as this satisfied the onlookers, Reenie gave Gwyn a slight look of annoyance.

"Thank you, Reenie. Take us to the prison immediately," commanded the king.

"But?!" called out Commander Merdan.

"Silence, Commander. There will be no more interruptions from anyone!"

As soon as the King of Wayan finished, all five necromancers stood to attention and formed a circle. With the mission's fate resting on their shoulders, Reenie knew she couldn't afford to make a mistake now that her reputation was in jeopardy. While they focused on conjuring a gateway from their Tarot cards, some members of the king's army noticed the earth tremble under their feet.

"King Marco, up ahead!" shouted Nathaniel as his rapa, Missy, carried him high into the sky.

The king followed Nathaniel's warning, and the sight before him was painful to accept, for rows of Naxthosian armed soldiers, some he'd grown up with and fought alongside, filtered out of the castle on horseback. Ready to advance on his army, the Naxthosians gripped their mystical weapons and shields.

So, it is final, he told himself. Lillian had instructed an army from his homeworld to attack King Marco and his wife's people. There was nothing to come back from. He knew he needed to accept that his sister was gone forever, so he delved into the familiar feeling of support from his Tarot cards. The king couldn't hold back now. His comrades depended on him.

"Nathaniel, take the wands into the air and strike from above," he commanded. The young Wayan instantly summoned his army into the sky. They flew towards the enemy, ready to fire deep brown energy from their wands.

The king turned to the other three leaders and told them to split their armies. The first group would protect the ground where they were, while the other half was to go with him to the prison.

With masterful leadership from Commander Merdan, Sir Stephan and ever so slightly from Maid Ella, the first half of their armies broke away and created teams of three, with one member from each land. At the front was a soldier from the Lands of Swords and Pentacles, who would work together with their array of weapons to fend off the Naxthosian soldiers. The last teammate, from the Land of Cups, would keep to the back and protect them with mystical water strikes.

As Wayan's forces took formation, they advanced upon Castle Naxthos, just as King Marco turned to Reenie, whose health was deteriorating rapidly.

"Are you okay?" said the king.

Before she could answer, Reenie fell to the floor, eyes severely bloodshot from her efforts to break through Naxthos's portal defences.

"I'm sorry," said Reenie. "There had been a barrier to the prison all along. But I've managed to remove it." A portal emerged in front of him and, catching her breath, Reenie confirmed this would transport them into the prison without fail. "I'm so sorry. I honestly don't know what happened," said Reenie, deeply troubled by her mistake.

King Marco delicately placed a hand upon Reenie's shoulders and told her to return to Wayan if needed, but Reenie refused. The esteemed necromancer scrambled for every last bit of energy inside herself and her Tarot cards. Rising from the floor, she refused to leave the king and commanded her necromancers to accompany them into the prison. Once Reenie cemented their camaraderie, the king turned to Commander Merdan, Sir Stephan, and Maid Ella, instructing them to join their remaining soldiers.

As the group filed through the gateway, on the other side the king was the first to arrive within the bleak prison deep under Castle Naxthos. The mood in the cavern was eerily quiet, as no one spoke or moved from inside the row of cells. As King Marco stepped forward to inspect the compartment in front of him, the commander, Sir Stephan and Maid Ella worked their way up the spiral staircase with their soldiers to check the rest of the cells on the other floors.

Through the gap between the bars, the king saw an unconscious figure sprawled out, lying head first on the floor, and because the prisoner's hair was cut short, he quickly identified an amethyst crystal around their neck. It glowed a wondrous purple, which confirmed to him and his onlookers that a star had infiltrated the prisoner's body.

The rest of Wayan saw the same scene inside the other cells, and this ignited a wave of relief and hope, for it looked like Sylvie's spell had managed to keep the prisoners unconscious. Satisfied all was stable, Reenie and her necromancers willed energy from their Tarot cards to unlock each cell and levitate the unconscious prisoners off the floor and through a portal back to Wayan.

The process seemed to be a success, and the king thought they had finally made progress, but his positivity was short-lived. He grew unsettled as he thought he'd seen the outline of his parents' bodies tied to a pillar across the cavern. The image disappeared, reappeared, and then disappeared. Nevertheless, he couldn't shake it away.

"Did anyone see them?" asked King Marco.

But while confused faces looked in the direction he pointed to, high above the cavern, Maid Ella and Erik were still focused on inspecting the cells on their floor. Without thinking, the young rebel tried to open the cell door closest to him, and to his surprise, it opened with ease.

"What are you doing?" asked Maid Ella.

"Inspecting the prisoner," responded Erik, who knelt beside the unconscious being.

"But you don't need to," she replied, sternly. "Reenie and her necromancers have it covered, so we just keep watch for any attack from Naxthos."

Erik was already close to the being and instinctively placed his hand on the prisoner's arm. Erik's hand went straight through the flesh, and his mouth dropped. The body wasn't natural; it was an illusion. Before Maid Ella repeated her words, Erik looked up and gestured for her to keep quiet. He subtly beckoned her to join him inside the cell, much to her annoyance.

"Look," whispered Erik, as he showed her the illusion with his hand, "it's not real."

Maid Ella looked concerned at what he'd discovered, and when she rested her mystical mace and shield down on the ground, she instructed him to remain silent.

"We need to warn everyone immediately," said Erik.

"Wait," whispered Maid Ella.

"Why?"

"We don't know who we can trust, so we need to remain calm."

As soon as she finished her words, they could hear Reenie below, who told her necromancers to focus on the second floor of the prison next, as everyone from the ground floor had been transported back.

"We need to do something," said Erik.

"We will. We're going to exit this cell and find Merdan and Sir Stephan."

"But you said we don't know who we can trust?" queried Erik, a little sceptical of Maid Ella's leadership.

"I know, but we have to start somewhere, and I think they are the best option right now." She had never looked so calm and composed. She nodded for him to exit the cell, and as soon as his back was turned, conjured a hidden, mystical dagger from her Tarot cards.

"Shall I warn the commander? And you warn Sir Stephan?" asked Erik as he turned to face Maid Ella, who expertly grabbed the back of his head and used the dagger to cut across his neck. Killed instantly, Erik fell to the floor in a heap. Hastily, Maid Ella checked through the gap of the cell to make sure no one on the outside had seen or heard anything. But the cavern remained calm, and the only sound came from Reenie, who kept everyone updated on their progress.

After a few minutes, the five necromancers had finally covered all prison floors, with Maid Ella claiming no one was inside the cell closest to her. And so that was it: mission successful.

A relieved Reenie signalled everyone to return to Wayan immediately through a portal she and her necromancers had conjured. As she instructed her group to focus on transporting Wayan's soldiers from the battlefield back home, King Marco had not moved or spoken since he'd first stood before the pillar.

Apart from the king, the last remaining Wayans in the cavern were Reenie, Maid Ella, Sir Stephan and Commander Merdan, who gave the king a look of concern, for he hadn't answered them in a long time. The commander placed a hand on King Marco's shoulder, and without warning, the king fell to the ground, unconscious.

"What's happened?" called Maid Ella, who showed a fake look of concern.

With haste, Commander Merdan and Reenie knelt beside their king, whose eyes were open, but their colour was forest green.

"It's like he is in a trance," said Reenie, confused.

"Is there anything you can do?" asked Sir Stephan.

"I don't know," answered Reenie. "The magic I can detect from his Tarot cards is hate, not from King Marco but directed at him."

"From the pillar, maybe?" said Sir Stephan. "He focused on that spot for a long time."

"We must take King Marco home immediately. We can't afford to stay here any more than we need," urged the commander.

After Commander Merdan spoke, the group nodded in agreement. Just as Reenie and the commander were about to hoist the king from the floor, the cavern shook violently. With every back turned to inspect the debris from above, Maid Ella swiftly knelt beside Reenie and left the dagger on the floor for her. With haste, Reenie concealed the dagger under her tunic and waited.

The sound of Sorcerer Saxthos could be heard from above as he commanded his soldiers to enter the prison and restrain those who'd crossed over from Wayan. This distracted Commander Merdan and Sir Stephan, allowing Reenie to plunge the dagger through King Marco's armour and into his chest. No sound came from the injured king, whose eyes were still forest green, and swiftly Reenie mystically wiped away the blood that seeped from his wound and repaired his armour.

On the outside, King Marco was still unconscious as the leaders of Cups and Swords carried him through the portal, but underneath his armour, he continued to bleed as his life ebbed away.

Meanwhile, Reenie and Maid Ella hung back in the cavern on Naxthos, and when Saxthos appeared beside them on the ground floor, all three acknowledged each other, for their plan to kill King Marco had worked.

Chapter Twenty-One

Heritage

On one tempestuous night in the middle of winter, the wind whipped ten-year-old Maid Ella's hair as she charged through the Royal Forest on her way to Castle Wayan. Eyes haunted and determined, she was only a mile from the castle gates, and her fourteen-year-old sister, Lady Helena, pursued her. Panicked and wild, Lady Helena picked up speed and gave everything she had in an attempt to reach her, for the family secret their father had entrusted her with for most of her childhood had finally been revealed.

It had not been an easy secret to keep, for since Maid Ella was little, she had always been curious, restless and suspicious of everyone around her, even the people she loved the most. It stemmed from when Maid Ella realised she was the only being within her pentacle clan, and others she'd met on Wayan, with pentacle tattoos over her body.

Years passed, and so the resentment built, for each time Maid Ella asked about her tattoos, her clan were dismissive and reassured her the tattoos were merely a fluke. But, deep down, she knew she was being lied to. She couldn't ask her mum, because she died just after Maid Ella was born, and her father and sister never gave anything away.

But this was the night that changed Maid Ella's world forever. The boredom and disdain she felt during their visit to Castle Wayan had taken its toll, and she needed some space within the Royal Forest. So, alone and surrounded by elm trees that glowed a mystical, spiritual white, a frustrated Maid Ella sat cross-legged on the snow-covered ground, wrapped up warm in wolf fur. As she breathed in and out, she looked up at the falling snow.

The cooling sensation from the delicate snowflakes that landed on her cheeks started to calm and help centre her. Eventually, she was ready to remove her Tarot cards from inside her tunic. As she held on to them tight, Maid Ella hoped the 'reading' she was about to conduct would finally explain the pentacle tattoos. Since she received her cards a year ago, she had tried desperately to gain as much information as possible about her family and the pentacle clan. But each time she 'read', all Maid Ella could see was fog that clouded the answers.

She shuffled her Tarot cards with brutish force while concentrating on the questions she was about to ask them. But before she could reveal the first card, the crackle of a snapping twig alerted her to an invisible presence. She scanned the forest as her heart beat faster, and she refocused on her mission.

From a distance, a shape formed and made its way through the snowflakes. It got closer, and eventually its presence was revealed. Lady Helena stood, her face consumed with worry and fear as she looked down upon her sister, then her stomach filled with dread, for Lady Helena knew she needed to stop her.

"Dear sister," said Lady Helena.

Maid Ella's eyes opened with haste as she looked up at her sister with a mixture of annoyance and hope. Lady Helena knelt beside her and placed a hand on her shoulder to comfort her.

"Please don't stop me again," begged Maid Ella.

"I'm just trying to help…" said Lady Helena with a delicate tone. "It pains me, dear sister, to see you like this. For you know that each time you use your Tarot deck, you don't receive the answers you want."

Maid Ella sighed with annoyance at her sister's words but remained silent as she knew Lady Helena had not finished the lecture.

"I keep reminding you that the cards are only there to guide you. You can't control what you want to believe. Otherwise, if you continue down this path, your unhealthy obsession will worsen."

"But my tattoos? Explain them to me?"

"As I've told you before, those tattoos are nothing. So please stop torturing yourself."

Maid Ella paused her Tarot reading and contemplated her sister's words, for deep down, she loved her very much. But, unknown to her, Lady Helena knew how to manipulate her sister's love, and that manipulation should have been seamless, like all the times before. But a rather unfortunate event happened that neither sibling had prepared for. The tattoos on Maid Ella's arms glowed a wondrous burnt orange.

"Er, what's happening?" said Maid Ella, concerned.

With sheer force, an array of energy blasts shot from her skin into the sky. Scared and speechless, Maid Ella rose from the floor and hunted for where the light had gone, while Lady Helena looked up in horror, for the secret her father had made her keep had risen to the surface.

"Ella, calm down. It must be your cards. They are having a mind of their own," she said as theories whirled around her head as to what had triggered her sister's powers.

"It's star energy! Isn't it?" called Maid Ella, as she realised she was sucking star energy from the night's sky. Even though Lady Helena was about to dismiss her sister's notion, it was apparent she was right.

With no way to talk herself out of the predicament, Lady Helena watched as Maid Ella left her and made a run for Castle Wayan. As tears trickled down Lady Helena's cheeks, she chased after her sister.

Upon reaching the castle gates, Maid Ella paused momentarily to assess where her father could be. Once she made up her mind, she travelled through the deserted courtyard to the grand entranceway of the castle. Inside, she bolted for the banqueting hall, and as soon as she pushed open the large oak doors, she saw her father sitting at the dining table. Next to him was his sister Queen Anya, and her husband King Peter. Sat across from them was their daughter, Princess Maria.

"Ella, dear? What's wrong?" said her father, Necromancer Gill, the leader of the Land of Pentacles.

"Star energy," panted Maid Ella.

Gill's face dropped at his daughter's words, and he cast a look of concern at his other daughter, Lady Helena, who appeared at the doorframe, ready to collapse from the sprint.

"My dear niece, are you okay?" asked Queen Anya.

"Something happened... it triggered my powers! I could feel a connection with the night's sky," said Maid Ella, looking directly into her father's eyes. "That's what my tattoos can do! They can draw energy from the stars." As Maid Ella caught her breath, she started to feel a little uneasy, and briefly thought she could hear voices in her head.

As Gill was about to answer and dismiss his daughter's words, Queen Anya rose from her chair, placed her hand upon his shoulder and squeezed it tight. They looked at each other with pain and sorrow, and then, finally, Gill nodded for Queen Anya to take the lead.

"I'm sorry you had to find out like this," said Queen Anya, as she walked steadily over to Maid Ella. "I promise you, we're trying to protect you."

Queen Anya paused when she noticed Reenie, alarmed and out of breath, appear behind Lady Helena.

"It's my fault, my Queen," said Reenie. "It was me that conducted a 'reading' on my balcony, and I foolishly tapped into a star energy spell by mistake."

"It's okay," she was reassured by Queen Anya, who gave a fleeting look of fondness at her most talented and hard-working new necromancer, who'd joined the High Council a year ago. Then, as the room fell silent, Maid Ella stepped in.

"Please, can someone just be honest, for once!" said Maid Ella, firm and defiant.

"I know you're frustrated, Ella. Please sit down, and I will tell you everything," Queen Anya reassured her.

Maid Ella's entire body shook as she pulled up a chair. Lady Helena and Reenie stepped into the banqueting hall and joined the others at the table. Once everyone was seated, Queen Anya began.

"A thousand years ago, a tyrannical entity called 'The Sphere' travelled through vast Tarot worlds. It hunted stars and stole their powers. A group of stars sought refuge and managed to find a way to fall to Wayan. Your late mother was descended from those stars. She could tap into star energy, as can you. But your sister hasn't shown signs of these abilities."

Maid Ella's mouth dropped. The revelation made sense, but why didn't anybody tell her sooner? Why hadn't she been entrusted with the secret? Anger brewing, she held her tongue and waited.

"Every star that managed to escape and take on a Wayan form had the same tattoos as yours. But a spell was found to successfully remove those star markings to keep their identity a secret. You were the first one in our history where it failed."

"Why me?"

"Honestly, we don't know why, and we've been cautious not to try anything else. We don't want to risk blowing this secret, for if the inhabitants of Wayan found out stars have lived amongst them the entire time, without them knowing, it would look bad."

"But I promise you. I won't reveal the secret. I wouldn't do that to you," pleaded Maid Ella, desperate to prove herself.

"It's okay. Calm yourself. I think we'd better call it a night," said Queen Anya.

"But wait! Please," pressed Maid Ella, determined to gather any last bit of information she could.

"There will be plenty of time in the morning, I promise," Queen Anya replied delicately.

The group filtered out of the banqueting room and into the hallway. Much to Maid Ella's annoyance, Lady Helena kept close and offered to accompany her back to her living quarters. But she refused. Her abruptness and disdain were cutting as she turned her back on her sister.

Once inside her living quarters, she closed the light oak door behind her and inspected the room to ensure she was alone. Resting on the edge of the bed, she stared down at the tattoos on her arms.

She had always assumed they were pentacles, it never occurring to her they were stars. *Tonight, it is a refreshing change*, she thought, *to not resent them.* They looked beautiful and delicate, words she had never used before, and then she wondered about the other fallen stars. Where were they? Were they, and her, still in danger from 'The Sphere'?

A tap on the door alerted her to a presence, and before she could answer, Reenie promptly entered her living quarters.

"What's happening?" asked Maid Ella, confused.

"Lower your voice, just in case," urged Reenie, who hurried to close the door behind her. She placed her hand on the wall and conjured protection energy to prevent anyone from reading or listening.

As the chaotic necromancer finally slumped upon a plush armchair, she gestured for Maid Ella to sit on an armchair opposite. Once seated, she looked hard into Maid Ella's eyes and eventually decided where she should begin.

"I knew you were still hungry for more answers," began Reenie.

"Er… yes I was," answered Maid Ella, sombre. Finally, she asked, "Why are you here?"

"I'll be brutally honest. I was sent here, on the orders of Queen Anya and your father, to wipe your memory of what you've just learnt this evening."

"I don't understand why? I told everyone I would keep their secret, so why would they want my memory wiped?"

"It's easier for them that you don't know. They want to protect their world, and you're a risk, but I want to give you a choice. A choice they weren't prepared to offer you."

"But why do you want to help me?" said Maid Ella, desperate. "What's in it for you?"

"I don't want you to be oppressed. It's as simple as that. I feel for you and your ancestors. My lover was descended from the stars, which fell to Wayan. Except, he told me that a group of Wayans had found out, captured some of them who attempted to flee, and tortured them," explained Reenie, with sadness in her voice.

"What?" replied Maid Ella, taken aback.

"I just worry about you. You should have the opportunity to find out who you are truly meant to be."

Her words were the final nail in the coffin as Maid Ella reflected on her family's secrecy. She was enraged when she leaned back in her armchair and looked up at the ceiling. Maid Ella contemplated her destiny and wondered if she would be forever subjected to a life of memory-wiping and dismissal if she didn't take a stand.

From the corner of the room, a portal began to form and take shape, and as Reenie assured her it was nothing to fear, Maid Ella kept her guard up. First, a silhouette slowly came into view from another Tarot world. As the shape crossed over, Maid Ella could see it was a man in his early twenties, of a similar age to Reenie, with kind eyes and a soft smile. He stood and waited patiently for Reenie to introduce him. He was Reenie's lover, Saxthos, and he'd just returned to Wayan from training necromancers in Naxthos.

"Hello, Maid Ella," said Saxthos delicately. "Reenie has told me about you and your heritage."

"Hello. Yes, I've just found out myself tonight. My head is spinning, but I want to know from you, is it true?"

"Is what true?"

"About your ancestors. Were they tortured?"

"I'm afraid so."

"I'm sorry to ask, but how did you find out?"

Saxthos smiled at her and removed a Tarot card from his tunic.

"One of the fallen stars transferred their memories in this card a thousand years ago. It had been passed down through the generations, and eventually, it came into my father's possession, and then into mine. It showed me the past and what the stars endured on their arrival upon Wayan."

"We believe," said Reenie, "that the card acted as a reminder of what the fallen stars went through so that they would never be forgotten."

As Reenie looked defiant, the fire in Maid Ella's belly grew, and she felt the urge to know the full extent of what the Wayans did.

"Can you show me?"

"Sorry?" asked Saxthos.

"Is there a way for you to show me what the card showed you? Please?" she begged.

"I don't know if you're ready for that, young maid. It's not a pretty sight," said Saxthos.

"I need to see. I promise you, I'm ready."

A worried-looking Saxthos turned to Reenie, who nodded. Saxthos held the card up in the air with both hands, closed his eyes and concentrated. He fixated upon releasing the memories, the floor began to tremble, and burnt-orange energy shot out from the Tarot card.

The light generated a scene from the past. At first, the card showed them the mesmerising moment when roughly forty genderless stars from the night's sky successfully lowered themselves onto Wayan. Their piercing yellow eyes were engulfed in a mixture of hope and distress, as they'd just escaped before 'The Sphere' had arrived in their Tarot world.

Maid Ella's eyes widened with shock as she saw how their bodies were dissimilar to the inhabitants of Wayan, for each had a different shape, with varying numbers of heads, arms, and legs. But each body glowed a mystical orange, and as they landed within the outer forest region of the Land of Pentacles, they set to work straight away. Their goal was to conjure 'protection energy' and change the shape of their bodies so they would look like members of the pentacle clan.

But before the protection energy was a success, the stars had failed to notice a young boy who had spied on them from high up in the trees. He silently worked his way back to his family's treehouse to warn them as soon as he figured the stars were there to stay.

What Maid Ella saw next made her skin crawl, for a group of rogue individuals from the pentacle clan had gone into the forest to capture the stars. A small group of stars escaped in time, but the clan managed to detain thirty.

Tied up and subjected to terrible mystical lacerations, the stars begged for mercy, but the pentacle group continued, telling them stars were not welcome on Wayan.

"Why?" pleaded one of the stars.

"We will not allow you to take over our world," commanded the group's leader, who gave the signal to kill them. "A star will never live amongst us."

As the lives of the stars ebbed away, the remaining ten who'd escaped watched from a distance. Shocked and scared, the survivors knew they couldn't help and eventually decided to delve further into the forest to complete the protection energy spell.

While Maid Ella's eyes welled up at the scene, Reenie turned to Saxthos to indicate Maid Ella had seen enough. Saxthos skilfully reeled the mystical energy back into the Tarot card and disbanded the memory scenes.

"I'm sorry you had to witness that, dear Maid Ella," said Reenie.

But Maid Ella couldn't hear her as she dropped to the floor, sickened by the scenes she'd witnessed. Her star ancestors had lived in fear, Maid Ella concluded. They'd been subjected to terrible ordeals, and the worst thing was that Queen Anya hadn't fought to include stars in Wayan society. It was far easier for the queen to keep the secret and live in cowardice. As anger engulfed her at the injustice of the situation, she asked herself why she should hide from who she was.

"Maid Ella... are you okay?" queried Reenie, concerned.

"I just need some fresh air." But, before she was about to leave, Reenie placed a hand on her shoulder and squeezed it tight.

"Please, don't take long, dear Maid Ella. Remember, Queen Anya and your father expect your memory to be wiped before morning, and you need to make the decision fast," said Reenie, her face desperate.

Maid Ella met the eyes of the necromancer. She nodded, quickly exited the room and tiptoed briskly down the lonely hallway through Castle Wayan, until she arrived at the courtyard. As grand and imposing torches were lit under the night's sky, she looked up wonderfully at the array of stars and felt a deep longing to meet them. She realised the snow had settled and wished for the cooling sensation of the flakes on her cheeks again.

Collating her thoughts, she knew that having her memories wiped wasn't ideal. But a small part of her had wondered whether it could cure her restlessness and help her find peace. However, the terrible events she'd witnessed in Wayan's past enraged her, and she was too involved to throw away everything she'd learnt that night.

As she continued to inspect the stars, she felt compelled to join forces with Reenie and Saxthos, but how would it all fall into place? Lost in thought, she hadn't noticed her sister standing under the entranceway that led into the castle. Calm, steady and with an air of giddiness, Lady Helena's mood was far from being upset since Maid Ella last saw her.

"Reenie told me where you were," said Lady Helena.

"Necromancer Reenie?" replied Maid Ella, confused.

"Yes. I bumped into her. She told me where to find you."

"Er..."

"I haven't seen you all evening. Have you been here the entire time? Let's get you inside. Our father asked the kitchen staff to be on standby for you, so there'll be food before you head to bed," said Lady Helena, her tone a little whimsical.

The cheeriness and elevation coming from Lady Helena is unusual, Maid Ella thought. Then Reenie appeared next to Lady Helena and smiled innocently.

"Ahhh, you found her," said Reenie. "I'm so glad."

"Yes, thank you," replied Lady Helena. "I was getting a little concerned. But everything is all right now. Everything is fixed."

Following her sister and Reenie inside, Maid Ella's face scrunched up in anger. *She used the word 'fixed'*, she thought. So, Lady Helena must have known the memory-loss spell would happen that night. The loving feelings she once had for her sister began to dwindle and were replaced with hate.

As they reached the banqueting hall, the kitchen staff entered the space with various dishes for Maid Ella, Lady Helena and Reenie to feast on. The group ate and exchanged light pleasantries into the early hours, when Lady Helena finally decided to call it a night and departed, leaving Maid Ella and Reenie alone.

Their faces were expressionless as they stared at each other across the dining table in silence, not to give anything away to anyone or anything on the outside. Then as neither one spoke, Maid Ella eventually gave a subtle nod at Reenie, who instantly reciprocated. They raised their colourful amethyst goblets, filled with honey-sweetened wine, high in the air and gave a silent toast, for they knew their journey together had only just begun.

"Cheers, Maid Ella," said Reenie, with a smirk.

"Cheers," replied Maid Ella, determined and eager to get to work.

Once all the wine was drunk and the food had been cleared, Maid Ella shook Reenie's hand before they retired to their separate living quarters. In her room, Maid Ella slumped back onto her bed. Legs and arms stretched out, she looked up at the ceiling and attempted to focus on the delicate-sized illuminating crystal chandelier to help centre her mind from the amount of wine she had drunk. Then came a deep sigh of contentment. That day, she knew, was the first day of the rest of her life.

As Maid Ella was consumed with happiness at claiming her life back, two floors up, Reenie was on an even higher plane of euphoria. She entered her room, cheerfully closed the door behind her and rocked from side to side with child-like excitement. *For this night*, she thought, *has been a complete success.*

From the spell she'd purposely cast on her balcony to ignite Maid Ella's star energy to the lie she told her about Queen Anya and Gill plotting to wipe her memory, it had been flawless. How she'd kept her cool was wondrous, for she'd practised her act on Saxthos many times before to get it just right.

But above all, Reenie had successfully instilled enough memory-loss magic, conjured by Saxthos, into the nightcap drinks. So, by the morning, Queen Anya, King Peter, Gill, and Princess Maria would not recall the events after Maid Ella's star powers were awakened.

Lady Helena, however, had already fallen victim. And with a pinch of happiness and elevation magic thrown into the memory-loss mix, Reenie thought it would help fuel Maid Ella's anger even more. She would believe everyone around her was glad her memories were wiped.

Reenie gingerly picked up a dazzling quartz decanter. She quickly poured the contents of the smooth, crisp liquid into an empty pair of wine goblets but couldn't wait for Saxthos. She needed to give a toast to herself first. Holding the goblet high in the air, Reenie took a gentle, satisfying sip and revelled in the night.

A delicate portal emerged at the far corner of the room. Reenie looked in admiration as her lover, Saxthos, crossed into her living quarters and breezed across the room to join her. They clinked their glasses with glee and looked at each other lovingly.

"Well done, my beautiful Reenie," expressed Saxthos.

"And well done to you. Your fake Tarot card was brilliant. Those scenes from Wayans past were expert trickery. Maid Ella gobbled it all up," replied Reenie.

"Thank you," said Saxthos cheerily. "It's about time the inferior Wayans are taught a painful lesson."

Chapter Twenty-Two

A Rapa Named Denk

The look in his sister's eyes was something else, Andrew reflected as he knelt over the small, curved balcony. The rage was terrifying, the complete opposite of Amy's gentle nature. Welling up, Andrew looked out at the beauty of Wayan's mountains, rivers and forests to centre himself.

He had to stay strong for Amy. She would be waking up soon. But he remembered being back inside the High Council chamber for a split second. Her body lay motionless in the centre and there was no sign of life. Andrew thought he'd lost her inside the amethyst plane. He was sure Star Maya had won.

Overcome with nausea, the morning rays of Wayan's sun began to pierce the top of his head, and he didn't know what to do or think next. As he became engrossed in imagining the worst possible scenarios, Amy called out from inside her bedchamber.

Turning his back on the outside world, he trod carefully into the tight-spaced room where Amy's bed dominated the centre. Wary as to whether Star Maya still controlled his sister, he was hesitant to approach. When Amy saw his distress, she slumped back into her pillow, riddled with shame.

Seeing the look on her face, he snapped out of it. He wasn't helping the situation. Kneeling on the bed, he took the lead and wrapped his arms around his younger sister and squeezed tight. In seconds, Amy burst into tears and clung to him.

In silence, save for the crying, he waited until she eventually looked up at him and asked a question she'd dreaded asking.

"Is Ben okay?"

"He's safe. He returned to Earth…"

"Are you sure?"

"Yes, he's fine. And you're safe now," he said, hoping to soothe her.

"But what if I'm not?" asked Amy with new-found assertiveness. "A portal could open out of thin air, just like what happened at Euston station?"

"That's highly unlikely here. For one, Wayan has their defences up, so it's not the same. Also, I'm with you."

"You're just as defenceless, even more so without a Tarot deck of your own."

"Woah! Only momentarily! I'll have one soon."

"But how long could that take?"

"As quickly as I can, you know that. Also, you're not an expert at your cards just yet."

"I have some experience. All I'm saying is we need to think of a backup plan for you, just in case you're unsuccessful."

"It will be fine," replied Andrew, trying to stay optimistic, but she still didn't look convinced. "Are you okay?" he asked. "All this negativity you're generating, it's not you."

"I'm just trying to be realistic."

"Again, that's not like you. The determined, creative, whimsical Amy would be marching out the door ahead of me, ready to take on the world."

"That was before I had to defeat a star to reclaim my body. You can't blame me for becoming a little more cautious."

As the last word left her lips, Amy fell hauntingly quiet, while Andrew couldn't believe the woman in front of him was his sister. Staring at each other awkwardly, a sharp knock on the door broke the tension.

Lady Helena breezed in, calm and composed as she shut the door behind her. Looking with fondness at Andrew and then at Amy, she gestured for them to remain quiet before they could speak.

Raising her arms in the air, the leader of the Land of Pentacles masterfully willed, from her Tarot deck, protection energy that shot out and consumed the room with dazzling light. Once satisfied, she nodded in approval and instructed the energy to retreat into her cards.

"Okay, we are safe to talk now," said Lady Helena.

"What was that?" asked Amy.

"It's called protection energy. It prevents anyone from listening to our conversation, even those who might wish to conduct a Tarot reading."

"What will they see, now?" asked Andrew.

"A cluster of dark, greyish clouds. I am here because times are growing desperate, and I need to talk to you both first before anyone else."

"Yes, of course," said Andrew.

Longing to complete his final task, Andrew waited, but his mouth dropped when Lady Helena instructed him to tell Amy about his childhood memories.

"Your childhood memories?" asked Amy.

"Er…" Andrew stumbled.

"Come on, Andrew. You need to hurry," said Lady Helena.

"Sorry. There's no easy way to say this…" said Andrew.

"I know, Andrew," said Amy.

"Wait?" replied Andrew, bewildered.

"On Naxthos, Queen Lillian awakened some of my childhood memories," explained Amy. "But I heard a revelation from inside the amethyst plane."

"Keep going," encouraged Lady Helena.

"Queen Lillian spoke to herself briefly," said Amy. "A star called Star Lisa has controlled Queen Lillian's body all this time."

"Amy, are you sure?" said Lady Helena.

"Yes. It trapped her inside an amethyst crystal. Before Star Lisa took back control, Lillian called out to me. She told me she loves us and we're from Naxthos."

"She's not the villain of Naxthos," said Andrew.

In the background, Lady Helena's mind was confuddled with worry and paranoia, for a star had tricked everyone into believing Queen Lillian was a tyrant, and no one had known. Or maybe someone had? What if someone else knew since the very beginning? Who could she trust now that Queen Maria was missing and King Marco hadn't returned?

As Lady Helena's mind spiralled, she knew she needed to consult her Tarot cards for guidance, but at Castle Wayan, she needed to be careful. There were too many opportunistic moments for eyes, ears, and Tarot readings to spy on her. So, what would her next move be?

"Amy, are you okay?" asked Andrew delicately.

"Yes," replied Amy, as she tried to fight back the tears.

"I don't think you are. You are putting on a brave face, but you must be feeling something?"

"What do you want me to say? I'm trying to come to terms with our lives in Aberaeron. You didn't care much for our town or our way of life, but I fought for it."

"I loved our childhood too, Amy."

"No, you didn't. You couldn't wait to leave."

"Woah! Where's all this come from?"

"This has eaten away at me for a long time, ever since you left home."

"You can't blame me for wanting to live my own life! I was allowed to leave."

"It wasn't about you getting your own life, Andrew. It was your attitude to it. Watching your pressure to make it in the big city was painful."

"I'm sorry I 'made' you watch. I was the one living it daily." As his last comment came from nowhere, he wondered if his true sense of self had finally reached the surface.

"Yes, you were. And you wanted everyone else to aspire to it. But I was happy where I was, and nothing was wrong with it."

"Maybe we should continue the argument elsewhere," advised Lady Helena. As Andrew and Amy paused for breath and looked at each other scathingly, Andrew realised Lady Helena's odd choice of words.

"Sorry," panted Andrew, and with one final glare at Amy, he focused all his attention on Lady Helena. "Somewhere else?"

"Yes, within the Land of Pentacles. My home. You can start work on your final challenge. But I will meet you there."

"Wait? Where will you be?" asked Andrew.

"Here, for now, but hopefully I can join you eventually."

"Why can't you come with us?" queried Amy.

"It's a little more difficult just to walk away, especially now," replied Lady Helena, slightly annoyed.

"Why? What is it you're not telling us?" asked Andrew.

"Nothing of importance."

"Why do I feel like–" said Andrew.

A sharp knock on the door interrupted them. Rather than wait for the presence on the other side to disappear, Lady Helena begrudgingly approached the large elm door. Slowly and carefully, she opened it and on the other side, standing hesitantly in the hallway, was her younger sister, Maid Ella.

"Hello, Lady Helena," she said, addressing her sister with the highest respect. "Sorry for the intrusion, but King Marco has returned, and he's injured. The High Council need you immediately."

"Yes, of course."

Turning to face Andrew and Amy, the leader of the Land of Pentacles saw Amy's agitated demeanour, and a wave of suspicion consumed her.

"Everything okay, Amy?"

"Yes, sorry."

"Are you sure?" Lady Helena encouraged her. "You can tell us."

"It's fine. You need to go."

But Amy was far from okay, for sparks of forest-green energy had shot out of her Tarot deck from under her duvet, and they were going stir-crazy. Working together, they conjured an image of Maid Ella's pentacle tattoos inside her mind. The tattoos glowed burnt orange as they released an unusual amount of power, and Amy sensed it was star energy. The vision was gone, and Amy looked a little disorientated.

"I'm sorry, but I must go now. The High Council need me," said Lady Helena.

"Why did they ask for you? Specifically?" pressed Andrew, still sure she hadn't told them everything.

"I am Queen Maria's cousin, so I am expected to stand in until she returns," she answered nonchalantly.

As waves of shock and admiration swept across the faces of Andrew and Amy, Maid Ella slithered into the hallway. Lady Helena followed her and closed the door behind them, leaving Andrew and Amy alone.

"She will tell them about Star Lisa?" said Amy.

"Of course, Amy," Andrew reassured her. "We just need to sit tight."

But, like Amy, Andrew was frustrated at being told to wait, and as he tried to keep his emotions in check, he wasn't ready for what Amy said next.

"There's something not quite right about Maid Ella. I felt star energy coming from her."

Stood in silence, unable to process a new problem, Amy sensed her brother was getting overwhelmed.

"I'm sorry," he said, finally. "I just need some fresh air." As the words left his lips, he hurried onto the balcony, took a deep breath, closed his eyes and tilted his head up. The warming sensation from the sun's rays struck his face, and as he began to calm down, he thought about escaping. Could they take a boat to the south-easterly side of the mainland and dock at the Land of Pentacles? Eyes glinting with hope, Andrew hatched a plan.

"Andrew!" called Amy from inside his living quarters, but he could not answer. "Andrew!" continued Amy. Eventually, he managed to tear himself away from the balcony. But, once inside, the scene before him threw his plans and shifted his focus entirely.

Within the centre of the room was an excitable, tiny, fluffy-winged rapa with baby-like mannerisms. He tripped over his legs and fell face-first onto the floor. Unfazed, the young rapa quickly picked himself up while Amy, out of bed and keeping her distance from the creature, grew anxious. Finally, the rapa gave her a playful smile as he knelt and, with sheer joy in his heart, kicked hard off the floor and began to charge towards her.

Skilfully dodging the little rapa's charge, Amy tried to calm him down while Andrew watched them both with amusement.

"Amy, what happened? What did you do?"

"I didn't do anything," panted Amy, still trying to dodge the creature. "He just appeared."

"Did you see or hear a portal?"

"No, there was nothing."

"I wonder if anyone knows he's missing?"

"Well, we can't know for sure right now, but Denk doesn't seem concerned, though."

"Denk?! Who is Denk?"

"The creature in front of us," replied Amy.

"He's called a rapa."

"Is that what he's called?"

"How do you know his name?"

"It says on his nametag," replied Amy, who pointed at the nametag made of solid gold around his neck.

"That looks like solid gold! He must belong to someone with money. So why has he suddenly appeared in this room?"

As Denk paused mid-charge to inspect his surroundings, he saw Andrew and instantly became buoyant, for he thought Andrew was about to play with him next.

"I think it's your turn." Amy chuckled. As Denk charged at Andrew, Amy's eyes were drawn to the top left-hand corner of his nametag, for it had begun to glow a wondrous yellow. His entire nametag was consumed in the same energy. "Er, Andrew, his nametag is glowing."

Andrew looked, and Denk took the opportunity to bulldoze into him, knocking him back onto the floor. The cheeky little rapa pounced on him and licked his face while Amy wistfully knelt beside them and took the opportunity to inspect the nametag. As she turned it around to see what was on the other side, she saw a mishmash of words appear and engrave themselves into the metal.

"How odd."

"To be fair, Amy, everything has been odd up until now."

They inspected the five words dotted around the nametag: 'pent, open, top, protect, close'.

"A weird choice of words," said Andrew, but Amy noticed each word lit up in a particular order.

"Did you see that? So, there's a three-second break before it starts back around at 'open'?" said Amy.

Then, as Andrew understood what Amy meant, he said the words aloud. "Open…"

"Wait!" said Amy.

"Why? It's worth a shot."

"We need to sit tight, Andrew, and wait for Lady Helena."

"But what if Denk was sent here by Lady Helena? He's here for a reason. I mean, the answer is staring right at us!"

"I still feel we should wait."

"What you mean to say is you should wait? Is there something you're holding back from?"

"It's just…" started Amy awkwardly. "What if I should stay here? Especially as Lady Helena is about to tell the High Council about Queen Lillian."

"But that's for Lady Helena to sort, Amy," said Andrew with suspicion. "Do you feel the challenge I have to complete will waste your time? Is that it?"

"I…er… it's just… what if my star energy can help? I feel I should stay if I can be of some use."

"But what if everything is in hand already, and you're just confining yourself to these four walls for no reason? Don't you want to see what's out there?" Before Amy could stop him, Andrew said aloud, "Open, protect, pent, top, close," and as soon as the last word left his lips, a sudden wave of protection energy in the shape of a pentacle burst out from Denk's nametag. Severely disturbed by the spectacle, Denk retreated and pushed hard against Amy's knees.

"Andrew!" shouted Amy, but it was too late.

The energy created a dazzling portal within the centre of the room, and Andrew didn't waste any time. He grabbed a dishevelled backpack off the floor, scooped a scared Denk into his arms, and carried the tiny rapa across the room to the portal.

"I'm going, Amy," he declared. "Are you coming?"

But Amy wouldn't budge, and he turned his back on his sister and crossed through the portal. Tears formed as Amy lost sight of him, but she knew, deep down, that whatever was on the other side wasn't meant for her. It belonged to Andrew.

Chapter Twenty-Three

The Reward

Andrew didn't look back at Amy in case he had a change of heart. He kept telling himself it was for the best. Of course, it was. What else was he meant to do? Just ignore what was right in front of him? Amy didn't want to join him. Simple as that.

As he arrived on the portal's other side, he congratulated himself for taking the lead. But then why, deep down, did he feel like the worst brother in the world for leaving his only sister? The reality of his actions accelerated towards him like an oncoming bus, and *bang!* What had he done? Where was Amy? Had she followed them through?

He saw the portal vanish, and Amy was nowhere to be seen. Shrouded in darkness, he held on to a terrified Denk as he wondered where the sunshine had gone.

A gust of wind whipped around him, and shots of cold tingles travelled down his spine. Then, as he stepped forward, the ground under him started to move. He instinctively reached for something to hold on to and wrapped his left hand around a wooden handrail. As he tried to steady himself, he swore he'd heard the faint noise of running water below.

"Are you okay, Denk?" he asked delicately, for the little rapa had started shaking uncontrollably in his arms. The gold nametag Denk still wore around his neck began to glow, illuminating the space in front of them.

Andrew followed the light, and from what he could make out, there seemed to be the faint outline of a forest. As he turned Denk's nametag downwards, the light revealed the surface of a rickety, ageing suspension bridge. Through a gap in one of the planks, he swore he'd seen the faint glimmer of an eclectic mix of colours within the water under them. Maybe it was the fish he'd seen when he first arrived on Wayan?

Denk wrestled with himself, out of control, and Andrew couldn't keep hold of him for much longer.

"Denk? What's happening?"

Shocked and bewildered, Denk started to make his way across the suspension bridge.

"Denk! Where are you going?"

The tiny rapa was dragged forward, and finally Andrew realised the nametag had a mind of its own.

"It's okay, Denk. I'll follow you; I promise."

Denk turned his head to look at Andrew, and with no choice, the tiny rapa was propelled forward along the suspension bridge, kicking and screaming. His dark panther paws made contact with the muddy ground, but with no time to recover, the nametag dragged him into the elm-covered forest.

"Hold on! I'm coming!" called Andrew as he struggled to keep up. He inhaled a quick swig of air as he fought a stitch. Ahead was a clearing out of the elm trees and into a wide-open space.

In front, Andrew saw Denk rooted to the spot on a patch of grass, and he let out a massive sigh of relief as he hunched over and clutched his stomach. Taking deep breaths, his heart rate slowed. The weight from the backpack felt like a tonne of bricks as he slowly approached the tiny rapa.

"Denk? Are you okay?" he asked delicately as he knelt before him.

The scared rapa managed to raise his head slowly and met Andrew's eyes. Consumed with fear, Denk was on the verge of tears as Andrew opened out his arms for him to fall into them. Grateful for a hug, Denk pressed the right side of his face against Andrew's chest, but through blurred vision, the other side noticed something peculiar ahead.

Unable to settle, the tiny rapa resisted Andrew's hug and gestured for them to inspect what he'd just seen. As Andrew turned to face a possible danger, he looked up in wonder at a two-storey cabin nestled within the centre of the woods.

"Wow!" he said as his eyes followed the short flight of steps that led up from the grass onto the front deck.

There was no sign of life inside the cabin, not a single light or movement, so Andrew decided to circle the structure. There was nothing else around, just them and the cabin surrounded by the elm forest.

"Sorry, Denk, but I think we are meant to go inside," said Andrew, eager to bound up the steps while Denk pretended he hadn't heard. "Come on, we need to," continued Andrew, travelling up the stairs onto the crystal decking. But before he approached the arch-shaped door, he momentarily turned his back. *It is undeniably peaceful*, he thought, *the view of the luscious elm trees from the deck, even if there is a slight air of creepiness about the whole situation.* But a wave of intrigue washed over him as he realised there was no star or form of light in the night sky.

"Okay, Denk? Are you ready?" he asked, snapping out of his trance.

Denk was far from ready and hadn't moved from the grass at the bottom of the steps. Andrew looked down at him, but the tiny rapa averted his eyes. Trying the handle on the front door, it wouldn't open.

"Right, okay, let's try again," he said, determined.

The door refused to open, and Andrew tried pressing his body against it, but with no luck. He continued to try while Denk started whining in the background. The whining got louder, and Andrew grew frustrated when he heard it more prominently.

"Okay, Denk, you don't have to come inside. I haven't even been able to get in yet."

Denk's whining turned to a wail, which made Andrew grow even more frustrated.

"Denk?! Come on, what's wrong?" he called, but Denk carried on, and Andrew couldn't take it anymore. Andrew spun around. The gold nametag around Denk's neck was glowing. Then, before Denk could back away, Andrew bounded down the steps and inspected the set of words that had appeared, engraved into the metal. Even though it had been the same process at Castle Wayan, where they glowed in a particular order, he noticed these words were completely different.

"Okay," he said, "let's give this a try… Unlock, enter, Aaron, task, reward."

The last word he read sent butterflies around his stomach as he felt close to meeting his Tarot cards. However, the euphoria quickly took a back seat as he heard a creaking sound behind. The front door started slowly opening, so he picked Denk up before the tiny rapa could escape and hurried back up the steps.

Through fear the front door would close on them, he bolted inside and as soon as he placed Denk down on the old, rickety wooden floor, the door closed abruptly behind them. A faint light ignited in the far-right corner of the space. It slowly grew, and he saw a delicate flame from a bulky, pentacle-shaped candle on top of a floor-length stand. Three more candles lit up the other corners of the room, and Andrew noticed the musty yellow wax looked untouched and fresh.

Looking around the wide-open space in wonder, he saw a mishmash of labourer's tools, including chisels, hammers and mallets, hung from crystal hooks along the walls. He saw two decaying wooden benches in the centre of the room, while in the far-left corner was a wooden spiral staircase.

Where should I start? Andrew thought. *Also, is anyone even in the cabin?* As he stepped forward, careful and calculated, he inspected the worker's tools around the room, and when he finally reached the workbenches, some peculiar objects rested on them.

Hunched over the first bench, ready to inspect, Andrew realised he still had his backpack on, so he decided to remove it and let it rest on the floor close to him. Meanwhile, Denk had joined him, much calmer than before.

Both of them settled. Andrew looked upon the first bench and saw, piled high and spread across the entire surface, an array of chunky circular wooden blocks made from elm. Compared with the other table, these blocks had little space, while the second workbench housed only a singular block.

Andrew scanned the singular block meticulously. On one side, a fully formed carving in the shape of a pentacle dominated the space, but as he turned the block over to inspect the other side, he was further intrigued by the situation he'd walked into. Whoever had carved into the block had abruptly left the pentacle shape on the other side half-finished. It was crystal clear. The line that travelled horizontally, away from the upwards-facing triangle, had ended.

"I don't think that was part of the plan," said Andrew. "It looks like they might have been forced to stop carving."

Volatile flames shot out of all four candles and struck the half-finished block in his hands. Shaking, he let go and retreated under the workbench, out of the firing line.

"Woah, what's happening?!" he yelled.

The candles continued to fire, but nothing happened to the woodblock. The flames strengthened in frustration and fired an energy blast. Silence.

"Okay, let's move, Denk," said Andrew, hurrying towards the spiral staircase, out of the way.

When a begrudging Denk joined him, they travelled up to the first floor, where the warmth from the wall candles filled Andrew with a brief moment of comfort.

A door was slightly ajar at the other end of the hallway, and he sprinted towards it with nowhere else to turn. The candles started to flicker with an air of mischief. "Need to keep going, need to reach the other end. Come on, you're nearly there," said Andrew.

When he finally reached the door, he was about to push it open, but the candles had other plans. Their energy conjured a wall of flames in front of Andrew, blocking him.

"Wait!" he shouted. His insides filled with anger at the thought of being thwarted. But before he released a tirade of abuse, the candles focused their light upon an array of oil paintings littered across the hallway walls.

Andrew wondered whether they had been there the entire time. Either way, it was apparent the candles wanted him to inspect the paintings first before he was allowed to discover what was on the other side of the door.

"Okay, what are we meant to find, Denk?" he asked, trying to keep calm.

He heard a slight moan from the spiral staircase. "Okay, let's get him," Andrew muttered under his breath. As he tilted his head down, he saw the tiny rapa curled up on one of the steps, desperate to avoid eye contact.

"Right, no more messing, Denk," Andrew encouraged him, picking up the tiny rapa and cradling him in his arms. "We'll do this together, nice and slow."

The first painting Andrew and Denk stood in front of was of the cabin, at night-time, surrounded by snow, with the figure of a woman in the centre, wrapped up warm. She held on to one of the wooden blocks in her hands. A fully engraved pentacle was on the front of it. He also noticed her expression – the woman's eyes beamed with pride as she held up the block.

"It's like it's her pride and joy," he whispered. He inspected the rest of the painting and noticed it had a peculiar border. Eight pentacles, cocooned within their respective circle, were spread evenly around the outer edges. He noticed the same border on the adjacent painting. As he slowly made his way down the hallway, he noticed a pattern: each piece of art featured the cabin, set against a night-time backdrop, with no stars or any other form of light, and on the outer edges was the same border. The only slight variation he detected was the change in seasons. Some paintings showed the leaves from the trees falling to indicate the start of autumn, and others had buds growing to symbolise spring. Another difference was the figure. Each individual never appeared in another painting. They had different clothes and ages, but their pride united them as they held up their wooden block.

Lost within the determined eyes of the woman in front of him, he hadn't noticed the wall of flames evaporate. But Denk had. The tiny rapa saw the door open further and wriggled nervously in Andrew's arms.

"Everything okay?" asked Andrew, placing him delicately on the floor.

Denk nervously indicated towards what he'd just observed, and Andrew loyally followed. "Okay, candles, please behave now," he said aloud as he reached the door and entered the space.

He was taken aback by the stale and uninviting room, littered with old books and beaten, decaying furniture. The smell of must sharply overpowered him. It felt neglected, which wasn't surprising, and also inhabitable, but a sharp wheezing sound alerted him to a presence.

Through an archway that led to another room, he saw a man, similar in age to him, alone in bed, with a tatty blanket strewn over him. Eyes closed, the man looked gaunt as he struggled with his breathing. As Andrew tiptoed closer, the man suddenly opened his eyes, clutched his chest, and tried to control his breathing.

"Is there anything I can do?" Andrew asked.

The man looked up at Andrew with a mixture of fear and wonder, and as he closed his eyes, he managed to control his distress.

"No." answered the man. "Unfortunately, there's nothing you can do for me, Andrew."

"How do you know my name? Are you sure there isn't anything I can do?"

"No, Andrew. But I have something for you from Lady Helena," he coughed. From under his blanket, he removed a piece of rolled-up parchment tied delicately with orange silk and gestured for Andrew to take it.

"Here," said the man.

"When did Lady Helena give you this?"

"When you first arrived on Wayan. It explains what you need to do to claim your Tarot cards."

Desperate, Andrew quickly accepted the parchment with gratitude and began to read while the man coughed again.

"Dear Andrew,

You have arrived at the House of Eight, and your task is simple.

Young Aaron, unfortunately, is coming to the end of his natural life. He is the last remaining member of the Iticus clan, whose ancestors have resided in this house for over three hundred years.

They were proud workers who'd isolated themselves from the rest of Wayan through fear of distraction. Their duty was to engrave pentacle shapes onto the blank circular wooden blocks you've no doubt already found.

Their magic inside the blocks inspires and encourages those to reach their fullest potential. And our motto has always been, 'You work hard, and you will get your reward'.

Now, young Aaron is about to die, and we did everything we could to save him. But the Iticus clan have always been recluses, so it is a shame it came to this. While we figure out which family will take over, you will be entrusted to run this house in the meantime. The blocks you complete will be transported to homes throughout the Lands of Wayan in desperate need of encouragement.

I know you can do this, Andrew, so please remember, when times are tough, 'You work hard, and you will get your reward'.

Love,
Lady Helena"

As he reread her words, he was about to ask Aaron where he should start but paused. Looking down upon the last remaining member of the Iticus clan, he saw Aaron's eyes were closed, finally at peace. *What had driven him to do everything on his own?* Andrew wondered. *Without any help?*

A gentle glow appeared upon the parchment before he was about to figure out his next move. At the bottom, under Lady Helena's signature, was a set of words.

"PS, please look after Denk."

He rolled up the parchment, popped it in his back pocket, and encouraged Denk to nestle in his arms. Once the tiny rapa mustered enough strength to accept his hug, he was carried away from Aaron, now consumed in mystical energy. Denk and Andrew took one final look while standing under the archway and witnessed Aaron disappear.

Once downstairs, Andrew rested Denk upon a pillow he'd acquired, and as the tiny rapa settled on the floor, Andrew explored the array of tools hung from the walls. Where should he start first? Well, a chisel was always handy, but the problem was there were about twenty of them. Was there even any difference? With no other choice, he selected one and decided to go from there. En route to the workbench, he picked up a hammer, too, for extra power. Who knew how tough the elm was?

Standing in front of the second workbench, he decided it would be a good start to complete the half-finished block first. Hovering over the edge of the line, he had his chisel ready. With his right hand, he lightly tapped the top of it with the hammer. But as soon as the hammer made contact with the chisel, both instruments wriggled out of his hands, flew across the room and hit the front door.

Not giving up, he picked the tools up from the floor and tried again, but the same thing happened, and for about an hour, he made no progress.

He tried a different chisel and a different hammer, but the instruments flew out of his hand, away from the workbench. Was it the tools or the block that was the issue?

He placed a blank wooded block next to the half-finished one and attempted to chisel it, but the tools did the same thing. This time, they flew away from him with even greater speed. So, what was he going to do?

"What do you want from me?" he asked, distressed. "I'll do anything! Please, just to get me started! What is it you want me to do?"

Silence, and even more silence. He stood over the workbench alone and frustrated. Was he meant to keep trying? As he was about to pick up a different chisel, he heard Denk shuffle.

"It's okay, Denk. You rest; I've got this."

But Denk rose from his pillow, determined, and made his way over to Andrew, for since his train of thought had come back to life, he had an idea. The tiny rapa gestured for Andrew to follow him up the spiral staircase, where he needed to show him something.

With nothing else to try, Andrew decided to follow him, and when they reached the hallway that contained the paintings, Denk stood rooted to the spot in front of one of them. Andrew scanned the painting and realised there was no figure, but as he waited, a picture of Aaron, who held a wooden block in his hands, appeared in front of the cabin.

Andrew inspected the scene and saw Aaron had worn a belt with a chisel and a hammer hung from it. The tools were slightly different, Andrew noticed. They had a delicate engraving of an unusual flower etched into them. The tools may be the ones that would work, and the blocks would accept.

With haste, he made his way down the hallway into Aaron's living space, but after searching everywhere, he still hadn't found the tools. He tried to think where they could be. Those tools were Aaron's bloodline; they meant everything to him, and he would have wanted them close to him to the very end. Andrew looked in the direction of Aaron's bed. The blanket hadn't disappeared.

He pulled back the top right-hand corner of the blanket and found a delicate chisel and a hammer with the same flower engraved into the metal. His eyes looked hopeful as he picked up Aaron's tools, and when he returned to the workbench, he executed the first blow on the half-finished block. The tools stayed in his hands.

Pumped with adrenaline, Andrew tried again, and when it worked a second time, he cheered aloud, making Denk jump.

As he set to work, Andrew picked up the pace until he eventually completed the block in less than four hours. Stepping away from his craftsmanship, he felt elevated as he looked down upon the completed pentacle. The candles came to life, and he ducked just in time before they struck the block, which disappeared.

"It's gone!" he called out, excited.

He grabbed one of the blank blocks of wood and placed it delicately upon the second workbench. Scanning the picture of the pentacle shape he'd drawn earlier on the parchment from Lady Helena, he used it to guide him into the night. As he worked, with no sign of light outside, or sense of time, he had no idea if he was working quickly, slowly or just right. All he knew was that it felt like hours, and he had only completed three blocks, with thirty left.

Without realising, he'd worked flat out for four days straight until he'd cleared the first workbench. But before he celebrated, a new set of blank blocks appeared. With no other choice, the work continued for a further two weeks, with Andrew fixated on his task until the blocks stopped appearing.

He desperately hoped this was it. He stood silently for a whole day and patiently waited for his next task. A fantastical ball of forest-green light appeared in the cabin's centre. It whipped mystical energy up into a frenzy and Andrew looked up in wonder. His Tarot deck appeared out of the ball and flew into his hands. His whole body was consumed in the same mystical energy, and as tears formed, he started to embrace his connection with the cards.

Once the ball of energy subsided and disappeared, he was euphoric. He thought of Denk and wanted to celebrate his victory with the tiny rapa who'd helped him. "Denk?" called Andrew, as he scanned the room, desperate to find him. "Denk! I've done it! But not without your help. It was a team effort!"

But Denk was nowhere to be seen, and Andrew started to worry. Where was he? He searched the cabin.

He burst through the entranceway and ran out onto the deck. "Denk!" he shouted in the direction of the forest.

But before he made his way down the steps, a Tarot card whipped out of his hands. Levitating, the card showed him an image of a figure consumed in stars against the night sky. Andrew looked at it with wonder, then felt a little dizzy. His body felt strange. Without knowing, the card had started to awaken his ability to draw energy from the stars.

Knelt on the floor, he looked at the sky, and for a moment, before he passed out on the crystal decking, thought he'd seen a cluster of stars draw closer, their light growing ever stronger.

Chapter Twenty-Four

Crossing Over

Stood alone, surrounded by Wayan's elm trees that dazzled against the pitch-black backdrop, Andrew sensed he was unconscious. *The energy,* he thought, *feels different,* for his mind was active, but his body had succumbed to an invisible resistance.

A cluster of stars drew his attention. He wasn't unnerved; rather, a strange sense of comfort ignited and then radiated into his soul. Maybe he'd started to connect with his star heritage?

Whatever the outcome, all he could do at that moment was soak in the wondrous stars as they continued their journey towards him. They seemed more like an emblem of hope, not hate, for a beautiful and magical sight. Not all stars were like Star Lisa, surely? Suddenly, the stars disappeared, as did the elm trees surrounding him.

Eyes opened, awake and groggy, Andrew looked at the ceiling inside the cabin. How did he end up back there? He turned on his side and used the palms of his hands to steady himself. As he stood up, his head throbbed, and he was desperate for water. He pushed the urge away as he scrambled to find his Tarot cards. He searched the pockets of his tunic first. Empty, and so were his trouser pockets.

His eyes scanned the room and he saw them nestled on the second workbench within the centre, the same area he'd spent the last two weeks carving pentacle shapes into the wooden blocks for the inhabitants of Wayan.

He made his way across the cabin and picked up the innocent-looking Tarot deck with relief as he fought back the tears. It had been a long time coming, and the thought of losing his cards so soon had filled him with dread. Calming down, Andrew remembered Denk. Where had the tiny rapa gone? He'd just vanished. The cabin was explored top to bottom, but Andrew had fallen unconscious just before he'd had the opportunity to explore outside. "Let's try again," Andrew muttered. But before he even attempted to open the front door, a sudden knock from the other side rooted him to the spot with fear.

Who was it? And what if they meant him harm? He was worried; he hadn't had a chance to connect with his Tarot cards and learn how to conjure his powers. He would lose in an instant. There was no other choice but to find a way to escape and buy some time. Another knock broke his attempt to hatch a plan.

Silence. The knocks ceased as sweat poured down Andrew's forehead from the build-up of worry and paranoia. The waiting game felt like a long-term jail sentence, but his Tarot cards, thankfully, took the lead and broke him free. They came to life and circled him with a confident force. Then an image appeared in his mind.

"The past, moments ago," calmly reassured the Tarot cards inside his head. "It's okay, you are safe," as they showed him a cluster of dazzling stars that edged closer and closer away from the night's sky. Eventually, two stars left the rest behind as they drew nearer to him. But before he could ask out loud who the stars were, the Tarot cards wiped the image from his mind.

Back in the cabin, the front door opened quickly and two men, who looked like they were in their early forties, stepped inside cautiously. Their sudden appearance astounded them as much as Andrew, and even though they had the same bodily features as him, Andrew knew they were not human, or Wayan, but stars. Their energy was uncanny – the same as he'd felt in the night's sky when unconscious.

"You called us?" said the star on the left, with an air of giddiness, as he spotted Andrew's Tarot cards.

"Er… I don't think I did," he answered, confused.

"Calo wasn't talking about you," said the other star, straight to the point. "Your Tarot cards called us and invited us into this place."

"Finally, we have been allowed to step inside the infamous House of Eight," said Calo, warmer and more understanding.

While the two stars were about to continue, a whirlwind of possibilities encroached on Andrew's mind as he looked at the figures before him. But before he could speak, Calo instantly cut him off and told him that he and his brother, Saco, were stars born on Wayan.

"The Iticus family, and families before them, never allowed light or other beings within this part of Wayan," explained Calo. "Instead, they kept to themselves through fear of distraction. So, we have watched this place from afar and longed to be a part of it."

"Maybe that's why we have been drawn to you?" added Saco. "Our desire to help."

As soon as the words left Saco's lips, Andrew's body felt a rush of excitement. He didn't know how or why, but his gut instinct told him they were genuine.

"We have always loved Wayan just as much as the inhabitants who live upon it," started Saco, "and if we can engrave the pentacle shapes upon the wooden blocks, it would be a great honour."

"We promise you. We are not like Star Lisa or any other star that wishes harm. We are different," said Calo.

"What do you know about Star Lisa?" asked Andrew.

"Star Lisa is toxic, hateful. Just like the Mystic who created it," answered Calo, with an air of hostility.

"The Mystic?" queried Andrew, with a jolt of adrenaline, as he felt he'd landed upon something fundamental.

"I must correct you, Andrew. It was 'A Mystic'," answered Calo, determined to keep the other Mystic's integrity alive. "There has never been one singular entity; rather, a group of higher beings responsible for giving birth to stars. But their influence plays a big part, and unfortunately, Star Lisa's creator wasn't ideal."

"It believed it was superior to all life forms on every Tarot world in existence," explained Saco, stuttering a little through fear, which caused Calo to cut in to help.

"Star Lisa won't rest," said Calo. "It needs to exert dominance, just like its maker."

"Well, it's controlling my mother's body," replied Andrew, his desperation growing, "and I need to help save her."

Calo and Saco looked at each other, a fleeting moment of concern, for they knew Queen Lillian would most likely die if she didn't give everything she had. But then a curious idea came across Calo, its worried eyes shifted to hope, and before Saco could intervene, the star began to pace around the cabin.

"I don't think this is wise, Calo," pressed Saco, while Andrew wondered why the star had started to inspect the array of labourer's tools on the wall.

"Calo, stop!" shouted Saco. "We can't intervene. It's not right."

"We can't just wait it out, brother, not this time," replied Calo, fixating on the task at hand until its eyes finally widened with glee at the sight of an old, beaten leather flask. "So, this is it!" Calo called out. Andrew wondered what was so significant about it, and the star replied, "You'll see."

Calo stood in the centre of the cabin and looked into Saco's eyes, not backing down. Eventually, its brother begrudgingly joined the star, knowing it had lost the fight. Their eyes closed as Calo unscrewed the top, and with immense force, mystical star energy shot out of their bodies and circled the room. The power concentrated down and formed a liquid in the flask. Once filled to the top, Calo screwed the lid tight and handed the flask to Andrew.

"You'll need to return to the castle with this," explained Calo. "Inside is our star energy, and it should help you to unravel Star Lisa's history."

"Star Lisa's history?"

"Yes, it may help Wayan for the fight to come," answered Calo delicately.

"And that's all you're getting," said Saco, desperate for the conversation to be over. "That's everything from us."

Before Andrew could thank Calo, his Tarot cards came to life with a new-found optimism due to the gift he'd just received. They flew swiftly into the air, circled Andrew, much to his wonderment, conjured forest-green energy, and generated a mystical portal inside the cabin.

"That's the signal, Andrew. You need to go," said Calo.

But Andrew hesitated, for he hadn't heard anything from Lady Helena about his next set of instructions. A small part of him worried he'd been too naive at accepting Calo and Saco so quickly, but what helped ground Andrew, at that moment, was his Tarot cards. They'd intended for him to cross, and Andrew needed to trust them.

"Okay," he replied, giving both stars a look of gratitude. "Thank you."

He held the flask tightly with one hand as he picked up his worn backpack. Behind him, Saco watched Calo with unease.

"Wait, Andrew!" called out Calo just as Andrew was about to step through the portal.

"Yes?" he replied, eager to obtain anything else useful before he departed.

"You need to find Paga first, before you seek anything else."

"Paga?"

"No, Calo!" interrupted Saco, who was ready to beat down its brother.

"Yes, Paga."

"What is it?"

"It's a world where stars used to be born," continued Calo, "and now it's abandoned. Star Lisa's homeworld."

Andrew paused. The force of the revelation nearly knocked him backwards. But before he could ask for more information, the portal started to close, and he had no choice but to leave them behind in the cabin. As he stepped into a murky backdrop, vision obscured, he instantly felt, in his hands, the Tarot deck that looked after him and the flask that contained the star energy. They were still there. "Check," Andrew muttered to himself. He inhaled deep. Where in the world was he?

An instant chill struck the uncovered parts of his skin, and as shivers travelled down his spine, he heard the sound of water droplets in the distance. They made contact with the stone floor quickly, and natural light started to flood down through the gap in the ceiling. The cavern lit up just in time to stop him from making assumptions about where he was, for he knew, clearly, he'd arrived inside the portal room underneath Castle Wayan.

He'd made it back in one piece. His Tarot cards had brought him back, and now, he hoped, the flask would be of some use. But in his absence, he wondered what important events he'd missed and whether he was too late to help. He heard footsteps in the distance. Their pace quickened, and two figures came into view out of the shadows. Even though Andrew had been well accustomed to their company, he was still taken aback by their appearance.

On the left was Lady Helena, eyes devoid of energy and her demeanour dishevelled. Had stepping into Queen

Maria's shoes taken its toll? Were things going from bad to worse? Even though Lady Helena's presence shocked him, it was the sight next to her that bewildered Andrew even more. His sister, Amy, looked almost unrecognisable. Her face, neck, and arms were covered in deep cuts and bruised swelling.

"Amy!" said Andrew, ready to explode with rage. "You were attacked?"

"Andrew, please," said Amy. "It's not what you think."

"How obvious can it be?" he said, not backing down.

"I haven't been attacked. I've been training."

"Training?"

"For the invasion on Naxthos," continued Amy, her face suddenly hardened with an echo of combat experience.

"We are going to war with Naxthos?" he asked, instinctively knowing it was a bad idea.

"It appears the High Council and the leaders from the Lands of Swords, Wands and Cups believe this is the only way," answered Lady Helena, a little sombre.

"We have tried to look at alternatives," added Amy.

"But time is running out, and Wayan needs to feel like it's doing something," said Lady Helena.

"What about Queen Maria and Uncle Marco?" he asked, dreading the answer.

"Queen Maria is still missing," said Lady Helena, "and your Uncle Marco... well, he's resting." Lady Helena paused, choosing her words wisely, so as not to upset Andrew even more. "And while he rests, his loyal comrades are working to retrieve the rogue stars that escaped from Naxthos's prison."

Lady Helena noticed the flask in Andrew's hand as it started to glow and dazzle. "Star energy?" she eventually whispered, trying not to sound unnerved at the prospect of a new problem.

"Yes," said Andrew, detecting her hesitation.

Recalling the scene with Calo and Saco in the House of Eight, he tried everything to reassure Lady Helena and Amy.

"I promise you; they were genuine. I'm certain this vial will show us Star Lisa's background. It can help us learn more and be better prepared."

But Amy was unconvinced.

"Give me the best reason you have as to why we should trust Calo and Saco?" asked Lady Helena, calm and collected.

"My Tarot cards invited them into the House of Eight," pleaded Andrew, "and they held off conjuring a portal back until I was given this flask."

"I don't like this," said Amy. "Lady Helena, please."

Lady Helena fell silent, deep in thought, and before she was given a chance to make a decision, Andrew simultaneously made up his mind for the three of them. No amount of reassuring words were ever going to make them feel at ease. He had no other choice but to act.

He unscrewed the lid, and as the star liquid shot out Amy lunged at him, but she was too late. The dazzling energy levitated, circled the group, and with a fizz, pop and then a bang, exploded and conjured a magnificent phantasmal orb within the centre.

"What have you done, Andrew?" exploded Amy as she reached for her Tarot deck. But just as her cards ignited and manipulated forest-green energy, Andrew's cards came to life too.

"Wait!" called Lady Helena, transfixed on the orb. "Both of you stand down." She looked upon the orb, took in its aura, and relaxed. *It feels pure*, she thought. After recent events, all conspiracy theories and trust issues began to melt away, and she needed every ounce of good intent.

"Calo and Saco said it would show us Star Lisa's history?" asked Lady Helena, with a hint of eagerness and new-found energy in her voice.

"Yes," begged Andrew, as he blocked out Amy's presence, "but Calo said we need to find Paga before we do anything else."

"Paga?" queried Lady Helena, making it clear she had never heard the name before. It ignited her intrigue and sense of adventure.

"A now abandoned world where stars used to be born," answered Andrew. "Star Lisa's homeworld."

A rush of hope travelled through Lady Helena's body, and a strong shot of adrenaline awakened her free spirit as she looked at Andrew with fondness. She nodded, stepped towards the orb, and looked closer, concentrating on the word 'Paga'. "Okay, let's give it a go," she said coolly. "Please show us Paga."

The orb conjured and whipped up three strands of energy in a flash. Each one scooped Lady Helena, Andrew and Amy from their positions and transported them inside the phantasmal matter.

It is all going to be worth it, Andrew thought, even though the sudden trip inside the orb made him ill. On the verge of throwing up, he knelt to catch his breath. Thankfully, he couldn't see the rage in his sister's eyes. Still wanting to have a go at him, Amy knew she needed to keep herself restrained until they were out of Lady Helena's company. With both siblings unsettled by their sudden departure, but for entirely different reasons, Lady Helena was surprisingly calm as she inspected their surroundings.

The group stood on a worn, shaggy carpet within the centre of an unkempt, oblong-shaped room. Medieval in aesthetics, the furniture was riddled with cobwebs and grime, while high shelves made of amethyst crystal housed an array of dust-covered books in varying shapes, sizes and colours. Lady Helena deduced they were in an abandoned library. When she craned her neck, she noticed a rusty door behind them. At the front was a foreboding tapestry hung over a cold, derelict stone fireplace.

The item that intrigued Lady Helena the most was the tapestry, and as she made her way over to the fireplace, the faint light from outside struggled to come in through the mucky, cracked, floor-length windows. Thankfully, there was just enough light for her to inspect the tapestry and read the words: 'Paga's First Order of Mystics'.

The words piqued Andrew and Amy's interest, and when they reunited with Lady Helena at the front, Andrew read over the words again.

"Calo said they were the group responsible for giving birth to stars," explained Andrew, "until they abandoned this place."

As Lady Helena and Amy soaked in his words, the light from outside suddenly diminished, and the group would have been thrust into darkness if it hadn't been for the orb. Instead, the phantasmal matter conjured a delicate ball of light in front of the tapestry, much to Lady Helena's relief, for she was about to decipher a set of symbols stitched on the outer edges. But the ball had other plans, for it drew the light away from the fireplace and flew confidently across the library.

With no other choice but to follow the light, Amy reached the ball first and cast her eyes over the array of books with unusual titles on the spines. *Let's select one at random*, she thought. *What's the worst that could happen?* If things go sour, she could always blame Andrew.

Amy picked up a magenta, leather-bound book with ashen-edged pages. She read 'Star 567: Pod 4. Creator: Mystic 7' engraved on the cover and spine. As she read the first page, she instantly became hooked. "How peculiar," said Amy.

"What have you found?" asked Lady Helena.

"It appears to be a handwritten log. The opening reads, 'I can confirm and approve the birth of Star 567....'"

While Lady Helena and Andrew listened to Amy, the ball of light moved up one shelf and six books along until it eventually paused and levitated in front of a deep violet, leather-bound book. Andrew removed it from the shelf, opened it delicately, and started to read. "I can confirm and approve the birth of Star Lisa. Pod: Not disclosed. Creator: Not disclosed."

Andrew's eyes widened as he realised the book he held in his hands was Star Lisa's birth log. As he continued to read, he became confused. "'And approve the final stage of metamorphosis and the unbreakable bond'. Unbreakable bond?" he whispered.

But before he had the chance to react, Lady Helena cast her eye over what he discovered and found it strange the author hadn't declared which pod Star Lisa had been born in and which Mystic was responsible. The author wanted those details hidden, she concluded.

"Amy!" called Lady Helena. "Does yours mention the 'unbreakable bond'?"

"Er, yes, mine does," she answered, quickly skimming back over the pages she'd read. "The unbreakable bond is to do with the pod the star was born in. They are forever connected. It is for birth and also for death."

"For death?" Lady Helena articulated as she met Andrew's eyes. Lady Helena was hopeful. If they destroyed the pod, there was a strong chance Star Lisa would die. If this happened, there would be no need to wage war on Naxthos and Wayan would avoid unnecessary bloodshed. Her eyes welled at the prospect, but she was interrupted before calling a meeting. The ball of light flew towards the front door, with Andrew and Lady Helena pursuing. Within seconds, Amy joined them.

"I'm guessing that's important?" asked Amy, who saw the book in Lady Helena's hands.

"It sure is," she replied, fighting back tears. "It's Star Lisa's birth records."

Amy looked at Andrew with sincerity as she began to realise going there was the right thing to do, and while she knew he deserved an apology, there was no time for that. The ball had grown and become more volatile until, eventually, Lady Helena decided to release the latch. In a flash, the ball propelled forward along a cold, barren hallway and arrived at the entrance to a monumental pair of amethyst doors.

With haste, Andrew was the first to arrive and pushed hard against the cool amethyst crystal, but surprisingly, the doors swung back with ease as Lady Helena and Amy joined him on either side. Inside, the oval-shaped space was jaw-dropping. A high ceiling, as far as the eye could see, housed rows of amethyst crystal cots on top of grandiose shelves made of marble. Large, bulky stepladders made each floor accessible as the group gazed in wonder at the sheer volume of pods.

Lady Helena looked up at the empty pods and thought about her mum and their star ancestors on Wayan. Not once had they mentioned originating from pods like these.

"Calo said Star Lisa's creator wasn't ideal. It had a toxic and negative influence. Maybe the first order abandoned this place because of that Mystic?" queried Andrew.

"And sparks theories as to why we couldn't find the details inside Star Lisa's records," said Lady Helena, her mind now back in the room with a clear head.

"What details?" asked Amy.

"The pod number and Mystic information are missing," answered Andrew.

Amy digested their words as she looked up at the sheer volume of pods with numbers inscribed on the front. It could take a while if they had to check each one individually. But what other choice did they have? Suddenly, Amy thought she'd seen a faint glimmer of purple energy and waited.

"Amy?" said Andrew.

"Did you see that?" she asked.

The faint glimmer reappeared, and she spotted a pod on the fourth floor, slightly smaller than the rest. Even though it could have been a trick of the eye, she needed to pursue it. But before she set off on her mission, Lady Helena gave her Star Lisa's record book and told her to be careful.

As she climbed the imposing ladder with the book, Amy paused at the fourth floor, pushed her weight off the ladder, and landed on the edge of the hard marble floor. Bent over the first pod, she saw it had a number inscribed, '456', but there was no glimmer. Working along, she reached the one pod that looked slightly smaller and saw someone or something had scratched out the number. On a whim, she opened the book, and in a flash, profound violet energy came off the pages, circled the pod, and brought it to life.

"I think this is Star Lisa's pod!" she called down.

"Careful, Amy!" called Lady Helena. "I'm still unsure whether the orb conjured a duplicate Paga for us to explore or whether all of this is real."

The pod began to shake violently. Intuitively, Amy closed the book, breaking the connection. The energy vanished, and Star Lisa's pod fell silent again, much to Amy's relief. Her complacency was short-lived when Andrew called up from below.

"Amy, hurry back!" he shouted. "Bring the book!"

With haste, Amy scrambled down the ladder and saw the orb had reappeared in front of Lady Helena and Andrew. It conjured three strands of energy, and while one of the strands swept the leader of the Land of Pentacles up instantly, Andrew dodged the other two strands. Just as Amy jumped off the last step and hit the ground hard, Andrew gripped her tight as both of them were transported inside the orb.

On the other side, Lady Helena was relieved at the sight of their safe return. "Well done," she said. "Don't worry about the book."

"What do you mean?" said a confused Amy. Looking down at her hands, she realised the book had vanished.

"I swore I had it," she said.

"It's okay. I'm sure we can remember the contents together," said Lady Helena.

"Yes. The unbreakable bond is the pod the star was born in. They are forever connected. It is for birth and also for death," reiterated Andrew.

"And Star Lisa is connected to that pod," said Amy.

"So, what if a group went to Paga and destroyed it?" queried Andrew.

"My only concern is Queen Lillian. I don't know if she would survive," answered Lady Helena with caution.

"Then we weaken the pod somehow?" added Amy.

"Exactly," replied Lady Helena. "Draw Star Lisa out of hiding. If the star shows, we can disband the amethyst plane inside the crystal. This will help Queen Lillian to fight back."

Andrew and Amy nodded, and as the group became hopeful, Lady Helena wondered if her tiny rapa, Denk, was safe. After he left Andrew within the House of Eight, she gave the little rapa his next mission: find Evie on Earth and bring her home.

Chapter Twenty-Five

Ettaler Forest

Powerful upward air currents carried water vapour into the evening sky. They generated an array of dark cumulonimbus clouds above Ettaler Forest, a remote wilderness area in the Upper Bavarian district of Garmisch-Partenkirchen. Heavy rain escaped from the turbulent clouds and descended upon a dozen tiled gable roofs well-equipped to drain high rainwater levels. Rarely flooded, the small two-storey farmhouses, known as Waldlerhaus, had protected and housed Erika's Tarot clan, Etta, for over one hundred years, and that night was no different.

Inside one of the farmhouses, an unconscious Lucy Jenkins rested upon a rustic rectangular oak table in the centre of the living room. Congregated around her, Evie, Ben, Erika and her great-grandmother Lina, stood silent, unable to move. Their energy was at rock bottom amid worry Lucy wouldn't make it if their plan didn't work. Eventually, Evie couldn't take it anymore. Desperate for breathing space, she made an excuse to leave the group and bound up the wooden staircase to the second floor, out of sight on the landing.

In just under an hour, she would come face to face with Susan Jenkins and her eldest son, James. They'd landed at Munich International that morning, rented a car, and began their journey to his location, when they touched base with Ben on the phone. Soon enough, Susan and James would see what happened to Lucy on Lixus, and Evie wasn't prepared for that. It had been her responsibility to protect Lucy, and she failed. Evie wondered how she was going to look Susan in the eyes.

Head spinning with guilt, she hurried down the hall towards the bathroom, locked the door behind her and slumped to the floor, exhausted. Overwhelmed by the sight of Lucy's throat being slashed by a Lixusian guard, the image frequently replayed inside her mind. The viciousness of the act had emotionally taken its toll, and every time she looked down at her hands and clothes, she saw them soaked in Lucy's blood.

Remembering the moment she'd carried Lucy through the portal, Ben and a necromancer were the first on the scene to greet them in the inner courtyard of Castle Wayan. Ben dropped to the floor and scooped Lucy up in his arms while Evie took a step back and allowed the necromancer to inspect the wound across her neck. From his Tarot cards, he conjured energy to stabilise the damage, but even though the necromancer tried various healing spells, Lucy didn't wake up.

"Is there anything you can do?!" said Evie.

"I've kept it contained, but the severity of the wound is great. The magic did quite a lot of damage," explained the necromancer.

"Please!" begged Evie, as she looked down at Ben in hysterics holding on to his baby sister. "Even if it's a long shot, we need to try."

"I think a blood-healing spell might be the only way," said the necromancer. "And for that to happen, she would need to be reunited with her mother on Earth."

"Wait!" said Ben, as he held tight to Lucy. "My mother has no idea any of this even exists. They need help, guidance," Ben trailed off, and suddenly he knew where they needed to go.

"Erika's clan in Germany," said Ben. "We need to meet there. They are the most experienced and the best hope we have."

The necromancer contemplated his words and nodded, while Evie was torn between going with Ben or going back for Queen Maria. But the necromancer sensed Evie's distress and decided to take the lead.

"I will gather a team to bring your mother back," encouraged the necromancer. "Evie, you're not alone."

Those words, "You're not alone," Evie remembered as she sat upon cold, hard tiles in an unfamiliar bathroom on Earth. How foolish had she been to believe him? He was only trying to make her feel better. Now, in the present, for the first time in her life, Evie had never felt so alone.

Outside the nightmare, the rain continued to pour down heavier, and lightning shots jolted Evie out of her spiral. Desperate for something familiar, now she was back in the room. She removed her Tarot deck from her tunic and buried her face in them. On the verge of tears, a tap on the door diverted her attention, and as the tapping continued, she managed to pull herself up and see who was on the other side.

"Are you okay?" asked Erika, her bright blue eyes consumed with concern at Evie's shaken body.

"I don't know," admitted Evie, voice low, as she held tight to her Tarot cards.

"I know you need some breathing space, but you would be cross at me if I didn't tell you Susan and James have just pulled up in their car outside."

"Just pulled up?" she queried, confused by the passage of time.

"Yes," replied Erika, in a gentle tone. "You have been gone for a while, and I decided to come and get you."

Erika's mouth radiated a smile at a delicate Evie, who knew she needed to get a grip now that Ben's mother and brother had arrived. Under their feet, they heard the latch to the stable door open, and as footsteps entered the rickety hallway from the cobbled rain protected path, a high-pitched voice with an undertone of anger called out for Ben.

That must be Susan, Evie and Erika thought, as they locked eyes with each other. Their camaraderie formed. Both women made their way downstairs, peered through the doorframe and watched the new arrivals in the living room. Within the centre, Susan was submerged in tears as she hugged Lucy's unconscious body, while James kept his arm around Ben for support. Eventually, Susan released her grip, and noticed sparkles of white energy hovering over Lucy's wound.

"Why is it doing that?" she stuttered, starting to wonder what was in the realm of the possible.

"It's to contain the wound, Mum," said Ben.

Eyes swollen and chest tight from the trauma of seeing Lucy, Susan looked up at Ben and James. "Has anyone heard from Cassie?" she asked, growing worried.

"She's not answering any of our messages," stuttered Ben as James kept hold of him.

As the Jenkins family were falling apart, Evie wondered what her mother, Queen Maria, would have done in that situation. 'Be brave' were the first words that came to mind. Her mother would have pretended to be brave for the sake of others. At that moment, Evie knew she needed to suck in the worry and step up.

"We have a way to save Lucy, Lady Susan Jenkins," started Evie, who stepped into the living space with an air of reassurance. "There is a strong chance it will work. Our necromancer from Wayan assured me."

"Wayan?" said Susan, confused.

"It is a Tarot world, Mum," said Ben. "It's real. Tarot is real."

"Oh my," said Susan, her despair now turned to shame. The innocent world of Tarot she'd started to take an interest in was merely the tip of the danger, and she'd unknowingly encouraged her children to be a part of it.

As the realisation hit Susan, Evie needed to push forward quickly, for everyone's sake. "We need to save Lucy," she interrupted. "I was given instructions to heal her, but I'm going to need all of your help."

"Yes, of course," answered James, determined to keep his family together. As Evie waited patiently for Susan and Ben to respond, they finally nodded.

Across the room, Erika joined her great-grandmother, Lina, behind their altar – a four-legged table with a white robe draped over the top, forged one hundred years ago. It was the centre of their clan's energy and Lina's pride and joy. Now the room had settled, Evie made her way to the front of the altar, where a collection of objects, prepared in advance for Susan and James's arrival, rested upon it. From left to right were a cup, a sword, a pentacle-engraved coin, a wand, and a couple of unopened Tarot decks.

"Before we start," said Evie, "does anyone need a Tarot deck?"

Susan and Ben raised their cards and showed Evie they didn't require one, while Evie handed an unopened deck to James.

"Everyone in this room will need to close their eyes and take deep breaths," started Evie. "Slowly shuffle your cards face down and clear your minds." But as Evie spoke, she looked down on Lucy's body and thought that was easier said than done. "You need to accept the cards. Your desire to connect with them must grow stronger," continued Evie, who hadn't noticed Erika shuffle uncomfortably behind the altar, for since the cauldron on Naxthos disbanded the energy from her original cards, Erika still found it difficult at times to embrace her new Tarot deck.

"Once your breathing is calm and steady, you can stop shuffling," instructed Evie, who was the first to stop, closely followed by Lina. Eventually James stopped, then Ben and Erika. The last person was Susan, still trying to suppress the worries she harboured for her children.

Satisfied by the group's first task, Evie moved swiftly on and said delicately, "Objects combine." Evie's cards glowed a reddish pink, as did the pentacle coin she picked up and held tight. Next, Lina's cards shone a dazzling, spiritual white, as did the altar. James picked up the sword, raised it high, and his cards came to life while he admired the Germanic craftsmanship. At the same time, Ben's cards gravitated towards the cup. The last object was the wand that belonged to Erika, and Susan was left with nothing.

"Is there something wrong?" said Susan.

"No, Lady Susan," Evie reassured her. "This is good."

"Evie, wait," said Erika. "How come everyone's Tarot energy is white, and yours is a reddish pink?"

Before Evie answered, Lina stepped in. "I think it's because we are from Earth, little Erika. We have harnessed a basic spiritual connection. Thus, our unique colours haven't manifested yet."

Evie nodded and continued the spell. "Everyone, please form a circle around Lucy. Lady Susan, you need to stand behind Lucy's head."

When Susan reached her position, Evie asked her to close her eyes, shuffle her cards, and focus on healing Lucy through sheer willpower. "When you have formed the connection, Lady Susan," Evie said, "you will need to stop shuffling and reveal to everyone the card on top of your deck."

Susan nodded. Her daughter's life was in her hands now, and Ben and James needed her. Nothing else mattered but her children.

Eyes closed, she shuffled her cards and focused on a steady rhythm. Briefly she thought she'd heard the cards whisper words of encouragement inside her mind. While outside, Evie and Erika watched each other nervously, for they knew which card Susan needed for the blood-healing spell to work.

With new-found confidence, Susan paused and revealed to the group the Magician card. It showed a man standing in front of an altar with tools representing all four suits: cups, wands, swords, and pentacles.

"Is this good?" asked Susan, a little unnerved by the silence.

"Yes, Lady Susan," replied Evie who, along with Erika, sighed with relief, "that's the card you needed. It will unite the energy from the objects we possess and strengthen our desire to heal. You will repeat the word 'restore' out loud while the rest of us focus on the words, 'heal Lucy.'"

The group nodded. Susan took a deep breath and called out, "Restore." Each Tarot deck glowed wondrously and brought to life the object that belonged to its respective owner. The altar, cup, pentacle-engraved coin, sword, and wand levitated, and the Magician card held by Susan drew energy away from them.

Overwhelmed, she lost concentration when the card directed the energy into her body. It was unlike anything she'd seen or felt before. The group saw the look of terror in her eyes, and the energy retreated out of her body and evaporated.

Ben and James tended to their mother to ensure she was okay, while Evie, Erika and Lina waited patiently for Susan to recover. What felt like centuries, in reality, was only ten minutes.

Susan was ready to try again. "Restore," Susan called as she stood behind Lucy. "Brace yourself," she muttered to herself, anticipating the onslaught of mystical energy that was about to enter her body.

The Tarot decks brought each object back to life while the Magician card directed their energy into Susan's body. This time, she managed to contain her fear as the energy infiltrated every part of her being. She concentrated hard on bringing Lucy back to consciousness.

The group looked at the spectacle with hope as the blood-healing spell was now in full swing. Still holding the card, Susan had successfully stepped into her role as the vessel, so why would it fail? But after two hours of endless attempts, Lucy still hadn't woken up.

Knees weak, Susan dropped to the floor, exhausted. It was too much as blood appeared in her eyes. The power was on another level. But what other choice did she have? A break, Evie suggested a break, but Susan refused.

"Lady Susan, I do think we…" began Evie.

"No!" shouted Susan. "Everyone, back to their positions!"

The tension in the room rose to new heights. Even though the group continued trying, they were no closer to saving Lucy.

"Why isn't it working?" screamed Susan. "Are we not trying hard enough?"

"Mum, please," said James as he attempted to wrap his arm around her but was pushed away.

"Is it the instructions?" said Susan. "Were they wrong? Or is it because we are on Earth?"

"I… er…" Evie stumbled, but Erika quickly jumped in and took the pressure off.

"The necromancers on Wayan were not able to heal Lucy. The spell is the same wherever we are."

"Then why is it not working? How am I meant to heal her if I am powerless?" said Susan.

"Mum, we can try again," Ben said, encouraging her.

"It's only day one," added James. "We've achieved so much already. So, let's call it a night and try again in the morning. We all need the rest."

Susan couldn't wait till morning. She was not abandoning Lucy. Her Tarot cards, however, had other plans. They came to life, withdrew energy from Susan and made her fall to the floor unconscious. In her mind, all she could see was red as she fought to wake up, but the cards pushed back harder until, eventually, Susan had no more energy left to give.

On the outside, Ben and James scooped their mother off the floor and followed Erika to a spare bedroom next to the farmhouse kitchen. Entering, the brothers spotted the single bed and gently laid their mother on the mattress, while Erika brought a duvet to protect Susan from the cold.

"I'm sorry I didn't stop her," said Evie as she appeared at the doorframe.

"It's okay," James reassured her, "we're used to it."

"We sure are," added Ben, as he sat upon a low stool and used the cold flannel Erika gave him to wipe the blood off Susan's face. "At least the bleeding from her eyes has stopped. So that's a positive."

Even though James and Ben intended to make Evie feel better, it hadn't worked. Instead, she wondered whether Susan was right, and she'd misunderstood the necromancer's instructions. Or was it the objects from Earth? Evie held the pentacle-engraved coin in her hand

and considered whether they were just not powerful enough. But the necromancer promised that wouldn't be an issue. As a dozen more reasons rattled around inside Evie's mind, she was still no closer to an answer.

"If you need time to gather your thoughts," said James, encouraging Evie, having picked up on her concern, "then feel free to go. Honestly, we can take care of Mum."

Evie was about to resist, but Ben swooped in and told her they had everything under control. Battle lost, Evie left the bedroom. Bounding down the hallway, she glanced at Lucy's body in the living room. Frustrated the blood-healing spell hadn't worked, she needed to escape into some fresh air.

Evie opened the latch to the stable front door and ran outside into the torrential downpour. She needed to feel something other than guilt; a shock to the system that would reawaken her back to the once confident Evie. The version who'd mentored Andrew when he first arrived on Wayan. Where had she gone?

Knelt upon the muddy forest floor, she glanced wildly at the farmhouses surrounding her. Some had lights on, while others were shrouded in darkness. Would they see her about to lose it? She didn't care. Evie looked up at the pitch-black sky, and as the rain hit her face, she located from the pit of her lungs all the anger and frustration.

Evie released a piercing scream into the air, overpowering the thunder from the lightning strikes, and as she continued, members of the Etta clan heard the commotion. Some peered through the windows while others, including Lina and Erika, opened their front doors to inspect the source. From their roof-protected porches, the residents watched Evie with unease, and before Erika could shut the door behind her, James and Ben stepped outside to join them.

Concerned looks swept across the entire community, and before Erika could intervene to help Evie, Lina stopped her. "It's okay, little Erika. She needs to be alone," said Lina, with warmth in her tone.

"But what if she's out of control? Who knows what powers she could unleash," said Erika.

"I promise you, the first sign of danger, and I will stop her," replied Lina, confident in her abilities. "Let's just watch and see."

Stood in silence, Erika, Lina, James and Ben watched Evie anxiously and hoped, for her sake, she would feel better soon. But all Evie could do was hold on to the pentacle-engraved coin as she continued to scream. Finally, the strength she thought she'd once lost started to awaken, and her Tarot cards responded. They came to life with tremendous reddish pink energy, flew out of her tunic and circled above Evie.

The cards were working together to build a connection with the Earth-made coin. It wouldn't be an easy process, but that didn't stop them from trying. Finally, they managed to feed off Evie's strength and sent electrical currents into the coin. "The coin is the issue, Evie," said the cards inside her mind.

"Are you sure?" whispered Evie as tears formed.

"Don't worry," encouraged her cards.

The Tarot deck flew higher and higher into the sky, out of sight, and as Evie looked up, all eyes around the community searched above too. After an eternity, the silence broke, and Evie felt her cards stir. Incredible reddish pink energy illuminated the sky and merged with the lightning. Then a single card lowered itself for everyone to see.

"What's the card?" asked James, sensing its importance.

"It's…" started Erika, vision blurred by the rain.

Evie said aloud with new-found excitement, "It's the eight of pentacles!"

"Is that good?" called James.

"Yes! It's The House of Eight," called back Evie.

"Is that better?" James whispered to the group, even more confused.

A fantastical portal opened within the centre of Erika's community. The Etta clan looked on in amazement, for they'd never seen a gateway to another Tarot world before. As Evie approached the portal, a frightened creature appeared. With the head and body of a panther and the wings of a raven, Evie was astonished at the sight of the tiny rapa, whose yellow eyes looked distraught from the sudden change in location. Sensing its distress, she tried to calm the rapa, but it was too frazzled. The tiny creature sprinted away from her, and before it escaped behind one of the farmhouses, she spotted the satchel on its back.

"Are you okay?" called Erika, running to Evie's side, with James and Ben not too far behind.

"Yes," said Evie, still in shock. "That was a rapa, a creature we have back home in Wayan. It must be here for a reason."

"The rapa looked terrified," added James, who tried to see where it had bolted to.

"Yes, it did. Let me try to approach it on my own. Can the rest of you split up and fall back? In case it decides to run for the forest. Nice and steady now."

As Erika, James and Ben fell back, Evie made her way slowly and delicately around the back of the farmhouse. She was certain someone had sent the rapa to help her, and something important was inside the satchel.

A flash of lightning revealed the tiny rapa's hiding spot in the shadows. Back pressed against the wall, Evie saw its yellow eyes lit with fear.

"It's okay, little one. My name is Evie, from Wayan. I think you were supposed to find me?"

Still caught up in hysteria, the tiny rapa looked away from the volatile weather and flinched. Evie kept encouraging it to relax until, eventually, the scared creature started to take deep breaths. After other words of reassurance, the tiny rapa bounded into her arms, desperate to be held.

"What's your name?" asked Evie, inspecting the nametag around its neck. "Denk. You're called Denk?"

The tiny rapa nodded and gestured for Evie to open the satchel on his back. When she released the drawstring, inside was a mystical wooden block with a pentacle shape carved into the centre. When she touched the object, hope and willpower seeped into her body, giving an energy boost.

"It's from the House of Eight," she whispered, extremely grateful for the gift bestowed upon her.

"Right, little Denk," said Evie, placing the block back inside the satchel, "we are going inside, out of the rain, where we will get you warmed up and fed."

Thankfully, it didn't take long for Denk to feel better. Back inside the farmhouse, Evie dried him off with a towel on the kitchen table while Erika, James and Ben watched in disbelief at the creature they never knew existed.

Finally, fur ruffled and heat restored, Denk was ready for food and Lina delivered; she'd prepared a dish full to the brim with leftover slabs of beef for the tiny rapa to feast on. Licking his lips with satisfaction, Denk was oblivious to the conversation around him as Evie explained the significance of the wooden block to the group.

"So, this block is from your homeworld?" asked James.

"Yes. A being must have made this in the House of Eight," she answered Evie. "Its purpose is to encourage willpower, and in return, you will get your reward."

"And you think we could use this for the blood-healing spell?" added James.

"Yes. I will switch out the coin for this pentacle-engraved block," she said, encouraging the group to take turns holding the object.

After, Erika, James, Ben and Lina each felt a sudden burst of positive energy and started to understand why the object was so unique.

United in their plan, all they needed was for Susan to wake up in the morning well-rested. But when the clock struck 11am, she was still unconscious in bed until, finally, her Tarot cards released their hold at midday and allowed her to wake up, and Susan's eyes opened. A little dizzy, she scanned the room and before she had a chance to speak, James gave her words of reassurance.

"When you are ready, Mum," began James, "we have something else to try and, believe us, it'll help."

James handed the wooden block to Susan, who felt its energy and smiled. She paused, looked up at Evie and apologised for her behaviour.

"I never blamed you, Evie," Susan reassured her. "I promise you, none of this is your fault. So, let's try again."

As the preparations came together, everyone returned to the living room, ready to begin the blood-healing spell. Susan's aura was calmer as she said aloud, "Restore." Again, the objects came to life, including the pentacle-engraved block, but the group felt different this time. The energy was more substantial and the path cleaner, like all the barriers had vanished. As soon as the Magician card directed energy from the objects into Susan's body, she felt awakened.

Everyone was relieved, including Denk, who was by the doorframe waiting patiently. The little rapa knew he and Evie didn't have much time left on Earth. There was no room for goodbyes.

Susan saw Lucy's eyes open, and her neck wound had fully healed.

"Lucy!" cried Susan, rushing to be by her daughter's side.

James and Ben followed suit, while Erika hugged Lina. The group sighed with relief at their victory in saving Lucy, but then a wave of uncertainty circled the room.

"Where's Evie?" said Erika.

The Jenkins family broke away from their hug and saw the space where Evie once stood. The pentacle-carved block from the House of Eight had been left behind on the floor.

"Also, Denk?" added James. "Both of them are missing."

The group cast each other worried glances for, unknown to them, Evie and Denk had already left Earth, soon to be reunited with Lady Helena on Wayan.

Chapter Twenty-Six

Working Together

Evie and Denk shielded their faces from the sun as they stepped out of the portal from Erika's living room onto the dry, grassy mound north-east of Castle Wayan. In front of them was the entrance to an underground burial chamber, one of many spread throughout the land that protected the bodies of the deceased. A long time had passed, Evie remembered, since she'd last visited this particular 'House of the Dead'.

A necromancer reached the end of her life due to a freak accident, and Queen Maria needed Evie's help to bring the deceased body to this protective space. A small group had gathered to pay their respects, including Reenie, who'd learnt and grown under the dead necromancer's wing.

It seemed strange to Evie that Reenie hadn't shown any emotion. She was cold and withdrawn. Maybe Reenie found it difficult to express herself? But the niggling feeling deep inside Evie never subsided. She was suspicious of Reenie. A gut instinct that never let go.

Back in the present, Evie grew fearful. Of all the places Denk brought her to, why did it have to be here? This was not good. Denk may have made a mistake. Evie returned to the entrance and headed down the mound towards the castle.

"Denk!" called Evie, pace quickening. "This way, little one. We're heading inside."

But as Evie reached the first archway into the grounds, she noticed the tiny rapa hadn't joined her. Looking longingly at the castle, Evie finally turned around, and saw Denk hadn't moved. Instead, he just stared at her. Evie tried to encourage him to join her but failed. She stepped forward; he backed away. She tried again, but he retreated further.

"Denk! Please stay where you are. No! Don't run off!"

The tiny rapa bolted inside out of sight, much to her annoyance. A small part of her considered leaving him to it. He was safe now in Wayan, but what about her mother and father? How would they react? The moral compass won. She begrudgingly turned to face the burial chamber and ran towards it. But she hadn't noticed, from afar, that a mystical force had taken control of Denk's nametag and forced him into the 'House of the Dead'.

Evie entered a narrow passageway, where paintings and inscriptions of Wayan's four suits – cups, wands, pentacles and swords – dominated the walls. Further down were a set of stone steps. The images on the walls had changed to Wayan's deceased leaders, with actual quartz crystals surrounding them.

Evie saw Denk sitting in front of two imposing stone doors. The rapa refused to budge, and Evie was no closer to returning to the castle. "Okay, have it your way," Evie said as she pushed open the heavy doors. Upon entering the circular space, Denk looked around at the sheer number of archways leading down into the catacombs on the outer edge. Evie, however, didn't care about the catacombs.

A recently prepared stone tomb on a raised platform drew her attention. Edging nearer, she wondered who had died. When she finally reached the tomb, something inside her felt compelled to push open the lid.

A body was concealed under a velvety, haunting drape, and a dark hole within the pit of Evie's stomach formed. Denk rubbed his body against her leg to comfort her until she eventually mustered the courage to reveal the person's face. She looked down upon her dead father, King Marco. Eyes shut and arms crossed, he looked at peace, save for the knife wound across his midsection.

"This isn't happening!" she said, firm and defiant. "Denk! This is a mistake. A cruel mistake."

But Denk didn't respond. Instead, he kept his head down, avoiding eye contact, as the mystical force controlling his nametag made him subdued. While Evie couldn't keep her eyes away from King Marco's wound, she wondered why no one had attempted the blood-healing spell. Anger building, she needed answers.

"Denk, we need to try and make a portal now, back to the castle. We have to fix this."

Evie's Tarot cards came to life and circled the air. But before they charged reddish pink energy, they quickly disengaged and flew back into her tunic. Caught off guard, Evie wondered what was happening. Before she had the chance to react, the doors to the chamber closed abruptly behind her.

Turning to face Reenie, Evie watched as the necromancer willed energy from her Tarot cards, blocking anyone attempting to leave or enter the room. Bemused by her cold behaviour, Queen Maria's daughter demanded an explanation.

"What's happening?" asked Evie, animosity building in her tone.

"I can explain..." began Reenie, whose cards circled the air, conjuring fantastical energy, ready to strike Evie dead.

"Well, I can only assume," continued Evie, "that by the look on your face and your intention to trap me, you had something to do with my father's wound?"

"Evie..." replied Reenie, voice low.

"What about the blood-healing spell? Did anyone think to try that?"

Ignoring her comments, Reenie focused on keeping to the plan. *Evie is alone and vulnerable*, the necromancer thought. *The perfect opportunity to finish her once and for all.*

"You need to let me go," said Evie, "or my cards will show you the door, literally."

"I doubt that."

Evie sensed something was off. Her Tarot deck felt suppressed. She tried again but still nothing, not even words of encouragement. Wait. Where was Denk? She realised the tiny rapa had been pulled away from her and was now forced to stand behind Reenie. Evie watched the terror wash over Denk's face, for he knew she was in the firing line.

Dodging energy strikes left, right, and centre, Evie took cover behind her father's tomb. The ferocity of the attacks grew worse as Reenie edged closer until, finally, she had the opportunity to kill Evie. But Evie reacted in time and, without hesitation, ran towards one of the archways leading down into the catacombs. She wasn't quick enough, being struck in the back and falling to the floor unconscious.

Ready to finish what she'd started, the walls around them started to shake violently, drawing Reenie's attention away. Whoever attempted to breach the burial chamber had help, and she needed to hurry. But a rumble rocked the space, and the two imposing entrance doors burst open. Out of the passageway, an enraged Lady Helena strode towards Reenie. Her Tarot cards generated fantastical energy, and Lady Helena repeatedly fired at the necromancer, who tried to block the attacks.

"Please! Wait!" called out Reenie, pleading to be heard.

But Lady Helena refused. From behind, her army of necromancers from the Land of Pentacles entered and surrounded Reenie, preparing to trap her with the energy from their cards. Maid Ella, the last person to enter the room, took her position further away from the others.

"Everyone!" commanded Lady Helena. "On the count of three..."

Her loyal comrades raised their arms high, unifying the entrapment spell they were about to inflict. But as soon as Lady Helena called out the number two, Maid Ella reacted. She hit one of the archways instead, claiming it was an accident, but Maid Ella knew she had every intention of creating a diversion, giving Reenie enough time to escape through a portal.

"Focus!" commanded Lady Helena, but they were not quick enough.

The room fell silent. None of the Land of Pentacles necromancers made eye contact with Lady Helena, but Maid Ella had no shame swooping in.

"I'm so sorry," she said, running up to her sister. "I don't know…"

"No," replied Lady Helena, with an air of strictness.

"But…" continued Maid Ella, becoming a little wary.

"I don't want to hear your excuses. You were told on the count of three. That's not an easy mistake to make."

Through all the times she wriggled out of situations, it hadn't worked for Maid Ella this time, so she needed to think of a different approach, fast.

"Again, I'm sorry," she said, forcing tears as she approached the entrance. This pained Lady Helena, who held back but considered calling out her name.

"My Lady," said one of the necromancers, breaking Lady Helena's train of thought, "we are ready."

Snapping out of it, Lady Helena scooped Denk up lovingly in her arms and signalled Evie to be carried through a portal into the infirmary room inside Castle Wayan.

"It's okay, Denk," reassured Lady Helena, "we are going home."

On the other side, the tiny rapa nuzzled into Lady Helena's neck as she watched Evie lying unconscious on one of the recovery beds. Before leaving them alone, her necromancers conjured energy to protect them, while the head of the group was sure Evie would wake up soon. But time was running out.

At that moment, Lady Helena's loyal comrades had gathered inside the portal room as Andrew and Amy worked together to unravel their ability to draw energy away from the stars.

Lady Helena thought maybe she could use the breathing space to her advantage; one last opportunity to conduct a Tarot reading and uncover anything she might have missed. It would need to be quick, though. But before she revealed her cards, she felt a new presence enter the room.

"Calum?" said Lady Helena. "Are you okay? Has something happened to Sylvie?"

Calum's eyes were bloodshot and puffy. He hadn't slept properly since his Auntie Sylvie was attacked on Naxthos.

"Er, no, nothing new," he said. "I thought I'd heard your voice, and I wanted to say hello."

"I see," replied Lady Helena delicately, knowing Calum was trying to keep a brave face. "Thank you for checking in. Unfortunately, Evie is hurt, but she will wake up soon. Please can you watch over her? I'll check on Sylvie."

"Of course," replied Calum, feeling slightly elevated that Lady Helena would place her trust in him.

"Thank you," replied Lady Helena, with sincerity, as she strengthened the protection energy inside the infirmary. She needed to keep them safe. There was no room for error. Once satisfied, she left them and made her way down the hallway, arriving outside Sylvie's private space.

Lady Helena scanned the room to ensure nothing had been tampered with and closed the door securely behind her. As Sylvie lay unconscious in bed, covered in cuts and bruises, Lady Helena removed her Tarot deck.

"What a predicament, dear Sylvie," said a subdued Lady Helena under her breath as she began slowly shuffling her cards. "This is my last chance alone. Let's see what we find."

While Lady Helena was working her magic next door, a nervous Denk lay on the edge of Evie's bed. Shuffling restlessly, the tiny rapa was ready to break down, but Calum was determined to keep their spirits up.

"She will pull through, Denk."

This hadn't worked. Denk started crying and couldn't stop. But the rapa hadn't noticed Evie's foot move. Denk was startled by the sudden motion and turned to face Evie.

Vision distorted and head spinning, Evie felt sick. Her insides churned as she tried to make sense of her surroundings.

"Evie," began Calum. "Hi, I'm Calum. I don't think we've met, but Lady Helena asked me to watch over you."

Unable to function properly, Evie struggled until, finally, she realised they had escaped the burial chamber. Lifting herself and looking around wildly for any sign of Reenie, Denk dived into Evie's arms, desperate for a hug.

"Where is she?" stressed Evie, anger returning and adrenaline pumping. "Do you know she's the enemy?"

"I, er... All I know is we're safe, and Lady Helena asked me to watch over you."

"Do you know where my mother is?" asked Evie, a little more delicate, as she sensed Calum was genuinely afraid.

Before he could attempt to answer, Evie saw Lady Helena enter the infirmary, calm and composed.

"So, whose side are you on?" asked Evie, throwing the bed cover off and reaching for her Tarot cards in case of an attack.

"Hello Evie. I'm on your mother's side. I saved you in time, but Reenie escaped."

"And–" fired Evie, but Lady Helena was too quick to answer.

"We don't know where your mother is yet. But we have a plan to find out, and once we locate her, we will attempt the blood-healing spell on your father."

"From what I saw, it was too late."

"I can assure you, it's never too late to try. But I'm going to be brutally honest. I can't afford to waste any more time. So, either you come with me or stay here out of the way. I can't risk you delaying us."

The strength of Lady Helena's spirit shook Evie, and with no other choice, she nodded. "Are we coming for Queen Lillian?" asked Evie delicately while hugging Denk.

"Yes and no," replied Lady Helena, conjuring a portal in front of Evie, Denk and Calum. "Let's join the others downstairs."

"I'm sorry," said Calum, deeply apologetic, "but I…"

"It's okay," said Lady Helena. "I know you need to stay with Sylvie. It's okay." But before she turned her back on him, she looked down at the tiny rapa and considered for a moment. Denk did everything she'd asked. He now needed to stay and keep himself safe. But the tiny rapa insisted on accompanying Lady Helena and Evie.

"It's okay, Denk," added Evie, supporting Lady Helena's decision. "Your next mission is to watch over Calum and Sylvie. They can't do this without you."

Denk, unconvinced, pretended he'd ignored their commands until Calum helped and encouraged the tiny rapa to stay. After further persuading, Denk huffed a little and begrudgingly gave up, following Calum out of the infirmary into Sylvie's room.

Now alone, Lady Helena squeezed Evie's hand gently, determined to reunite Queen Maria with her daughter one day. "Let's go. We'll do this together," said Lady Helena.

On the other side of the portal, Lady Helena and Evie travelled down a set of stone steps into the portal room, deep underground. Within the vast space of the cavern, groups of individuals were immersed in their tasks, including Andrew and Amy, whom Evie eyed straight away.

"I'm guessing Andrew claimed his cards?" asked Evie, beaming with pride.

"He sure did," replied Lady Helena.

Both women watched as Andrew and Amy faced one another, engrossed in training. Their Tarot cards circled them as they practised working together to draw star energy away from the cards that housed the 'star' symbol. Their confidence grew until, finally, they were successful, as they were now starting to connect with their birth father's powers.

"So, Queen Lillian's children," said Lady Helena, pointing at Andrew and Amy, "they have been practising drawing away star energy. Queen Lillian once thought she could use them as weapons, but we have turned them into Wayan's allies. By the way, it's not Queen Lillian, you know? A star entity called Star Lisa has been controlling her body all this time."

"Sorry, what?" asked Evie, out of the loop on recent events. But before she could repeat her question, Lady Helena walked off. Evie needed to catch up.

"We are going to the star's homeworld, an abandoned planet called Paga, to weaken it. And your auntie will have the opportunity to reclaim back her body."

"And my mother?" asked Evie, confused. "Sorry, where does she fit into all of this?"

"If we save Queen Lillian, she might know your mother's whereabouts," replied Lady Helena, hopeful. "Please follow me."

In a flash, Lady Helena's Tarot cards came to life and made their presence known in the air while she passed her comrades down below. When she reached the far end, with Evie by her side, she turned to face everyone. All eyes were now on her as she stuck to her plan. She would not reveal to anyone what her Tarot cards showed her earlier. Not even Evie, Andrew and Amy would know.

At the front, Commander Merdan, Sir Stephan and Nathaniel waited patiently, as did their soldiers, who lined up behind them. While on the far left, three of Wayan's most esteemed and trusted necromancers stood next to half a dozen necromancers from the Land of Pentacles. Nestled behind them, Lady Helena saw Andrew and Amy standing to attention and gave them a look of pride. But her mood dropped slightly at the sight of Maid Ella, positioned at the back, away from the others.

"Greetings, everyone. First of all, Evie has returned to Wayan safe and well," started Lady Helena, as Evie looked at the familiar faces in the crowd with a beaming smile. Especially Nathaniel.

"But we still need Queen Maria," continued Lady Helena, staying strict. "Our mission to Paga is simple. Draw the star entity called Star Lisa out of hiding and weaken it.

This star has controlled Queen Lillian's body for the last twenty years. It is why rogue stars are out there right now controlling individuals from other Tarot worlds."

She paused, waiting for any sign of resistance, but to her surprise, everyone remained silent and listened intently.

"For now, we need to defeat Star Lisa before we attempt to deal with the mess it made. Andrew, Amy and my necromancers will accompany me to Paga. The rest of you will stay and defend Wayan if Star Lisa attempts to breach our world." Those in the room nodded as she continued. "If we save Queen Lillian, there is a strong chance she will know where Queen Maria is. But I must stress, as soon as I bring down the amethyst plane Queen Lillian is trapped in, it's all on her to defeat Star Lisa."

Lady Helena paused and silently contemplated her next move. Just as she'd successfully united everyone in her plan, was this the right moment to say something a little more controversial? "Before we cross, I need to be completely honest with all of you."

At the back, Maid Ella looked up at her sister, confused. This wasn't the woman she thought she knew, the one with the guts to tell the room not all stars in the night's sky wished them harm.

"Two stars, Calo and Saco, helped us, and I am very grateful," said Lady Helena.

Her heart spontaneously elevated, and Maid Ella felt hopeful. The truth might finally come out.

"They returned to the night's sky and wished us well," continued Lady Helena, trying to keep upbeat, but inside, she was frustrated. They would have been worthy replacements for the House of Eight, but she needed to tread lightly for now.

Just as hope ignites, her sister quickly takes it away. Reenie and Saxthos were right. Wayan and other Tarot worlds would never accept higher beings living amongst them. Accepting things will never change, Maid Ella had never hated her sister so much.

Chapter Twenty-Seven

The Journey

Another day broke, and a dizzying rush of excitement filled the air. The birds nestled on tree branches, singing melodic tunes while the light of dawn eagerly seeped into Queen Lillian's bedchamber through an oval window. It looked like a pleasant start to the day, filled with the prospect of new hopes and dreams, but Queen Lillian's mind and body were not euphoric.

In bed, unable to move, her eyes remained tightly shut. She couldn't afford to lose herself today. She tried to remember none of it was real. Fighting back the tears, she finally mustered the courage to roll onto her back and look at the ceiling.

At a glance, nothing appeared out of the ordinary. The colourfully painted beams, showcasing former leaders of Naxthos, were the same display she'd woken up to every morning since she was a child. But if you paid close attention to one of the tastefully decorated Tarot cards nestled within the centre of the picture, you would see a slight change in appearance. Eyes tense, Queen Lillian waited, and finally, she saw a faint flicker of purple, mystical fog. That could mean only one thing: the amethyst forcefield was still active.

Trapped in the same four walls for the last twenty years, it had undoubtedly taken its toll. A painstakingly slow ordeal, Queen Lillian heard, on rare occasions, Star Lisa conspiring on the outside with various individuals. Finally, they'd managed to infiltrate and manipulate the citizens of Naxthos, but their quest to find her children hadn't been easy. Lately, however, the room had fallen hauntingly quiet, as if the star found a way to prevent her from eavesdropping.

Longing for change, Queen Lillian sat upright in bed and begrudgingly surveyed the all-too-familiar space around her. Against the wall, on the far right-hand side, was a meagre, decrepit bookshelf housing only a handful of children's fairy tales known throughout Naxthos as *The Naxthosian Tales of Old*. Since she was a little girl, they'd been Queen Lillian's favourites, transporting her to faraway lands where determined heroes battled rancorous foes. However, the reversions inside the forcefield replaced energetic sweeping prose with the hero's demise and, inevitably, death.

Dismissing the books, she climbed out of bed and made her way across the room to the imposing oval window. She looked down upon a polished, elm writing desk, avoiding the forged view outside of idyllic, verdant hills and quaint, winding streams.

Star Lisa's cruel housewarming gift, a leather-bound, forest-green notebook, regal in aesthetics, rested on top of the desk. Anxious, she opened it and flicked through the pages littered with handwriting that didn't belong to her. Eventually, she stopped at the first blank page and waited.

That day's date and year of imprisonment appeared in the top left-hand corner. It was close to twenty-one years without her Tarot cards. Thankfully, the cauldron on Naxthos hadn't managed to disband their energy, but she still worried whether she would be able to connect with them again. Dark, negative thoughts brewed, but before the strength intensified, the walls drew her attention.

She told herself to stay focused. *The specks of purple, mystical fog you thought you saw weren't real.* The mist reappeared and grew to cover all four walls around her. Head spinning, she wondered if something had happened to the forcefield. Straining her ears, she couldn't hear any commotion outside, just silence.

Heart beating intensely, the ground under her feet shuddered, knocking her off balance. What had happened? She noticed the rolling hills and streams outside vanish and the writing desk disappear. The notebook fell to the floor with a loud thud.

Not once, out of all the years in captivity, had she experienced this. Was the forcefield growing stronger, perhaps? But wait! That voice. Yes, the one belonging to Star Lisa, she could hear it. The tone was angry, desperate.

Attempting to make sense of the puzzling situation, a swish, quickly followed by a terrifying flash, invaded the space. She blinked, and her mouth dropped. Stood in the centre of an oval-shaped room, she was surrounded by rows of amethyst-made crystal cots resting on top of exquisite marble. *The sight is monumental*, she thought. Was she in another Tarot world?

Her attention was drawn to the fourth floor, where three desperate necromancers hunched over a slightly smaller cot. They worked on maintaining a spell while their Tarot cards deflected energy shots fired from the other side of the room. *Are they from Wayan?* she wondered, recognising the pentacle sigil on their cloaks. But who were the two figures positioned above them? Taking a closer look, she saw Andrew and Amy.

Beaming with pride, she watched her children as they worked together to conjure energy from their Tarot cards. She started to feel stronger, and Star Lisa's hold over her body subsided. Then a thought dropped: where were her Tarot cards?

Delving into the pockets of her cloak, she desperately tried to find them. Had Star Lisa left the deck on Naxthos, perhaps? She continued to look. Feeling their weight, she'd found them. Tears of relief streamed down her face as she held on to them tight. They were finally reunited.

The ground shook violently, and an intense, mystical battle erupted on the other side of the room. With ferocity, Saxthos, Reenie and Emerea fired mystical energy into three other necromancers, who quickly blocked their attacks. *Is there anything I can do to help?* Queen Lillian wondered, looking down at her cards. It was now or never. She needed to try, at least.

Shuffling from side to side, she pushed her worries down to the bottom of her stomach and stepped forward. Attempting to connect with her Tarot deck, a sudden presence from behind startled her. Turning to face them, she gazed upon two women standing firm and defiant. But before she had the chance to speak to them, her vigour plummeted, and the star took back control. Returning to the forcefield, hope ignited inside her soul. Would she be able to enter the amethyst plane soon? Pacing the room, pumped full of adrenaline, she couldn't wait any longer.

Checking the window, the hills and streams hadn't reappeared, but the walls had started to return to normal. Had her chance been taken away? She could hear screams seep into the forcefield, and with a flash, she was back on Paga, lying face down upon the cool, hard ground.

She rolled onto her back. It felt like the wind had been knocked out of her. Head spinning, she touched her forehead delicately and saw blood on her hands. She thought she must have been wounded from when Star Lisa took back control. Looking around wildly at what she'd missed, the two women were now aiding the necromancers on the ground, still under attack from Saxthos, Reenie and Emerea.

Taking in their features, Queen Lillian realised one of them was Lady Helena, who called the other woman Evie. *Who's Evie? Her daughter, perhaps? No, she's Queen Maria's. The resemblance is uncanny. But where is Queen Maria?*

Thinking fast, Queen Lillian decided to avoid the battle and join the other necromancers on the fourth floor. At least she would be immersed in the weakening spell, with Andrew and Amy aiding from above. Ready to execute her plan, Queen Lillian picked herself up and dusted herself off as she hobbled towards the nearest stepladder. But an eerie young woman silently emerged behind the ladder, hidden in the shadows. She grabbed Queen Lillian's cloak and pulled her into the darkness.

"Star Lisa," said the young woman, voice low, "I'm sorry it took me so long to arrive on Paga. Are you okay?"

Queen Lillian stayed silent, not giving anything away. It was obvious the young woman was conspiring with Star Lisa, so Queen Lillian waited for her to make the first move.

The silence unnerved Maid Ella, who worried whether Star Lisa was angry with her. "Er," stuttered Maid Ella, ready to break down, but her fear suddenly turned to deep hatred for Lady Helena. *It is all her fault*, Maid Ella thought, *for the onslaught on Paga and attacking Star Lisa*. Enough was enough! Removing a mystical dagger from her belt, Maid Ella turned to locate her sister amid the battle.

Queen Lillian knew the woman was hungry for blood, and it was directed towards Lady Helena. But why would she want to hurt her?

"Stay in the shadows and bide your time," instructed Queen Lillian, pretending to be Star Lisa. "You can't expose yourself."

Taken aback by the star's words, Maid Ella felt torn as she stood on the spot, unable to move. Then, inhaling deep, she tried with all her might to see Star Lisa's point of view, until she eventually mustered the strength to accept the command. At that moment, Maid Ella was desperate to find some peace in the turbulent world around her. But her eyes lowered, and she saw the Tarot cards in Queen Lillian's hand.

"Why do you have those?" asked Maid Ella.

Queen Lillian followed her gaze. Staying calm, she focused on connecting with her cards before it was too late. As both women saw specks of crackling, forest-green energy coming out of the deck, Maid Ella was trying to decipher what that meant.

"You're drawing energy from your cards?" said Maid Ella, confused. "But why would you need to? You're a star?"

Before the realisation hit, Queen Lillian needed to act fast. Willing her cards to levitate, they did so in a heartbeat and generated fantastical energy, ready to strike down Maid Ella. But as she was about to release the onslaught, Queen Lillian didn't feel so good. Across the vast space of the birthing room, Saxthos had successfully struck and killed one of the necromancers conducting the weakening spell.

Fighting internally to keep hold of her body, Queen Lillian couldn't hold on anymore. Falling to the floor, Tarot cards in hand for comfort, she looked up at Maid Ella, who held the mystical dagger tight. "You'll regret your decision," said Queen Lillian. "If you go out there and hurt Lady Helena, there'll be blood on your hands."

Maid Ella listened, but instead of answering, she walked away.

"No!" Queen Lillian called out, but it wasn't enough. Maid Ella charged towards Lady Helena, who was too invested in protecting Evie to register her sister's intent to kill her.

"Helena!" shouted Queen Lillian, desperate to be heard, but the scene around her disappeared, and she was back inside the amethyst forcefield, shaking uncontrollably. She looked around wildly, desperate to be freed.

As the screams on the outside amplified, they quickly turned into battle cries until, finally, there was silence. Queen Lillian rose from the floor and looked around the room. Everything had returned to the way it was, and nothing appeared out of the ordinary. Had Lady Helena failed? It was hard to tell.

"Don't lose yourself. This can't be the end," said Queen Lillian.

After an eternity of waiting, the sound of an explosion rocked the room. She turned to find a newly conjured, emerald-painted door, backed with diagonal bracing and strengthened with long, iron hinges. She released the latch and opened the door with ease. Blocking out everything around her, she left the fabricated prison and stepped through into the purple, mystical fog.

Crossing over into the grounds of Castle Naxthos, the mood was eerie against the backdrop of purple haze. No fire pits were conjured to combat the chill, and she shivered under the miserable weather as dusk settled. *It feels real*, she thought. Naxthosian winters were always dire, but years spent inside the forcefield taught her mystical trickery was everywhere. Star Lisa thrived on mind games, and this was more than an ideal opportunity. "Stay alert," Queen Lillian muttered to herself, "don't drop your guard."

Surveying her home, the drawbridge was raised preventing escape, while the inner courtyard was stripped of life. As she made her way towards the entrance, she noticed two bodies tied to the foreboding pillars on either side. Dangling like rag dolls, their faces were obscured. She welled up at the cuts, burns and bruises across their skin. Confident they were dead, Queen Lillian wondered if Star Lisa had tortured them. She told herself, "Don't ask any more questions. This is not real."

But then why did a wave of unease wash over her? Instantly recognising the jewellery around their fingers and wrists, she knew they belonged to her mother and father. Anxiously, she lifted their heads in turn and saw the faces of her dead parents. Horrified at the scene, her mind spiralled. Had Star Lisa kept their murders hidden from her all this time?

Unable to make sense of the grief, she looked around for any sign of Star Lisa. No more games, this had to end.

"Show yourself!" Queen Lillian called out. "Come on, now!"

But as she was about to continue, her attention was drawn to her parents' legs. They were on fire. The flames licked and grew with delight, making their way up to their chests and along their arms. She looked out across the vast space of the courtyard for anything that could be of use. Preparing to inspect the area properly, the ground started to rumble and a malevolent wall of flames rose from the floor in front of her.

Blocked in, the fiery wall edged closer. She didn't want to leave them but had no choice; she needed to take shelter inside the castle. Making her way towards the entrance, she glanced behind and saw her parents were now entirely consumed by fire. Rattled, she lost her footing and landed sideways upon a cold, tiled floor as the entrance doors closed, trapping her inside.

She rested sideways in the foetal position, shell-shocked with grief. Star Lisa had killed them. Finding it hard to breathe, her mind spiralled. She couldn't see a way out. "But, of course, that's because there is no way out." And there they were: the words she'd fought to bury deep inside herself.

Inside the vast, grandiose parlour space, littered with waning candles on top of forest-green pillar stands, Queen Lillian kept her eyes closed, unable to move. Even the faint whispers coming from the other side of the room hadn't drawn her attention away from despair. Hurried and distorted, the voices grew louder, but no one was visible. She was alone.

A separate voice pierced the air and overpowered the others. It was a man's voice, calling out to her, telling her to open her eyes. The voice repeated, "You need to listen to me," but Queen Lillian refused. When the man's voice became more noticeable, she realised it sounded like her brother, King Marco.

"You're not real," she called out, but before she could continue, a door leading into a separate room opened with haste. "I need you," repeated the voice. "I need my sister."

Fighting back the tears, she mustered the strength to rise from the floor. Even though the ordeal shook her, she had to keep going. Turning to inspect the parlour, she didn't remember there being an entrance into another room. It didn't feel right. She stepped inside and saw heavy, draped curtains blocking the night's sky, while a tomb lay in the centre upon a raised stone platform.

Edging closer, she stood before the tomb and lifted the lid. Hands pressed against her mouth in shock, she looked down upon her deceased brother, a knife wound visible across his midriff. "Wait!" she called. "This isn't right! You told me you needed me! My brother isn't dead."

A different voice emerged from the shadows. This time it sounded exactly like hers and answered back with a harsh tone. "Your brother 'needed' you," replied Star Lisa, calm and calculated.

"Stop with the mind games," said Queen Lillian, staying strong, for she knew it was the only way to escape the amethyst plane.

"I'm impressed," continued Star Lisa. "I thought your dead brother would have finished you off."

"Until I escape and uncover the truth, I will not accept anyone's death. If this is the worst you can do, forget it. Show yourself now, and we'll settle this."

"One final point," said Star Lisa.

"No!" answered Queen Lillian, anger brewing. Scanning the room for any sign of the star, Queen Lillian kept her guard up, ready to block an attack, but Star Lisa's voice vanished. Queen Lillian was left alone with her brother and wondered if she should stay or explore the rest of the castle.

The only other power at play would be to see Andrew and Amy hurt, but they were safe the last time she saw them. So, she decided to stay and not encourage Star Lisa. Nothing else could shock her now.

Settling into her plan, she kept looking around the space for any signs of entry. All was silent and cold. The whispers in the distance were no longer apparent, and King Marco's body lay in peace. She kept her guard up as the entrance door closed abruptly in front of her. Still nothing. But then she heard faint groaning noises coming from the other side of the obstructed window, outside.

Louder and louder, the groaning sounds transformed into hateful shrieking until, finally, they called out for Queen Lillian. Edging closer towards the heavy, draped curtains, she pulled back the scene. Clawing at the window were her parents. Their corpses looked at her angrily as they attempted to break through the glass.

Queen Lillian couldn't take it anymore. Shaking uncontrollably, she released her hold on the drape as it fell and obscured the window. "They're not real," she muttered to herself. "It's just another one of Star Lisa's parlour tricks. Everything will be okay."

As her breathing calmed down, the sounds of her deceased parents began to disappear. Filled with relief, she started to relax but failed to notice that King Marco had woken up.

From behind, her brother sat upright and surveyed the room. Once he saw her, he silently lifted himself out of his tomb and walked steadily towards her, arms outstretched. At the same time, she remembered the tomb behind her and turned to inspect it. Before she could react, King Marco wrapped his hands around her neck, squeezing tight. She struggled to break free, but her energy dropped as he continued to squeeze.

After a few more escape attempts, she lost the fight and blacked out. Unable to overthrow the mythical imposter on the outside, she desperately wondered what her mind could do to help. Remembering how she felt on Paga, she fixated on her Tarot cards. Their beautiful covers, detailing the four suits of cups, wands, swords and pentacles, were both familiar and breathtaking.

She concentrated on those feelings, and as the cards settled visibly inside her mind, briefly, she managed to connect with them. A sharp electrical crackle of forest-green energy appeared and disappeared.

Opening her eyes, she was no longer inside Castle Naxthos. Instead, the ground under her fallen body felt stiff and uncomfortable as small stones and pebbles dug into her skin. Was she out of the amethyst plane? As she surveyed the cold, dark cave, she wondered where Star Lisa was.

"Lillian?" said a confused voice in the shadows. "Is that you?"

"Stop!" shouted Queen Lillian as she scrambled to her feet. "Star Lisa, show yourself!"

Looking hard into the pitch-blackness, Queen Lillian saw the outline of a figure come towards her. A dishevelled, bearded man with kind eyes and healed scars across his face and arms drew closer. She couldn't move or think. It had been over twenty years since she saw her husband, Nicholas, the star who'd dropped from the sky onto Naxthos and fallen in love with her.

"No!" she squirmed. "Not this." Consumed in tears, she couldn't take the pain anymore.

"You're not real," she said.

"I love you, Lillian," said Nicholas, determined to hold on to the moment.

"Please, enough," she replied, her face looking down to the floor.

But Nicholas didn't stop. Instead, he wrapped his arms around her and hugged her tightly. A wave of love consumed his entire being, and as the moment lingered, he knew he needed to act quickly.

"You're right. I'm not real. I'm merely a being conjured by Star Lisa. But I can feel Nicholas's pain and yours."

Queen Lillian looked up, desperate to meet his eyes, as she wondered whether this being on the amethyst plane had the same memories as the real Nicholas. Maybe it knew where he went and if he was still alive?

"Where did Nicholas go?" she asked, desperate.

Before Nicholas could reply, he dissolved into thin air, and Star Lisa appeared in front of her, in the form of Queen Lillian. "Naughty, naughty," taunted Star Lisa.

Enraged, Queen Lillian grabbed Star Lisa, who retaliated and overpowered her. With one swift movement, the star threw her against the cave wall. Disorientated, she tried to stand up, but the star punched her in the face, and when she fell to the ground, Star Lisa hovered over her, ready to kill her once and for all.

Looking into the eyes of the being who stole her life, Queen Lillian's eyes started to close, and everything went dark.

Chapter Twenty-Eight

Help Is Coming

Andrew thought the moment had finally come – the chance to prove himself to everyone. All he needed to do was stick to Lady Helena's instructions and maintain the image of the Star card inside his mind. *Let the Tarot deck draw star energy away from Star Lisa and, whatever you do, don't open your eyes. Don't break the connection.* But as soon as Andrew's best intentions left his head, a loud explosion from down below rocked the birthing room on Paga with incredible force.

Andrew felt torn when hearing Evie's cries on the ground floor and Lady Helena's intent to help her. Another explosion followed another until Evie's cries had grown painstakingly unbearable and desperate. He watched as fantastical energy shots were fired between Lady Helena's necromancers and Star Lisa's followers, lighting up the air in a dazzling array of colours.

As the colours diminished, he was mortified at the mystical bloodbath raging on. Still, before he could identify who was close to winning, a hand grabbed him from behind. Turning to face his sister, he could tell Amy was annoyed.

"Now we have broken the connection with our star cards," said Amy. "Our birth mother could have been transported back inside the amethyst plane forcefield."

"I'm sorry, Amy." But before he could continue his apology, the rickety wooden platform under them grew more unstable. It rocked abruptly, and both siblings clung to each other in an attempt to steady themselves.

"Andrew, you need to focus."

"I know, it's just…"

"No, Andrew, you need to snap out of it, for all our sakes," said Amy, letting go of him.

Torn by the sounds and images, he froze. Stumbling to close his eyes, Amy gave him one final spur, and finally, he obeyed. Closing their eyes, both siblings fixated on their respective Star cards. Andrew didn't feel able. The root of the problem was Amy. Since he had reunited with her on Wayan, he'd tried to suppress a hefty amount of negative thoughts. He worried she was stronger than him. What if he couldn't catch up? What if he held her back?

For such a long time, he'd kept his career and family separate but, now he was working alongside Amy, it threw him off considerably. She was excelling, and it was scary to feel weak next to her.

As the spiral grew deeper, he couldn't find a way out, and his Tarot cards decided they had no choice but to intervene. The deck circled him faster and faster, and they whispered in his ear for a fleeting moment. He heard their encouraging words tell him to concentrate on his mission only, and it wouldn't do anyone any good if he broke down completely. Their overwhelming desire to comfort and support him began to seep into his being.

The Tarot deck continued to circle him, gaining momentum while generating a different kind of fantastical energy, more powerful than anything he'd experienced. The colour changed to sage green, and for Andrew, it was liberating – a unique power only meant for him. Keeping his eyes closed, he embraced new-found confidence, withdrew from the outside world and focused on the task he needed to complete.

Sensing Star Lisa becoming weaker, he tried to home in on its hiding place inside the birthing room. He was confident he could locate it, but as he got close, a flash followed by a mighty rumble distorted the image of the Star card in his mind.

Raising a hand to shield his vision from the blinding light outside, Andrew looked out of an imposing, oval-shaped window. He made out the endless, luscious green rolling hills and idyllic streams in the distance. This place doesn't look or feel like Paga. He could hear birds singing!

Thinking back to Lady Helena's instructions, she hadn't mentioned anything about this place. Was it a mistake? Or was he meant to do something here? Looking down upon the polished elm writing desk, he saw a forest-green notebook. Opening the cover, he flicked through the pages listing dates as far back as twenty-one years, with a note next to each one detailing how many days his birth mother had been imprisoned.

An overwhelming sense of sorrow filled the air as he began to understand the scale of torment Queen Lillian had endured all that time. The notebook started to rattle violently on the desk, snapping him out of his trance. A group of handwritten words appeared across the page: 'behind you'.

With one swift movement, he followed the instruction and turned to face Queen Lillian, who stood eerily quiet in front of him. Eyes cold and mouth pressed shut, Andrew sensed her disdain at his sudden arrival. It would have been a warm and happy reunion in an ideal world, but he knew without question the woman in front of him wasn't his birth mother.

"I'm assuming you're not pleased to see me?" said Andrew.

"I wasn't pleased you and your sister dragged me back inside the amethyst plane forcefield," sniped Star Lisa, "but I'm pleased I managed to pull you in with me momentarily."

"And you will stay here until Lady Helena brings down the forcefield. You've held on to my mother long enough."

"I don't think so," taunted Star Lisa. "And for clarity, she's only your birth mother. Your 'real' mother, Grace, and her husband Henry, are currently trapped in a box underground on Earth."

"I'm not falling for it. This is another one of your tricks."

Ignoring him, the star gazed around the prison, admiring its handiwork, especially the reversions of *The Naxthosian Tales of Old*, and chuckled.

"Your birth mother's favourites as a child," explained Star Lisa, pointing at the books, "*The Naxthosian Tales of Old*. Originally, a collection of folktales about gallant heroes overcoming the odds. But we need to understand first, Andrew, why the authors chose those individuals to be the 'heroes'?"

"You think you're a hero?" asked Andrew, confused by the star's statement.

"I think it's complicated," said Star Lisa, falling hauntingly quiet. Finally, the star said, "It's true. Grace and Henry are buried underground. Amy wouldn't have known because I tricked her into believing they were safe."

"You're just trying to rattle me."

"No, I'm not," replied Star Lisa, aloof in tone.

Andrew could hear cries coming from Grace and Henry, and they sounded like they were in a lot of pain. He ignored it. Star Lisa was trying to trick him. But the cries sounded genuine, and it was uncomfortable to listen to. Eventually, he couldn't take it anymore. Anger building, he was about to lose it, and Star Lisa was pleased with itself.

"It's real," it taunted.

Charging towards Star Lisa, demanding answers, he nearly grabbed the star, but an overwhelming sense of nausea knocked him off balance. The space around him evaporated, and Star Lisa's final words before he left were, "I'm going to be seeing you very soon on Paga."

Still determined to grab hold of the star, he dived forward, but he hadn't realised he was back on Paga. Accidentally stepping off the rickety wooden platform, he woke up in time to grab hold of the edge while the rest of his body dangled in the air.

"Amy!" called Andrew. "Amy!"

Where was she? She had told him to keep to their positions! Andrew said, "Okay, let's try lifting yourself." A fantastical energy shot hit the platform, and as he clung on, his heart was beating wildly. He tried to lift himself again. "Come on; it shouldn't be this difficult!" Still struggling, he grew more frustrated, and as he was about to try again, he heard Queen Lillian call out from below.

"Lady Helena!" shouted Queen Lillian. "Be careful! A woman's coming for you! She has a weapon!"

The warnings stopped, and a rumble shook the room. With great force, a burst of forest-green energy rose and lingered under his feet. Screams pierced through the attack, and he could hear Lady Helena call out to her necromancers, "Star Lisa is back! Necromancers, get into position!"

Andrew scrambled onto the platform, while a separate burst of forest-green energy flew past him. Narrowly missing the attack, he was thrown off balance and fell back into the air. Descending at great speed, he waved his arms wildly, terrified at the prospect of plummeting to his death. "Amy!" he called out, desperate for help, but she didn't come. *Is this it?* Andrew worried as he continued to fall, and then a sudden beacon of sage-green energy emerged from above.

It grew brighter and brighter, and much to his relief, his Tarot cards flew towards him. They drew closer, and when they reached Andrew, the cards manoeuvred under him and conjured an array of fantastical strands of energy. Wrapping themselves around his arms and legs, the strands pulled him up and threw him over the side onto the fourth floor.

Landing with a violent thud on the exquisite marble floor, his entire body ached from the shock. Coughing and spluttering, he mustered the strength to roll onto his side and take up the foetal position. Breathing deeply, his eyesight returned to normal, ready to take in his surroundings.

A bloodied and burnt necromancer, devoid of life, was sprawled out on the floor nearby while his Tarot cards lay motionless around him. He wasn't breathing, and the cards looked dead, too.

Certain the necromancer was one of Lady Helena's comrades responsible for the weakening spell, he wondered where the other two were. Lifting his head to survey the space around him, he saw the others strewn over the ledge with the same injuries as the first.

Andrew was growing more concerned. There were none left to conjure the weakening spell on Star Lisa's cot. Where was Amy? He needed to find her, quick. Lady Helena couldn't do everything on her own. Eyes scanning the birthing room, he was about to ask his Tarot cards if they could go looking for his sister. But, hearing a turbulent uproar of incredible energy from above, he paused and followed the commotion.

Dazzling, forest-green energy, a different shade to the one fired from below, deflected a ferocious onslaught of burnt-orange energy. As the two figures lingered in the air and came into view, he recognised them without fail. Amy was flying! He looked up in amazement. He didn't know she could do that! But then again, he didn't think Amy knew she could either, from the unsettled look on her face.

Willing her cards to deflect Sorcerer Saxthos's onslaught, Amy attempted to fire forest-green energy back. Frazzled and desperate, she wasn't quick enough, and Saxthos used the opportunity to launch himself towards her.

Andrew was desperate to help; he took in the sorcerer looking for any sign of a weakness. Frantically scanning the spectacle, he wondered where Saxthos's Tarot cards were. He hadn't used or needed any against Amy. *Could he possibly be a star? But then why hadn't Amy managed to weaken him? Maybe she didn't know*, he wondered.

Eyes closed, Andrew fixated on the Star card and willed his Tarot deck to draw star energy away from Saxthos. "Please do this for me," he begged, clinging on to hope. He kept going as he withdrew from the outside world and into the spell inside his mind. "You can do this," he said. After a while, the silence started to unsettle him. *Is the plan working?* he wondered. *Has Saxthos been disarmed?*

Nervously, he opened his eyes and levitating in front of him was Saxthos, very much alive, unhurt, but mostly annoyed at Andrew's efforts. Next to him, also in the air, was Amy, bruised and dishevelled as strands of burnt-orange energy wrapped around her bruised body. The energy burnt into her skin every time she struggled to break free.

Crying out in pain, Amy looked at her brother, pleading for him to make a run for it, but he didn't budge. *I would never leave her. She should know that.*

About to ask his cards for help, Saxthos chimed in. "You were right," he said to Andrew. "I am a star. Well, a part star. I only felt minor goosebumps down my arm when you tried to draw star energy away from me."

"Please, Andrew," jumped in Amy, "you need to get out of here."

"He can make up his mind," replied Saxthos, direct and cold in tone. "Well, I would have thought he could."

Ignoring the sorcerer's quip, Andrew closed his eyes and willed his Tarot cards to try again, but as the deck attempted to draw star energy away, they were still no closer to succeeding. The sorcerer had had enough. With one swift movement, Saxthos conjured strands of burnt-orange energy, bloodthirsty in nature, and instructed them to wrap around Andrew. While they took care of him, a separate set took hold of his Tarot cards and imprisoned them with Amy's, inside a mystical box floating in the air.

Struggling to break free, Andrew suffered the same pain as Amy. The burns were unbearable, but he refused to give up, while Amy pleaded for him to stop and conserve his strength. No closer to escaping, both siblings were at boiling point, and as they were about to have a full-blown argument, Saxthos cut in.

Commanding the burnt-orange energy wrapped around them to follow him into the birthing room, all three quickly landed on the ground floor. While Saxthos took great enjoyment in the devastation around him, Andrew and Amy welled up in anguish – all Lady Helena's necromancers were dead. Their bodies were scattered around the space; some had limbs missing, and almost all were unrecognisable because of the blood and deep cuts.

The mystical massacre was all too much, and as tears streamed down their faces, Andrew and Amy saw Lady Helena on the other side of the room in distress. Knelt before a severely wounded Evie, the leader of the Land of Pentacles attempted to heal the deep scorch marks across the young Wayan's chest. But no amount of spells seemed to work. Struggling to breathe, Evie tried with all her might to stay strong, but Lady Helena knew Queen Maria's daughter was terrified.

Preparing to try another healing spell, Lady Helena was struck in the arm by a powerful hit of forest-green energy. Reeling from the attack, she slumped next to Evie, who rolled onto her side despite the pain across her chest and reached for Lady Helena's hand. While the young Wayan hoped she was okay, Andrew and Amy followed the direction of the attack. It came from Star Lisa, who entered the birthing room from the hallway. The star held on to its birthing log from the Mystics' library and looked content as it glided towards Lady Helena and Evie across the room.

While en route, Star Lisa glanced at Andrew and Amy and watched as both siblings struggled to break out of the burnt-orange strands. Closing his eyes. Andrew willed his Tarot cards to break out of the mystical box.

Just as he felt his cards gain the strength to resist Saxthos's magic, Star Lisa swooped in and intervened. The star conjured a small, less powerful ball of forest-green energy from its hands and struck Andrew's chest, propelling him back across the space.

Colliding with one of the stepladders, he fell to the floor in a heap while Amy cried out. Star Lisa ignored her and told Saxthos to strengthen the magic wrapped around both siblings.

"Where's Emerea?" asked Star Lisa, concerned. "Is she safe?"

"She hasn't come back yet," replied Saxthos, calm and composed.

About to press for more information, the sound of approaching footsteps from the hallway averted Star Lisa's attention. Turning around, a sudden wave of love hit the star as Emerea entered the room.

"We've checked everywhere. The place is abandoned," said Emerea, as Maid Ella followed her inside. "We're the only ones left."

"Thank you," replied Star Lisa, who held out its hand for Emerea to take.

Now that Star Lisa and Emerea are reunited, it is time to break away, Maid Ella thought, moving gingerly towards Lady Helena. She couldn't miss another chance. It needed to be final.

Holding the mystical dagger tight, Maid Ella relished the butterflies in her stomach. It had taken a while to craft the weapon. Finally, Star Lisa, Saxthos, Emerea and Reenie combined an intricate number of spells into the knife, whose sole purpose was to murder Lady Helena. The time had come. Star Lisa, Emerea and Saxthos made their way across the space, forcing Amy to join them. They took front-row seats, ready to watch Maid Ella carry out the act.

Growing more and more desperate, Amy knew they needed help. If Lady Helena hadn't managed to communicate with her comrades back on Wayan, she should try, but the issue was Saxthos's magic.

But wait, Amy thought. Saxthos imprisoned her cards to block any attempts to weaken him or Star Lisa. What if she intended something different? Especially now that the sorcerer was distracted by Maid Ella. Could she ask her Tarot cards to create a portal instead?

Trying not to draw attention to herself, she imagined a portal opening in front of her. Ignoring the box holding her Tarot deck prisoner, she worked tirelessly to tap into her card's energy. Shortly after, she felt a tingle as it started to work. She could feel Wayan's energy at last.

While Amy continued with her plan, the scene around her escalated. Stood firm and defiant in front of her sister, Lady Helena wasn't shocked or surprised by Maid Ella's animosity towards her. It was expected.

The leader of the Land of Pentacles couldn't keep making excuses. She'd tried to reason with her sister for a long time, but no amount of words or promises would ever help Maid Ella find peace.

"I've tried, dear sister," said Lady Helena, "but if I have to choose between you and protecting Evie, it will be Evie."

Maid Ella's anger boiled over, and as she charged towards Lady Helena, her sister reacted with ease. Willing her Tarot cards into the air, Lady Helena instructed them to generate her infamous, fantastical energy, light orange with a yellow hue. The Land of Pentacles' leader opened fire on Maid Ella.

"This is for the victims in this room whom you conspired to kill," said Lady Helena.

Suppressing her fear at the oncoming onslaught, Maid Ella kept going, and as the first set of energy strikes drew close, Star Lisa, Saxthos and Emerea intervened. Swiftly joining forces, they combined their magic to create energy shields, protecting Maid Ella.

Drawing closer, Maid Ella raised the dagger, and as Star Lisa blocked another energy strike, she tried to stab Lady Helena. Dodging the blade, she fought back with her energy, but Star Lisa, Saxthos and Emerea blocked her attempts. Maid Ella took her chance and plunged the dagger deep into Lady Helena's stomach. The puncturing sensation left Lady Helena with the wind knocked out of her as she stumbled back onto the cold, hard ground. Struggling to breathe, she mustered the strength to press hard against her wound. The sticky blood travelled out, trickling down her fingers and sides.

Across the birthing room, Amy was close to conjuring a portal. Finally, one started to appear behind her, next to Andrew, who stirred. "Here come the reinforcements," Amy muttered. "We should be okay. Just hang on, Lady Helena, please."

The portal grew more expansive, and a figure came into view from the other side. Andrew looked up, and his mouth dropped as Reenie stepped into the birthing room, pleased with herself.

"Distorting portals coming in and out of Wayan is my speciality," quipped Reenie. "You're coming with me." Conjuring fantastical energy, Reenie willed Andrew to accompany her towards Star Lisa and the others, while Amy was shell-shocked at her failure to call for help. Overwhelmed with guilt, she looked sideways at Andrew, who stood beside her.

Taken aback by Lady Helena's life ebbing away, Andrew looked wildly around the birthing room. What were they meant to do now? No one else was more powerful than Lady Helena to go up against Star Lisa and its followers! Along with Andrew, Amy was desperately trying to find a way out.

Evie couldn't even move, for Star Lisa had willed her injuries to worsen, and the pain was unbearable. With tears streaming down her face, Evie thought she'd faintly heard Lady Helena's voice in the background. Words distorted, she struggled to listen to what the leader of the Land of Pentacles was saying before falling unconscious.

Gesturing for Maid Ella to go closer, Lady Helena whispered in her ear. "Help is coming," said Lady Helena, "and you're not going to like it."

As Lady Helena gave her sister a mischievous wink, she closed her eyes, took her last breath and passed away. Feeling unnerved, Maid Ella worried about what her dead sister had planned. She needed to warn Star Lisa. But, before she could speak out, she heard a faint rustling from Lady Helena's tunic pocket.

Scrambling for the source, Maid Ella retrieved a deck of Tarot cards which had fallen on the floor. She wondered who those cards belonged to. The deck came to life, as did Lady Helena's. "That's impossible," said Maid Ella. Why had her sister's cards come back to life?!

Both sets flew into the air, intertwined, and cast a sizeable, fantastical ball of multicoloured energy. They were conducting a spell. What had Lady Helena done?

Andrew and Amy looked up in awe at the spectacle, while Star Lisa and its followers grew unsettled. Finally, Emerea reached for the star's hand and suggested they leave right then. But as Reenie was about to conjure a portal for them to escape Paga, she was thwarted. Both sets of Tarot cards had picked up on her plan and willed fantastical energy from the ball to strike Reenie dead.

All nervous eyes in the room were on the multicoloured energy. It grew outwards, becoming more powerful, and suddenly both sets of cards merged and formed one mighty deck. Preparing for an attack, Saxthos and Emerea stood in front of Star Lisa, ready to protect the star, while Maid Ella backed away, unable to process what was happening.

A figure came into view out of the ball, and Andrew and Amy were dumbfounded when they realised it was Sylvie. The newly awakened sorceress, ready to tip the balance, embraced the powers she'd obtained from Lady Helena's Tarot cards, and Lady Helena's memories and past experiences.

Communicating with the mighty Tarot deck in the air, Sylvie knew the former leader of the Land of Pentacles had read her cards in Wayan's infirmary and understood her potential demise. So, Lady Helena had set in motion a backup plan: trade her life for Sylvie's and merge their Tarot decks.

"Andrew, Amy," snapped Sylvie. "Back away, please."

As both siblings obeyed, Sylvie swiftly conjured an array of incredible energy from her newly formed Tarot deck and hit Saxthos and Emerea before they could defend themselves. With the wind knocked out of them, Star Lisa's followers struggled to get up from the floor. Before they could attempt to conjure a portal to escape, Sylvie hit them again and again until, finally, they were knocked unconscious. With Saxthos down, the strands of magic wrapped around Andrew and Amy subsided, and their Tarot cards were released from the mystical box.

Star Lisa, still clinging to its birthing log, attempted to conjure a separate portal, but Sylvie was too quick. Manipulating strands of multicoloured energy from her mighty deck, the all-powerful sorceress willed them to wrap around the star and tie it to one of the stepladders.

"Andrew! Amy!" called Sylvie. "Draw star energy away."

With no time to think or worry about whether they were up to the task, both siblings just carried out Sylvie's order. Fixating upon the image of their respective Star cards inside their minds, they worked together and drew star energy away from Star Lisa, weakening it.

The star struggled to break free, crying out in pain; its energy was dwindling from Andrew and Amy's powers. "We need to finish this," Sylvie told the siblings. With one swift movement, the mighty sorceress disbanded the amethyst crystal around Star Lisa's neck and brought down the forcefield inside the amethyst plane.

"Goodbye, Star Lisa," said Sylvie. "For I have every confidence in Queen Lillian right now to take back her life."

Chapter Twenty-Nine

A Different Day

Deep inside Queen Lillian's mind, the eerie purple fog from the amethyst plane crept in and surrounded her. Opening her eyes, still reeling from Star Lisa's attack in the cave, she thought of Andrew and Amy, and how much she wanted to see them again.

"And Nicholas. He could still be alive," said Queen Lillian.

Straining to survey the uninhabited space around her, the encroaching fog distorted her vision. She tried again, desperately thinking of more incentives to help reignite consciousness.

She watched anxiously as a fog-walled dome formed ahead. Queen Lillian was afraid as she recognised the soul-sucking energy behind the covering. It was a mystical abyss. She needed to get out of there! She tried to wake up with every ounce of mental fortitude, but nothing seemed to work. The deep purple mist slowly seeped out of the dome towards her. Time was running out.

Turning, she hunted for a way out of the fog. But the mist launched itself at her with considerable velocity. Struggling to break free, she was overpowered until, finally, her mind went cold.

Silence. The mist carried on without mercy, but before the abyss killed her, the sudden arrival of an unknown force thwarted it. Above the fog, many forest-green energy strands blasted their way through and struck the fog-walled dome. A whirlwind of dazzling Tarot cards entered the space and continued a full-scale energy assault.

The entity tried to fight back, but Queen Lillian's cards were persistent. They'd found a spiritual breach inside the amethyst plane and were determined to look after their owner. The Tarot deck refused to back down. With one final energy hit, the abyss couldn't hold on to her any longer. From its core, it released an innocent-looking amethyst crystal. It rolled along the floor towards Queen Lillian and stopped next to her face.

In the blink of an eye, a shell-shocked Queen Lillian was back inside the cave, lying face down on the ground. Her body shook uncontrollably from the ordeal, with no recollection of how she had escaped.

Looking around wildly, she saw the amethyst crystal on the floor and reached to pick it up. *So, this is the end*, she realised, hatefully fixating upon the crystal for the stress it had caused her. Placing it safely inside her pocket, she rolled onto her back and saw a forest-green forcefield covering the entirety of her body. It was acting as a barrier between herself and Star Lisa, who stood over her, face fuelled by annoyance.

The star just watched and waited impatiently, while Queen Lillian noticed for a brief second that images of her Tarot cards appeared across the forcefield and then disappeared. She realised their energy had found her, and her heart was filled with hope.

"Your cards can't protect you forever," said Star Lisa, suppressing the urge to lose her temper. "They don't belong here."

Pretending to ignore the star's comments, Queen Lillian grew restless. Deep down, she knew her Tarot cards had not physically travelled to the amethyst plane. They had only managed to find a spiritual breach. Clinging to their warmth for comfort, she whispered delicately to them, "It's okay. I will see you soon. I promise."

But despite their limited time in the amethyst plane, her Tarot cards refused to bring down the protective forcefield.

"My dear cards," she encouraged them, rising from the floor, confidently meeting Star Lisa's eyes. "Disband."

The forcefield was gone, and she charged at the star in a flash. With adrenaline pumping through her veins, Queen Lillian grabbed hold of its shoulders and threw it against the cave wall with considerable strength.

Disorientated from the impact, the star tried to collect its surroundings, but Queen Lillian was too quick. Hands interlocked behind Star Lisa's head, she initiated one swift knee kick to the face. The star fell back, while she dived forward and repeated the move with more severity.

Unable to pick itself up off the floor in time, Star Lisa watched in horror as Queen Lillian, eyes wild and demeanour stormy, placed her hands over the star's face.

With ferocity, she smacked its head against the cold, hard surface of the cave floor and kept going. Eventually, it became apparent Star Lisa wouldn't wake up again.

Short of breath, Queen Lillian paused and, as the red mist of anger evaporated from her eyes, she looked down upon the star's lifeless body. Choked up and unable to think straight, she began to sob. The pent-up torment she'd suppressed for such a long time was finally released, and she couldn't bear to stay in the cave a moment longer.

Queen Lillian wondered whether any of this was real. Had the fight with Star Lisa been a trick? Was she still trapped inside the amethyst plane? "No" she said, as she removed the amethyst crystal from her pocket. She had to stay focused. All was not lost. Just wait and be patient.

But, as the minutes ticked by, the silence was tense, and Queen Lillian couldn't take it anymore. Picking herself off the floor, she inspected her gloomy surroundings. There was no way out! What was she meant to do next?

Head spinning with uncertainty, her attention was diverted towards a desperate cry for help in the distance. Queen Lillian turned to inspect the source and saw an entrance to a narrow passageway that wasn't there before. The cries for help grew louder.

"Help us!" shouted the voice in the tunnel.

Queen Lillian knew who that voiced belonged to. She couldn't just sit back and do nothing. She left Star Lisa's bloodied and beaten body on the floor and entered the cold, dark, narrow passageway with caution. She eventually found an exit by winding through the tight space and ducking under the ever changing, rugged formation.

Arriving inside a smaller cave, her eyes darted towards a mystical, rainbow-coloured wall on the opposite side. It shimmered and lit up the cave in an array of wondrous colours, but she was hesitant to accept something so innocent looking.

Taking a small step forward, she heard the cry for help behind the rainbow-coloured wall. She didn't know whether this was from inside the amethyst plane or a gateway into another Tarot world.

Edging closer until her face was inches away from the wondrously lit wall, she waited. Then, all of a sudden, the colours evaporated. She realised it was a window into another Tarot world, and a bloodcurdling scene threw her off guard.

"Maria?" she said, alarmed at seeing her injured sister-in-law struggling to stand on top of a rugged mountainscape. Queen Maria glanced at the sky in fear as volatile flames surrounded her, thwarting escape.

With a piercing cry, an opposing army of winged, demonic beings prepared to dive and charge towards her. As the first creature, with silver skin and eyes of purest white, set towards an unnerved Queen Maria, a loud rumble rocked the mountaintop.

A young, abrasive half-human with extraordinary Lixusian wings propelled through the air and punched the demonic being hard in the face. Desperate to protect Queen Maria, the young half-human continued to fight off the army.

"Maria!" Queen Lillian called, desperate to reach them. But before she could do anything, purple light from the amethyst crystal shot out of her hand. The scene vanished, as did the cave around her. Instantly, Queen Lillian was lying on her back, looking up at an unfamiliar elm ceiling with rustic beams painted a deep red.

Surrounding her was an adornment of gently flickering pillar candles that gave the bedchamber a comforting warmth – a hopeful attempt to evoke a peaceful and unthreatening space. Queen Lillian couldn't let her guard down.

Eyes squinting at the ceiling for a faint gleam of purple, mystical fog, she waited, but the top remained untouched. "Okay, that's a good start," she told herself, ready to inspect the unfamiliar bedchamber.

She first noticed no bookcase housing *The Naxthosian Tales of Old. Again*, she thought, *another positive*, still a little on edge.

Eyes scanning the walls, she looked upon the old tapestries of Wayan's former rulers, and a faint smile appeared on her face. She thought maybe this was real, and she'd finally escaped. But wait, she realised, fixating upon Queen Maria's portrait; what had happened to her sister-in-law inside the cave? And the young half-Lixusian with her?

"Maria," she murmured, deeply concerned for Queen Maria's safety.

But before she could reflect even further, a soft voice from the balcony entered the space and disrupted her train of thought. "Mum," whispered Andrew, delicately, as he stepped inside, away from the evening night's sky.

Welling up at the sight of her son, Queen Lillian didn't want to get her hopes up. She wanted him to be real. Her heart breaking as he smiled at her.

"It's okay, we're here," said Andrew.

Amy appeared from the balcony and made her way over to her birth mother, arms outstretched, ready to hug her.

"Mum," whispered Andrew, as he sat on the stool next to her, "you're safe now."

Accepting his hand, she squeezed it tightly while Amy sat down on the other side of the bed and hugged her. That was the moment she let go. Pulling Andrew in, tears of gratitude trickled down her cheeks. She held on to them tight as Andrew and Amy breathed a sigh of relief.

While a happy family reunion radiated from inside the bedchamber, Sylvie hadn't mustered the strength to tear herself away from the balcony. Instead, she watched as thousands of pentacle-shaped lanterns rose from all four corners of the land and lit up the night's sky as a sign of remembrance for Lady Helena.

Looking out at the vast expanse of Wayan, Sylvie could feel Lady Helena's memories. Since their powers merged, she understood what made Lady Helena happy and what made her sad. But, above all, Sylvie knew Lady Helena had kept a brave face to the end, even with her decision to bring Sylvie back to consciousness.

While her enhanced powers heard sobs, cries and anger across the lands, the lanterns continued to rise and consume the night's sky. Contemplating her next move, she was aware the people of Wayan were not going to accept her so easily. She had a lot of work to do.

Sylvie stopped her train of thought when Andrew called out to her from inside the bedchamber. Taking a deep breath for the inevitable reunion, she exited the balcony and saw three teary faces looking up at her.

"Sylvie, I'm..." Queen Lillian started to say.

"Are you okay?" asked Sylvie, growing worried.

But Queen Lillian couldn't process anything around her as her eyes fixed upon the right-hand pocket of Sylvie's tunic as it glowed a wondrous forest green.

A playful smile spread across her face and Queen Lillian knew what was inside Sylvie's pocket.

In a flash, her Tarot deck flew out of Sylvie's pocket in a flurry of excitement. They circled the room and willed fantastical energy to release the clasp from Queen Lillian's neck and remove the amethyst pendant necklace.

Half expecting the chain to burn into her neck, Queen Lillian gazed down upon the lifeless object as it landed on her lap. In the background, her cards fired delicate crackles of forest-green energy into the air in celebration.

Finally starting to relax, Queen Lillian looked at Andrew, Amy and Sylvie with gratitude for everything they had done for her. "This is real," she said, awash with acceptance as she embraced the love and warmth in the room.

While everyone fell silent and gave her breathing space to take in her new-found freedom, the slight agitation in Sylvie's demeanour woke Queen Lillian from her peaceful moment.

"I know I can't rest for too long," said Queen Lillian, remembering the flashback of Queen Maria.

"But..." said Andrew, determined to make her birth mother rest.

"It's okay, Andrew," said Queen Lillian. Looking hard into Sylvie's eyes, Queen Lillian knew the fight wasn't over. "I know, deep down, you're desperate to start fixing the mess Star Lisa caused," said Queen Lillian.

"I…" Sylvie stuttered.

"It's okay," replied Queen Lillian, embracing her Tarot cards as they circled her with determined force. "Let's begin."